Prescription for Disaster

By
John Avanzato

Also By JOHN AVANZATO
HOSTILE HOSPITAL

Credits

Prescription for Disaster by John Avanzato

ISBN-13: 978-1-939961-22-8
ISBN-10: 1-939961-22-X

First Edition

Publisher: Michael Fabiano
KCM Publishing
www.kcmpublishing.com

KCM Publishing

a division of KCM Digital Media, LLC

Prescription
for
Disaster

Contents

In Memory

of

Isabelle Avanzato

1923-2014

Devoted wife and loving mother

She now rests in the arms of the Lord and we will cherish her memory always.

She was special beyond words and kind beyond description.

Her life can be summed up with one word.

Love

Acknowledgements

I would like to thank the early readers of Prescription for Disaster for their time and input which I found to be invaluable in helping me craft and fine tune this story. Most importantly, I would like to thank my wife, Cheryl Avanzato MD. Wife, mother, doctor and now full time literary consultant, what would I do without you?

I am deeply grateful to everyone for their comments and sage advice. Thank you, Lorraine Frances Avanzato, Marianne Arseneau MD, Lori Matts, Fiona Jarrett-Thelwell-Dunphy DC, Michelle Pedersen Robbins, Director of Program Development at the Seneca Falls Library, Mara O'Laughlin, Paul Kisatsky MS Physics, Mark Rego MD, and Russell Harris.

A special thanks to William Greenleaf, of Greenleaf Literary Services, my first editor and unparalleled instructor of creative writing as well as Michael Fabiano, of KCM Publishing, who had the courage to give me a chance.

PATIENT NAME _____

ADDRESS _____

_____

_____

Prescription

Rx is the universal symbol for a medical prescription. It is thought to be derived from the Latin word, recipere, meaning "to take or receive".

Rx is defined by Merriam-Webster's Dictionary as a written direction for the preparation and administration of a medicine.

Rx is defined by Dr. John Cesari as a method of persuasion using a combination of verbal wit and heavy objects made of iron.

SIGNATURE _____

DATE _____

Prologue

"I'M sorry, Mom." I stood there, tears streaming down my face, ashamed for having disappointed her.

She looked at me, stunned. I had just entered the house, panting, and was disheveled, blood on my white shirt, my knuckles badly bruised. She came running over and threw her arms around me. "Che successo, Giovanni?" (What happened, Johnny?)

"Ho fatto una cosa terribile, Mama." (I did a terrible thing, Mama.)

She studied me carefully as she nudged me into a chair so she could better hug me. At seventeen, I was nearly six feet, 180lbs. and in good shape. I worked weekends and summers as a laborer with my uncle who was a mason. Swinging a sledge hammer and wheeling barrels full of cement all day in the hot sun made you hard. My mom was in her early forties and barely five feet tall with shoes on. As a single parent, she did the best she could, but I was a handful and I often wondered where she got the patience.

She stroked my hair and said sympathetically, "Tell me everything, Johnny, all right?"

Glancing over at the picture of Jesus on the wall, I nodded. My mother was a devout woman who believed that all problems big or small could be solved through prayer. It was midsummer, and we were in the basement of our small row house in the Bronx, New York. I had interrupted her doing the laundry with my abrupt arrival.

An hour before, she had sent me to the store to pick up a few groceries. The front of our little brick home faced Allerton Avenue. Leaving the house, I'd turned left and walked to the store along Eastchester Road, which was a larger four lane street. There was more traffic on the road and more people on their porches than on the side streets. In the Bronx, more people meant more witnesses, which meant safer. When I left the store, I decided to swing around Mace Avenue and return home down Woodhull Avenue, a smaller street, barely enough room for a single vehicle to travel down. I liked Woodhull better because there were lots of trees, making it a more appealing stroll in the summer. It was a beautiful day and I couldn't resist.

I was staring up at a robin perched in a maple tree and got lost in the moment. When I turned my attention back to the path ahead, I saw them. More importantly, they saw me. Two were leaning against a parked car; one had a cigarette dangling from the corner of his mouth, and the other, a toothpick. They were just feet away from the narrow sidewalk. The leader stood on a patch of grass, facing them from the other side of the cement path, his back to a row of hedges. I would have to walk between them to get by.

Slowing my pace, I rapidly calculated my options. Turning around or crossing the street would, at a minimum, invite ridicule. Showing that kind of fear might also provoke them into chasing me down. It was the law of the jungle. I shifted the brown paper bag in my arms and continued toward them.

I lived in a mixed neighborhood in the Bronx, which meant that there were Jews, Italians, Irish mainly, and a smattering of other people of European descent. No blacks. The black neighborhood started at Gun Hill Road, several blocks away, where the concrete playgrounds were. The playgrounds were a neutral zone where it was acceptable to mingle and be friendly, play basketball, etc., but once you were done, you went home and that was it. After the games were over, they didn't cross the line and neither did we. To do so would get you an ass-kicking you would never forget. Everybody was racist in those days and in those neighborhoods. "Racist" wasn't even a bad word then. And no one ever called the cops. If you crossed the line and got beat up, black or white, then you deserved it.

These guys in front of me were Italian, but not all Italians were created equal I found out. I was Sicilian, which placed me in the not quite Italian, not quite trash category in their eyes. There was that old joke that Sicily was an island that had broken off from North Africa and floated towards Italy. A lot of people, including most Italians, felt that Sicilians belonged on the other side of the line.

The guy in charge here was Ron DeMatteo, or Big Ron as he was known. He was the neighborhood tough guy. They called his right fist sledge and his left, hammer. We were the same age and went to school together. I had learned a long time ago to keep my distance from him and his pals. Except for grunting at each other in the hallway, we barely ever spoke, and I was hoping to keep it that way today.

I walked deliberately, not making eye contact, but felt their gaze burning into me. As I passed, Ron, who was on my left, said something. His friends chuckled. I wasn't sure if he was talking to me or to them. Every cell in my body tingled and told me to ignore it and keep moving, but I stopped and turned towards him. I felt as if I had no control over my actions. Inside, there was a voice screaming to get the hell out of there, but I was never good at controlling my temper.

Standing calmly in front of him, I said. "I didn't hear what you just said. Care to repeat it?" I was enveloped by an unusual sense of calm that belied the imminent danger I was in. I was one of those guys that was either all in or all out. There were no half measures with me. I had already made up my mind. I wasn't going to take it anymore.

He hadn't expected me to respond, and suddenly seemed a little unsure of himself. He glanced at his friends to bolster his confidence. He started to say the word again but didn't get past the first syllable. I tossed the grocery bag at him to confuse and distract him. Before the bag even reached him, I launched my right fist, with all my weight behind it, directly into the bridge of his nose. It made a crunching sound as he hurtled backward into the hedgerow. He sprawled back into the bush, his arms flailing and trying to regain his balance, but it was already too late because I was on him in a flash. I followed the right with a hard left to the jaw. Then it was right left, right left, and right left until I was too tired to throw any more. He had stopped moving long before I had stopped punching. His face was a bloody mess, and so were my hands and shirt. I got off him and stood up, facing the other two, who just stood there speechless and wide-eyed. The whole thing had taken less than a minute. Focused energy and ferocity was like that.

"Either of you guys got a problem?" I asked, my chest heaving as I sucked wind. I must have been a frightful sight. Neither one said anything as they both stood there frozen. The toothpick fell out of the guy's mouth.

He finally said, "His brother Tommy's going to be pissed." I wasn't sure if that was a warning or a threat. Tommy DeMatteo, Ron's older brother, was an animal they let out of its cage just to play varsity football. I stepped toward them and got in their faces.

"Well, I wouldn't want to be the one to tell Tommy that his baby brother got his ass kicked while his two best friends stood by and watched," I hissed.

The cigarette fell out of the other guy's mouth and he made no attempt to catch it. Ron opened his eyes and looked at me as I retrieved my groceries. He was still too dazed to speak, so I took off fast, my heart racing. I was scared yet exhilarated. I was also very, very upset. I had promised my mother that I would not get into fights unless I was defending myself.

As I finished my story, my mother held me tight and asked me if I was all right.

"I'm fine, Mom."

She examined my knuckles. "They're starting to swell. We'll have to put them on ice, but first I want you to go shower and change into some clean clothes. Is the other boy going to be okay?" It wasn't the first time she had had to ice my knuckles.

"I think so. His friends will probably take him to the hospital. He was starting to come to when I left."

She shook her head. "Gianuzzu, che farò con te?" (Johnny, what am I going to do with you?)

"I'm sorry, Mom. I really am. Please don't be mad at me." I couldn't bear the thought of upsetting her. She was too good to me and I worshipped her, but I had a problem and we both knew it.

She smiled, gently wiped a tear from my eye, and kissed me. "Tu sei buon, mio figlio. Tu sei buon. No I'm not mad at you, but I am worried about your temper. Now go clean up and we'll talk some more. Are there going to be police knocking on our door again?"

"I'm not sure."

She nodded with resignation. "Go clean, and remember that I love you. There is no greater love than a mother for her child."

"I love you too, Mom, more than anything."

Years later, I reflected on that day and realized that I had learned a lot. I learned that when confronted with greater odds, it was important to act decisively. I learned that bullies frequently folded like cheap suits. I learned that shopping bags full of groceries can be used as weapons, but most importantly, I learned that my mother had more love, compassion, and understanding in one finger than all of the world's religions combined.

Rx 1

Present Day

THEY say there are no atheists in foxholes, and they're right. Just as true is that, in every man's life, there comes a time when he has to decide whether all the things he thought about himself are true or just a load of bullshit that he's fed himself to bolster his ego. Staring down the barrel of handgun was one of those moments that tended to shed light on that subject. Was I going to run, fight, cry or wet myself? Was I a tough guy or was I the guy who got prison tats even though I'd never even had a parking ticket?

It was Sunday night in New York City, and he was pointing the gun straight at me. It looked like a nine millimeter, maybe a Glock. It was dark out, and I wasn't sure. Many thoughts raced through my mind as I tried hard to maintain eye contact with him. He was very nervous and sweating, probably drugged up or in desperate need of some. He'd caught me by surprise and herded me into a deserted alley, demanding my wallet. I wanted to give it to him. I really did, but I was awkwardly holding a bag of groceries. It was 10 p.m. and Kelly had sent me for some ice cream, so I'd figured I might as well pick up a few other essentials while I was out.

"Give me the damn wallet, asshole," he ordered gruffly. He looked edgy and his eyes darted back and forth nervously. Yeah, he was a cokehead or on something, maybe meth. He was thin, slightly taller

than me, maybe six one, 160lbs. of skin and bones. Greasy and disheveled hair; he was dirty and reeked.

"You told me not to move," I answered calmly and wondered if tonight would be the night I would die. Another casualty of the streets,
the victim of some senseless crime that would spark public outrage for
about the time it took to finish your morning coffee, assuming anyone
would even care at all.

He looked at me and twitched a little. "Move just enough to get
the fucking wallet," he growled. "And don't do anything stupid."

I looked around the dark alley. It was just ten feet wide, fifty feet
long and dead ended in the brick wall that my back was up against.
There were no windows in the buildings on either side. A large metal
dumpster was to my left, and light filtered into the alley from Bleecker
Street. Background traffic noise could be heard in the distance. The
Smith &Wesson .38 holstered in the small of my back called out to
me, and I was considering how I could best get at it. It was positioned
in such a way that I could quickly release it with my right hand, but I
was hampered by the groceries. I thought about the bag of groceries
and a kid named Ron DeMatteo from a long time ago. I sighed deeply
at the memory.

"Hey pal, when was the last time you ate a decent meal?" I asked
as I shifted the grocery bag to my right arm and reached for the wallet
in my back left pocket.

"I'm not your pal and it's none of your business, so shut the fuck
up," he said. He was having trouble concentrating and was very ir-
ritable. I guessed he needed a fix of whatever it was pretty badly. He
blinked and twitched again.

"No reason we can't be civilized about this," I said reasonably. "I
want to help. I know what you're going through." Keep him talking.

I stretched my hand out with the wallet, and just as he was about
to snatch it, I let it drop to the floor. Distracted by its trajectory, he
briefly took his eyes off me. I tossed the grocery bag at him, causing
him to reflexively throw his hands up in a defensive posture. I charged,
grabbed his gun hand, and flung him back into the dumpster. The
force of the impact shook the gun loose to the floor and knocked the
wind out of him.

Without the weapon, he was no match for me. I was six feet tall
and outweighed him by at least fifty pounds. Compared to him, I

was a tank. He was malnourished and starting to exhibit withdrawal symptoms. On the other hand, he might have a backup weapon. I didn't want to hurt him, but he needed to be searched, and still had too much fight left in him. So, I cocked my right fist and gave him a measured three quarter blow to the left side of his face, enough to stun him and convince him to stop moving.

He groaned, relaxed, and I kicked his legs out from under him, laying him face down on the floor. A quick pat down failed to reveal any other weapons. I had my knee in the small of his back and most of my weight resting on him as I perused his driver's license, which was the only item of interest I found. His name was Ed Talbot.

"Hey man, I wasn't going to hurt you. The gun wasn't even loaded," he said.

It was difficult in the dark, but I eventually spotted the pistol about five feet from where we were. "Don't move, Ed," I said as I got off him and picked it up. It wasn't loaded, and I dropped it into the dumpster.

"Can I turn over?" he asked.

"Stay where you are unless you really want to get hurt," I commanded as I retrieved my wallet and collected the groceries, which had sprawled out of their bag.

Once I had organized myself, I told him to stand up. We had reversed positions in the alley. His back was now to the brick wall, and I was blocking him from leaving. I looked him hard in the eyes. "Look, I'm not going to pretend that I can solve all your problems because I know I can't, not in the middle of the night in a dark alley. You have got to want to get better. That's the only way. Right now you're in the early stages of withdrawal and it's only going to get worse if you don't get treatment and food."

He was twitching and jerking even more.

"Walk with me to Saint Matthew's Hospital. It's just a few blocks from here. I'll go in with you and make sure that you receive proper attention, all right?"

He stared blankly at me. "Who are you, fucking Mother Theresa?"

"Look, asshole, I just want to help you, nothing more. Would you prefer I just beat the shit out of you and throw you in the dumpster as payback for sticking a gun in my face?" He could tell that I was deadly serious about that option.

"What if I told you I can't go to that hospital," he said more politely.

"Why?" I asked, suddenly interested.

"Because they'll kill me."

I thought maybe he was in a more advanced stage of withdrawal than I had previously assessed. He was paranoid and maybe starting to get delusional.

"Why would anyone there want to kill you?"

"It's complicated."

"Well, I'm a physician, and I work at Saint Matt's. My name is Dr. John Cesari. We'll walk to the emergency room together, and I promise I won't let anything happen to you. Even better, rather than walk, let's take a cab together. My treat, okay?" I was starting to worry about this guy. Who knew what he might do if he was delusional?

He was quiet for a moment. "Are you really a doctor?"

"Yes, I am. I'm a gastroenterologist, and I really think you should let me help you."

He mulled over his options. I really couldn't force him to seek medical attention if he didn't want to, but he didn't know that. He was probably wondering what would happen if I called the police. That was a good question. He didn't know that I'd left my cellphone on the kitchen counter. Besides, I was the one with the illegal Smith & Wesson on his person.

Even worse, I didn't really have that great a relationship with the authorities. I had a rap sheet from a misguided youth and last year Kelly and I had been at the epicenter of a storm involving criminal activity at an upstate hospital where we worked. My medical license had been suspended for six months because of that episode, and although I was never formally charged with a crime, federal and local law enforcement had made it abundantly clear that I had better not ever show up on their radar again. So, we'd packed up and moved to Manhattan where we now lived in a one-bedroom apartment in Greenwich Village. When my suspension finally ended, I was able to obtain work again at Saint Matthews's as a staff gastroenterologist.

He looked like he was starting to trust me. "You'll stay with me the whole time, right?" he asked.

"The whole time. I promise."

"What's the matter?" he asked, noticing a perplexed look on my face as I observed a quivering red dot on his forehead, barely a split second before his head exploded in front of me.

He went down in a heap, and I threw myself down to the ground after him. The second shot, meant for me, hit the brick wall at the end of the alley. I crawled over Ed Talbot's lifeless body and tried as best as I could to hide myself behind the dumpster. Another shot from the silenced weapon hit the dumpster with a metallic sound. I had the .38 out now, but knew that it wouldn't do me any good against a high powered rifle unless they decided to come looking for me in the alley.

I saw the red dot again flickering along the brick wall behind me, probing. I pulled the corpse closer to me to act as a buffer. Who the fuck was this guy? Was he the primary target or was I? It was pretty dark in the alley. Were they using night vision equipment? Who uses night vision equipment anyway... the military, law enforcement, any asshole with a credit card? I had pissed off a lot of people last year and most of them had long memories, but mob guys generally didn't use high powered rifles and night vision equipment. Plus, they'd had plenty of opportunities to catch me alone. Why wait until there was a witness? No, the only thing that made sense was that he was the target and I was part of the clean-up. It seemed like my friend, Ed Talbot, knew some very unpleasant people.

I waited.

The red dot disappeared, and after about ten minutes of inactivity, I decided to make my move. I pushed Ed off of me and peered around the dumpster carefully. I pulled back quickly, anticipating a slug in my direction, but there was none. I stood up slowly.

Nothing.

Inching slowly forward with my back along the wall, I made it to the entrance of the alley. I looked at my watch. It was 11 p.m. There were people walking on both sides of the street and the usual New York City traffic. There was nothing out of place. I put the .38 back into its holster under my shirt, which I wore outside of my pants. It was a beautiful summer night, and the city appeared undisturbed by my distress.

I looked around then, wondering where the shots had come from. I was near the corner of Bleecker and McDougal Streets, just a stone's throw from the grocery store that I had been shopping at, and about two blocks from my apartment. Kelly would start to worry soon. An ice cream run shouldn't have taken this long.

I held my breath and stepped out quickly from the alley and took off sprinting in the direction away from my apartment, just in case someone was watching me. I didn't want to lead them straight back to Kelly. I reached the corner and made a sharp right and doubled around back. About a block away from where I lived, I stepped into the shadowy entranceway of an apartment building and waited to see if I was being followed. I wasn't, so I continued home.

****

"What means, 'diamonds is missing'?" Hissed the man slowly with a thick Russian accent, menace oozing off every syllable. He sat back comfortably in the large, black leather chair in front of the magnificent mahogany desk that wasn't his. A man approaching sixty stood submissively on the other side. It was his desk and chair, but he was in no position to point that out.

The older man tried to contain his fear as beads of sweat formed on his forehead. "I am sorry, Sergei. Some lowlife drug addict ambushed me just as I was leaving the hospital. He put a gun to my head, but don't worry. I know who he is."

Sergei grinned. "I no worry. You worry for me, yes?"

"Yes, of course. That's what I meant. This guy works at the hospital. I recognized him. He won't get far. I promise. I have somebody looking for him right now."

Sergei was a large, evil looking man of about forty years. He was fair skinned, heavyset, muscular, and about six feet tall. He had a jagged scar running down the left side of his face and was missing his right ear. His wounds were the result of two years at the corrective penal colony at Yavas, five hundred miles east of Moscow. Sergei sat quietly, contemplating the other man who stood before him, head bowed, on the verge of panic.

"Who is somebody looking?"

"My nephew. He's a New York City cop. He and his partner have the guy under surveillance as we speak."

"Call nephew now. I want speak to him."

The older man took out his cell phone and dialed. "Rick? Yeah, this is Uncle Reg. Sergei is here and would like an update on what's going on with Talbot."

"That asshole Sergei is there?"

"Yeah, and I'm going to put him on the phone now. Just tell him what's going on and don't leave anything out."

"Uncle Reg, you don't understand. We're up to our eyeballs in shit down here."

"I don't give a rat's ass. Sergei wants to talk to you, and that's all you need to know. Just tell him everything. Understand? Now here he is." Reg's voice cracked from the stress. He handed the phone to Sergei.

"Speak."

"We followed the guy down to Greenwich Village where he met a friend. They went into a dark alley, and it looked to me like he was about to give the diamonds away."

"What you do?"

"I made the decision to stop the exchange... so I shot him."

"You killed man who stole diamonds?"

"Yes."

"And friend?"

"He got away, but I have a picture of him."

"And diamonds?"

"Haven't found them yet. We just finished searching the alley, and we're in the process of cleaning up the scene. I think the guy has them."

"What mean 'cleaning up' scene?"

"I cut the dead guy's fingertips off and knocked all his teeth out so they won't be able to identify him. Just another dead crackhead who pissed somebody off."

"Where is other guy?"

"I don't know, but we'll find him. We have a description of him, and a photo, albeit a poor one. He's probably pissing in his pants. I'm going to call the shooting in to the precinct along with the local news. That should flush him out. Then we'll go back and search the dead guy's apartment. We almost caught the son-of-a-bitch there earlier today while he was having dinner, but he spotted us coming and took off."

Sergei hung up and placed the phone down on the desk. He was visibly angry.

"Look at me," he commanded.

Reg's gaze unconsciously drifted towards the missing ear.

"You see?"

He nodded.

"Work camps in Russia very hard, very cold. Hungry, always hungry. Man die, we eat. Sometimes, no die. We still eat. Men try eat me. Make soup with ear."

Reg collapsed into a chair behind him, trembling. He didn't like where this was going. "I'm very sorry to hear your troubles."

Sergei nodded. There was a framed photo on the desk and he picked it up to get a better look. "Very pretty. Who is she?"

"It's my daughter, Catherine," Reg whispered hoarsely.

Sergei thought about that for a while. "She has nice ears. Make good soup."

"Please, Sergei. I'll get the diamonds back. I just need a little time."

"Is good to have understand each other."

The smell of the older man's terror permeated the room as he sat in silence, digesting the threat.

Finally, Sergei stood up to leave. "I go back Russia now. When return, you have diamonds, yes?"

"Yes, I will have the diamonds."

"I know you will." He gave the older man a villainous smile, revealing rotting teeth and a poorly fitting bridge that appeared to be hand-carved from wood. As he walked toward the door, he was followed by the two even larger men who had been standing behind him.

Reg sat back in his chair, exhausted and drenched with perspiration. Warm urine ran down his pants leg.

R℟ 2

KELLY looked at me, horrified. "What happened to you? Are you hurt?"

I was breathless, sweating, and had Ed Talbot's blood all over me. "I'm fine. I was in the process of being mugged when somebody blew the head off the guy that was mugging me and then took a few shots at me."

"Oh my God! You can't be serious. Are you sure none of that's your blood? Take your shirt off." She came over to me and started poking and prodding me as I undressed.

Kelly and I had grown very close last year when we were targeted for extermination by the mob. We had uncovered an illegal prescription drug ring at the hospital where we'd worked. The bad guys went to prison and some of their ill-gotten profits found their way into my bank account.

I stood there while she walked around, inspecting me for damage. "Take the pants off, too," she ordered. "They're filthy and you smell. And would you lock that gun up? You promised me you wouldn't walk around with it." Once she was satisfied that I was okay, she threw my shirt and pants into the trash and sat on the sofa, observing me.

"Where did this happen?"

"I got trapped in a dead end alley on Bleecker not too far from the grocery store."

I started to sit next to her and she pushed me back. "Whoa. You're not sitting on the furniture until after you clean up. Just stand there for now and tell me everything. Start from the beginning, and don't leave anything out," she said.

I didn't leave anything out, but I did feel a little silly standing there in my underwear recounting the assassination I'd just witnessed.

She looked very disturbed. "Do you think it's the mob?" she asked.

"I thought about that, but honestly, I think the guy in the alley was the real target. I just happened to be collateral damage. They could easily have shot me first if they had wanted to. Besides, the guy was acting really strange. He said he couldn't go to the hospital because he thought somebody there would kill him. I thought he was just being paranoid from drugs and withdrawal, but now he really is dead."

"Who was he?" she asked.

I picked up my wallet from the coffee table and fished his driver's license out. I had held onto it for security in case he didn't agree to coming with me to the hospital.

"Edward R. Talbot, age 35, lives at number 4 Mercer Street, apartment 5E," I said. "That's just a few blocks from here."

"I think you should call the police and let them sort it out," she said.

"Yeah, I agree. I'll call it in anonymously, though. I really don't need any new problems. Besides, I just started this job a few months ago and I don't think something like this would go over well." There was a six-month probationary period during which I could be dismissed without cause. They had made it very clear that, because of my previous legal difficulties upstate, they would be keeping a close eye on me.

"Why don't you clean up first?"

"Yeah, I'll do that right now."

As I walked toward the bathroom, Kelly giggled. "I could get used to keeping a man around, barefoot and naked."

"Don't forget to chain me to the kitchen table."

I locked the .38 away and showered quickly, putting on a pair of pajama bottoms. When I returned, Kelly was watching television to see if the shooting had made the news yet. I wandered into the kitchen for a glass of water and to make the call to report the incident.

I hadn't even finished dialing the number when Kelly shouted from the living room, "John, come quickly. I don't believe this." She

15

was staring at the screen. There was a reporter at the scene as well as several police cars and an ambulance. More importantly, the reporter was describing a possible suspect that eyewitnesses had seen fleeing from the alley. I hung up the phone.

"The victim is yet unidentified. The suspect is described as six feet, two hundred and twenty pounds, white male with short, dark brown hair, mid-thirties and clean shaven. He is considered to be armed and dangerous," the woman said into the camera, and then there flashed a grainy, long distance photo of me peering out of the alley just before I took off at a full gallop. It had been dark, though, and, at that distance, you really couldn't tell it was me from a million other guys.

I looked at my watch. It was 11 p.m. The incident happened less than an hour ago. That was amazing. A photo and a fairly accurate description.

Kelly had curled onto the sofa, her legs tucked underneath, and I sat down next to her.

"Damn," I said.

"How could they have all this information already?" She asked. "It just happened a short time ago."

"I don't know. It was a silenced weapon, so I don't think anyone heard the shots. Heck, I was the one being shot at and I couldn't hear them. Maybe someone happened to go in the alley just as I left and found the body. Still, it's remarkable how fast everyone responded, and they even have a photo and a halfway decent description of me. The sketch artists will be working overtime tonight."

"What now, John?"

"I'm not sure," I answered truthfully. "I haven't really done anything wrong, and circumstances dictate that I should just turn myself in, but there's something wrong with all of this. It smells too much like a set-up."

High powered rifles with laser sites and night vision equipment? Rapid police deployment and media coverage? Geez, I didn't like this at all. Who was Ed Talbot and why was he suddenly dead?

R℞ 3

"I think this is a very bad idea, Cesari," Kelly said apprehensively as we walked down W. Houston St. toward Mercer St. and Ed Talbot's apartment building.

"I know, Kel, and you're probably right. But I'm curious as to who this guy was and why he just had his head blown off. Besides, if I'm being made the fall guy here, I think I have a right to know what's going on."

She sighed deeply as we crossed Greene St. "Aren't you being just a little paranoid?"

"Somebody just took a shot at me, Kel. I would hardly call that being paranoid."

"I know, but isn't it possible that this was just some random drive-by shooting? It happens all the time all over the country."

"Random shooting?" I thought about that. "That was a hell of a random shot; dead center of the forehead in a dark alley with a silenced rifle using laser sights. Still, you do make a valid point, but what a coincidence that someone got a description of me and a photo to the police within an hour. It just doesn't seem right. New York doesn't work like that."

It was almost midnight, and the village was jumping. It was a beautiful night in August, and the streets were crowded with throngs of people looking for entertainment. Every now and then someone would gaze at us just a little longer than seemed appropriate, which never failed to irk Kelly.

She shook her head in annoyance. "You'd think they'd never seen an interracial couple before. For God's sake, this is Manhattan and people still stare."

I laughed. "Oh Kel, they're just staring because you're so beautiful. You could be a model, you know?" She was five foot three, slender and perfectly shaped. She had big green seductive eyes and long, wild black hair that drove me crazy.

"You are so full of it, Cesari. Did you know *that?*" she said, and wrapped her arm in mine. We had been through this conversation many times before, and it always ended the same way. She thought people stared because she was black and I wasn't. It was my opinion that people stared because she was drop dead gorgeous, and they were wondering what she was doing with a loser like me. I would've stared, too.

We turned right onto Mercer St. and found his apartment building in the middle of the block. It was a very old ten-story brick structure in a low income, rent controlled neighborhood; maybe a half step up from being a crackhouse. We entered the main foyer and shut the door behind us. It was way too late to just start pressing door buzzers randomly, so I decided that a little old-fashioned breaking and entering was in order. There were no security cameras or doormen. I glanced around quickly, and using my shoulder and hip, lurched against the old wood door. The lock gave in easily and fairly quietly under my weight.

I looked at Kelly and said, "C'mon, we're in."

"Great. I want you to know that I don't find skills like yours very attractive."

Once inside, we found an elevator and took it up to the fifth floor. It was noisy and opened into a dimly lit hallway. There were five apartments on this floor. The one we were looking for was at the other end of the hallway, directly opposite the elevator. The wood floor groaned and creaked as we approached his apartment.

We stood in front of the door, considering our options while staring at the obscene graffiti on the walls.

I whispered, "Man, this place is a dump."

"What if he has a roommate or a girlfriend?"

I hesitated. "I'll knock first before breaking in, okay? If anyone answers, we're just returning his driver's license."

"At midnight?"

"Shhh."

I listened carefully for any sounds coming from inside the apartment and didn't hear any. So, I reached up and gently knocked on the door and, to my surprise, it swung slowly inward. Kelly and I looked at each other apprehensively.

We stood at the threshold and peered inside. As our courage grew, we furtively stepped into the apartment, closing the door behind us. I signaled Kelly to stand by the entrance while I checked around to see if we had company. It was a small one-bedroom apartment, and we stood in the central living area that opened into a separate kitchen space. The only other door led into the bedroom, which I quickly found was without an occupant.

I turned on a table lamp next to the sofa, and we could see that the place was a mess.

Kelly said, "This is disgusting. How could anyone live like this, and shouldn't we be wearing gloves by the way?"

She was right on both points. The sofa cushions were on the floor. Clothes were strewn everywhere. The carpet was stained, and the place reeked of cigarettes, pot, and booze. Paint was peeling off the walls and ceiling.

The kitchen was worse. After the roaches ran for cover, we observed dishes with partially eaten food on a small table. There were more dirty dishes in the sink, and the kitchen drawers were on the floor with their contents spilled out. The refrigerator door was open.

"You're right about the gloves, Kel. I should have thought of that. There are some kitchen towels we can use to touch things if we have to and we can use them to wipe down the room when we're done. So far, we're only talking about a door knob and lamp, but let's be careful, all right?"

She nodded. "What do you think?"

"I think the guy was probably a crackhead but I also think someone searched the place. Maybe he wasn't as strung out as I thought."

"Do you think they found what they were looking for?"

"Hard to say. You check out the living room and kitchen, and I'll search the bedroom more thoroughly. You never know what we might find. It would be nice to know what we're looking for, but that's how it rolls sometimes."

She started turning over sofa pillows and looking through the piles of clothes that littered the floor. I did the same in the bedroom, inspecting overturned drawers and empty shoeboxes. I found lots of drug paraphernalia such as needles, bongs, pipes, and a couple of vials of crack. I also picked up an employee photo ID that said he was an orderly at Saint Matthew's Hospital and pocketed it.

Kelly and I converged back in the living room.

"Find anything interesting?" she asked.

"Only this," I replied, showing her the ID badge. "And some drug stuff."

She studied the ID. "He worked at Saint Matt's?"

"How about that? Finding anything in here?"

"Nothing much, unless squalor counts."

I looked around the small living room and said, "Now what could this dirt bag possibly have that would be worth killing him over? And where would he hide it in such a small place like this?" I drifted into the kitchen area and looked around.

Kelly followed me. "God, what a disaster."

"Nothing grosses me out more than someone else's dirty dishes and half eaten food lying around," I said.

"I know. You tell me that all the time," Kelly smiled. Dirty dishes were one of my favorite pet peeves. I couldn't even sleep at night unless all the plates and silverware were washed, and the countertops wiped down. Trash bags had to be knotted up and anything edible sealed tightly and put away. I couldn't help it. I grew up poor and fighting off the nightly invasion by roaches and other night crawlers was a constant battle. The best defense was strict adherence to cleanliness and proper sanitation.

"If you ever want me to leave, just do this," I said, panning around.

"Okay, enough already. The guy was a slob. I get it. Are we done yet?"

There was a plate on the table with a partially eaten cheeseburger and fries on it. Nearby sat a Wendy's bag and two glasses, one with water, the other half-filled with Jack Daniels, the uncapped bottle next to it.

On the stove was a covered metal quart pot. I took the cover off and saw that the pot was half-filled with cold tomato sauce. There was an open jar of Ragu next to it on the counter top. This struck me as odd, but why?

Kelly saw my furrowed brow. "What's wrong?"

"I don't know exactly. There's something wrong with this scene, but I can't put my finger on it."

I circled in place, soaking it in and trying to make sense of it all. I stopped and took a few steps back to see it from a different perspective. I looked in the refrigerator and then all of the cabinets.

It was a small kitchen: a table with two chairs, a half-eaten burger with fries from Wendy's, and a glass of whiskey with an open bottle. There was cold tomato sauce on the stovetop and empty drawers with their contents all over the floor. Nothing in the fridge but a carton of milk and some vegetables. Bare cupboards.

"Kelly, what's the impression you get when you look at this kitchen?"

She scanned the room in much the same fashion I had. "He didn't finish his meal. So, he wasn't very hungry or he got interrupted. He was a slob but he wouldn't have just left it there, would he? The same for the whiskey."

"Agreed. Something came up in a hurry, causing him to cut his meal short. What else?" I asked.

She thought about it hard, eventually coming to the pot of tomato sauce on the stovetop.

She looked at me and said, "There's no pasta anywhere."

"Exactly, there's none in the refrigerator, cabinets, or even the trash. So why would he be heating up tomato sauce when he was in the middle of chowing down on a cheeseburger?"

We both looked at the pot on the stove carefully. I touched the side of it gingerly to make sure it wasn't hot. It wasn't. I leaned over and sniffed it. Nothing unusual.

"Aren't we getting carried away here?" Kelly said. "So he decided to heat up some sauce to go with his burger. Maybe he was experimenting with his cuisine."

I looked at her like she was crazy. "Yeah, right. Maybe he was going to be the next *Iron Chef.*"

I stood over the pot and hesitated. Oh, what the heck. I plunged my hand into the sauce and fished around the bottom, eventually coming across a small, hard, faceted object.

"Bingo," I said, and Kelly's eyes lit up with excitement.

"What is it?"

I pulled my hand out of the sauce, rinsed it off in the sink, and we examined the largest, most beautiful diamond either one of us had ever seen. It was round, white, more than a half-inch across, and dazzled brilliantly in the light.

"Wow," Kelly said. "I've never seen a diamond that big before. Do you think it's real?"

I held it up to examine it more carefully. "I don't know too much about diamonds, but it certainly looks like the real deal."

"Real or not, he was trying to hide it from someone. That's for sure."

"He most certainly was, wasn't he?"

Kelly said, "He must have known they were coming for him, and he was out of time. Pretty clever ruse. Open a jar of sauce and toss it in. With all this mess, who would know? I kind of admire his ingenuity."

"I have to agree. Pretty quick thinking for a crackhead."

"Where do you think he got it?" she continued.

"I don't know, but I'm getting the feeling that he died because of it."

R̶X 4

"**OKAY,** at least we know why he was killed," I said. "On the other hand, if you're the one looking for the diamond, why kill him if you don't have it yet?"

Kelly thought about that.

"I don't know. That doesn't seem to make sense—unless it was for revenge for stealing it."

I suddenly got nervous.

"Or maybe they figured out where the diamond was and decided they didn't need him anymore."

We looked at each other. "C'mon, let's get out of here," I said.

We walked over to the door, and I opened it. As I did, the elevator doors at the other end of the hallway opened. Two large men stepped out and froze when they saw us, but only for a second. They reached under their sport coats, retrieving handguns, and charged toward us. I slammed the door shut and quickly engaged the series of deadbolts that lined the inside of most New York City apartments, including this one. There was one at the top, one in the middle, and one at the bottom. I grabbed Kelly by the hand, and we bolted toward the bedroom.

"The bedroom window opens onto a fire escape," I said.

The men started banging on the door and slamming their shoulders against it.

In the bedroom, I opened the window and helped Kelly onto the metal landing. She was petite and easily fit through, scampering her way down. I quickly followed, and we made it to the bottom uneventfully. Once on the sidewalk, we started running as fast as we could. We heard a voice shouting at us and looked back. One of the guys was squeezing himself through the window. He held a pistol in his right hand.

On West Houston we jumped into a cab.

"Go, go, go," I said to the driver. "Anywhere." I tossed a couple of twenties at him.

Kelly exhaled slowly, "Shit. Who were they?"

"I don't know. They could've been cops, but why would they draw weapons on unarmed civilians?"

She glared at me.

"What?"

"Are you unarmed, Cesari?"

"Yes, I locked it up like you told me to. You can frisk me if you want."

"Put your hands on your head while I search you."

I did as I was told.

"Now spread your legs."

I saw the driver watching in the mirror. "Drop us off at Washington Square Park by the Fifth Avenue entrance and keep your eyes on the road."

"Sure thing," he said.

A few minutes later, we stood beneath the archway of the park, which was crowded with musicians, artists, students, revelers, and the homeless.

"What now and why did we come here?" Kelly asked.

"I felt the need to be surrounded by people. If it looks like no one followed us here, we'll head home. Let's grab a bench and listen to that guy over there playing the guitar."

He was thin, skanky, and not half bad, playing and singing "Hotel California." His guitar was an old, beaten-up acoustic. I dropped a five in his guitar case, and he nodded 'thank you' while he sang. We'd sat there for about ten minutes when I observed two men enter the park, twisting their heads in every direction looking for something. They were big and Nordic looking. Short hair, clean shaven, one was blonde. Assholes.

I put my arm around Kelly and kissed her so I could look in their direction better without being too obvious.

"Now that's what I'm talking about," she meowed. That's what I liked about Kelly. Anytime, anyplace.

"Those guys are here," I whispered into her ear, and she suddenly became alarmed. "They're behind you and to the right. Don't turn around."

"But how?"

"I don't know. Let's go. They're searching the other end of the park first. Goddamn, I can't believe it."

We hustled quickly out of the park and made our way up Fifth Avenue.

"How could they have known where the cab dropped us off?" She asked.

"Not sure. They might have called the yellow cab company, demanded to know if one of their cabs had just picked up a couple on West Houston and where they dropped them off. Only the police and certain government agencies have that kind of pull, though."

"Then they might really have been the police."

"Yeah, I guess, but why so jumpy with the guns? I mean they drew their pieces as soon as they saw me. Why would they do that? I wasn't threatening anyone. Besides, I've been in a lot of hairy situations, and there was something definitely wrong about those guys. I know the look when I see it, and I could see it in their eyes."

"What look is that?"

"The *I'm going to kill you look,* and they had it."

She chuckled. "Bronx intuition again?"

"You can laugh all you want, but it's kept me breathing all these years."

"So, if you can read people's eyes, what are mine saying right now?" She stopped and turned to look at me. She had the most beautiful green eyes, and she knew damn well that I was powerless when I looked into them.

"They're saying that you want me to buy you an ice cream cone."

She shoved me. "They're saying that it's almost one in the morning and I am too tired to walk all the way back to the apartment. So what are we going to do?"

"I don't wish to be paranoid, but if those guys have pull with the cab companies, they could just as easily have told them to check in if they pick up a white man and a black woman, say, within a five-block radius of the park."

"So what are we supposed to do if we can't take a cab?"

We had just reached W.11th Street. "Let's turn left here. There's the Larchmont Hotel toward the end of the block. I stayed there once a long time ago. They may have a room available."

"We're going to stay in a hotel when our apartment is less than a mile away?"

"Like I said, I don't think it's safe to take a cab. It might lead them right to our apartment. And as tiny as you are, I don't think I can carry you the whole way home."

R⬩X 5

WE entered the lobby of the Larchmont shortly after one a.m. and booked a room.

"You're lucky this is off season. We're usually booked solid," the receptionist said. He handed me the room key and pointed out the elevators. "There's complementary coffee in the lobby all night."

"Thank you," I replied. "Do you have a computer room I can use?"

"There's free Wi-Fi in all the rooms and there's a business center just down the hall. You can use your room key to access it."

"Thank you again."

"It's a really nice hotel," Kelly said, looking around. It had a European flare to it. There was plush red carpet in the main lobby and gold-framed paintings decorating the walls with sconces on the side. There was a huge crystal chandelier in the center of the ceiling. The wallpaper had a dark floral pattern to it.

"They've really upgraded it since I was here last. Back then you used to have to share bathrooms with the other guests."

We walked the fifty feet to the elevators and got on. "We're in room 701." I said, and she pushed the button for 7.

The room was fairly spacious with a king sized four poster bed and a window overlooking W.11th Street. There was a desk and a large flat screen television.

Kelly was pooped. "I'm going to take a quick shower and go to bed. I have to be at the hospital at seven sharp. Somebody's got to work around here."

She worked in the St. Matt's emergency room and pulled three twelve-hour shifts a week. Financially, we were doing okay now that I had started working again. I had a significant amount of money in an offshore account, but couldn't really touch it. It had belonged to the mob guys we'd run into last year. Their accounts had accidentally fallen into my hands. They didn't know where the money was, but I felt it was still a little too hot to handle just yet, except for emergencies.

"Kel, would you mind if I went down to the computer room to do some research? I'm a little wound up, and want to Google up who might be missing a very large diamond. I won't be long."

"No, I don't mind, but why don't you just look it up on your smartphone?"

"I prefer to read on a larger screen, and I think I'd like some coffee." I had some business at the front desk that I didn't want to worry her with.

"Coffee, at this hour? Are you insane? You know, Cesari, babysitting you is becoming a full-time job. Drink all the coffee you want. I don't care. Now go, I'm tired and need to get to sleep. Just make sure you don't bother me when you come back." She yawned, and disappeared into the bathroom.

I chuckled to myself. Just for that, I was definitely going to *bother* her when I returned.

Down in the lobby, I handed the desk clerk a fifty dollar bill. "If two big guys come in tonight looking for us, I'd appreciate it if you developed amnesia and maybe give a call to the room. Think you can handle that?"

He pocketed the bill. "Sure. I guess I don't want to know why."

"No, you don't, but if we get through the night without any problems, there'll be another fifty waiting for you in the morning. Deal?"

"Deal."

I grabbed a small cup of coffee and let myself into the business center. For only ten dollars I could use the computer there for thirty minutes. I slid my credit card into the receptacle and gave my approval to charge my account.

I started with a general query about diamonds, robberies, thefts and so on. A variety of hits came up about jewelry store robberies and home break-ins. Mostly, the stories were old and small potatoes. Nothing big like heist of the century. I then googled diamond prices. Hmm. Difficult to say without an appraisal. It all depended on the color, clarity, and degree of perfection. I took out the diamond and looked at it carefully. I had no way of measuring it exactly, but it looked wider than a half inch, which would make it roughly about five or six carats although, strictly speaking, carats were a measure of weight and not size. It was round and sparkled in the light. Assuming this was a perfectly flawless white diamond, it might be in the $500,000 or more range, according to the online chart I was using as a reference. Now, man-made diamonds were a different issue. They weren't nearly as valuable, but apparently were just as pretty. Any diamond dealer worth his salt should be able to tell the difference. I looked up the nearest diamond dealers, and jotted a few names and addresses down before logging off.

As I finished my coffee, I thought about who those guys chasing us might be. In another life, I had rubbed elbows with all sorts of the wrong people and had developed a feel for who the bad guys were. Those two certainly triggered off my early warning system.

It was close to 3 a.m. Better get some sleep. I was pretty tired and starting to come down from all the excitement. Looked like Kelly's off the hook after all. I smiled and left the business center.

I let myself quietly into the dark room. She had shut the curtains, and it was pitch black. I undressed, and snuck into my side of the bed by feel. I gently inched over to where she lay. I figured a little spooning wouldn't hurt, right?

"You're a pain in the neck. Did you know that?" she said, annoyed. "I told you I need to get some sleep. I'm exhausted."

"I'm sorry," I whispered. "Go back to sleep. I'll be as quiet as a door mouse."

"Oh, shut up and come over here. Let's get this over with."

R⃥x 6

IT was 9 a.m. when I finally woke to find Kelly had already left for work. I jumped up and took a quick shower. I would change into surgical scrubs when I got to the hospital. I only had one colonoscopy scheduled today and a series of orientation meetings. Almost 6 months under my belt, and I still barely knew where the bathrooms were.

I checked out of the hotel quickly, and dropped off the room key at the front desk. The clerk from the night before had already left, so I made a mental note to settle up with him in a day or two. I owed him another fifty. On Fifth Avenue, I caught a cab to St. Matthew's on the lower east side. It was one of the older hospitals in Manhattan, and despite its name, had long since shed its religious affiliations. The main lobby was spacious and crowded. There was a Starbucks off to one side, and I bought myself an Americano with a croissant. I really liked coffee. The stronger the better.

I meandered up to the third floor operating room area where I found the doctor's changing area. I threw my belongings, including the diamond, into my locker and put on a pair of blue scrubs. With my pager on my waist and stethoscope around my neck, I was ready to face the day. The coffee was good, but the croissant, not so much. It could have benefitted from a little crisping up in an oven and maybe some strawberry jam, too. As these thoughts crossed my mind, I heard my name paged overhead to the endoscopy room.

"Good morning, Dr. Cesari."

"Good morning, Gina. Good morning, Mary. How is everyone today?"

"We're great."

Mary and Gina were my endoscopy nurses today. Mary was about fifty and very business-like. Gina was in her late twenties and distractingly attractive. This was a big hospital and there were many OR nurses, so I was just starting to get to know them. They had just wheeled Mr. McCormick in for his colonoscopy. He was seventy-five years old and had a history of colon polyps. He'd been pre-sedated by anesthesia and was already snoring.

"Hi, Kirk, what have you given him so far?" Kirk Anderson was the anesthesiologist. Tall and blonde, he towered over everyone else in the room.

"I only gave him two milligrams of Versed, and he's already almost completely out. Sorry, Cesari. I won't do that again."

"It's okay, Kirk. All right, ladies, let's roll him into position and get started." I had told Kirk previously not to snow my patients before I had a chance to say hello, but everything these days was about efficiency and speed. Kirk was young, fresh out of training and meant well. He'd get the hang of things. The lights went out and I started the case. The patient had two small polyps, which I removed, a mild case of diverticulosis and some hemorrhoids. Thirty minutes later, they wheeled him into the recovery room, and I went to dictate my report. This is what it was all about: saving lives, one colonoscopy at a time.

Kirk sat down next to me as I finished dictating. He was broad-shouldered, blue-eyed, and athletic. He liked to compete in those iron man events. I put the recording device back into its cradle.

"What's up, Kirk?"

"I just wanted to say I'm sorry again about sedating the guy before you saw him."

"Forget about it. I'll visit him in his room later. He'll be fine. How are things going with you here? You're almost as new here as I am."

"Things are good. My wife and I are adjusting to life in Manhattan. To say the least, it's been challenging."

"I'll bet. Where are you two from?"

"We both grew up in a small town in Vermont. We were high school sweethearts."

"Nice. Vermont, huh? The Green mountains. I didn't know that. Where exactly in Vermont are you from?"

"A little place called Woodstock. It's in the middle of the state, lots of trees, squirrels, and your occasional moose."

I chuckled. "Woodstock? Like the town in upstate New York where they had that big rock concert in the sixties?"

"Yeah, spelled the same way, only nothing that exciting ever happens up there."

"Interesting. Is it worth a visit? My girlfriend Kelly has been bugging me about taking a weekend trip to Vermont in the fall to go leaf peeping." I made a face.

He laughed, "Yeah, the foliage is a big thing up there. Their whole economy revolves around New Yorkers coming up to see the fall colors. If you ever do go, there's a great bed and breakfast called the Reluctant Panther you may want to look into. It's on the main street, and quite a historic home with a beautiful setting; I bet your girlfriend would love it."

"Thanks for the tip. Say, Kirk, I don't mean to change the subject, but do you know a guy named Ed Talbot? I think he's an orderly here."

I fished his driver's license out of my pocket and showed it to him. "I found this on the floor of the locker room, and wanted to return it."

He studied the picture carefully. "Yeah, I've seen him around. Real skanky looking guy. I'd like to know what his HIV status is. I know he dates one of your nurses, or used to anyway."

"You're kidding? This guy? Which nurse?"

"The one you worked with this morning, Gina."

I was incredulous. "You can't be serious. She's so beautiful. It's hard to believe she'd ever be caught dead with this guy."

"Birds of a feather flock together, Cesari."

"What's that supposed to mean?"

He leaned closer in a conspiratorial manner and lowered his voice. "Everyone in the OR suspects she uses."

"Really? Well, I'm sorry to hear that."

"Why? Were you thinking of tapping that?"

He made me laugh. "No, it's just that..."

"Just that you were thinking of tapping that." Now he laughed. "Don't worry, Cesari, your secret's safe with me. Just make sure you wear a condom."

"Enough with the tapping. So, where would this guy's locker be? I'll just slip it under the door for him."

"I don't know exactly, although I've seen him change along the far wall several times." He pointed to a row of numbered lockers about twenty feet away.

"Thanks, I'll check with another orderly to figure out which one."

R℞ 7

I**T** was 11a.m. when I called Kelly. "Hi, Kel. How's your day going?"

"It's going. Any idea yet about what's up with that diamond?"

"No, nothing yet. I'm on my way to a mandatory seminar on sexual harassment. All the male employees have to attend. I did find out something interesting about one of the OR nurses, though. I'll fill you in later. There are too many people around. It'll be time for lunch when this lecture is over. Can you get away for a bite?"

"Maybe. Call me when you're done, and let me know if you learn anything."

"About what, the diamond?"

"No, sexual harassment! I'm exhausted because of you. I couldn't get back to sleep after you woke me up. I'm serious. You've got to stop pulling that little trick at three in the morning."

I chuckled. "I'm sorry. I slept like a baby."

"Shut up, Cesari."

"Okay, bye. Got to go. They're ready to start." I entered the basement classroom, and grabbed a chair in the back row near the exit in case I got paged out —or fell asleep.

There were about ten guys in the rectangular classroom, mostly physicians, and about twice as many empty chairs. An empty podium stood in front of us next to a large screen and a projector set up for a slide show.

After about a minute of waiting, the head of Human Resources, a guy called Bill Tarson, walked in accompanied by a thirty-year-old stunning brunette wearing a tight skirt, high heels and black hose. As she took the podium, I turned to the guy next to me and whispered, "I think that I've just died and gone to heaven."

Fred Bergstresser, one of our orthopedic surgeons, chuckled. "Cesari, meetings like this were meant specifically for guys like you."

I countered with, "Please, dear God, tell me she's not going to talk to us about sexual harassment. She's not even wearing a bra."

"Would you prefer a Romanian Olympic discus thrower on steroids?"

"It doesn't seem fair, Fred."

"Shhh."

Bill Tarson was a suit-wearing fifty-year-old man. He was corporate all the way. "Gentlemen, Doctors, I would like to introduce you to Dr. Pamela Gottlieb. As you may know, one of the ever-present dangers in the workplace today is the constant threat of sexual harassment. In the last year, there have been over 1.4 billion dollars in settlements nationwide because of this scourge. We here at St. Matthew's do not intend to take this problem lying down. Our position is to be proactive and aggressive in our approach. We have, in this hospital, a zero tolerance policy towards such behavior. Dr. Gottlieb has a PhD in human psycho-sexual behavior and has numerous publications on this subject. She is on the faculty at NYU, and has graciously agreed to share with us her thoughts on this vexing issue. Let's all give her a warm welcome."

We all clapped politely as she took the podium.

I leaned over to Fred. "I think I'm in love."

He chuckled quietly. "Fucking Cesari, you're not going to be happy until we're both suspended."

The lights went out, the slide show started and I zoned out. I had been to dozens of these things. The bottom line was that, if a woman didn't like you, almost anything you said or did could be interpreted as sexual harassment. These meetings weren't so much to prevent sexual harassment as they were to mitigate settlements by demonstrating good faith with the courts. I found it amusing that a woman could do anything she wanted to a man, including grabbing his crotch in the middle of a colonoscopy, and there was absolutely nothing he could do about it other than politely decline the offer. It was assumed that a man should be able to defend himself. Maybe they were right. The take home message was that you had better make the girls you work with like you or you're fucked. An hour later the lights came on and somebody woke me up.

We all clapped and signed the attendance sheet. I looked at my cell phone and saw a text from Kelly that the ER was a madhouse and she couldn't break away for lunch. So, I headed back to the locker room and found an orderly who told me which locker belonged to Ed Talbot. It was in the corner, locker number 45. It had a combination lock dangling through a hook. It was a big hospital, and if anybody knew he was dead, they weren't letting on, not even Gina. She looked fine this morning. But then again, if Ed was a crackhead, prolonged absences might be expected.

I inspected the lock. It was light-weight and inexpensive looking. The kind you might get at Walmart. All I needed was a hammer or chain cutter. As I studied it, another physician entered the locker room. Reginald Griffin III M.D., the senior gastroenterologist on staff, chair of the department. There were ten gastroenterologists at Saint Matt's. He was the boss man.

"Ah, Cesari. Good to see you. How are things coming along? Adjusting to St. Matt's?" He opened his locker and starting changing in front of me. Not exactly a pleasant sight. He was in his late fifties, tall and potbellied, with skinny legs and a pasty complexion. His hair was graying and he wore glasses. His accent and demeanor screamed North East money. His reputation was notorious, especially with the younger nurses, who referred to him as Uncle Reg.

"I'm adjusting real well, sir. I really like it here so far." I stood stiffly, not sure what to do.

"Well, that's good. I'm hearing very positive things about you, so keep up the good work. You're Italian, right?"

"Sicilian."

He seemed puzzled. "What's the difference?"

"The Italians don't like us."

"Why is that?"

"Because we're better than they are," I grinned.

He chuckled. "Being Sicilian sounds a lot like being Irish."

"Exactly."

He finished putting on his scrubs and closed his locker. "I'm glad I ran into you, Cesari. I've been meaning to talk to you about your productivity. Your colonoscopy numbers are pretty dismal. I realize you're new and all that, but I think there are a few things you could be doing to market yourself a little better, if you know what I mean?"

"I'm all ears." We started walking toward the door together.

"For starters, have you thought about giving a series of lectures on colon cancer screening to the primary care docs? You know, raise awareness and all that. Maybe going to their offices and press the flesh. Bring them lunch and the like. Let them get to know what a great guy you are. You know, when I was your age, Cesari, I beat the bushes hard for business. You young guys today just don't seem as motivated. I don't know... maybe we're just paying you guys too much. You just don't seem as hungry as you ought to be."

"I'll try harder, Dr. Griffin. I promise. Those were very good ideas you gave me, and I'll work on it."

"You do that and don't be afraid to get a little edgy. I used to take my biggest referrers out for drinks once a week; get them trashed, the whole nine yards. Hookers came in handy, too. You know how boys are." He laughed at that, and put his arm around my shoulder as he continued his fatherly advice.

"Come Mondays, my office would be flooded with colonoscopy consults. It was well worth the investment. What I'm trying to say is that you do whatever you have to, Cesari. Think outside the box. Remember, healthcare is just a business like any other. The Japanese like to say that business is war, and it is. Have you ever heard that?"

"No, I haven't, but I promise to keep that in mind."

"Well, if there's anything you need, Cesari, you let me know, all right?"

"Thank you, Dr. Griffin. You must have a case now, so I'll be on my way."

"Yes, I have a colonoscopy, sort of a V.I.P. case, and then I'll be heading over to the office. If you see Gina out there, could you tell her that I'll need her to scrub in with me on this one? I don't want anybody else but her."

"Yes, I will Dr. Griffin." We parted company as he headed toward the endoscopy rooms, and I toward the OR lounge.

It didn't take long to figure out what the pecking order was at St. Matt's. The bottom dwellers like myself didn't get to pick and choose which nurses we worked with. I opened the door to leave, and practically ran into Gina in the hallway as she walked by.

"I'm sorry Gina. I didn't see you there."

"That's okay, Cesari. No harm, no foul." She was as hot as they came. Late twenties, five four, long dark hair, round in all the right places. Great ass. It was hard to believe she was a drug addict, but you could never tell with these things.

"I just left Dr. Griffin, and he asked me to tell you that he'd like you to assist him with his colonoscopy. He's heading over to the endoscopy room as we speak."

"Oh, okay. Thanks." She looked startled or upset or something.

"Everything okay, Gina?"

"Yeah, sure. Everything's fine. Thanks for asking."

That was strange. If I didn't know better, I would have thought she was about to go into the men's locker room. I briefly wondered if I should tell her about Ed but decided that would open up a can of worms I wasn't ready to deal with. Like how did I know he was dead when no one else did?

******

"Any news?"

"We've got a lead, Sergei. We think the guy checked into a hotel called the Larchmont. We'll have his identity soon."

"I call tomorrow."

R_X 8

I cruised down to the first floor to say hi to Kelly in the ER, but she was too busy to do anything but wave back at me. It was lunch time, so I decided to go to the cafeteria and grab a bite by myself while I thought about what to do next. Breaking into Ed Talbot's locker in the middle of the day didn't seem like a good idea, but I was getting eager to find out what it had to offer.

I bought a ham and cheese sandwich and a cup of coffee. A corner table beckoned me, so I sat down facing a wall, my back to the room. The cafeteria was filled with employees and visitors. I didn't know too many people yet, so I politely stared at nothing in particular while I ate.

"May I join you?" I turned, and all I could see was a pair of thighs up to the ceiling.

"Sure," I said. It was Dr. Gottlieb, the sexual harassment lady. She sat opposite me with her lunch tray.

I reached across the table to shake her hand. "Hi, I'm John Cesari."

"Pam Gottlieb."

"Great lecture this morning, Dr. Gottlieb. I really learned a lot."

"Really, is that why you slept through the whole thing? And please call me Pam, John."

Silence.

I squirmed in my chair. "I'm sorry. I was up all night taking care of sick patients. When the lights went out, mother nature just kind of took over." It sounded weak.

She looked at me sympathetically. "Uh-huh. Relax, John, I know this kind of stuff seems silly to you, but it has to be done."

"Yes, I realize that."

"Well I'm glad we're on the same side. Some men can be very difficult about these things."

"Not me. I'm very progressive." I was starting to cheer up. She wasn't so bad after all.

"That's good to hear. I knew we were going to get along."

"Thanks for letting me off the hook like that, Pam."

"I didn't say I was letting you off the hook." She took a forkful of her salad.

"You're not?" I didn't like the ring of that.

"This hospital has a mandatory counseling program for those men that have been identified as high risk for reprobate behavior."

"And what exactly does that mean?" I asked warily. Reprobate was a big word for a guy from the Bronx.

"It means that sleeping through a mandatory lecture on sexual harassment places you in the high risk category. Don't feel bad, though; studies indicate that at least ten percent of all men need to be in preventative counseling for this kind of thing."

"I need counseling even though I haven't done anything? Oh c'mon. You can't be serious."

"Oh yeah. You need it more than most. And by the way, I am wearing a bra. I also have outstanding hearing." She took a sip from her bottled water.

"That was a joke, Pam." I had suddenly lost my appetite.

She smiled. "Really. Well, the next time you make a joke, be sure to tell me, so I'll know when to laugh."

She reached into her bag and came out with a business card, which she slid across the table at me. "Look, John, this won't be so bad. We can meet Wednesday nights. I have an office on the tenth floor in the Givelber building over at N.Y.U. It's not hard to find. The counseling sessions generally go for about an hour, from six to seven for a total of eight weeks. If you don't show up, I'm required to call the director of Human Resources and the chair of your department to report you. I should let you know that failing to attend the counseling sessions could result in your immediate suspension. At the end of the eight weeks, you get a certificate stating that it's safe for you to be around women again." She smiled and I groaned.

After she finished her meal, she stood to leave. "See you Wednesday, John, and don't be so glum. It's not the end of the world."

I nodded. Great. How was I going to explain this to Kelly? Pam was wrong. It was definitely the end of the world.

I left the cafeteria and went down to the maintenance department in the basement of the hospital. There were a couple of guys in dark brown uniforms standing around a work table. The room was painted a drab green, and smelled of machine oil and sweat. There were drills, saws, hammers, and other tools attached to peg boards on the walls.

"Hi guys," I said, announcing myself.

"Hello, Doctor, how can I help you?" The guy in charge asked. He looked about forty and had huge hands that were blackened from grease.

"I was just wondering if you guys had a small chain cutter I could borrow. I have an old lock on my gym bag that I forgot the combination to. I'd like to get rid of it."

"Sure do. Let me just take a look over here." He walked to the other side of the room and returned with a small chain cutter that looked like a large pair of scissors. "This should do the trick. You'll need to sign for it, okay?"

He put it in a small duffel bag for me, and I signed a sheet of paper on his clipboard. "You don't want to walk around the operating room with that out in the open, Doc. God knows what the patients will think," he chuckled.

"Thanks. I'll bring it back in about thirty minutes."

As I left, the guy said, "Next time just bring your bag down here and save yourself a trip."

"Thanks."

R 9

I waited until just after 4 p.m. The OR was nearly deserted by then as the typical workday was from 7 a.m. to 3 p.m. There was just one operating room in use now. The vascular surgeon was in the middle of an aortic graft procedure and wouldn't be done for another two or three hours. The locker room was empty.

Using the chain cutter, I easily clipped the lock off of Ed Talbot's locker. Inside was some loose change, a comb, a pack of cigarettes, and a USB memory stick. I reached for the memory stick and accidentally bumped the little box of unfiltered Camels, causing a jiggling sound. I pocketed the memory stick, and picked up the pack of cigarettes. Opening it, I found no cigarettes, but ten more diamonds roughly the same size or bigger than the one I already had.

Damn!

I put the pack of Camels with the diamonds in my pocket, and tossed what was left of Ed's combination lock into the trash can by the door. I hesitated. Maybe I should replace the lock. Why? Who would notice and would anyone care? I wrestled with the pros and cons of this on the way down to the ER to see Kelly.

She looked frazzled when I caught her attention. "Rough day, Kel?"

"It's been a zoo down here all day long. It's a good thing we have healthcare reform. Now everyone thinks they're *supposed* to come to the ER for any reason. I just spent most of my day with some guy who dreamt he was having a heart attack, so he thought he better have it checked out. He's healthy as a horse, has no symptoms, and just took up a room in the ER for hours, costing God only knows what for the rest of us. He refused to leave until a board certified cardiologist saw him. The cardiologist was terrified of being sued for malpractice, so he wouldn't clear the guy for discharge until he did a cardiac echo and a CT angiogram of the chest. Can you believe what's going on, and they wonder why everyone in healthcare is so depressed. I'm sorry I wasn't able to have lunch with you. How has your day been?"

I smiled at her frustration. We've all been there. Patients who are absolutely fine but require thousands of dollars' worth of tests before they will accept it. We stood at the nursing station in the center of the room. Doctors, nurses, and support personnel were busy at work all around us. It was a noisy, big city ER, and there were at least thirty patients being attended to at the same time.

"I'm sorry you're having a tough day, Kel. Mine was pretty boring, actually. I only had one colonoscopy to do and three orientation meetings. No consults yet." This wasn't the time to tell her about the diamonds I'd found in Ed's locker.

"What are you going to do now?" She asked.

"It's almost five. I was going to leave now and stop at the grocery store. I'll make dinner for us. Are you in the mood for anything special?"

"No, use your imagination. I'll see you at around seven, all right?" She signaled for me to bend down for a kiss, which I did.

I walked out of the ER onto 3rd Avenue. Our apartment was on Thompson Street near Bleecker. Very walkable from here. I pulled out the slip of paper from last night that I had written the names of the jewelers on. There was one on E. 9th St. just one or two blocks away. Practically on the way home, so I headed over there.

It was a small store. There was a sign on the window that read Schwartz and Schwartz Jewelers. Inside, there were two old, bearded men with yarmulkes and thick eyeglasses sitting behind a counter. They looked up in unison when I entered.

"Are you still open?" I asked politely. It was after five.

One stood up. "Of course we are still open. That's why the door wasn't locked. Can I help you?" he asked in a thick Yiddish accent.

"Yes, I recently inherited a piece of jewelry from my aunt who passed away. I'd like to have it appraised. It has a great deal of sentimental value for me. I doubt that it's worth much, though. Is this something you can help me with?"

The other old guy stood up. They looked like a pair of bookends. It crossed my mind that maybe they were twins. "Of course we can help you, young man. The sign on the window says we are jewelers, does it not? What kind of jeweler can't appraise jewelry?" He turned to the other bookend, "Hesh, what kind of a jeweler can't appraise jewelry?"

"Not a very good one, Avi. Not a very good one. Young man, do you have the jewelry with you? I am sure we can help you. My brother and I have been in the jewelry business since the first grade."

"That's right. My brother is right. We have been in the business since the first grade. You are right, Hesh."

They both stood there smiling at me. These guys were too funny. Okay, I thought. I reached into my pocket and took out one of the diamonds, and laid it on the glass counter in front of them.

They both stared at it without touching it. Then they looked at me a little bit more carefully. One finally turned to the other. "Hesh, why don't you lock the door. I think it is time to close."

I was puzzled. "Is everything okay?" I asked, watching Hesh lock the door and pull the blinds.

"Maybe," Avi said. "You are a very trusting young man to walk in here with such a very large diamond."

"Are you going to rob me?" I asked jokingly.

Hesh returned to stand by his brother and said, "No, we are honest business men, but not everyone in this business is. Do you understand what I am saying?"

"I guess so. Look, it might not even be real, guys. Like I said, my aunt left it to me, and she wasn't that wealthy."

Avi smiled wryly and nodded his head. "I wish I had an aunt that wasn't as wealthy as your aunt. And if it's not real, then why did two men who looked like Gestapo agents come in here earlier today, asking us if a man that looked just like you had come in here with a very large diamond?"

Silence.

"Really?" I asked, genuine surprise written all over me.

"Really. And if it's not real, then why is my brother-in-law, Chaim, in Antwerp, ringing my ears off every day about stolen Russian diamonds worth a fortune?"

"Really?"

"Really."

"I didn't know these things," I said truthfully.

Hesh said, "Do you mind?" He pointed at the diamond.

"Go ahead, that's why I came here."

He picked it up and put on the monocular magnifying lens called a loupe that jewelers use. Holding it up to the light, he studied it for a minute before handing it to his brother for inspection. They put it on one of their electronic scales, weighed it, and then placed it back down on the counter in front of me.

Hesh said, "We will need to run some more sophisticated testing on it, of course, but at first glance, it appears to be five and a half carats and perfect in every way."

"Perfect?" I asked.

"As in flawless," Avi said.

"And what does that mean?"

"It means two things, young man. One, this diamond is roughly worth five to six hundred thousand dollars, maybe more, and two, your life is roughly worth shit, maybe less."

R℞ 10

I stopped at the grocery store and picked up all the ingredients I needed. I still had an hour before Kelly got home. Plenty of time for my specialty, *Fettuccine Bolognese*.

The stock pot was simmering on the stove top, and the cutting board was in position. Here we go. I started chopping onions, carrots, and celery while the pancetta and ground beef browned in a sauté pan. The robust aroma of a classic Italian dish filled the room. I had turned the stereo on and was listening to Italian dinner music, dancing while I chopped. I reached into the refrigerator for a bottle of Pinot Grigio, and I was all set. Some for the ragu and some for the chef. I turned on the oven to crisp up the bread. That Kelly was one lucky girl.

When she walked in the door at seven-thirty, I had the table set for two with a candle lit in the center. I had switched the music to Frank Sinatra, and tossed the fresh pasta into the boiling water. I greeted her at the door with a kiss and a glass of wine.

"You're in a good mood," she laughed.

"That's because you are so irresistible and..."

"And what?"

"I made two new friends today."

"Really? Who?" She threw her bag on the sofa.

"Hesh and Avi, they're brothers who own a jewelry store over on E. 9th St."

"I see, and why does that make you so happy?"

We walked over to the kitchen table and I pulled out her chair for her. "I brought them the diamond to take a look, and they told me all sorts of interesting things."

"Like what?"

"Do you want the good news first, or the bad news?"

"Start with the good. I've had a long day."

I went over to the stove, strained the pasta, and placed it in the pan with the sauce, mixing it thoroughly. Kelly sipped her wine as I transferred the pasta to a large bowl and brought it to the table, serving her a healthy portion. We watched the steam from the hot fettuccine rise and perfume the room.

I said, "It seems that diamond we found is worth at least half a million dollars and technically has no owner."

"What about the dead guy in the alley? Wasn't he the owner?"

"Bread?"

"Sure, one slice. Thanks."

"The dead guy stole it. Cheese?"

"Yes, thanks. But he stole it from someone who must have been the owner."

"Not exactly. He stole it from someone who stole it from someone else." "Cesari, what are you talking about, and how is this good news? There's already one dead guy because of this diamond."

"That's the beauty of it. It doesn't belong to anyone in particular. Apparently, there is a large diamond mining company in Russia called Alrosa. It's a poorly kept secret that the silent partner in Alrosa is the Russian Mafia. Well, apparently, someone over there has been stealing their diamonds and smuggling them out to various parts of the world, but primarily to Antwerp and Manhattan. The Russian mob has been going nuts trying to stop the leak, but they haven't been able to figure out who or how they're smuggling the diamonds out. The Russian mob can't complain to anyone because they stole them in the first place."

"Tell me when the good news starts. The fettuccine is to die for, by the way. You really outdid yourself this time."

"Thanks. Kel, don't you get it? The net effect is that these diamonds don't exist. They were stolen right out of the ground, and then, in, turn stolen again. There's no real record of these diamonds. You can't steal something that doesn't exist. Alternatively, there's no one you can return them to either."

"Oh good, I'm sure the Russian mob would agree with your line of reasoning. Is that who those guys were last night, chasing us?"

"Maybe, but not necessarily. It's not clear who those guys were. Hesh and Avi say they can unload the diamonds for only a ten percent cut."

"What do you mean diamonds, plural? I thought there was only one. And what's with all this Hesh and Avi stuff? All of a sudden they're your best friends."

"I broke into Ed Talbot's locker at the hospital today and found a USB memory stick along with ten more diamonds like the one from last night."

"Wow." She stopped eating.

"I see I have your attention now. And you'll like Hesh and Avi. They're cute. They're from the Ukraine. They've been in the diamond business their whole lives and have family over in Antwerp also in the business. That's how they know all this stuff. It's a relatively small community and word spreads fast. More wine?"

"That's not what I meant when I said *wow*. I meant I can't believe you broke into Ed Talbot's locker."

"Oh."

"Well, did you check out the memory stick, and where are the diamonds now?"

"Yeah, that was the first thing I did when I got home. Nothing on it but a list of numbers."

"What kind of numbers?"

"There were five series of eight numbers. No particular pattern. I'm not sure what it means. I'll have to give it more thought."

"You didn't answer me. Where are the diamonds now?"

"It was too late to open a safety deposit box at the bank, but I will do so first thing in the morning."

"So where are they?"

I nodded at the big bowl of fettuccine covered in Bolognese sauce.

"Really?"

"They're at the bottom in a little plastic bag."

She shook her head and sighed. "So what's the bad news?"

"I have to go to counseling for sexual harassment every Wednesday night for the next eight weeks."

"Really? What did you do?"

"I fell asleep during the lecture on sexual harassment, and the woman giving the talk didn't appreciate my unique sense of humor."

Kelly chortled. "That's too funny, but I'm not clear on how this is bad news. You've needed something like this for a long time, Cesari."

I wasn't amused. "Gee, thanks for your support. I'm glad that news brought some joy into your life."

"Well, I'm still annoyed at you for waking me up last night at 3 a.m. I had to work a twelve hour shift today, totally exhausted from the get-go. You had better let me sleep tonight."

"I can't make promises like that, Kel... I'm all wound up."

R_X 11

I stood in front of the Givelber building on W.3rd Street and looked at my watch. It was almost six, and I was pissed. Preventative sexual harassment counseling. More left-wing bullshit. No wonder we can't get anything done in this country. I pushed open the glass door and entered the lobby. Students and academics were clustered in small groups here and there, talking over the day's events. I found the main elevators and went up to the tenth floor. When I got out, I looked at her card one more time. She was in room 1005.

I found her office and knocked politely. No response, so I let my-self in. There was no one at the reception desk, so I took a seat in the small waiting room. After about a minute, the door to her inner office opened and Dr. Gottlieb came out.

"Hello, John. Would you come this way?"

"Hi Pam...Dr. Gottlieb."

"Pam is fine."

We shook hands, and she held the door open for me as I walked past her. Her inner office was about twenty-five square feet. There was a modern glass desk and a high-back, black leather chair off to one side. Her floor to ceiling windows gave her a nice view of Washington Square Park. In the center of the room were five chairs arranged in a circle for counseling. The walls were a soothing light blue, and there were multiple framed prints on the walls.

I broke the ice. "I see you like the Impressionist period."

"And I see you know your art, John."

"Monet is okay, but I'm more of a Van Gogh type of guy. I grew up in the Bronx, and I think his type of insanity would have fit in well there."

She chuckled. "Please, have a seat. We'll get into the whole Bronx thing later. I have a feeling that it will probably be important when we do RCA on your problem."

"RCA?" I asked.

"Root Cause Analysis."

"Oh, and I didn't realize I had a problem by the way. I thought this was to prevent me from having one."

"John, what is the difference between someone who is thinking of committing a felony and someone who actually does?"

"About five to ten years in a federal prison, Pam. What kind of a question is that?"

"Yes, but psychologically they are one and the same."

"I beg to differ. Psychologically, one's got a pair of balls and one doesn't."

She sighed deeply as I sat down and glanced around at the empty chairs.

"Don't worry, you're not alone. There's another patient on the way, and then we'll get started."

Patient?

"I wasn't worried at all, Pam."

"Please excuse me while I make a phone call."

"Go right ahead."

Her hair was dark brown, shoulder length and wavy. She was about five feet six, and I didn't see a wedding band. I watched her saunter over to her desk and pick up the phone. What an ass. Jesus, how was I going to survive eight weeks of this?

She turned towards me, sat on the edge of her desk, and crossed her legs. She was wearing another short, tight skirt, revealing way too much thigh. Damn, she had great legs. What was she trying to do, anyway?

She finished her call and studied me over her glasses. I squirmed under her gaze.

"What did I do now?" I asked.

"You just don't get it, do you?"

"Get what?"

"That was a phony call I just made to see how you would behave if you thought I was distracted."

"And?"

"You were staring at me, objectifying me. You wouldn't have done that if I were a man talking on the phone."

"Oh, c'mon. You have got to be kidding. You're a beautiful woman and look how sexy you're dressed. It's impossible not to stare."

"That's exactly the kind of behavior and attitude I intend to beat out of you—Dr. Cesari. How a woman is dressed should not influence your behavior or demeanor toward them."

"Now you're being ridiculous. Why don't you just cut off my testicles prophylactically and we can spare ourselves eight weeks of agony?"

"Don't give me any ideas, and I have the authority to make it twelve weeks if I think it's necessary." We both heard the door to the reception area open. "That's probably the other patient." She went to greet the newcomer, and I breathed a sigh of relief. We hadn't even started yet, and I was exhausted.

In walked an attractive blonde, in a very conservative, navy blue business suit. She was about thirty, five feet four, with shoulder length hair and blue eyes. Oh my God, but I was really starting to have a bad day.

I stood up. "Hello, Cheryl."

She froze in her tracks, surprised at the sight of me. She rolled her eyes, but recovered quickly. "Hello, Cesari. I see they finally caught up with you."

Great. I was going to sexual harassment counseling with an ex-girlfriend.

"I see you two know each other," Pam said, surprised.

"Sort of," Cheryl answered gruffly.

We stood there uncomfortably for a few seconds, and Pam suggested we all take a seat and begin the session. I'd last seen Cheryl about a year ago. She was one of the assistant D.A.'s in Manhattan. We had dated for a while a couple of years back, but it hadn't ended well.

"I thought sexual harassment was just a male disease," I said jokingly.

Pam replied, "It primarily is, although we're starting to see more and more cases of it in women who are in traditional positions of power. Would you care to tell us why you are here, Cheryl? John is here because his attitude suggests that he is at high risk to offend women in the workplace." "Only in the workplace? You should see him in action at parties," Cheryl said wryly.

"That was unnecessary. Don't you think?" I asked Pam.

"The truth hurts, doesn't it, Cesari?"

I looked at Pam. "You gonna help me out here?"

Pam finally interjected. "Okay, break it up, you two. Cheryl, would you tell us what brought you here?"

"Do I have to?"

"No, you don't, but it would help us get to the root issues if we're open and honest. You see, sexual harassment is a form of anger. It is frequently an expression of inner rage and frustration. In men, it usually masks underlying fears of sexual impotence. In women, we are finding that it can be a projection of their feelings of inner worthlessness."

Cheryl and I looked at each other and simultaneously roared in laughter. Dr. Gottlieb wasn't amused and jotted down a few notes on a clip board.

We settled down and Cheryl said, "All right. It was no big deal. I sent flowers to a female co-worker. Her husband had just left her, and she was feeling down in the dumps. Everyone at work felt bad for her, so I thought I would cheer her up. Well, the flowers arrived in the middle of the workday with everyone around. She was embarrassed, misinterpreted my intentions, and filed harassment charges against me. I tried to explain myself to her and she flipped out. We were in the female bathroom at the time, and it caused quite a commotion at the D.A.'s office. So here I am."

I chuckled and wagged my finger at her. "Ha, you have inner rage. I knew it."

She laughed as well. "Oh, shut up, Cesari."

Dr. Gottlieb looked at us seriously. "I'm not sure how well this is going to work out."

R̩x 12

❝So, how have you been Cheryl?" I asked. We were sitting in a Starbucks down the block from the office for the prevention of sexual harassment. After the session with Dr. Gottlieb, Cheryl and I had decided to catch up over coffee. We had just now finished exchanging phone numbers and getting our drinks. It had been almost a year since we'd last saw each other. She had been instrumental in the takedown of those mobsters who had tried to kill Kelly and me.

"I'm fine. This whole thing just burns me up. Eight weeks of this nonsense over nothing." She had a latte, and I sipped an espresso.

"Yeah, I know. My crime was falling asleep during a mandatory lecture on the subject."

"Yeah, but you probably would have eventually done something to wind up here," she laughed. "Just think of it as getting a head start on things."

"Thanks."

"How's Kelly? Are you two still together?"

"She's fine, and yes, we are. We're shacking up in a one bedroom in the Village. My suspension finally ended, and I've been working at St. Matt's for the last six months."

"Staying out of trouble, Cesari?"

"You know me."

"That's why I asked."

"Hey, Cheryl, do you mind if I pick your brain about something?"

"Shoot, but make it quick. I have a meeting with the DA in half an hour."

"What do you know about the Russian Mafia?"

She took a sip of coffee and studied me carefully. "Why are you asking? Your mob friends in Little Italy starting to feel insecure?"

"No, but my friends in the diamond district are. What's that all about?"

"I'm not sure what you mean?"

I put my espresso down and lowered my voice. "There are rumors about diamonds being stolen from the Russian mob and smuggled into New York."

"That is interesting. I don't really know much about that. However, it's common knowledge that the Russian mob controls much of the diamond business over there. It's even more corrupt than the sanitation business on Long Island. Stealing from the Russian mob is dangerous business, Cesari, and I wouldn't stick my nose into it if I were you. Didn't you learn your lesson last year?" She paused, giving me a careful look. "Look, I've got to run. If I hear anything I'll let you know. I guess I'll see you next week. Thanks for the coffee."

We stood up together, and I wasn't sure what to do. I stuck my hand out awkwardly, which made her laugh. "Oh, brother, this sexual harassment stuff is really getting to you, isn't it, Cesari?"

"Yes, it is."

"We slept together for a year; I think you can give me a hug." She put her arms around me and whispered, "I don't hate you anymore."

"Thanks." Well, that was an improvement, I thought as she walked away. Our breakup hadn't exactly been mutual, and I hadn't been sure if she was still harboring a grudge.

I looked at my watch. It was almost eight o'clock. I was supposed to meet Kelly for dinner at Portofino's near Waverly Place. Just a little too far to walk, so I hopped a cab and was there in five minutes. Kelly was already sitting at the bar sipping on a Cosmopolitan from a martini glass. The red liquid looked delicious with the lime wedge on the side.

"What's a hot chick like you doing all by herself?" I said, sneaking up behind her and squeezing her gently. She looked great, as always.

She turned and smiled. "I was waiting for some good looking guy to have dinner with, and you're lucky you showed up when you did because this place is crawling with men."

I leaned down and gave her a smooch. The bartender came over and asked me if I would like a drink.

"I think I'll have a Cosmo, too."

"Would you like a pretty little orange umbrella in it, or straight up?" he deadpanned.

"Straight up will be fine. Thanks."

He walked away and Kelly laughed.

I said, "Asshole."

"Oh, calm down. He was just joking."

"No, he wasn't."

"Sit down. How did the meeting go?"

"The usual psychobabble. All she wanted to talk about was whether I hated my parents and had trouble potty training."

"Really?"

"Really. Cheryl was there."

"Your ex-girlfriend, the assistant D.A.? She's in sexual harassment counseling with you?"

"Yeah, too funny, isn't it?"

"I don't know if I like this."

"She's over me. She said so."

"You talked about it. Just like that?"

"It came up during the potty training stuff. So, how was your day?"

"Busy as always. I'll be glad to have tomorrow off, and don't change the subject. I don't know if I'm going to let you hang out with an ex-girlfriend once a week, and I don't care who ordered it."

The bartender brought my drink. There was a pink umbrella in it. He said, "I couldn't remember whether you said with or without." Pretty funny guy.

"Thanks. Did you run out of orange umbrellas?"

He looked at me. "Want me to go get you one?"

I thought about throwing the drink in his face, but decided against it.

Kelly laughed out loud. "Enough, I think it's cute. Now pay the man."

"That'll be $18.00 for the two drinks, and I think your table is ready." I settled up with the wise guy, and a waitress led us to our table. The dining room was a bustling, modern Italian bistro type place. There was an open kitchen with a wood-fired oven, and the walls were covered from floor to ceiling with wine racks. Our server handed us the menus, read a list of specials, and promised to return shortly.

Kelly reviewed her options. "Yummy. Everything looks so good."

"Not to beat a dead horse, but I have no choice as to whether I attend these meetings or not."

She didn't look up from her menu. "Yeah, well, I need to think about that, and then I'll let you know what you're going to do. What do you think about an appetizer? Maybe some calamari?"

"Sure.... I think I'll have the rack of lamb with rosemary and black truffles." I decided to drop the subject.

"God, that sounds so good, but I can't eat a whole thing like that," she said. "I'm going to have the farfalle with lump crab meat in the light cream sauce, but I'm going to have to taste your lamb, okay?"

"Of course. How about we just stick with the cocktails and forget about wine tonight?"

"That's fine with me, Cesari. You know, I was thinking about the numbers on the memory stick while I was working in the ER today." She reached into her bag and came out with a list of eight numbers written down on an index card. Seemingly eight random numbers, like on the memory stick.

I looked at it. "So? What's this?"

"I was looking at series of numbers like that all day. They're medical records numbers. They're on every page of every chart."

I took a big sip of my Cosmo and sat back in my chair. "That's interesting."

"It's a possibility, isn't it?" She said.

"Definitely worth looking into." I smiled at her. "Good work, Sherlock."

* * * * * * *

"Talk to me, Dr. Griffin."

"My nephew Rick found out the name of the guy who checked into the Larchmont. His name is John Cesari. He's a doctor, and I know him. We're just not sure if he's the same guy, or if it's just a coincidence that he was at the hotel on the same night."

"And what you do to clarify situation?"

"My nephew and his partner Murph got a good look at the guy the other night when he ran from the apartment. So we're going to try to make visual confirmation before we act. We don't want any unnecessary collateral damage."

"It was foolish for nephew to shoot man."

"I agree, Sergei, but what's done is done. We're going to get the diamonds back. I promise."

R⃰ 13

THE next morning, I left the apartment while Kelly slept. I performed four colonoscopies and three inpatient consults on the general medical wards. By the time I was done, it was almost noon. I scooted down to medical records in the basement of the hospital, eager to see if those numbers on the USB stick matched any hospital records and what that might mean.

I let myself in and saw a twenty-year-old girl in jeans, by herself, filing patient charts onto large wall racks. I had seen her around from time to time, but had never been formerly introduced. She would definitely know me by sight. She was on the tall side with short blonde hair and broad, athletic shoulders. Maybe a swimmer. No make-up. She was attractive, but I guessed she probably didn't like guys, which was fine with me. I had enough headaches, and she seemed harmless enough.

It was a big room and there were numerous file cabinets and desks with computers. I walked up to her. "I thought everything was electronic these days?"

She looked up startled and then chuckled. "Hello, Dr. Cesari. Yeah, right. Every time they go 'electronic' they have to hire a hundred more file clerks like me to take care of the paper they generate. What can I do for you?" She looked me up and down.

Was she checking me out?

"I was wondering if you could do me a favor and get these charts for me. I need to review them. I'd really appreciate it." I handed her a slip of paper with the five eight-digit numbers that I'd gotten off of the USB stick.

She looked at the paper, and then at me. She then glanced over at the partially open door. "It'll cost you, Dr. Cesari."

I chuckled. Everybody's a capitalist. I reached for my wallet.

She giggled. "That's not what I meant, doc." She walked over to the door, locked it, and then, leaning back against it with her hands behind her, she eyed me hungrily.

Uh oh.

"You can't be serious?" I said. So much for stereotypes. I needed to nip this in the bud before it got out of hand.

She walked over to me. "C'mon, doc. We're grownups."

"Well, one of us is anyway. Look, can I take a rain check? I really have a lot of work to do, and it's the middle of the day. Somebody might walk in." I was starting to get a little nervous. With the door closed, this was already a very compromising situation.

"Everyone's at lunch. They won't be back before one, and the door is locked. Do you want the charts or not?" She smiled seductively, put her arms around my waist, and nuzzled in close.

I let out a deep breath and looked her straight in the eyes. "Isn't this what they call sexual harassment?"

She laughed. "Sue me."

"I don't mean to be rude, but I don't even know your name."

"It's Lori, feel better now?" And she moved in for the kill.

My cell phone went off, and I gently pushed her lips away from mine.

"Hello, Cesari here."

"Hi, it's Harry Santelli in the ER. They tell me you're on call. We've got a bleeder in trauma room 2 with your name on it."

"How bad?"

"Big time. As in he will exsanguinate soon if you don't do something."

"Details, Harry," I said as I tried to untangle myself from Lori.

"He's a fifty-year-old white male with known alcohol and substance abuse. No significant medical history other than that. He binged last night and woke up this morning throwing up blood. The paramedics found him hypotensive in the field, but he responded to fluids. He's more or less stable at the moment, but blood is pouring out of his nasogastric tube."

I moved away from Lori, who was still trying to snuggle, and was tugging on my zipper. I signaled her to knock it off. She pouted, but didn't move away or stop pressing herself against me.

"What are his vitals and labs, Harry?"

"His blood pressure is still a little soft. It's hanging in the nineties systolic, heart rate in the one-hundred-and-fifty range. We got blood coming and saline running wide open. Like I said, he's stable, but may not be for long. First hematocrit was twenty-five, but I'm sure it's going to drop. His platelets and coags are fine. You'd better get down here."

"I'm on the way, Harry. Look, keep pouring fluid into him and make sure he's typed and crossed for at least four units of packed red cells. Start him on an intravenous protonix drip. Would you mind calling for an ICU bed, also? I'll be there in five minutes."

"Will do, Cesari. Are you going to scope this guy down here or up in the ICU?"

"I'll know better when I see him. Keep him alive." I hung up and looked seriously at Lori. She had her arms around my waist again and was resting her head against my chest.

"Okay, Lori. You heard. I have to go now and take care of a sick patient." I put my hands on her shoulders and gingerly separated us. I didn't want to make too much contact. "It was really nice meeting you. If you wouldn't mind getting those charts for me, and maybe just leaving them on the front desk over there by the door, I'd appreciate it." I smiled at her, and she finally got the message.

"Maybe some other time?" Her eyes searched mine.

I didn't say anything to that.

She added. "Are you going to tell anybody?"

"Tell anybody what?"

"You know..."

"I don't know anything. I came here for some charts, I met a nice girl, and she got me the charts. That's all I know."

She smiled. "Thanks. I'll leave them by the door."

As I walked over to the ER, my cell phone went off again. "Hello."

"Reginald Griffin, here."

"Hello, Doctor Griffin. What can I do for you?"

"Do you think we could meet for cocktails this evening, Cesari? I was thinking about our conversation the other day, and it's about time we got to know each other better. Say about seven. There's a place called The Blue Danube. It's not too far from the hospital. Lots of fun. I go there all the time. Heard of it?"

"Yes, but I've never been."

"Good. You'll love it. You married?"

"No."

"Gay?"

"No."

"Because if you are, it's okay."

"I'm not."

"Then what's your story? Good looking guys in their thirties don't usually last long in this forest. Too many female predators, if you know what I mean."

"I know exactly what you mean. I have a girlfriend. Can I bring her?"

"Sure, why not? Is she hot?"

"Very."

"Then I'm going to warn you now. Two martinis and I turn into a werewolf. See you at seven."

"Great."

R̷X 14

THE room was dark, and we focused our attention on the video monitor in front of us. The only sounds were from the beeping of the patient's heart monitor and the suction machine on the wall. I inserted the tip of the endoscope into the patient's mouth, advancing it along his esophagus and into his stomach. As I entered the duodenum, bright red blood filled the screen.

"There it is, Terry," I said to the nurse standing to my right. "Hand me the needle with the epinephrine, please."

"What are we looking at, Dr. Cesari?" Asked one of the three medical students standing behind me.

"At six o'clock on the screen, Denise. There's a small, maybe one centimeter duodenal ulcer along the posterior wall. It's magnified, of course, but you can see the clot in its periphery and blood oozing out from the edge. The blood vessel that's responsible for all the bleeding is just underneath the clot. Everybody see what I'm talking about?"

The three medical students answered in unison, "Yes." As part of my responsibilities as a staff physician, I spent time teaching medical students rotating through from NYU.

"I'm going to inject the base of the ulcer with epinephrine, a vasoconstrictor. This will slow the bleeding down. Then I'll cauterize the vessel with electrical current, and hopefully that will solve the problem. If it continues to bleed, I will place a metal clip on it." The patient was heavily sedated and snored loudly. His third unit of blood was running in his IV. I looked over at the other nurse, Katie.

"How's he doing?" I asked.

"Vitals are stable and oxygen saturation is in the mid-nineties."

"Thanks."

I injected the base of the ulcer with epinephrine, and then pressed the tip of the heater probe up against the vessel, stepping on the floor peddle to apply the electrical current. After several attempts, I was still only partially successful in cauterizing the vessel, and eventually wound up placing two metal clips on it in order to stop the bleeding.

By the time I finished in the ICU, it was almost five. The guy had stabilized and was doing a whole lot better. I thanked my nurses for their help and spent a few minutes reviewing the case with the medical students. I then called Harry in the ER to give him an update.

"Yeah, he's doing great, Harry. He had a small ulcer. It was bleeding like stink, but I was able to stop it. I'm going to transfuse him a couple of more units of blood tonight, but he'll be fine. Greg Mason will be covering for me if you need anything."

"Thanks Cesari. Great job. I owe you one. Have a great night."

"Thanks, Harry."

I walked back down to medical records, and before entering, peered around cautiously. I didn't want to fall into that trap again. Lori was gone. There were several other people there now as well as a stack of charts with my name on it sitting on a desk.

A middle aged woman approached me. "Are you Dr. Cesari?"

"Yes, I am." I flashed my ID at her. "I believe those charts are for me."

"Yes, they are. I'll need you to sign for them, okay?"

"Of course. Can I return them in the morning?"

"Certainly."

I signed for the charts and tucked them into my briefcase.

"Have a good night, Doctor."

"Thank you."

I left the hospital and walked down 9th Street towards the village. I passed Avi and Hesh in their little jewelry store. I waved to them and they waved back. Hesh opened the door and said, "Any decisions yet, young man?"

"Still thinking about it, Hesh. I might be going away for the weekend to mull things over. I promise I'll get back to you no later than Monday or Tuesday."

"Take your time. It is never good to be in a rush. It is bad for the intestines. Right, Avi?" He called back to his brother who suddenly appeared in the doorway.

"You are right, Hesh. Rushing is bad for the intestines. We had an uncle who used to rush, and he had an ulcer. You take your time. We will still be here. Where would we go?" And he shrugged his shoulders.

"Avi is right. Where would we go? You have a nice weekend, young man. But where are you going, and why would anybody want to leave this beautiful city?"

I said, "It's not decided yet exactly. I was going to bring it up with my girlfriend tonight. We've been wanting to spend a weekend in Vermont. You know... shopping, antiquing, maybe a little hiking. Clear our heads. That kind of stuff. A small town called Woodstock. Ever heard of it?"

"Never heard of it. Hesh, have you ever heard of it?"

"No, Avi, I never heard of it. Hiking? Sounds like work."

"You are right, Hesh. It sounds harder than work."

"All right then, guys. I'm glad we settled that. I'll talk to you Monday. Have a good night." I waved goodbye.

I cut through the NYU complex and found my way to the apartment.

"Hey Kel, I'm home." I took the charts out of the briefcase and threw them onto a desk in the living room. It was 6 p.m., so I'd review them later. We were meeting Dr. Griffin for drinks at seven.

"I'm in the bathroom getting ready," she called out. "How sexy do you want me to be?"

"That depends on you. If you don't mind a pasty, old white man with a Boston accent groping you, then go for it. He already warned me to watch out."

She laughed. "A girl needs to be groped once in a while, if you know what I mean."

"No, I don't know what you mean. What are you getting at?" I had entered the bathroom and was watching her put her make-up on.

"You've been missing in action the last few nights, Cesari. That's all. I'm kind of looking forward to being groped," she said, smiling.

"The other day you told me I'd better leave you alone, and now you're looking forward to being groped? I don't understand."

65

"And you never will, so stop trying and just do what I want when I want it. Okay?"

I sighed. I hated these kinds of conversations. "Sure, but I've got to warn you. I've seen Dr. Griffin in the locker room, Kel. Trust me. He's not your type, and here I've been trying to be nice to you by letting you get your rest. I know how hard you've been working."

We both laughed at that. She said, "Right. I make one little comment in jest and you disappear for a week. You expect me to believe that you're that sensitive or sympathetic. I can practically set my watch by how fast you fall asleep."

I put my arms around her and she squealed. "Stop, you're going to mess up my hair and make-up." I leaned down and gave her a big wet kiss on the lips.

"That's for saying mean things."

She smiled. "Maybe I should be mean more often? It turns you into a tiger."

"Speaking of tigers, we both have the weekend off. I was thinking that maybe we could take a drive up to Vermont and do the bed and breakfast thing you've been wanting to. It's August, so we won't see the fall colors, of course, but still it might be nice to get away, and if we like it, we could always go back for the colors. One of the anesthesia guys recommended a B&B in his home town, Woodstock. It's called the Reluctant Panther. It sounded really nice."

She thought about that. "Hmm. I think I really like that idea. When would we leave, and what's that got to do with tigers?"

"Tomorrow is Friday. We could leave in the morning, and come back Sunday afternoon. I'll call now to see if they have a room. And you know, tigers, panthers, big cats."

"That's a ridiculous association. No wonder the psychiatrists can't figure out what to do with you. By the way, have you heard from Mark?" Mark Greenberg was my psychiatrist who lived on the upper west side with his wife, Sarah. He was also my friend.

"No, not for a while. I'll give him a call next week when we get back."

R̲X̲ 15

THE cab let us off on the corner of 5th Avenue and W. 20th Street in the Flat Iron district, and we entered The Blue Danube at seven sharp. There was standing room only in the bar, and the crowd seemed pretty upscale, judging by the way they were dressed. Lots of suits, high heels, and bling. Kelly looked ravishing in a low-cut black dress and pearls. Her Valentino bag caused every woman in the place to stare as she walked by. Waves of long black hair flowed over her shoulders, and the scent of her Chanel was already driving me crazy. I wore dark slacks, a white dress shirt and a beige sport jacket. Your basic go-to doctor outfit.

I put my arm around her waist to signal the guys there that she was mine. "You look so gorgeous," I whispered into her ear.

"Thanks."

"You're like an African princess."

"That's enough, thank you."

I chuckled. "Are you sure?"

She glared at me. "If you go into your African princess routine tonight, Cesari, you're going to sleep on the couch. Got that?"

"Got it."

The bar was large, dark and very modern. There were at least four bartenders, and three times that many waitresses running around serving numerous thirsty customers. High-backed leather booths and wood tables wrapped around the room, adjacent to the bar. Heavily sedated jazz music piped in overhead.

"I can't believe the way these waitresses are dressed," Kelly said, noting the skimpy outfits the girls were all wearing. Blue miniskirts, bustier tops, white heels and stockings.

"What's wrong with the way they're dressed?"

"You'd better look at me, not them. You've been warned."

"Duly noted."

I spotted Reginald Griffin at the bar. "There he is, Kel. Tall guy with the dark blue sport coat sipping an over-sized martini. Looks like he should be on a yacht."

We slipped over to him through the crowd. "Hello, Dr. Griffin."

"Call me Reg, Cesari, we're not at work. And who is this gorgeous creature with you?" He practically pushed me to the side to get at Kelly. He was about six feet four inches tall and 250 lbs. He grabbed her hand and bent over to kiss it. "Reginald Griffin at your service."

"I'm Kelly." She played along and politely curtsied, which was like throwing gasoline on a flame.

"Cesari told me you were lovely, Kelly, but words simply can't describe your kind of loveliness."

Jesus Christ, Reg is a player.

"Well, thank you," Kelly said, eating it up.

He put her arm through his and escorted her up to the bar with me pulling up the rear. The bartender approached and nodded to Reg.

"What would you like to drink, Kelly? And you, Cesari?" Reg asked politely while ogling Kelly.

"I'll have a Cosmopolitan with Grey Goose please," Kelly replied.

"And I'll have whiskey on the rocks. Jim Beam will be fine."

The bartender looked at me suspiciously. Reg was annoyed. "For Christ's sake, Cesari, does this look like the bowery to you? They don't have Jim Beam here. Upgrade your order before the bartender gets insulted and asks us to leave."

Kelly chuckled, and I turned eight shades of red. I looked up at the shelves with the liquor bottles along the wall behind the bar. "Okay, make it the Jefferson Presidential Select. The eighteen-year-old bottle. The bartender approved and started making our drinks. Unbelievable. Now I had to impress bartenders in order to get a drink.

"Nice recovery, Cesari," Reg said. "I was starting to feel embarrassed for you."

A minute or two later, the bartender handed Kelly her Cosmo and me the whiskey.

I said, "You forgot the ice."

He looked at me contemptuously, and then at Reg, before walking away without saying anything.

"What the fuck was that all about?" I asked, my famous temper starting to flare.

Reg said, "Relax, Cesari. He was doing you a favor. He didn't want to humiliate you any further by pointing out your ignorance. High-end bourbon like that, you're supposed to drink neat and not drown in ice. So, put it behind you and let's grab a booth."

We chose a table close to the bar and sat. Kelly slid into to the booth and Reg slid in beside her, giving me no choice but to sit by myself across from them.

"Cheers," Reg said, raising his glass and then downing a huge gulp of vodka.

I said, "When did you get here, Reg? I hope we didn't keep you waiting."

"I got here at six sharp, Cesari. Like I do every Thursday."

"I'm sorry. I must have misunderstood. I thought you said seven."

"I did say seven, but I like to get a head start on the libations and scope out the talent," he said, eyeing a voluptuous blonde cocktail waitress as she walked by.

"That's Vanessa. We're in luck tonight. This is her table." He looked at his watch. "The action will start soon." He was right about that.

"What's with the outfits on these girls?" Kelly asked, watching Vanessa walk away. "What's the theme?"

"They're supposed to be German barmaids. Get it? Like the kind you might see during Oktoberfest," Reg explained.

Kelly rolled her eyes. "German barmaids or German porn stars? I don't think I heard clearly."

"C'mon, Kel. Get in the spirit," Reg said.

She wouldn't let go of it. "I'm sorry, it's just that I didn't realize your average German barmaid was a 38 double D and wore stilettos."

Reg winked. "God, Kel, if that were the case, I would've moved to Berlin years ago, but boys can dream, can't they?"

"So, Reg, what's going to happen?" I asked, judiciously changing the subject.

"You'll see, Cesari. Drink up. You're already three cocktails behind me, and the night isn't getting any younger."

Out of the corner of my eye, I saw two big guys at the far end of the bar eyeing us. They turned away quickly when I spotted them. At first glance, I didn't think much of it. I figured they'd caught sight of Kelly, and were just checking her out. Can't blame them for that, but there was something about them, and the way they were looking. And what's with Reg? I could understand him being a little relaxed after work, but wasn't he overdoing it?

We engaged in idle chatter like that for about another fifteen minutes when, suddenly, a loud buzzer sounded. The smooth jazz music that had been playing stopped and all the waitresses put their serving trays down, drawing chairs alongside their respective tables. Vanessa up close was quite the sight. About five feet ten with spiked heels, long blonde hair and a killer smile. She climbed onto her chair and then onto our table. A second buzzer sounded, and loud rock and roll blasted into the room. Vanessa and her colleagues broke into a classic high energy go-go dance. Reg brazenly looked up her skirt, and I didn't even want to know what he found. Kelly frowned at me, and my eyes begged for forgiveness.

I shrugged and mouthed, "I had no idea."

Thankfully, this only lasted a minute or so because I didn't think Kelly would last much longer. Just as abruptly as it had begun, the music stopped, and Reg helped Vanessa down, placing a twenty in her cleavage. He signaled me to do the same and I politely placed a twenty into her hand, thanking her for her effort. The jazz music kicked in again, and we resumed our conversation.

Reg looked at us, beaming. "Wasn't that great?"

Kelly tossed the rest of her Cosmo down in one gulp. "Well, it was interesting, that's for sure. I don't know how I ever survived without such entertainment."

He chuckled. "I knew you'd like it. They do that every half hour all night long. I think we need another round of drinks. Everybody in?"

Kelly said, "Oh yeah, extra strong this time."

The two guys at the bar were staring again. Fuck, that was rude. I mean, the first time, I understood. What did they want?

I said, "Excuse me, I'm going to the men's room. I'll be right back."

"Take your time, Cesari. I'd like to get to know Kelly." He smiled at her, and she politely smiled back.

I stood up and walked down the length of the bar, trying to get a better look at the two guys. The lighting was poor, and they were sitting hunched over their beers, pretending not to notice me. I couldn't see their faces well, although they definitely seemed familiar. They were both in their early thirties, maybe a hair over six feet, clean shaven, two hundred plus pounds, wearing dress slacks and sport coats. The bathroom was at the end of the bar and I went in.

Very nice. It was spacious and clean with decorative mosaic tiling on the floor and walls. There were four stalls and the same number of urinals. I stepped up to one to do my business, and out of the corner of my eye, saw one of the guys enter the room behind me. He was stocky with short blonde hair and a pasty complexion. Looked a little like Reg. He went to one of the sinks to splash water on his face, but it was obvious that he was just trying to get a better look at me.

I finished and went over to the sink to wash my hands. He was still freshening up, and looked at me in the mirror. He said, "Great place, huh?"

Was this the guy from the park? I wasn't sure. I'd never really gotten a good look, but if he was, how did he find me here?

"Yeah, it's pretty hot," I replied, and saw the bulge of a handgun in his shoulder holster.

"I'll say. Some of these waitresses aren't wearing any panties."

"That would explain the steep cover charge," I laughed. "Well, take care."

"Yeah, you too."

I returned to the table to find Kelly merrily engaged in deep conversation with Reg.

Kelly said, "We ordered some appetizers while you were gone. If we keep drinking like this without food, we're going to get drunk."

"In that case, cancel the food," Reg said, slapping the table, and both he and Kelly thought that was real funny. Kelly was already a little tipsy, and I saw that she was drinking her second Cosmo even faster than the first.

"Dr. Griffin is so funny, Johnny. He's got me in stitches. I told him that we're going to Vermont tomorrow, and guess what? He's stayed at the Reluctant Panther, and says that we are going to love it. It's very romantic."

"Is that so?"

"Sure is, Cesari. A little steep, pricewise, but worth every penny, but if it's romance you want, then stick around. They have a dance floor in the next room, and around ten, they start playing Salsa. The place really starts to jump by then. You know how to dance, Cesari?"

"Not really," I answered truthfully.

Kelly was starting to bounce around in her seat like she wanted to dance. "Reg, are we ready for another round of drinks or what?" she asked playfully and pointed to her near empty glass.

"I'm always ready, little lady." He signaled Vanessa, the German bar wench.

"Well, Cesari, you had better learn how to dance if you're going to take pretty girls like Kelly out to chic Manhattan clubs. What about you, Kelly, care to shake your booty with me later?"

"Sure, why not? I've never done the Salsa, but I'm a fast learner."

"And I'm a great teacher. If Cesari doesn't mind?"

Kelly answered for me. "He won't mind at all."

Great.

℞ 16

It was 2 a.m., and the three men huddled in a booth at The Blue Danube. "Well, was that them or not?"

Rick said, "There's no doubt about it, Uncle Reg. I'd swear on a Bible. They were under a street light when they left that guy Talbot's apartment and looked right up at me. I got a really good look at him in the men's room tonight. There's no doubt about it."

Murph chimed in, "I agree, Dr. Griffin. That's them all right. I didn't get quite as good a look as Rick, but I would bet on it. Why didn't we just take them here while we had the chance?"

Reg looked at him sternly. "Because I don't want any of this coming back to me, is that understood?"

"Yes, it's understood, Uncle Reg."

"All right then. Tomorrow, they're going to a place called the Reluctant Panther. It's a bed and breakfast in Woodstock, Vermont. They're leaving first thing in the morning, and they'll be on the road all day. That'll be the perfect time to search their apartment. If you don't find the diamonds there, you head up to Vermont after them and then you have my permission to do whatever it takes to find out where the diamonds are. I'd prefer to do this without any more casualties, but if it gets nasty, keep the mess up there and away from me. Sergei will be back in town next Friday, and I don't need to tell you what's going to happen if we haven't recovered the diamonds by then."

＊＊＊＊＊＊＊

"Kelly, you're drunk." She was sitting on my lap with her tongue in my ear. I looked at the cab driver. "Is there a problem?"

"No, sir." He turned his sights back on the road ahead.

"Did kitten have a good time tonight?" I cooed.

"Did I ever! That was great. We should go there every week."

"I'll pencil it in."

"And we're going to start taking dance lessons, Cesari, so next time I can dance with my boyfriend and not some old guy. He was really good, though. Did you see him out there?"

"Unfortunately, I saw every jiggle."

"He's a wild man. I wish I had a boss like that."

"He's not like that at work, Kel. He tends to be a bit more subdued when he's sober."

The taxi pulled up in front of the apartment building and we got out. She danced and swirled all the way up to our apartment.

I opened the door and saw the pile of hospital charts on the living room credenza where I had left them. Hmm. I had promised to return them tomorrow, but I was a little too tired to review them all right now. Plus, I was pre-occupied with the question of who those guys in the bar were. If they weren't the same guys from the other night, wasn't it quite a coincidence that they were carrying guns and staring at Kelly and me? On the other hand, we weren't that far from the 10th precinct. The Blue Danube might simply be the preferred watering hole for law enforcement. They could just have been horny cops out on the town and couldn't keep their eyes off Kelly. Yeah, I told myself, that's probably all it was.

"Hey Kel, I'm going to look at one or two of these charts before coming to bed. All right?" She didn't answer, and I presumed she had passed out on the bed.

Sitting down on the sofa, I opened one of the charts for review. It was a patient named Ivan Cheveneskai, a forty-year-old Russian here on a work visa. Generally, he was in pretty good health and wasn't on any medications. About six weeks ago, he developed a sudden onset of rectal bleeding and came to the St. Matt's emergency room. He spent the entire day in the emergency room under observation. According to the ER records, all his labs were normal, and he physically appeared well. That night he underwent an emergency colonoscopy, which was normal. His rectal bleeding resolved, and he was sent home that same night after his colonoscopy. That was it. Pretty thin.

The file didn't contain the actual operative report, only a summary of his stay at St. Matt's. That seemed a little strange, but not that strange. The op-note might have been scanned in electronically. As it stood, I had no way of knowing who did the colonoscopy, who assisted him, or what exactly had happened, although it sounded pretty routine. I put the chart down and went over to my desk. I powered up my laptop and waited for it to log onto the internet. I then accessed the St. Matthew's website, and was in the process of entering my password, when I felt a pair of hands on my neck.

I looked up. "Hi, Kel."

"Looking at porn again, Cesari?"

"Now why would I do that when I have you here?"

"Because men are all the same—disgusting."

I turned to her. She was wearing a short, lavender silk robe. She came around and sat on my lap, blocking my view of the screen. "I was just going through one of those charts I brought home and realized that part of it is only available for review in the electronic medical record."

She put her arms around me and gazed at me as if I was speaking a foreign language. "Listen up, Bub. It's two in the morning, and we have a long ride ahead of us tomorrow. There are at least a hundred little shops on the way, and I intend on stopping in every one of them. So you had better not be tired tomorrow." Her robe opened up while she spoke, and I could see that she wasn't wearing anything underneath. My right eye met her left nipple and I stopped thinking about patient charts. I felt a tingling sensation as I took a deep breath.

I looked at her.

She looked at me.

I looked at her nipple again. I knew I was a drunk, but I could have sworn that it winked at me.

Kelly said, "Well?"

I said, "Let's go to bed."

R_X 17

THE aroma of a freshly brewed pot of French roast coffee beckoned me to wake up. It was 9 a.m., and Kelly was already up and busy in the kitchen. I jumped in the shower, and was in the process of shaving, when Kelly came into the bathroom with my favorite mug brimming with joe.

"God, that smells good, Kel. Thank you." I kissed her good morning.

She smiled. "You're welcome. Now get the lead out. It's a five-hour trip, and according to my calculations, we are already behind schedule. I've been online Googling all the things we can see and do up there. We have to stop in this town called Grafton for lunch. It's got an old-fashioned country store, and it looks adorable. It'll be like walking back in time."

"Sounds great. I'm on it." I hurriedly finished up in the bathroom and threw on jeans and a cotton shirt. We packed a few things into a small suitcase and went down to the garage. We pulled the blue Camry out onto Houston and headed over to the West Side Drive. In less than half an hour, we were northbound on the New York State Thruway, hauling ass up to Vermont. It was ten o'clock and we estimated our arrival time at the Reluctant Panther at around three. If we stopped an hour for lunch, we'd get there by four at the latest. We had dinner reservations for 8 p.m. at the Prince and the Pauper restaurant on Main Street. Plenty of time.

Kelly was reading some novel on her Kindle. She looked up just long enough to say, "Step on it, Cesari." I was already doing eighty.

"Boy, if just the thought of shopping makes you this aggressive, I can't wait to see what happens when we get there."

She smiled at that. "Did you have to bring those charts and the laptop? I thought we were just going to relax and enjoy the fresh country air?"

"We are going to do just that, but I just figured that when we had a little down time, I could do a little research. I promise I won't let it interfere with our plans. You just reminded me, though. I have to call medical records to let them know that I'm going to keep the charts over the weekend."

By noon, we had passed Albany and were ahead of schedule. We eventually found ourselves on Route 7, heading straight into the heart of Vermont and the Green Mountains, which ran the length of the state.

"Sure you don't want to stop for something to eat, Kel?" I was getting hungry.

"Keep driving. Grafton's only an hour away at this rate. We'll stop there, okay?"

I had inched the speedometer up to eighty-five. The roads were fairly empty, and we hadn't seen a cop yet. The Camry rattled a little, but didn't spring any leaks.

******

"There's nothing here, Rick," Murphy said.

"Fuck." Rick looked around Cesari's apartment and observed the devastation they had wrought. They had cut open the mattress, overturned the armoire and smashed all the lamps and vases.

"Want to go through it again, Rick?"

"Go through what again, Murph? We've already destroyed all the furniture and trashed anything worth trashing. We've emptied the closets, drawers, and refrigerator. I'm not sure what more we can do here."

"What about the Schwartz brothers?"

"The old guys with the yarmulkes? You think they were lying to us?"

"Yeah, I do, Rick. I think they played us like a piano. Their jewelry store is right on 9ᵗʰ St. This guy Cesari must walk past it every day on the way to the hospital. I find it hard to believe that he wouldn't have gone in there to ask their opinion. Maybe he even left the diamonds there for safekeeping."

"That's a thought, but uncle Reg doesn't want any more collateral damage. We're lucky no one's figured out who the crackhead in the alley is yet."

"If we don't find those diamonds before the Russians come back, we're the ones who are going to be collateral damage. Besides, if those geezers have got the diamonds, then we could save ourselves a trip to fucking Vermont."

R℞ 18

WE pulled into Grafton at 1 p.m. Ancient oak trees lined the main street, which was only about twenty feet wide, and stretched for about two hundred yards. That was it. Not even one street light. There were a few antique shops and art galleries lining the strip, but the main attraction was far and away the Vermont Country Store. Judging by the number of people jostling in and out of its front door, one might have guessed that most of Vermont was in sudden, desperate need of cheddar cheese and flannel shirts.

"What a cute town." Kelly marveled, and indeed it was. There was a big red barn that had been converted into a tinsmith's shop on one side and a Christmas store on the other. Wood-framed, colonial-style homes, with colorful shutters and doors, dotted the landscape, accented by their perennial gardens and white picket fences.

"Yes, it is." I concurred.

"Look at all these people. We're a month and a half away from peak season, and it's already a madhouse." She grabbed my arm. "I'm so excited, John. This looks like fun."

We walked up the front steps and into the store. The old pine floor boards, some of which were close to two feet wide, creaked noisily under our weight. It was like a carnival atmosphere inside the store with throngs of customers walking about examining the mostly handmade merchandise. There was even a section with old-fashioned toys and kid's games.

I said, "I have to admit, this is pretty cool. You don't see places like this anymore." There were giant kegs of maple syrup, harvested locally, next to homespun pajamas, next to a guy making kettle corn. There was a counter selling sandwiches of local cheeses and sausages.

"What do you think?" she asked.

"I think that if I don't eat something soon, I am going to pass out," I answered truthfully.

"All right, how about some cheese, bread, and apple cider?"

I looked at her. "You're really buying into this country shtick, aren't you? Cheese is fine, but get some sausage, too. I said I was hungry."

"Fine. I'll go wait in line, and you try to get us a couple of rocking chairs on the front porch. That would be fun."

She went to get our lunch, and I went back outside. All the rockers were taken, but there was a wood bench free, so I sat on that and waited. There was a kid trying to fly a kite he had just bought down the main street, and I noticed for the first time that there were no telephone poles or power lines to obstruct him. They must have run everything underground. Interesting how easily I'd missed that. Power and telephone lines are such a routine part of modern life that their very absence subliminally suggested by-gone days. Boy, they had nostalgia down to an art here. I couldn't wait to reach Woodstock.

I took out my cell phone and called the medical records department to let them know that I still had the charts.

"Hello, this is Dr. Cesari."

"Hello, Dr. Cesari. This is Lori."

"Oh. Hi, Lori. Look, Lori, remember those charts I signed out yesterday?"

"I've been thinking about you, Dr. Cesari."

"Well, that's nice. Anyway, I was supposed to return the charts today, but I forgot, so I just wanted somebody to be aware that I still have them and will return them Monday."

"I could come to your apartment to pick them up if you want?"

"Thank you, but that won't be necessary. Would you please make a note of that somewhere?"

"Anything for you, Dr. Cesari. When will I see you again?"

"Look, Lori, I think you may have misinterpreted things a little. Hold on. I have another call coming in." I looked at the caller ID. It was Cheryl, my ex-girlfriend from sexual harassment counseling. "I have to go now, Lori. I have to take this call. Bye." I switched calls.

"Hello, Cheryl. How's my favorite assistant D. A.?"

"Hello, Cesari. I'm fine."

"What can I do for you? Looking for some extra counseling before next Wednesday's meeting?" I chuckled. I had a bad habit of laughing at my own jokes.

"Very funny. No, I'm calling to give you a heads-up."

"About what?"

"Well, I'm sure you remember Lou Barazza and Vito Gianelli."

"How could I forget? How is Big Lou doing?" They'd been the guys who ran the prescription drug ring out of the hospital I'd worked at last year. Vito was now in witness protection, and Lou was permanently brain damaged, or at least I hoped he was.

"He's on a feeding tube and still in the coma you put him in."

"Whoa, I never admitted to any of that. And Vito? Still behaving himself, I hope?"

"Yeah, but the point is, we and the FBI sealed all the files. If anybody searches their names, it comes up as restricted access and triggers an alarm for us. There are still a lot of people down in little Italy pissed off about what happened last year."

"What's that got to do with me?"

"Well, for your protection, we also added your name to the security system. So that if anybody searched your name in our database, it would also trigger an alarm. We didn't want anybody taking pot shots at you, at least not without us knowing it."

"I appreciate that. You got my attention now. So what happened?"

Kelly sat on the bench next to me and unwrapped some cheese. She offered me a drink of apple cider, which I accepted. She took a bite of cheese, and people-watched while I talked to Cheryl. She'd also gotten us a couple of apples as well. Great. I'm starving and she brings me cheese and an apple.

I mouthed, "Where's the sausage?"

"This is better for you. Sausage is all fat."

I rolled my eyes in disbelief and took a savage bite from my apple.

I returned to my call. "I'm sorry, could you repeat that?"

"Pay attention, Cesari. I said somebody searched your name this morning. Of course the file was restricted, as I just said, but the point is that somebody is looking for you, and I don't know who or why. "

"Well, thank you for the heads-up, but I don't know if it's anything I should lose sleep over just yet. It could've been anybody, right? Maybe somebody at the hospital was curious about me?"

"No, not anybody. It would have to have been somebody in law enforcement or somebody with a friend in law enforcement. They would need to have at least a minimum security clearance. Not just anybody can search our database, but there's something else. Something I can't talk about on the phone. Where are you?"

I looked at Kelly, who was starting to pay attention to the conversation, and I could see the beginnings of a scowl as she stopped eating.

I sighed. "I'm in Vermont with Kelly. We both had the weekend off and thought we'd do a little antique shopping."

She chuckled. "Are you kidding? Antique shopping? Oh, brother. Which town are you in? This is pretty serious."

"We're staying at the Reluctant Panther. It's a bed and breakfast in Woodstock."

Kelly shoved my arm, and rolled her eyes disapprovingly. "Who are you talking to?"

I covered the phone. "Cheryl."

She shook her head. "I knew it. It's starting already."

"How far is it, Cesari?"

"About four and a half hours from Manhattan. Why?"

"It's two o'clock now. I can get there by eight. I just have to finish up a few things first."

"But Cheryl, this was supposed to be a romantic weekend away for Kelly and me. And besides, we have dinner reservations for eight."

"Where?"

"A place called the Prince and the Pauper. Why?"

"Great. I'll call them and add my name to the reservation."

Rx 19

THE Reluctant Panther was just outside of Woodstock on Route 4, the main road running through town. It was a large, stately, timber-framed, two-story house that proudly displayed a sign declaring that it was built in 1795. It was white clapboard with blue shutters surrounded by very old sugar maples.

We turned into a narrow driveway that led to a small parking lot in the rear of the house. There were three other cars parked there as I maneuvered into the tight space. I had filled Kelly in on my phone call with Cheryl as we completed the last leg of the trip.

"Why do you think people are asking about you? Do you think it has anything to do with the diamonds?"

I opened the trunk and retrieved our suitcase. "I don't know. There's something going on that Cheryl didn't want to talk about on the phone. Something she felt I should know about. I'm sure there are people looking for the diamonds, but they don't know who I am. How could they? And if they did, I'm sure we would have heard from them by now. Don't you think?"

"I don't know if I like this. Maybe we should just turn them in or give them away."

I closed the trunk door and looked around. There was a garage at the far end of the parking lot, presumably for the sole use of the owner. I didn't see a rear entrance, so we traipsed back around to the front of the house.

"Who would we turn them in to, Kel? I don't know anybody in the Russian Mafia. Do you? We could just give them away I suppose, but then we would just be placing somebody else in danger. Look, I'm just thinking out loud. Like I told Avi and Hesh, let's think it over, and on Monday, I'll do whatever you feel comfortable with. Okay?"

"Maybe Cheryl's just using this as an opportunity to see you again."

"Oh, please. It's over and it's been over."

"Maybe it's not that clear to her."

"No way would she drive all the way up here for that. Trust me; she's not even remotely interested in me in that way anymore."

"You don't know anything about women, Cesari."

I turned suddenly, put the suitcase down and wrapped my arms around her, kissing her long and slow, like in the movies. We eventually had to come up for air. I said, "I know that I adore you Miss Kelly, and that I would walk a thousand miles through barbed wire and minefields to be near you. I would rather give up oxygen than lose you. You have power over me and I'm not even going to pretend that I can fight it."

She giggled triumphantly. "Humph. Talk is cheap, Cesari. We'll see if you can walk the walk."

"Why don't we check in while we think of ways for me to prove my devotion?"

The winding brick path leading up to the entrance was lined by mature hydrangeas in full bloom, showing off their large pink and blue flower heads. We followed this up to the front door, which was painted blue to match the shutters.

"Oh, John, it's so beautiful here. I love it already. Look at all these flowers."

The house was surrounded on all sides by perennials and annuals. Most of the perennials were spent, but the petunias, geraniums, marigolds and zinnias were in full bloom as were hordes of black-eyed susans and day lilies. There was a vegetable garden nearby as well, and dozens of vine-ripened tomatoes were ready to be plucked.

There was a brass, colonial style knocker in the center of the door that no one responded to, so we let ourselves in. Off to one side of the reception room was an antique wood desk with a bell on it. The room was decorated with period furnishings, and an old, deeply faded rug covered uneven, pine floor boards. Several oil paintings depicting Revolutionary War figures hung on the walls. There was a musty old house smell. I put the valise down and rang the bell on the desk. Soon, a robust, middle-aged woman with gray hair appeared wearing a kitchen apron. She looked about sixty and hard. Her cheeks were flushed, and I guessed she had been working vigorously somewhere, probably the kitchen.

Without smiling, she stepped behind the desk, took out a ledger book, and greeted us with a thick German accent. "Do you have reservations?"

I said, "Yes, the reservations are under Cesari. Two people for Friday and Saturday night."

She opened up the book and traced her finger down the page. "Ah, here it is. Cesari, John, for Friday and Saturday night. Very good. Pleasure to meet you. I am Hilda Weber, the proprietor." She still didn't smile.

"I'm John Cesari and this is Kelly Kingston."

Kelly said, "Hello."

We all shook hands. Very formal.

"Your room is ready. If you will just follow me please."

Kelly gave me a sideways glance, and I smiled. For an innkeeper, Hilda was a tad short on social skills. She showed us to a room on the main floor that looked out into her garden. The placard on the door read The Panther's Lair. It had a canopied king bed and an adorable working fireplace framed with decorative tiles. There was a small couch, a couple of Queen Anne style chairs and a fairly large bathroom. The wall covering was off-white with a floral pattern. She lit a cinnamon scented candle for us.

Hilda said, "Breakfast is served promptly at 7 a.m., and the kitchen closes promptly at 9 a.m."

"What happens if we're late?"

"Don't be."

Kelly pushed me. "Never mind him, Hilda. He likes to joke."

She eyed me warily. "I see."

As she turned to leave I said, "Oh, Hilda."

"Yes?"

"Where do we get firewood?" I pointed to the three twigs that were lying beside the fireplace.

She walked over to the fireplace and examined the wood. She then looked at me sternly. "Why do you need firewood, it is August?"

"I thought it would be romantic."

She looked at the meager collection of wood by the hearth again. "That should be enough."

On that note, she turned and left the room. After the door closed, Kelly and I broke out laughing.

"Oh my God. Is she for real?"

"I can't believe it, Kel. I think we found us a real live war criminal hiding out right here in Vermont."

"Could she possibly have been less friendly?"

"Und dat iz eenuff vood for *you*," I said in a mock German accent. "Jesus. I'm paying three hundred and fifty bucks a night, specifically for the fireplace, and that's all the wood I get? Who cares that it's August? She should lower the price if no one uses the fireplace during summer. Well, she doesn't know me at all. I'll go chop down that maple tree out front tonight if I have to."

We both laughed again, and Kelly threw her arms around my neck, pulling me down until I fell on top of her on the bed. "Take it easy, Cesari. I'm already having the best time of my life."

"I can't help it. I'm all fired up."

She kissed me and stuck her tongue in my mouth.

She smiled. "Did that calm you down?"

"No, and now I have an erection."

"I can tell. Why don't you take a deep breath?—That's it. Feel better?"

"No."

She laughed and pushed me off. "How about we freshen up and go explore the town before dinner?"

I poked her gently in the side. "How about we take care of this erection first?"

Too late. She had her Vermont guidebook out. "Later, if you're good."

I laughed. "How about another kiss at least?"

She thought about that and climbed on top of me. She grabbed my wrists and leaned her head close to mine, letting her hair fall into my face. She aimed her green eyes at me and I stopped breathing as her lips slowly approached mine. Our lips locked and we both moaned. I couldn't have moved if I'd wanted to.

We lay there for a while enjoying the moment, when out of the blue, she asked, "Do you think that maybe Hilda had an attitude because of— you know?"

"If you mean, maybe she copped an attitude because I'm Italian. Well, the thought did cross my mind."

"Oh, God. Here we go. That's not what I meant. But go ahead, why on earth would she cop an attitude because you're Italian?" she asked derisively.

"It's a well-known fact that the Germans blame the Italians for losing World War II. It's like they think we threw it on purpose."

"Explain yourself." She got off me and put the valise on the bed, opening it while she listened.

I sat on the edge of the bed, watching her unpack. "Well, Hitler and Mussolini were best buds in the nineteen-thirties. In fact Benito Mussolini was Hitler's role model for how to oppress people. So, when they teamed up in World War II, Hitler thought he had a strong ally covering his ass in southern Europe."

"He got it wrong, I gather?"

"Boy, did he ever. What he didn't understand was that Mussolini was just a gorilla stuffed into a human costume. He also didn't understand that, even though the Italians liked marching up and down in parades, they had lost their stomach for real war a thousand years earlier. Once the shooting started, and their uniforms got dirty, they wanted out. And then there were millions of Italian immigrants living in America who thought Mussolini was a total asshole and sided with America. They enlisted in the U.S. Army in droves to prove they were loyal Americans. This didn't go over well back in Italy because many of these GIs like my grandfather still had family back there. Meanwhile, Mussolini's army folded like a cheap suit every time someone pointed a gun at it. So that, my dear, is why the German people dislike the Italian people," I concluded.

She looked at me funny, and then laughed. "That is the silliest thing I have ever heard. You have told me some whoppers before, but that one takes the cake. I have never, ever, in my entire life, heard that German people dislike Italian people for any reason. You made that whole thing up. Admit it."

"It's common knowledge, sweetheart. Ask anyone in the Bronx."

She shook her head and hit me with a pillow. "Stop, you're giving me a headache. I thought that maybe Hilda was put off because we're not married, and maybe also because of the black-white thing. You know how that generation can be."

"Might be a little of that, too. The Germans aren't exactly known for their racial tolerance. But truthfully, I think there's a much simpler explanation for her behavior than racism or decades old feuds about who caused who to lose the war."

"And what's that?"

"I think she's a bitch on wheels because she probably hasn't gotten laid in twenty years."

"And how do you know she hasn't got laid in twenty years?"

"Did you see her face? Besides, most women get cranky when they're not getting any."

"You're making me mad now, Cesari. Every time a woman is a little off her game, you say it's because she's not getting any or she's having her period. That's a sexist attitude, and I don't like it. And I don't think I like you very much right now either for saying that, so apologize."

"Apologize? Me? I didn't do anything."

She furrowed her brow, got quiet, and stormed into the bathroom, slamming the door behind her.

I sat on the edge of the bed, bewildered, trying to understand what had just happened. I didn't think I did anything that bad. Was she really upset because of what I said or because I wouldn't apologize when ordered to do so? Why would she defend Hilda anyway? I'm the one without any firewood. And what's with this sudden women's solidarity stuff? Then it dawned on me. Maybe it was that time of the month. Better not take any chances.

I took a deep breath, went over to the bathroom and gently knocked on the door. "Kelly?"

Nothing.

I knocked again. "Kelly?"

"Go away."

"I'm sorry," I said softly.

Nothing.

I knocked again. "I'm really sorry, and—I'm an asshole."

The door opened, and Kelly gave me a severe look from inside. "Give me a minute, and we'll go check out the town."

℞ 20

WE strolled leisurely into town along the main street. Historic old homes lined both sides of the road. They were charming and authentic. Some were brick, some were wood. Their manicured lawns, along with masses of day lilies, roses, and wisteria vines, made for a breathtaking vista, suggesting great pride from the homeowners.

It was a beautiful afternoon, and the center of town was setting up for a festival. Woodstock was a small, quaint village nestled in the heart of Vermont on the eastern side of the Green Mountains. It had managed to preserve much of its historic charm despite the march of time in and around it. Because of that, it had become a major tourist destination for those who wished to take a peek at how things might have looked and felt in small town America a hundred years ago. It was like being in a Norman Rockwell wet dream.

The village green was a small park that dominated the core of the town, and today it was filled with vendors and their carts, preparing for the weekend-long party. Woodstock teemed with small art galleries, book stores, clothing with moose designs, novelty shops, and restaurants. If it was eclectic and impractical, you were sure to find an entire store devoted to it. Which, of course, made it all the more fun.

"It's adorable," Kelly said, as we walked hand in hand along the sidewalk. "Let's go in there, all right?" She motioned to an old brick home that had been converted into an art gallery.

"Sure."

We entered and were greeted by a well-dressed woman in her early forties.

"Good afternoon."

"Good afternoon," we both responded in kind.

"Enjoying the beautiful weather?"

"Yes, we are. This is such a lovely town," Kelly said.

"Thank you. Is this your first visit to Woodstock?"

"Yes, it is."

"Oh, how nice. How long are you here for?"

Kelly said, "Just for the weekend. We just arrived."

"I am sure that you are going to enjoy yourselves. These are all original oils and watercolors. The artist has a studio upstairs. My name is Joyce, and if there is anything I can help you with, please let me know."

"Thank you," I said.

She moved away to assist another customer.

"Look at that," Kelly said, pointing to large oil painting of a man in a gray suit and bowler derby, but with the face of an elephant. He was holding an open umbrella over his head even though the sun was shining in the background.

We moved closer to better inspect it. Kelly said, "It must be a metaphor for something."

I chuckled. "Maybe it's a warning to young artists about the dangers of dropping acid when you're painting."

"Will you relax and enjoy the moment? So, it's a little weird. I kind of like it."

It was six feet tall by four feet wide. I noticed the price tag at the bottom. "Wow, only $12,000. It's a steal."

"We could hang it in the living room. It would be quite the conversation piece."

"I'm warning you now, Kel. There isn't enough room in all of Manhattan for this painting and me."

"Really? Because I was thinking the same thing about me and your ego."

She thought that was real funny, and I had to admit, as far as zingers went, it wasn't too bad. She was really coming along in the humor department.

"That wasn't very nice. Don't you care about what I think?"

"Stop whining. I was just joking." She giggled and put her arm through mine.

We moved deeper into the gallery, eyeing the varied collection of pop, modern, and traditional art.

We finally found something that I found appealing, and I noted my approval. "This is the kind of art I like."

It was a simple country scene of a white farmhouse set on a two foot wide canvas. There was a red barn and grain silo in the background; couple of cows, a corn field, the setting sun. No people.

Kelly wrinkled her nose. "Not my style. Sorry. Boring." She feigned a yawn.

"What's boring about it?"

"It just is. So forget about it."

We spent a few more minutes wandering around, said goodbye to Joyce, and she handed us her business card as we left. We walked in and out of a few more shops, browsing.

"There are quite a few people out and about. Don't you think?" Kelly asked, noticing the throngs of people milling about. We stopped in front of a small cheese shop on one of the side streets and took in the atmosphere.

"Yes, there are. I have a feeling it's tourist season all year round up here. Hey, Kel, how do you think I would look in one of those hats?" I nodded in the direction of several men walking with their wives, wearing wide brimmed hats for sun protection; not quite cowboy hats and not quite *Raiders of the Lost Ark* hats. They stuck out like sore thumbs as tourists.

"Over my dead body, Cesari. You'd look ridiculous. You can wear a baseball cap if you want."

"What if I get one anyway? You can't tell me what to wear," I said playfully.

"Fine. Get one if you want, but don't walk next to me wearing one of those. I wouldn't want people to think we're together."

"I have rights, too, you know."

"Are you trying to make me mad again? Didn't you learn your lesson earlier?"

She was smiling, but I decided to shut up anyway.

"Let's take a look in here," I said, nodding toward the cheese shop.

We entered the bustling *fromagerie* and were met by the delightful scents of artisanal cheeses, cured meats, fresh bread and wine. Hungry customers enjoying their purchases gathered round a large wooden table in the center of the room. There were several workers behind a long counter taking orders, making sandwiches and retrieving bottles of wine for thirsty patrons.

"Mmm, everything smells so good in here."

"Yeah, seems more like a delicatessen than a cheese shop, although cheese does seem to be the big seller. I can't believe how many choices there are for such a small shop."

"I didn't know you could open a bottle of wine and just start drinking it in a store like this."

"You can't in New York State." As we talked and scanned the refrigerated bins of cheeses, we couldn't help overhearing the shopkeeper in a heated debate. He was a heavyset man in his late-forties with a handle-bar mustache and a fairly obvious French accent.

He was lecturing a much younger man. "I am telling you, Pierre, the people here will never accept you as one of their own. I have been living here twenty-five years and still feel like an outsider."

"I disagree strongly, Jacque," replied the much younger man sagely. "It is all about how you comport yourself. If you are aloof, then you get what you deserve. My wife, Marie, is now seven months pregnant, and our child will be a true Woodstock native, no different than anyone else."

The shopkeeper waved his hand in exasperation. "Pierre, you are my sister's only child, and I love you like you were my own son, but in this you are terribly naïve. Putting a kitten in an oven does not make it a blueberry muffin."

Kelly and I studied some foie gras, trying hard not to laugh.

I leaned in close and whispered, "What the hell was that supposed to mean?"

She elbowed me. "Stop. You'll get us thrown out of here."

"Can I help you?" The shopkeeper asked politely, noticing us. The other man stepped to one side, allowing us a better view of the cheeses.

I asked, "Do you have anything French and stinky?"

He chuckled, and wiped his fat hands on his apron. "I have a cousin in Paris who would fit that description, but nothing here. I am sorry. I carry mostly local cheeses and what I make myself. I do have several imported cheeses you might like, such as Camembert and Brie, but they're not very stinky. Unfortunately, there is not a big market here for your more pungent cheeses, despite the fact that they are so delicious."

"How about a small wedge of Brie then? Enough for two, and a baguette."

"Certainly, I'll wrap it up. Anything else?"

"Yes, can you tell us where the Prince and The Pauper is? We have reservations for dinner tonight."

"It is only about another fifty yards up this same street. The entrance is off to the side, and there is a sign out front that you cannot miss. You are going to love it. The food there is heavenly, very sophisticated and very French. I have dined there many times."

"Thank you."

We settled up and said goodbye.

Once outside, Kelly said, "Are you going to be okay at this restaurant tonight?"

"What do you mean?"

"It's French."

"I'm not sure what you're getting at."

"You're not going to be able to order chicken parm there. I don't want you going nuts."

"I'm insulted at the implication that I won't know how to behave in a nice restaurant."

"It's not that. It's just that I know you can take the boy out of the Bronx, but you can't take the Bronx out of the boy."

"I'll behave. I promise. Besides, they might have chicken parm there. You won't know until you ask. They might even make it special for me."

"Oh God, please promise me you won't do that."

I laughed. "What are you worried about?"

"That you're going to offend the entire French population of Vermont."

"Offend the French? Sweetheart, the Italians taught the French how to cook in the first place. They owe us big time. The least they could do is make me some chicken parm."

"Oh, brother. I feel another tall tale on the way."

"It's true, and if you had paid attention in history class you would already know this. At the height of the Renaissance, in the fifteen hundreds, Catherine De Medici of Florence married the French King, Henry II. She brought all her chefs with her to France where they passed on their culinary skills and techniques. Soon after her arrival, dinner became a fine art and there followed a great gastronomic awakening in the French as they embraced their new and beloved queen."

"Are you through?"

"Yes."

"Are you going to behave in the restaurant or not?"

"I'll try my best."

"Thank God. Well, it's just about six already. Maybe we should head back to the room and start getting ready for dinner. I'd like to spruce up a bit, and that cheese is going to need to be refrigerated."

"Hey, Kel. Do you think we could just stop in that bookstore across the street for a few minutes first? It looks interesting." I pointed at a large wood sign over a doorway which read Ye Olde Bookshop.

She shrugged. "Sure, why not, but not too long. Okay?"

Kelly and I loved to read fiction, and browsing bookstores was something we both enjoyed, but this was rapidly becoming a thing of the past with the onset of digital media. I'd thought I would never get used to reading on a Kindle, but that was all I ever used now. We entered the store and noted that every inch of space had something crammed into it. There were eight long, narrow aisles, and each wall had floor to ceiling shelves that could only be accessed by ladder towards the top. Several aproned employees busied themselves with customers. We found the fiction section and slowly cruised up and down the aisle.

Kelly looked around. "Wow, it's as big as most Barnes and Noble's in here."

"Yes, and there's another floor upstairs," I said, noting an escalator to one side of the store. "From the outside, I thought this was going to be a small, intimate mom and pop bookstore like the one we had upstate in the town of Penn Yan. That place was cool, and the bookseller there, Jim, was even cooler. This place feels like Walmart."

"You know, Cesari, I'm reading a really good book now on Kindle. I wonder if they carry it in paperback. I think I would like to get a copy before paper becomes extinct."

"I doubt that paper is going to become extinct, Kel, but sure, get one if you want. Who knows, maybe we'll bump into the author one day and have it signed."

She searched for a few minutes and decided it might be faster if she just asked the store manager, a woman named Penelope, who she found at a desk toward the back of the store. Middle-aged, short and frumpy, she was not particularly pleased to be distracted from the cookie she was eating while reading the local newspaper. It was getting near closing time and she looked tired.

Kelly addressed her. "Hello, I was wondering if you carried a novel called *Temperature Rising*? I couldn't find it on the shelves. It just came out a few months ago. It's very good."

Penelope sized us up, turned to a computer screen nearby, punched a few keys and asked, "Do you know the author's name?"

Kelly answered, "Give me a second. He's very new and it's his first book. I think he may even have self-published. I'm not sure of the spelling, but I've been reading it on my Kindle." She reached into her bag and pulled out the device, turning it on as Penelope rolled her eyes in disgust. Kelly saw that and said, "I'm sorry, did I do something to offend you?"

Penelope ignored the question. "I doubt that we carry your book, miss."

Kelly looked surprised and puzzled. "But you didn't even look?"

The woman shook her head and scolded her. "If it's a new author and he self-published, then it's probably just an e-book, and as a matter of policy, we don't carry print versions of e-books. The sign out front, in case you didn't notice, said Ye Olde Bookshop, not Ye Olde E-Bookshop. We only work with traditional publishing houses. You e-book people are all the same. You just don't get it. You come waltzing in here all the time with your little Kindles and Nooks, thinking you're going to find hard copies of the books you've been reading. It doesn't work like that. This is a bookstore, not RadioShack. The books here are written by real authors, not some hack who was able to get published simply because he has a laptop and access to the internet. We sell books here, the kind people like to hold in their hands and feel the pages with their fingers, and sometimes if you're really lucky, maybe even smell the ink."

Kelly stammered. "I guess I don't understand?"

"Well, I'll explain it in plain English then. Traditional publishing houses have overhead. They have buildings, warehouses, printing presses and employees. Bookstores also have overhead. Guess what overhead e-books have? That's right—almost nothing. And you can't compete against nothing. Bookstores are closing all over the country because you can't compete against nothing. The print book industry and everything I have devoted my life to is passing into the pages of history right before my eyes and e-books are the reason. I feel like the old south in *Gone with the Wind*. Now do you understand? I shouldn't have to explain this to you, either."

Kelly was speechless at the woman's ranting. But I could see that her shock was about to turn to real anger, so I stepped in between. "Thank you for your time, Penelope. I think we'll be leaving now, right, Kel? We have dinner reservations and a cheese that needs to be refrigerated."

It was a fifteen minute walk back to the Reluctant Panther, and that was good because it took that long for Kelly to calm down. She said, "I don't understand why she was so obnoxious. What did I do to deserve that?"

"You didn't do anything to deserve that, Kel. Traditional bookstores are a dying industry gasping for their last breath. Digital media such as Kindle is the future; everyone knows it, even the book sellers like Penelope, but a lot of them can't accept it, so they cling to the hope that it will all just go away. They're all feeling very threatened right now by the new technology, but that doesn't mean she had the right to berate you like that. When she saw your Kindle, she unloaded all her fears and insecurities about her own future onto you. People like her remind me of when digital cameras first came along. Kodak put its head in the sand trying to ignore them, and when they finally pulled their head back out again, they found out that instead of being leaders in the industry they had once ruled, they were bankrupt. But her reaction was uncalled for, that's for sure. You were just a customer asking an innocent question. She needs to relax a little, for sure."

Kelly scowled. "Humph, I know what she needs all right."

I chuckled. "I'm not falling for that one twice in one day, Kel."

"Did you see her face?"

We both started laughing at the same time.

I said, "How about we put this little incident behind us?"

"Fine, but she didn't have to call me an e-book person. That wasn't nice. What does that even mean?"

I put my arm around her. "If it's any consolation, I'm an e-book person, too."

That made her smile and she pulled me close as we walked. "Maybe we'll have little e-book children someday?"

I stiffened and she hung on tightly, chuckling. "Relax, Cesari, it was a joke. Let's put that one behind us, too."

As we approached the B&B, I spotted something of interest towards the back of the old house.

"Kel. Look over there."

"What? I don't see anything. Just the garage."

"What do you see by the side of the garage?"

"I don't know. What? A pile of wood?"

"No, Kel. Not a pile of wood— a woodpile." Neatly stacked along the garage in back of the house was a large pile of cut wood, partially protected from the rain by a tarp.

"Cesari, you're not going to start in again about the wood, are you?"

"Kel, I paid to have a romantic fireplace for us, and I intend on using it! Look, the window to our room is right over there on the same side of the house as the wood pile. Later tonight, I'll go out, gather some wood, and pass it through the window to you. We won't need that much. She'll never miss it."

"Oh my God. I can't believe you. You're going to get Hilda mad at us."

"Let me worry about Hilda, all right? Speak of the devil." We had just entered the B&B when Hilda appeared.

"Oh, hello," she greeted us.

"Hello, Hilda, may we store this cheese we bought in your refrigerator?" I asked politely.

She looked at the items I was holding. "Certainly. I will take care of that for you."

She extended her hands, and I gave her my package.

I thanked her, and we started to walk toward our room.

As we passed her, she turned. "Did your friends find you?"

We stopped. "What friends?" I asked.

"Two gentlemen checked in about an hour ago. They said they were friends of yours. I told them you were probably exploring the town."

"Do you remember their names, Hilda?"

"Yes, I do. One was Billy Clanton, and the other Frank McLaury."

"Are you sure about that?" I asked.

"I am very sure. I wrote the names down in the registry."

"And they were looking for us, not some other couple?"

"I couldn't remember your names right away so they described you both. They said they were looking for a very pretty girl and an unusually ugly man. Who else could they mean?"

Kelly chuckled.

"That's what they said?" I asked incredulously. That was kind of harsh.

"Yes, I am certain."

"Can you tell me what room they are in?"

"I put them on the second floor, rooms seven and eight, but they are not here right now. I think they went out to look for you."

"Did you tell them which room we were in?"

"Of course I did."

"Thank you, Hilda."

Inside our room, Kelly burst out laughing. "I think you're very handsome. I don't care what Hilda said. I wonder who they are, though... It sounds like a mistake. I never heard of those guys, have you? Well, I'm going to take a quick shower and then get ready. I can't wait to try this restaurant, even if your ex is going to crash the party. What are you doing, Cesari?"

I was throwing our stuff back in to the suitcase and didn't answer.

"I asked you what you're doing."

"We can't stay here, Kel. I don't know who those guys are, but I doubt that they're our friends."

"Relax, Cesari. It's probably just a mistake." She started taking stuff out of the suitcase again. "You're obviously not the guy they described. You're very good looking." I must have looked upset because she touched my arm gently. "Are you going to be okay?"

"The names of those guys Hilda just gave us. I do know who they are."

"And who are they?"

"The question you should ask is who were they? They've been dead for over a hundred years. They were killed at the OK Corral by Wyatt Earp and Doc Holiday."

R_X 21

"OH stop, you're being paranoid now. The OK Corral. For heaven's sake. I'm not going anywhere. It's just a coincidence." She took the bag from me. "That's enough. You're letting your imagination run away with you, and I'm not going to let you spoil the weekend. If you keep it up, I'm not going to let you read any more spy novels."

She went into the bathroom with the suitcase, and soon I heard water running. I wasn't happy at all. I had left my .38 in its lockbox in New York. Browsing antique stores didn't generally require concealed firearms. I suddenly felt very exposed, so I left the room in search of a weapon. In the parking lot out back, I observed four other cars besides my Camry. Two were from Massachusetts, one from Colorado and the last was a black Cadillac from New York.

In the garage, I spotted a Volvo with Vermont plates. Hilda's car. I looked around and found what I needed in a corner leaning against the wall, a maul. Half sledge hammer, half axe, this one was old and heavy. The metal head was rusty and weighed about six pounds. I returned to the parking lot and looked at the Caddie. It didn't seem familiar, and I couldn't recall if it had been there when we'd arrived.

I walked up to it and peered inside. Nothing on the front seats or on the dashboard. The rear was clear as well. Just an ordinary car, or was it? Something just didn't seem right. It was too clean. What did that mean? I would've loved a more careful inspection, but there was still too much light out to start smashing windows. I walked over to my car and looked in. There were empty coffee cups, a napkin on the floor, and phone chargers in their jacks. It looked lived in. Same for the other cars. People who drive long distances are usually pretty road weary by the time they reach their destination, and cleaning out their car is not necessarily their high priority. Unless you weren't ordinary travelers. I looked in the Caddie again. It was spotless. My cell phone went off.

"Hi, Kel."

"Where are you? It's almost seven."

"I'll be right there. Could you open the window, please?"

"Cesari, are you still obsessing about that wood? I'll open it, but I expect to see you here in five minutes."

I walked around to the side of the house and slipped the maul through the open window. I then went around to the front of the house and let myself in. Kelly was still in the bathroom, and I hid the maul under the bed.

As I stood up, she entered the room. "Hi, Kel."

"What have you been up to?" she asked suspiciously.

"Just admiring Hilda's garden."

"Yeah, right. Get changed, will you? I'd like to get there a little early and have a cocktail."

"Okay, I'll hurry." I stripped down and started to put on a pair of dress pants.

"Oh, no, you don't. Get in the shower," she ordered. "We've been driving and walking around all day. You need to clean up. I'm going to be all dressed up, and if you want to come near me tonight, you're going to have to be clean and looking sharp."

Unbelievable. A woman with a towel wrapped around her head was giving me orders.

"Do I have to wear a tie?" I called out from the shower. "I don't think I brought one."

"I packed one for you."

Great.

Fifteen minutes later, I slapped on some aftershave and was ready to go.

"How do I look?" I was wearing khakis, penny loafers, a white button down dress shirt and a solid blue tie.

She came up to me and straightened my tie. "You look nice, but you need to comb your hair better. Your sport coat got a little wrinkled on the way up, but it'll do. And how do I look?"

She looked great as she twirled around for inspection. She wore an orangey-yellow summer dress with spaghetti straps and had a matching bag and shoes. Her hair was gorgeous, wavy and smelled great. I knew she spent a lot of time on her hair, but I had learned a long time ago not to ask too many questions about it or to touch it without permission. That was a problem for me because I liked to touch things.

"You look like a supermodel that just got kidnapped by an unusually ugly man."

She laughed. "Stop and get over it. We're going to have a great night."

"I can't get over it. I think Hilda made that part up just to piss me off."

"You think she's smart enough to do that?"

"I think she still mad because of World War II."

"You're driving me crazy with that. Let's go."

We left the B&B and drove the one mile to the restaurant. Kelly didn't want to walk in heels. We arrived at fifteen minutes of eight and announced ourselves to the hostess. Our table wasn't ready, so we sidled up to the small bar off to the side of the restaurant.

"This place is really old," Kelly said, looking at the ancient, timbered ceiling.

"And old school," I added, noting that all the waiters were wearing black jackets, white shirts, and ties. All the patrons wore formal attire as well. I felt just a bit underdressed, not wearing a suit.

The bar was dark and poorly lit. Candles glimmered in sconces on the wall and in pewter holders. Several leather chairs and a sofa adorned the room and swivel stools lined the bar itself.

"Where do you want to sit, Kel?"

"Let's sit at the bar. I really like the ambience in here."

"I do, too. It has the feel of an eighteenth century tavern."

I helped her onto the bar stool and stood next to her. Nearby was another, much older couple. They had white hair, and she wore a diamond necklace with matching earrings. He wore diamond cufflinks and tie pin, and they sipped dirty martinis from over-sized crystal glasses.

We nodded hello, and the bartender asked Kelly what she would like to drink.

"What do you think, Cesari? I always get Cosmos. I want to try something different."

"How about a Manhattan, or an Old Fashioned?" I offered.

The bartender was thirty-five years old, good looking with long, brown hair in a ponytail. His name was Aldo, and I already didn't like him.

He said, "I make a great Sidecar with Remy XO. I guarantee you'll love it. If not, it's on the house. It's an elegant drink for an elegant and beautiful woman." His eyes lingered on her for just a little too long.

Holy Shit!

She smiled. "Thank you, Aldo. I think I'll try that. I've never had one."

"It's always good to try new things. And you, sir, what would you like?" He spoke to me, but was still staring at Kelly.

"I'd like my girlfriend back, for starters," I grumbled, and Kelly gave me a quick kick.

"Ouch."

"He's always joking around like that, Aldo. I'm sorry," Kelly said. "Tell the man what you would like to drink, John." She gave me a very seriously annoyed look.

I took a deep breath and rubbed my leg where she'd kicked me. "Yeah, I like to kid around. How about Jim Beam on the rocks?"

No reaction.

"I'm deeply sorry sir, but we don't carry Mr. Beam. Would you care to make another selection?"

Oh for God's sake. I could feel the old couple next to me staring. The old man said under his breath, "He'll probably request a Bud light or some such thing next. I daresay, they're going to love this one at the club."

My cheeks began to flush from embarrassment. I looked at the bar and saw a row of high-end, single malt scotches.

"Scotch, neat. Anything from that shelf over there." I nodded toward the bottles lined up behind him..

"Anything, sir? Are you certain?"

"Yeah, you pick for me, Aldo."

He mixed Kelly's drink first and then poured my scotch.

"So, what did you decide on for me?" I asked civilly.

"Glenfiddich, 1937, sir. I hope it is to your liking. He showed me the bottle."

"I swirled it around and sniffed it before taking a sip. "Wow. That's outstanding. Very smooth. Thank you, Aldo. This was an excellent choice."

"You're welcome, sir. Will there be anything else?"

"Out of curiosity, what does a bottle of that go for?"

"About $20,000."

Kelly and I looked at each other concerned. I didn't want to know how much it cost per glass.

R̷x 22

IT was a quarter past eight when we were finally seated at a corner table. The restaurant was very crowded and Cheryl hadn't arrived yet. We finished our cocktails and enjoyed the scenery.

Kelly said, "Wouldn't it be great if she got lost and never showed up?"

"That's not very nice, Kel. Cheryl's only trying to be helpful"

"I know. It's just that I was hoping to have a nice romantic dinner with you alone, if you know what I mean?" She batted her eyes and to emphasize the point, ran the side of her foot up my leg.

She smiled and asked again, "Do you know what I mean?"

"I think I do. And trust me, I'm no happier about this than you are. She didn't exactly give me a choice. She said she had something important to tell me and couldn't do it on the phone. Before I could even respond, she hung up."

Our waiter came up and greeted us. He was tall, lean, and looked like a runner. His hair was jet black, and he carried himself with an air of authority. "I am Pascal and it is my entirely good pleasure to service you this evening," he said stiffly and with a French accent. I noticed that he was the only server without a name tag. Instead, he had a white rose pinned to his lapel. Maybe he was important, or maybe it was his birthday. He handed Kelly her menu, and me, a wine list as thick as a chemistry book.

"Will you be desirous of bottled water or tap?" he asked.

I glanced at Kelly, who shrugged. "Bottled water would be nice."

"Gas or no gas?"

I stared at him.

"Bubbles or no bubbles?"

I stared at him.

Kelly said, "No gas, please."

"Thank you, Mademoiselle. If you have any questions, please do not hesitate to ask to me. I return now quickly with your water, no gas." He waited politely as we thanked him, and then walked away.

Kelly laughed. "You've never ordered bottled water in a nice restaurant before?"

"When he said 'gas or no gas', I thought he was explaining how the menu was organized."

"You're impossible, Cesari."

She studied her menu. "Everything looks so good. What does poularde mean?"

"I'm pretty sure that's french for overpriced chicken. Geez, will you look at these prices?"

"I'm worth it, aren't I?" She smiled, and reached across the table to hold my hand.

I didn't answer fast enough, and she kicked me gently under the table. Not as hard as before.

We both laughed. "This is nice," I said.

"Yes, it is."

"How sweet. Move over, Cesari. Hi Kelly." Cheryl had found us. I let go of Kelly's hand and slid further into the booth. She wore a dark blue, knee-length skirt with a white blouse, very little make-up and gold earrings. Her hair was tousled from her recent car ride. Probably had the windows open. She looked good.

Kelly and I greeted her. I said, "Just got here, I gather?"

"Haven't even found a place to stay yet." She picked up a breadstick and started eating. Pascal came over with our water and introduced himself to Cheryl, handing her a menu. Another waiter came over with a tray of appetizers which Pascal called amuse-bouche. Little bits of something wrapped in something else.

"Have you selected a wine, sir?" he asked.

"Haven't even had a chance to look, Pascal. I don't suppose you have any Chianti here?"

"I am afraid no, monsieur. We serve only the highest qualities of wine so that they may pair the more well with our cuisine."

I felt my face turning red again, but I managed to maintain my composure. "This is a very extensive wine list, Pascal, but I don't read French."

May I assist you in this regard?"

"Even better, Pascal. Why don't you pick a wine for us? I trust your judgment, and I think we'd prefer a red if you don't mind." Kelly nodded in agreement.

Pascal bowed courteously. "Thank you, monsieur. You will not be dissatisfied." As he turned to walk away, his eyes lingered on Cheryl.

We studied the menus and made our decisions. Pascal returned a few minutes later and uncorked a bottle of burgundy, Chateau something or other, and gave me a taste. It was very good. Cheryl's napkin slid off her lap to the floor, and Pascal quickly bent over to pick it up. She reached out for it, thanking him, and he pulled it away.

"I will have a new one for you immediately," he said and quickly grabbed a fresh napkin off of a nearby cart. He placed it in front of her, bringing his face within inches of hers.

"Thank you, Pascal," she said.

"No, thank you for bringing your most beautiful self to this undeserving restaurant. Will mademoiselle be joined by a gentleman friend— her huz-band perhaps?"

"No, Pascal, I'm not married." Kelly and I watched this little scene.

He smiled a little French smile. "How fortunate for all the single men in this great country." The color in Cheryl's cheeks rose.

Damn. Another smooth talker. Only now with a French accent. I was going to have to be careful in this place. I was outclassed by a mile.

Pascal filled our wine glasses and took our orders.

After he left, Kelly giggled. "Oh my goodness. He was pouring it on thick with you, Cheryl, wasn't he?"

"He was kind of cute. I like him," Cheryl said, smiling. "He seemed like a real gentleman."

"Enough already, girls." I was annoyed. "Want to tell me what's going on now, Cheryl?"

"Relax Cesari. I've had a long ride." She took a big sip of wine. "Hmm, nice. Okay, this is the deal. This morning we got notified that someone did a search of your name in our database. We don't know who exactly, but it has to be someone in law enforcement, as I told you. That, by itself, only narrows it down to thousands of people all over the country. The problem is that your name was linked to Barazza and Gianelli's files. I'm sure you remember them, Kelly. The two guys who ran the drug ring in that hospital you worked at. Gianelli's hiding somewhere in witness protection, and Barazza is getting all his nutrition through a feeding tube. All he does is drool and stare straight ahead all day. Nice work, Cesari." She paused to take another sip of wine.

I sidestepped the accusation. "When they searched my name, what did it come up with exactly?"

"Just that we have a file on you that cannot be accessed without approval from the Department of Justice. It can be done, but requires a formal request in writing. The website also let the person know the case number that you were involved in. Accessing the case number would pull up Barazza and Gianelli's files, which also cannot be accessed casually."

"Okay, so far it doesn't sound like that big a deal. Somebody searched my name, and found out nothing except that I'm known to the FBI and somehow associated with the Barazza case. So what?"

Pascal came with some fresh, warm bread and whipped butter while we spoke and nibbled on the amuse bouche. He refilled our wine glasses and discreetly retreated.

"Yes. Well, the big deal is a guy called Salvatore Moretti. They call him Boom Boom. After Barazza and Gianelli left the scene, he stepped in to fill the power vacuum left behind. He promised the other families that he would, among other things, get to the bottom of what happened last year and seek vengeance against those who needed it. In addition, there's about ten million dollars in misplaced mob money they're seeking to get back. No one knows where it went, and Barazza can't tell anybody anything."

Kelly looked at me furtively and Cheryl caught the look. "Anything you forget to tell me, Cesari?"

"No, not really," I lied. Five million of that money was sitting in a bank account with my name on it in the Cayman Islands, and the other five was sitting next to it, in an account belonging to my psychiatrist friend, Mark Greenberg. Mark had helped me hack into Barazza's laptop last year and transfer the money over to us.

Pascal returned with our dinners, and we paused while he served us. Kelly had the Chilean Sea bass with sautéed baby carrots and potatoes au gratin. I had the grilled veal chop, medium rare with truffle butter, roasted fingerling potatoes and ratatouille. He served Cheryl last and most dramatically.

"And for the beautiful mademoiselle with no huz-band, we have the soft shelled crabs sautéed in garlic and butter, roasted asparagus with rosemary and Parmigiano Reggiano and a timbale of eggplant layered with whipped Yukon gold potatoes. I personally selected the soft shelled crabs for you. They are the best we have to offer. Bon appetit."

The girls just stared at the food after he left. Kelly said, "It looks too good to eat."

"I know what you mean," Cheryl added. "God, it smells so good, too. Why can't men smell like this?"

Kelly thought that was funny, and they both laughed.

I swallowed a mouthful of veal. "So, Cheryl, you haven't told us why you drove all the way up here. I don't understand all this cloak and dagger stuff, and what does this Boom Boom character have to do with this? He's not the one who tried to access my file, is he?"

"No," Cheryl said. "But we've had his phones tapped for the last couple of months, and this morning, about one hour after the hit on the website came, someone called Boom Boom to ask him if he knew who you were."

Kelly and I stopped eating.

Kelly said, "You're kidding?"

I said, "Shit."

Pascal said, "Another bottle of wine?"

R̽ 23

"**WHAT** else did they say?" I asked, now genuinely concerned.

"Well, Boom Boom didn't know who you were, but was very interested in the fact that you were associated with Barazza and Gianelli, which he hadn't known. The other guy also told him that you were going to Vermont this weekend with your pretty girlfriend."

"Great," I said, now alarmed. "Hey, wait a minute. So, you already knew where I was when we spoke earlier today?"

"Not exactly. We heard the guy say Vermont, but couldn't make out much else because of sound distortion. Besides, I needed for you to confirm what we'd heard in case the guy was blowing smoke in our direction."

"Damn, how did they know that?" Kelly asked anxiously.

"I have no idea," Cheryl replied. "There was loud background music playing and the pick-up was poor. Eavesdropping is still an imperfect science. Well, anyway, I just wanted to give you a heads-up because you're now on the radar, and I don't know how serious it is."

"Thank you," I said sincerely. "But it sounds pretty serious to me."

"Yes, thank you. Cheryl," Kelly added. "That was nice of you to drive all the way up here to warn us."

"You're welcome, Kel. These are some nasty characters we're talking about, and if they keep snooping, they may find out that they have an axe to grind with you, Cesari. I don't know what you can do, but at least you've had a warning."

I looked at her, puzzled. "Why exactly did you drive up here, Cheryl? Why couldn't you tell me all this on the phone?"

She hesitated, looked over her shoulder instinctively and lowered her voice in a conspiratorial manner.

"For several reasons. First of all, we've wire-tapped that asshole, Moretti, without a court order. So I couldn't exactly say how I knew what I knew, not out loud on the phone. You never know who might be listening. Secondly, we have significant concerns about the loyalty of some of our people. This guy who searched your name and called Moretti is undoubtedly NYPD or FBI. The question is, how high up and is he alone? Thirdly, I owe you from last year. You both did us a big favor in helping us take down Barazza and Gianelli, and I would prefer that you didn't get killed because of some turncoat in law enforcement."

"Thanks, I appreciate it."

We finished our meals and had a round of coffee.

"Anybody want anything else, like dessert?" I asked. "Or should I just get the check?"

"This on you, Cesari?" Cheryl asked. "I don't mind paying my own way."

"After the favor you just did for us, not a chance. In fact, let me pay for your motel, too. Hey, why don't you stay with us at the Reluctant Panther? It's a beautiful B&B just down the road from here, and it's only half filled with guests because it's off season. It's late, but I don't think the owner would mind the extra income."

Kelly said, "Yes, please stay with us. I feel like we owe you that much. You know, I had mixed feelings when I heard you were coming up, but I am truly glad you did. I would feel bad now if you had to stay in some dirty motel."

Cheryl laughed. "Wow. Dinner and a night at a nice B&B. I'm going to start crashing your dates more often Cesari. Sure, why not? I wasn't looking forward to sleeping in some truck stop anyway."

Before I could signal Pascal for the check, he approached, pushing a small, elegant cart with a silver serving tray. On the tray were four cognac snifters and a bottle of Armagnac, vintage

1964. He poured out three hefty glasses without asking and served them to us.

"Compliments of the house," he said. I looked at my watch. It was almost eleven-thirty, and the place was starting to clear out.

I said, "What the hell. In for a penny, in for a pound. Thank you, Pascal. Look, I don't want to get you in trouble with your boss, but would you care to join us? You've been a great waiter and made our experience here quite memorable."

He smiled and took a polite bow. "I thought you would never ask. That is why I brought the extra snifter. I wouldn't worry about my boss either, since I am the owner." He poured himself some Armagnac and sat next to Kelly, who slid over in the booth. I watched him stare at Cheryl.

It was well after midnight when we all finally arrived at the Reluctant Panther. I was fine, but the girls were flying high from the wine and after dinner drinks. Cheryl left her car in the parking lot of the Prince and The Pauper and rode with us in the Camry. This suited her just fine as it gave her the perfect reason to go back and see Pascal again.

We entered quietly, trying to be respectful of the hour.

"Should I wake up Hilda?" I whispered, while we stood in the reception area.

"How else are we going to get Cheryl a room?" Kelly asked.

"Yeah," Cheryl chimed in.

I went behind the desk and opened the inn's registry. There were a total of eight guest rooms. Five were occupied, three downstairs and two upstairs. Hilda slept on the main floor toward the back of the house. I read through the registry and saw the names of all the guests staying here, including the names Billy Clanton and Frank McLaury, registered in rooms seven and eight upstairs. Next to each name was the make, model, and license plate number of the car they were driving. Hilda didn't like unauthorized persons using her parking lot, and I guessed that during peak season that might be a problem. The guys from the OK Corral were driving the black Caddie I had seen earlier. I had forgotten to mention them to Cheryl, but would tomorrow when she was sober.

"So what's the plan, Cesari?" Cheryl giggled. "Do I get a room or turn tricks on the street all night?"

"Give me a second. I'm thinking, and keep it down."

Cheryl looked at Kelly. "He's thinking." And they both started laughing.

"Shhh," I said. I opened the desk drawer and saw multiple sets of keys.

There was a legal pad on the desk, so I wrote Hilda a brief note telling her that we had an unexpected guest and to go ahead and charge my credit card for an additional room. I would explain in the morning. I took out my credit card and left it in plain sight with the note. I found the key to room four on the main floor.

"C'mon girls. Follow me."

They stumbled down the hallway after me and we found the room. It had a brass placard which read The Panther's Womb.

Cheryl looked at the sign. "You've got to be kidding me."

"Our room is called The Panther's Lair," Kelly said, making a growling sound and waving a clawed hand in the air like a panther. The girls started laughing again, and I shh'd them again. Kelly trying to be tough on a good day would arouse as much fear as a kitten playing with a ball of yarn.

After glancing around the hallway, I opened the door and we went in. I breathed a sigh when I saw that the king bed was fully made up. I didn't want to have to search for bed sheets and pillows.

"Okay, you're good to go."

"Wow, this is so gorgeous," Cheryl said. "Thank you again, John, and you too, Kelly. Well, have a good night, all. I'm going to take a quick shower and hit the sack. I'm drunk and exhausted."

"Good night, Cheryl. We'll see you in the morning. Wait 'til you get a load of Hilda," I said. Kelly wished her goodnight as well, and we went to our room.

R~X~ 24

BACK in our room, I closed the door and put my arms around Kelly in the dark. She was facing away and nuzzled back into me. I kissed her gently on the neck.

"I've been wanting to do that all night," I whispered. "You looked so hot, I could barely see straight."

She liked that, and purred. "And I've been waiting for this all night."

She reached up and backwards, clasping her hands around my neck. She pressed the length of her body into me. I could feel my blood pressure rising and falling in various parts of my body, depending on where you measured it. She turned around to face me, and I leaned down, giving her a long wet kiss.

She smiled and pressed into me even more. "Are those your keys I feel?"

I shook my head. "I don't think so."

"Let me go clean up a little. I have something special that I want to wear for you," she whispered softly.

"I promise I won't go anywhere."

I turned on the small lamp by the night stand, which shed a little light into the room. It was only a forty watt bulb. Kelly went dancing off into the bathroom. I looked at the fireplace and then remembered the maul. I had work to do. I went over to the bathroom and knocked gently.

"Kelly," I whispered. "I'm just going to get us a handful of wood for the fireplace. It'll be romantic. Okay?"

"I thought you got some earlier?"

"Not enough. I won't be long."

"You'd better be back by the time I come out or I'll start without you," she giggled through the door.

"Understood."

Retrieving the maul from where I had hidden it under the bed, I looked around for something to muffle the sound and found a throw blanket on one of the Queen Anne chairs. I left quietly and made my way to the parking lot in back of the house. It was quite dark out, and only the sound of crickets could be heard. The black Caddie was still parked in its space.

I went to the passenger side and threw the blanket over the roof, letting it drape down over the window. I glanced around quickly, and saw no one. All the lights in the house were out. Standing to one side of the passenger door, and using the sledgehammer side of the maul, I smashed the window hard in its center. The sound of it shattering inward was muted well by the blanket. I prepared to run, but there was no alarm.

Reaching inside, I opened the door and swept broken glass off the seat. I sat down and opened the glove compartment using the blanket to prevent leaving finger prints.

Bingo.

There was a large .357 magnum with a four inch barrel. It had a black rubber handle and felt good in my hand. I made sure not to touch the barrel or trigger with my fingers. It was loaded and weighed about two and a half pounds. Who goes to a B&B with a loaded handgun in their car? Bad guys, that's who. Cops? A cop would never leave a loaded pistol in his car. But why would anyone leave a gun in their car? Maybe it was a backup piece. I laid the weapon gently in my lap and fished around until I found the car's registration and insurance card. They indicated that the vehicle belonged to a Michael Allenby of Mahopac, New York, not Billy Clanton or Frank McLaury. I replaced the gun, registration and insurance card back in the glove compartment.

I looked at my watch. I had to hurry or Kelly was going to be pissed. She had quite the temper and might even lock me out of the room. I saw anger management in her future. On the other hand, you should never keep a girl waiting when expectations were running high. I ran to the wood pile by the side of the garage. It was twenty feet long and about four feet high. The wood was split into nice foot-long logs which should catch fire quickly and they appeared well seasoned. I rested the maul against the far end and gathered as many pieces of wood as I could carry in my arms.

Returning to the window of our room, I knocked gently and whispered, "Kelly."

Nothing.

I knocked a little louder. "Kelly."

She came to the window and opened it. "What took you so long?"

"I'm sorry. Here, I'll pass them to you one at a time. Watch for splinters."

When we were done, she closed the window and I walked around to the front of the house. On the way, I used my cellphone to make an anonymous call to the local police, reporting a stolen Caddie and loaded weapon in the rear of the B&B. I picked up a handful of twigs for kindling and made my way to the room. Kelly was in the bathroom, probably washing her hands from the wood. There was a box of fatwood near the fireplace along with matches. I reached inside the fire box, opened the flue and positioned the kindling on top of the fire-starter. It caught and started flaming briskly, so I added two of the smaller logs. I watch as the flame licked upward, and after a minute or two, added a third log for good measure. Behind me, the lamp clicked off. I turned around and saw Kelly standing by the bed, illuminated by the glow of the fire.

She was in black stockings, heels and nothing else. The flickering light of the fire made her seem almost surreal. I froze at the sight, breathless and helpless, anticipation surging through my body. Without saying a word, she slinked towards me, stopping just inches away. Her green eyes roamed over me seductively, and I felt my pulse race. Neither one of us spoke as I watched her breasts rise and fall with her shallow breathing. She took my right hand and placed it on her left breast, and we both sighed deeply. I hated to show favoritism, but I actually did prefer the left breast to the right for some reason. But as I played with her nipple, squeezing it gently and pulling on it with my index finger and thumb, I knew that before the night was over, I would have to give the guy on the right equal time. Kelly arched backwards with pleasure and I started to ache all over. The room was spinning and I was getting lightheaded.

"Do you like?" she asked gently.

"Oh yeah."

I put my arms around her and kissed her gently. "You are so beautiful, Kelly. I can't believe how lucky I am."

"Well now's your chance to prove it," she said, smiling and wrapping her arms around my waist. She pressed herself against me and giggled.

I picked her up and carried her to the bed, laying her down gently and caressing her.

"Take off your clothes," she ordered. "I want to feel you next to me."

I fumbled clumsily with my shirt buttons while she undid my pants. I kicked my shoes off and almost fell to the floor in my haste to undress. I jumped back in the bed and held her down under me.

We were both breathing heavily, and I was seeing double from the excitement. Our hands raced up and down each other as tongue explored tongue.

She moaned, "Now. Please. Now."

Thirty minutes later, we lay there looking at each other, frustrated. It was two in the morning, and I had failed her.

"I'm sorry, Kel."

"It's okay," she replied sympathetically. "This happens to men sometimes when they're under stress. I saw it on Oprah. It doesn't mean there's anything wrong with you. We've both had a long day. We'll get a good night's sleep and try again tomorrow, okay? I promise." She leaned over and kissed me.

"I'm pissed. It's not like me."

"You're just going to make it worse if you get all worked up about it. You have to relax and then all the pieces will fall into place."

"Thanks for being so understanding."

The flashing lights of a police car, no, two— make that three police cars, shone through the window as they pulled up to the front of the house.

We both jumped up and ran to the window.

"What's that all about?" Kelly asked.

"I think our friends, Billy Clanton and Frank McLaury, are about to find out what the inside of a Vermont jail looks like."

"What did you do?" She eyed me suspiciously.

"Only what I had to. C'mon, put on a robe. I want to get a good look at these guys."

We got out of bed and quickly put robes on. I heard heavy footsteps pound through the front entrance. With my door slightly ajar, I saw a ruddy-faced Vermont sheriff talking to Hilda, who was demanding to know what was going on. Her hair in curlers, she was very upset at the disturbance and starting to get loud.

Cheryl and the other guests were ordered back into their rooms. Hilda pointed up the stairs, and two officers in combat gear went up in tandem. One held a shotgun with a pistol grip, and the other an assault rifle. Guarding the front entrance were another pair of heavily armed, large Vermont country boys. The flashing lights in and around the sides and back of the house suggested that the building was surrounded. I hoped these guys upstairs weren't stupid.

They weren't. There were sounds of a commotion and then quiet, but no gun shots. Soon, two groggy men in pajamas came down the stairs with their hands cuffed behind them. They were big, mean-looking fucks with dark hair and complexions. Definitely Italian.

Hilda followed them to the front reception area, scolding the officers for their intrusion, and I brought up the rear with the other guests who had emerged again from their rooms. I studied the guys carefully before they were brought outside. I'd never seen them before. The officer in charge conferred with Hilda, who was almost hysterical by now.

He said very contritely, "I'm sorry about the disturbance Mrs.Weber, but we had to act quickly. We received an anonymous tip that there were two armed men staying here who had registered under false names. We ran the plates on their car in your parking lot and it was reported stolen two days ago. We found two illegal handguns in their rooms and another in the car. I think you should be thanking us instead of threatening to file a report that we used excessive force."

I'm glad I'm not a police officer, I thought. Talk about a thankless job.

"I am personal friends with the mayor, and I am going to call her first thing in the morning," she threatened. "You could at least have waited until they paid their bill."

Hilda, just shut up and go back to bed.

To his credit, the officer remained professional and respectful. "We'll be leaving now, Mrs. Weber. Once again, I am sorry for having disturbed you and your guests."

From the door, I could see a tow truck pulling into the driveway to impound the Caddie. I turned around and saw Cheryl, Kelly and several other sleepy looking guests standing around wide-eyed, listening to the exchange.

"Holy mother of God," Cheryl said. "I can't believe it. Right here in the middle of nowhere. Who would have thought it? This place is as bad as Manhattan. Who were those guys, Cesari?"

"I have no idea, but without a doubt, they were up to no good. Well, I'm going back to bed," I yawned. "Good night, everyone." Thankfully, in all the commotion, Hilda didn't notice Cheryl. Tomorrow morning ought to be fun.

Kelly and I went back to our room. I turned off the light and stoked up the fire.

She asked, "What do you think?"

I tossed my robe to the floor and stood there in my birthday suit. "I think I want to try again, right now."

She giggled. "Ooh, I'm going to call the cops on you more often."

R⅟X 25

I woke up early Saturday morning a very contented man. So content, in fact, that I let Kelly sleep in while I reviewed the hospital records that I had brought with me.

All five charts were of people who'd had colonoscopies performed for rectal bleeding and had nothing found at the time of their procedures. The operative reports were only available electronically, so I fired up my laptop and accessed the electronic medical records of St. Matt's. It took about an hour to review them all, and when I finished, I sat there pondering the information. Now that was interesting: Reg and Gina were involved in all five cases. What did that mean?

It was nine o'clock when Kelly finally woke and looked at me sleepily. Her hair was all over the place.

"You look a mess," I joked.

"Thanks. And how do you feel this morning?"

"Like a million bucks. I told you there was nothing wrong with me. I just needed a little coaxing is all."

She shook her head and smiled. "Is that all men care about, whether they get the job done or not?"

"No, we care about food, too."

She looked at the clock on the night table. "I'm hungry. We missed Hilda's breakfast. How about we go find some place in town?"

"Sounds good. Let's get dressed.

Someone knocked on the door. "I'll get that, Kel. Why don't you go clean up?"

It was Cheryl and Hilda, and neither looked like they were having a good morning. Cheryl was dressed, but looked like she had done so in a hurry. "Good morning, Cesari."

"Yes, good morning also," Hilda said, frowning.

"Good morning, Hilda. I see you met my friend, Cheryl."

"Yes, and I am not happy either. I am a moral woman and I don't believe in any hanky panky business."

I looked at Cheryl, a little confused.

She explained, "Apparently, Hilda thinks that we are a threesome, if you get my drift."

I chuckled. "Hilda, Cheryl here is my sister. She is also good friends with Pascal, the owner of the Prince and The Pauper. You can call him. I assure you that there is no hanky panky going on here. She arrived late last night by surprise, and I didn't want to wake you. I'm sorry."

Hilda looked at me annoyed, and then at Cheryl. "Well, next time you wake me. I don't like people sneaking around my house in the middle of the night. We've had enough trouble here to last a lifetime."

"I'll be sure to remember that."

"I will leave your credit card on the desk. Will you be staying to-night as well?" she asked Cheryl.

"No, I don't think so. I have to get back to New York."

Hilda waddled away and I heard her say, "Humph."

"Want to come in?" I asked. "We're just waking up."

"No, my phone's been blowing up all morning already, and I have a hangover."

"What's going on?"

Despite what she'd just said, she stepped inside the room anyway and shut the door behind her.

"I received a call from New York just a few minutes ago. I was just about to come talk to you when Hilda banged on my door and accused me of being your whore. Those two guys last night were Boom Boom's men. They called Boom Boom at six this morning to let him know they got pinched, and we picked up the call. The good news is that they didn't confirm contact with you. I'll try to keep you in the loop as information comes in. In the meanwhile, try to keep a low profile."

"What's the word on what happened last night?" I asked.

"It seems that someone broke into their Caddie, probably kids. When they found a loaded handgun in the glove compartment, they pissed their pants and called it in to the police. When the police came, they ran the plates and realized that the car was stolen and gun unregistered."

"Lucky break for me, huh? What do you think they wanted?"

"Answers, I guess. Right now, you are Moretti's only lead as to what happened to Barazza last year and the missing ten million dollars."

"Why would they use a stolen car to come up here?"

"You're the gangster. You tell me."

"Ex-gangster." I corrected.

"Great. Ex-gangster. Maybe they were planning on putting you in the trunk after they finished talking to you. Now might be a good time to tell you why they call him Boom Boom. It seems his preferred weapon is the Colt .44 magnum, the big one, weighs about five pounds or more, and when he uses it, he always puts two bullets in his victim's brains even though they're dead after the first. Get it? The gun is so big and noisy, it sounds like boom boom."

"Sounds like a fun guy. By the way, I'm not their only lead. Gianelli is still out there."

"Yeah, but they know where you are, not him."

"Where is he anyway?"

"I couldn't tell you even if I knew. That's FBI witness protection. Not my jurisdiction."

"Yeah, but I bet you could find out if you wanted."

"But I don't want to. Look, thanks for dinner and the night here, but I've got to go. Tell Kelly I said goodbye."

"I will. Have a safe ride home."

She looked at me funny and then returned to her room. Hmm. That had been an odd look on her face just then. I wondered what she's up to.

Kelly came out of the bathroom and said, "Your turn and don't lock the door."

"Why would I lock the door?"

"Because you're paranoid that I might walk in on you." She laughed as I locked the door.

She banged on it. "Open it now."

"You have control issues. Did you know that?" I said, letting her in.

"No one keeps me from my make-up."

I jumped in the shower, and she decided that this would be a good time to start talking to me.

"So what was that all about?" she asked.

"Hilda just found out about Cheryl and was pissed off."

She laughed. "Not much of a surprise there."

"No, not at all, but she's okay now. Cheryl was with her and told me that she found out who those guys were."

"And?'

I stuck my head out of the shower. "They were Boom Boom's guys."

She looked at me.

I continued. "Yeah, she got a call about them this morning. Sorry."

"What did they want?"

"I assume they were on a fact-finding mission. Probably wanted to ask me a few questions. Well, we're not going to have to worry about them for a while unless they have a great explanation for all the guns and the stolen car."

"Great. It's never a dull moment with you, Cesari."

"Yeah. Hey, look at this."

She laughed as I flexed a wet bicep for her.

"Is that supposed to turn me on?"

"It works on all the others."

"Remember, you're awake now, okay?"

I ducked back into the shower laughing.

"Hurry up. I'm hungry."

R̨ 26

WE left the B&B around ten and walked the half mile to the center of town. It was another beautiful summer morning and a balmy seventy degrees with just a few clouds sprinkling the sky. The tree-lined street was serene, and tourists were just starting to make their appearances. We walked under the shadow of a densely forested mountain called Mount Tom. In the village, we found a quaint café at the corner of Elm Street and Route 4 and went in for breakfast.

The place was old-school and not that big. Small, white tables with wood chairs were lined up like one might see in a school cafeteria. With pencils positioned over their ears, waitresses chewing gum buzzed back and forth. There was a hairy, short-order cook in a T-shirt and white apron sweating over a hot griddle.

"What on earth are they doing here?" I said, surprised, as we waited to be seated.

Avi and Hesh were sitting at a table eating breakfast. They saw me as well and waved excitedly for us to come over and join them. The waitress signaled that it was fine with her.

Kelly asked, "Who are the little old guys with the black eyes?"

We reached the table, and I introduced her to them. "Avi, Hesh, meet Kelly. Kelly, meet Avi and Hesh. What are you two doing up here, and what happened?" I asked, noting their bruises. They jumped up to say hello and shake our hands. They were very upset and spoke fast.

"I can't believe how lucky we are that we found you, young man. We drove up here as fast as we could last night, even though it was the Shabbos. We had to warn you, but we didn't know where you were staying. We figured that you must eat, so we came here." They both had coffee and partially eaten bagels with cream cheese in front of them. The waitress came over and handed us menus.

"The specials are on the wall." She pointed to a chalk blackboard.

Kelly and I ordered coffee.

I turned to the older men. "Okay, slow down, you two. Tell me what happened?" They both had fresh shiners. Avi had a matching set and Hesh had a fat lip to go with his.

Hesh spoke first, "Yesterday, those Gestapo men we told you about came back and roughed us up right in our own store. They wanted to know where the diamonds were. We told them we didn't know. They called us liars."

Avi joined in. "That's right. They called us liars."

Hesh agreed. "Can you believe that? Of course, we were lying, but they didn't know that."

"How could they?" Avi said.

Kelly said, "What's this about Gestapo men?"

"The day before, two thugs came to their jewelry store asking about the diamonds and a guy that looked like me," I explained. "I didn't say anything because I didn't want you to worry. Sorry."

The waitress poured our coffees and we ordered breakfast. I had pancakes and country sausage. Kelly had an egg white omelet with whole wheat toast.

I turned to the Schwartz boys. "Look guys, I'm sorry about what happened. Could you describe these animals a little better? For instance, did they have dark hair and complexions like me, or were they fair skinned? Were they tall or short? Fat or skinny?"

"We already told you," Avi said. "They looked like the Gestapo. Tall, big shoulders, fair skinned. One had short blonde hair. Real mean looking."

The guy who'd followed me into the bathroom at The Blue Danube?

Possibly.

"Okay, where are you guys staying?"

"We checked into a motel outside of town. The sign said there was a swimming pool, but it wasn't in use, not that I know how to swim because I don't," Hesh said.

Avi added, "Neither one of us knows how to swim. So don't ask why the sign caught our attention. We were just driving and Hesh said, '*Look Avi, there's a swimming pool at that motel. Why don't we go there?*' So we did."

I said, "Well, I appreciate your coming all the way up here to give me a warning."

"Not at all. It's the least we could do to protect our fifteen percent cut," Avi countered.

I looked surprised. "When we last talked, you said it was only ten percent?"

"That was before the Gestapo men came and beat us up. The price just went up."

Hesh agreed, "That's right, young man. The price just went up. And if we get beat up again, the price goes up again."

Kelly laughed.

I thought that one over. I appreciated their logic and their spirit. These guys were tough. "All right, you have a point. Fifteen percent it is. Are you going to stay today or head back?" "We were just talking about that when you walked in. We are very tired and very sore. It might be a good idea if we rested another day."

"Look, why don't you two come with Kelly and me back to the B&B we are staying at. I know they have rooms available, and you'll be more comfortable there. I want to keep an eye on you so that you don't get beat up again. Besides, I can't afford the exchange rate."

"Sounds good to me. I haven't had a black eye since the third grade. That's almost seventy years ago," Hesh said.

"That's right," Avi agreed. "A girl named Reina gave him a black eye in third grade. I'll never forget it. I was so embarrassed. My brother gets beat up by a girl. She was such a tiny little thing, too."

Kelly was very amused. "Why did a girl beat you up in third grade, Hesh?"

"She was in love with me, only I didn't know it," he explained, and we chuckled.

The waitress brought our breakfast, and I savored the aroma of fresh pancakes and real maple syrup. A guy could get used to this.

"So what happened to Reina, Hesh? Did she ever tell you that she loved you?" Kelly persisted. Girls love this kind of stuff.

"Boy, did she ever," Avi interjected. "She told him every day for the next fifty years."

Kelly and I said together, "Really?"

Hesh got teary and nodded. "We married right after high school. It was the best fifty years of my life, and every single day she told me how much she loved me." He sniffled, and wiped his eyes with a paper napkin. "She passed away two years ago."

Kelly said, "I'm so sorry." She extended a consoling hand across the table.

"Let that be a lesson to you, young man. If a girl punches you in the eye, it means she loves you," Avi said.

I looked at Kelly and said, "I'll keep that in mind, Avi."

R̞X 27

WE checked Avi and Hesh into the B&B for the night. We were surprised to learn from Hilda that Cheryl had changed her mind and had paid to stay another night. Since Avi and Hesh each got their own room, Hilda was actually making out okay and seemed to be in better spirits. The place was almost full up. By the time they finished all the paperwork, it was almost noon. Kelly and I went to our room to freshen up while they dealt with Hilda. We met them later as we left to go hiking.

"All settled in guys?" I asked. Kelly stood next to me, looking pretty damn cute in shorts and sneakers.

Avi said, "I think we are going to lie down for a nap. That cute innkeeper offered to make us some lunch when we woke up."

Cute innkeeper?

"She did?"

"Yes, she is very sweet. She said to make ourselves at home, and that we could help ourselves to anything in the kitchen, anytime. Where are you two young people going?"

"We're going to hike up Mount Tom. It's a small mountain nearby, and then maybe we'll head over to the Woodstock Inn for a cocktail before dinner. We don't really have any set plans, just a little sightseeing and exploring," I said.

"That sounds like too much work. Hiking up a mountain? Why would anyone want to do such a thing? Hesh, why would anyone want to hike up a mountain?"

"I cannot think of even one reason, Avi. Well, we will now do what old people do best. Sleep. Have a good time and don't fall off the mountain."

We watched them as they walked upstairs to their rooms.

Outside, we both started laughing.

"Oh my God. '*That cute Innkeeper is going to make us lunch.*' I couldn't believe my ears."

Kelly said, "Stop it. I think it's sweet. Those guys are adorable."

"I can't help it. They're only here ten minutes and Hilda's already treating them better than me."

She wrapped her arm in mine while we walked. "Don't be jealous, Cesari. Do you think that might be us one day?"

"Kelly, there aren't enough stool softeners on the planet to make me want to live that long."

She pushed me. "Enough with picking on old people. C'mon, we have some hiking to do. I want to work up an appetite for dinner. Where are we eating dinner, by the way?"

"I don't know. There are lots of nice places listed in the guide book. If we stay locally, there's the Jackson House or the Woodstock Inn. If we want to travel a little, there's the Simon Pearce restaurant in a town called Quechee. It's just a few miles away."

"I don't care. You pick."

After about ten minutes, we turned onto Mountain Avenue, walked under an old covered bridge and reached the entrance to the park, which wasn't very far from the town center. The well-worn trail started at the base of the mountain and was well demarcated. Spirits high, we began our afternoon adventure.

"Are you sure we're dressed appropriately for hiking up a mountain?" Kelly asked. I wore blue jeans and a cotton polo shirt. She wore shorts and a blue camp shirt, sleeves rolled up. We both wore Nike sneakers.

"Yes, Kel, we'll be fine. This isn't exactly Mount Everest. Even old people hike this mountain. In fact, there are two trails leading to the top. One of them is actually called the cardiac trail, and winds up nice and gently for the older, less conditioned hikers. I think the top is only about twelve or thirteen hundred feet above sea level. Most real mountain climbers wouldn't even consider this a mountain, more like a hill."

"Yeah, well. If I can't make it to the top, you're going to have to carry me."

"That would be my pleasure, but there would be a price if it ever came to that."

"Oh yeah, and what would that be?"

"You're not ready yet to hear my deepest, darkest fantasies."

"I may pretend to be injured just to find out."

We had walked upward about a hundred yards along the winding, heavily forested trail that slowly zig-zagged its way up the mountain when I abruptly turned around, causing her to walk into me. I put my arms around her and kissed her. She glanced around instinctively to see if anybody was watching. We were alone in the woods and she smiled. "What was that for?"

"That was because I like your face."

"Well, I'm glad for that."

We changed places, and she walked ahead of me now. This worked out better because it prevented me from walking too far ahead, and now I could watch her butt without being accused of sexual harassment.

After about an hour of mild to moderate exertion, we approached the summit. It was very humid, and the temperature had reached eighty degrees. We were perspiring pretty vigorously and needed a breather. At the pinnacle, there was a clearing with a large boulder that we sat on. From our vantage point, we looked down at the town while drinking from our water bottles. In the distance, I noticed dark clouds moving in.

"We're going to get soaked on the way down," I said.

She looked at the dark clouds. "If my hair gets wet, I am going to kill you, Cesari."

Before my brain had a chance to think it through, I commented, "It's already starting to frizz up from the humidity."

"Stop, or I'll kill you now before it starts raining. I swear I will, and no one would blame me."

We both laughed. "I love your hair, Kel. Straight, frizzy, or nappy. It doesn't matter to me."

She smiled. "Thanks. I'm glad you like it. It's just that it takes so much work to get it straight." She looked around and said, "This is so beautiful up here."

We heard music drifting up from the village green where the weekend festival was taking place. The afternoon bands were starting to play.

"Yeah, it is nice. Different from Manhattan, that's for sure."

"So, did you find out anything interesting from those charts this morning? I heard you hmm hmming in my sleep."

"Oh, I'm sorry about that. Actually I did, but I don't know how it relates to the diamonds. What I found out is that over the course of the last six months, all five of those patients presented to the ER with lower GI bleeding, and were admitted for observation. They all underwent colonoscopies the same night of their admission and went home right after they recovered from the sedation. Nothing was found on any of their examinations, and the bleeding was attributed to hemorrhoids."

"I don't know enough about stuff like that. Is that odd?" She asked.

"Well, yes and no, Kel. Someone having a minor rectal bleed from hemorrhoids is exceedingly common and happens all the time. What caught my attention was when I looked up the operative reports in the electronic medical record. It seems that they all came in on the one day a month the chief of the department takes call."

"Dr. Griffin?"

"Exactly. And he chose to perform all of their colonoscopies late at night, in fact, close to midnight for some reason, rather than wait until the next morning. Another thing is that Gina was one of the OR nurses on call every time he was called in. That's an odd coincidence, too."

"Hmm."

"See what I mean? It makes you go 'hmm.'"

"Yeah, I see why now."

"The call situation is skewed heavily in Reg's favor, which is why it's such an anomaly. There are ten gastroenterologists on staff, but call is proportioned according to seniority and rank. Since I'm the most junior person on staff, I take the most calls and the most weekends throughout the course of the year. The boss, Reg, takes a nominal one day a month call, an occasional weekend and no holidays.

If similar patients came in to the hospital every day, then it also wouldn't be that strange, but that's not the case either. I looked it up.

There were a total of ten lower GI bleeds admitted to St. Matt's during the time period we're talking about, and Reg got five of them. That's a ridiculously high percentage considering how infrequently he takes call. The fact that he elected to perform a colonoscopy on all of them that same night also doesn't make sense. I mean, why not wait 'til morning? None of them seemed particularly urgent. It's peculiar. See what I'm getting at?"

"Yes, I do. But what does it mean other than Reg has bad luck whenever he takes call?"

"Bad luck? By any standard, that would be extraordinarily bad luck. But you know something, Kel, I take call ten out of thirty days and at least one weekend, sometimes two, every month because I'm the new man there. That's ten times as much call duty as Reg, and I haven't had to come in and do even one emergency colonoscopy at night. Most gastroenterologists would rather have their eye teeth pulled without anesthesia than do a colonoscopy in the middle of the night. Yet, the chief comes in at midnight every time he's on call. That just doesn't seem logical, and why would Ed Talbot have a memory stick with those charts on it?"

I looked at Kelly. She had a mischievous look on her face as she panned around.

"Maybe he noticed the connection between those patients and was trying to understand it."

"Why would a crackhead care about anything Reg does when he's on call?" I asked, thoroughly puzzled.

"Ed Talbot was an orderly in the OR and would have had to clean up the mess after those procedures. He may have noticed the odd co-incidences we're talking about. Maybe you're not giving him enough credit. Just because he was a drug addict doesn't mean he was stupid. He may have noticed some strange goings on and decided to investigate it himself."

I thought about that. She was right. Maybe I had unfairly pre-judged Ed Talbot's intellectual capacity.

"Okay, fair enough. So this guy, Ed, is a drug addict, but when he's sober he's pretty sharp. He works at night, and notices a pattern of late-night colonoscopies being performed by Reg. He decides to look into it further and makes a list of the medical record numbers of the patients involved. Does that seem plausible so far?"

Kelly had lain backward, staring at the sky. "Very."

"Then what was he planning on doing with the list, and what does any of this have to do with those diamonds?"

"I have no idea, Cesari, but it might be a good idea if you put your arms around me."

I noticed again the naughty look on her face. I reclined back next to her, and we looked at the gathering clouds. "What are you thinking about, Kelly girl?

She smiled. "If we did it up here, would that make us members of the mile high club?"

I laughed. "No, not even close. We would only be members of the quarter mile high club, and there's way too many people tramping around to take a chance like that. I can't even imagine how much of a commotion that would cause in a small town like this if we got caught. We could even get arrested for that, you know."

"You worry too much, Cesari," she whined. "C'mon, I thought you were a tough guy?"

"I don't know, Kel..." She was looking at me with those big green eyes and I knew she was trying to hypnotize me. I was starting to tingle again.

As we lay there weighing the pros and cons of her suggestion, the sounds of people approaching caught our attention, so we stood up. Soon, the heads of two men appeared in the wooded trail about fifty feet below our position. They seemed to be having great difficulty as they slowly wound their way upward. I stood on tip-toes to get a better view, and noticed that they looked ridiculous wearing sport coats. They were tall with big shoulders and one had blonde hair.

Uh-oh.

Drenched in sweat, swatting flies and mosquitoes, they were not happy campers. They hadn't yet seen us, so I made a quick decision. There was a trail leading down the other side of the mountain, and I grabbed Kelly's hand, dragging her with me.

She didn't have a chance to react or object. She sensed my fear and instinctively understood that something was wrong, even though she hadn't seen the men. Within seconds, we were hidden from view by the thick forest. This trail also meandered slowly, back and forth, down the mountain. The quickest way down would be to cut across it and go straight down the side. It would be steeper and more hazardous, but there were plenty of trees and boulders to hold onto. The decision made, I pulled Kelly into the underbrush with me. Off-trail, we slid, ran and stumbled rapidly downward, plummeting toward the bottom.

"What's happening?" Kelly gasped.

"We got company. Save your breath and keep moving."

We were about one hundred feet from the top when we heard them shouting. I looked back and caught a partial glimpse of them through the foliage. They had some type of snub-nosed revolvers out, possibly .38's, I guessed. At this distance, it would be a miracle if they hit us.

"Faster, Kel."

"I'm moving as fast as I can," she panted.

One of the guys yelled and cursed as he fell down. I looked back again and saw his friend helping him up. We were putting good distance between us, and I guessed they were wearing dress shoes. Assholes. We reached the bottom in half the time it took us to get to the top and hunched over, gasping and sweating profusely from the exertion. The two guys were still halfway up, and one of them was limping badly. Probably twisted his ankle.

We didn't waste much time recovering and took off at a run. A sign read that the Billings Farm and Museum was about a mile away, and we raced along Elm Street in that direction. Near exhaustion, muscles burning, but pumped full of adrenaline, our legs kept churning. But less than a half of a mile into it, Kelly could no longer keep pace and abruptly stopped, holding her side as she sucked wind.

I watched her sympathetically. I was out of breath as well.

"Kel, we've got to keep moving quickly. We're too exposed out here on the road. Who knows what kind of backup those guys might have?"

She gasped. "I can't. I need to rest. Who were they, anyway?" She bent over, her hands resting on her knees.

I searched the road furtively in both directions. An old, red pickup was heading our way. "I think they were the guys who beat up Avi and Hesh. They might even be the same guys who chased us out of Ed Talbot's apartment. I have an idea."

I stepped into the road and flagged the pickup down.

The rusted truck pulled to a stop, and I noticed Vermont plates and a full load of cut firewood in the back. There were two unkempt thirty year-old men in the cab.

The driver asked, "Everything all right, friends?" They looked like farmers and wore dirty overalls and green John Deere hats.

"We need a ride. We ran into some car problems and were trying to make our way back to town before it started raining, but we're running out of gas ourselves. Any chance you could help us out?"

He looked at his companion and then returned his gaze to me. "I don't see why not. The little lady looks plum tuckered out. We weren't going to town, though."

"Anywhere you're going is fine."

"Me and my brother, Clem, we was heading to the Billings farm to drop off a load of firewood. We could take you there, but there's only room for one more in the cab."

"Can I ride in the back with the wood?"

"Can't 'low that. Too dangerous, and if the troopers stop us, it'd be six or seven points on my license. Sorry."

"How far is the Billings farm?" I asked.

"Less than half a mile up this here road. Off'n to the right. Can't miss it."

I looked at Kelly. She was a little better, but any further running was out of the question.

"Kelly, why don't you go with them? The Billings farm isn't that far, and I'll catch up to you in ten minutes, okay?"

She was too exhausted to argue. She nodded, and the guy on the passenger side got out and helped her into the cab where she sat between them.

"Thanks, guys."

"No problem, mister. We'll see you there in a few minutes."

The truck drove off, and I jogged after it. Seconds later, it was out of sight. There was a sudden, loud clap of thunder which shook the ground, and I looked upward.

It started to pour.

R_X 28

I entered the Billings farm soaked. The brief, intense thunderstorm had subsided and settled into a light, steady downfall. I looked around, but didn't see a red pickup. It was two o'clock, and there were only a few people milling about with umbrellas. The rain had put a damper on visitor traffic. Inside the museum, I found a worker and asked him where someone might drop off a load of firewood. Gary was a polite, fifty-year-old man wearing overalls. He didn't look too sharp, but seemed friendly enough. He looked at me, and I realized that I must have seemed an odd sight. Sopping wet from head to toe and breathless, anxiety was written all over me.

"Why would we need firewood? It's August."

"You weren't expecting a load of wood this afternoon?" I asked, my heart starting to pound with apprehension.

"Not that I know of, but let me ask Martha. She's in charge." We walked over to a matronly-looking older woman with gray hair smoking a corncob pipe. I couldn't help wondering if she was for real or in character for the museum.

Gary asked, "Martha, were we expecting a load of firewood today?"

"No, not that I know of. Why?"

"This young man says he was supposed to meet somebody here who was delivering a load of firewood for the farm."

136

She eyed me, trying to decide why I looked such a mess. "Why would we need firewood? It's August."

"I know that, but I met these guys in a pickup truck who told me they were coming here to deliver firewood. Why would they say that?" I didn't like the feeling I was getting in the pit of my stomach.

"What did those men and the truck look like, Mister? Let's start there and maybe I can help you."

"It was a beat up old, red Chevy pickup, rusted out on the sides, Vermont plates and an NRA bumper sticker on the back. There were two white men in their mid to late thirties with scruffy beards. They looked like farmers and wore John Deere hats. They both looked like they needed a dentist."

She laughed and slapped her knee. "Sweetheart, you just described most of the men in Vermont, but I think I know who you're talking about. It sounds like them no-account white trash McNealy brothers, Earl and Clem."

I got excited. "Yes, that's them. One of them was named Clem. The other one said that he and his brother, Clem, were coming here to deliver the wood."

"Well, they were yanking your chain, friend. They didn't come here, and we didn't ask for no firewood."

"Could you please tell me where I could find them? It's important." Somewhere in the back of my mind, I remembered hearing a statistic about how much time you had from the time someone was abducted to the time they turned up dead. It wasn't very long.

"They live in a trailer about two miles from here. What they do, boy, rob you?"

"Something like that. Could you be more specific when you say about two miles from here?" I could feel my pulse quicken and my senses sharpen.

"You keep going up Old River Road, that's the road outside the entrance to the farm, until you reach the Cushing Cemetery. You can't miss it, even in the rain. You turn left there onto Cloudland Road. Their trailer is about a half mile on the right. You can't miss that either. They have a big sign on the front lawn that says *Guns don't kill, we do*. Real assholes is what they are. You be careful with them boys. They're real rascals."

"Is there any chance I can borrow a car? I'd pay you." I pulled out my wallet. I had about two hundred in cash, and offered it to her. "You can have it all."

They both looked at me and said, "No."

I stared at them blankly.

"Please, this is very important. A friend of mine might be in trouble." I was starting to get very nervous and it showed.

Martha said, "We don't have a car for you to borrow, but you can use my truck, and it won't cost you anything. Just promise to bring it back, and pay for any damages. Let me see your driver's license."

I took my license out of my wallet and handed it to her. She tried saying my name, but had trouble so I helped her.

She nodded. "Sounds Eyetalian."

"Yes, it is."

She studied me carefully. "Are you in the Mafia?"

"Not anymore."

"If you don't mind, I'll hold onto your license until you return my truck."

"I don't mind."

"Come with me then."

We walked out to the barn where she kept her pickup. It was a spanking new, silver Ford 350. Damn, it was enormous. I climbed in, and she handed me the keys. Something out of the corner of my eye caught my attention, so I got back out of the cab and walked over to it. There was a maul leaning against the back of the barn door, which I picked up and hefted in the air, testing its weight. At least 5-6 lbs. That should do nicely.

"Do you mind if I borrow this?"

"Be my guest," she said.

I hoisted it into the passenger side of the cab and made myself comfortable in the driver's seat. The engine roared, and I signaled Martha to stand clear.

She looked up at me. "Are you going to kill them McNealy's?"

"Only if they don't return what belongs to me."

She thought that one over and nodded. "Sounds fair. Just remember, that's how I feel about my truck."

I looked at her seriously. "Sounds fair."

As the truck surged forward, I calculated that I couldn't be more than half an hour behind the McNealy's. People have been raped and murdered in less time than that. I was starting to freak. When I reached the farm's exit, I turned onto Old River Road and let the motor rip. Eighty miles an hour down a small country road in the rain. I hoped no one was traveling in the opposite lane. Cops I didn't mind. I would just let them chase me to the McNealy's. The rain was starting to pick up again as I reached the cemetery, and lightning flashed brightly over the farmland. I veered left without stopping and almost slid off road into a ditch. I gunned the engine until I spotted the trailer set way back from the road. The belligerent sign on the front lawn that Martha had told me about was barely visible in the deluge and with the darkened sky above.

I was no more than ten minutes from the Billings farm, but it seemed like I had just landed on another planet. There were no other homes or trailers in sight, and I could see the red pickup parked behind the trailer. They had covered the wood in back with a protective tarp. Thunder clapped loudly as I brought the Ford to a stop by the side of the road. At night I would have easily missed this place.

Holding the maul in one hand, I glared at the trailer from where I stood. I wasn't just angry; I was consumed by rage. As the rain pelted my face and lightning ripped through the sky, I knew that I was in danger of acting injudiciously.

I took a deep breath, crept slowly up to the front entrance and tested the door. It wasn't locked. Turning the handle slowly, all sounds muffled by the storm, I cautiously let myself in. Off to one side was a bed with Kelly on her back. The McNealy's faced away from me, holding her down. One guy had picked up her shirt and was fondling her breasts while he kissed her. The other was in the act of pulling her shorts down while she kicked and struggled. She was obviously weak from exhaustion or else just resigned that nobody would hear her and wasn't even trying to cry out. They hadn't noticed me.

On the other side of the trailer was a hard looking, greasy-haired woman of about thirty sitting at a table and holding a baby. She stared blankly into space and didn't even acknowledge my presence or the crime being committed just a few feet away. The place reeked of pot. So this was how the other half lived.

I charged them silently with the maul over my head and brought the sledge hammer side crashing down hard on the back of the one pulling her shorts off. I heard his vertebrae crack with a gruesome sound. He moaned and went limp. The other one turned and froze, trying to understand what had happened. Before he could react, I rammed him dead center in the face with the top end of the maul. The 6 lb. steel head broke his nose and knocked him backward off the bed onto the floor, stunned, blood pouring down his face. The first guy groaned in pain and rolled off of Kelly onto his back. He wasn't moving so well, and I suspected that I might have paralyzed him. I swung the maul down hard on the front of his face, and teeth flew out of his mouth as his jaw shattered. He went limp for real this time. The other guy started to get up, holding his nose and blood covered face. He cursed and spat at me.

I paused momentarily to catch my breath and saw that Kelly had instinctively curled herself up into a ball. She lay there wide-eyed, trembling and quiet, watching the awful scene unfolding before her.

Wanting to feel his flesh, I dropped the maul, grabbed him by the hair and dragged him toward the center of the trailer. I flung him down on his back and sat down on his chest, straddling him. His ugly, inbred face sneered at me in defiance, and I could see that he just didn't get it. So, with all my might, and all the force I could muster, I delivered a blow designed to remove his head from his neck. It didn't, but it came close. So I tried again. The back of his skull slammed into the floor of the trailer with a thud and he lost consciousness. That was too bad because I wanted him to feel every punch.

With both hands, I pummeled him mercilessly, raining down blow after blow into the bloody mess that used to be his face. I felt bones crunch and saw blood splatter, but I didn't stop. I didn't want to stop.

Kelly placed a hand on my shoulder. "It's over, John," she whispered gently.

I looked up at her, exhausted, and nodded in agreement. My knuckles were bruised and sore, covered with red, sticky McNealy fluid. Underneath me, he gasped and gurgled on his secretions, but was still alive. I stood up and held Kelly tightly. My chest heaved from the exertion, and I knew that I was still out of control. Anybody that came near her right now was in danger of having their head ripped off.

"Are you okay?" I asked.

She nodded, "Yes. What about you?"

I nodded.

We turned to leave, but found ourselves staring down the barrel of a .12 gauge shotgun. The woman I had seen at the table had put the baby down in a crib and was now standing in front of us, blocking our exit. She cocked the trigger, and I couldn't help thinking how much life had to suck to die like this. She had the same blank expression on her face as when I first saw her. Meth, I thought. We held our breath, waiting. No one moved and no one spoke.

Then, without signaling her intention, she stepped away from the door, waving the gun toward it. "Go now, before I change my mind."

We walked out into the driving rain, and before we reached the truck, we heard a shotgun blast from inside the trailer. A few seconds later, we heard the weapon discharge a second time. I helped Kelly into the cab of the truck and we drove off.

R͓X 29

WE had a lot to think about as we drove slowly, in silence, back to the Billings farm. By the time we arrived, the rain was easing up, and the sun starting to peak through. It had been just over an hour since I'd first borrowed the truck, but it felt like a lifetime. When I pulled it into the barn and cut the engine, Martha and Gary were there waiting.

They stared at us, wide-eyed. We were a mess,: disheveled, dripping wet, bloodied, and visibly distraught. Kelly's eyes were puffy from crying, and her clothes ripped and torn.

Martha held my hands and studied the swollen knuckles. "We're going to have to get some ice on those." And the way she said it and held my hands reminded me of how my mother used to do the same thing.

"Thank you, Martha."

"They're dead aren't they?" She asked.

"I think so. There was a woman there. She finished them off with a shotgun. I think she's in shock right now. She's going to need help. There was a baby there, too."

Martha nodded. "That would be Emily. I've known her since she was a child. She was a great kid before the drugs got to her. She's been in shock ever since she took up with them assholes."

She went over to Kelly, who was shaking, and put an arm around her. "There, there, you poor thing. Everything's going to be all right. Is she what they took from you, Mister?" Martha asked as we walked into the fully restored farmhouse.

"Yes, Martha. This is Kelly."

Kelly started to sob and Martha sat down with her on a bench, holding her.

"Gary, lock up the museum. We're closing early today."

"Sure thing, Martha," Gary replied dutifully, and walked over to lock the door.

"You're going to be okay, young lady. We'll get you into some warm, dry clothes and clean you up. How about I put on some tea?"

"Thank you. Tea would be nice." Kelly said softly, collecting herself.

Martha sprang into action as she came to a conclusion. "You did the right thing, Mr. Eyetalian man. Gary, take the truck and go get Emily and the baby. Bring them here and we'll figure out what to do next. She should've shot them two varmints a long time ago as far as I'm concerned. No point in making a bad situation worse by calling the law. You two come with me. If you walk into town looking like that, you'll get arrested on the spot."

Gary left to get Emily. The rain had driven all the visitors away, so there was no one around to ask questions. We cleaned up as best we could. Martha and Gary kept changes of clothes around for when things got messy at the working farm. She loaned us some poorly fitting garments. Gary was a medium and I was a large. Martha was a large and Kelly was a small. But they were dry and clean and helped improve our spirits. By the time Gary returned with Emily and the baby, Martha and Kelly were having tea while I bathed my hands in a bowl of ice water.

It was four o'clock, and the sun had made a full comeback.

Martha instructed Gary. "Drive these two nice people back to their bed and breakfast. When you come back, we'll take Emily and the baby home with us." She was now holding Emily tightly, who was, in turn, holding her baby tightly. They were all crying. "Everything's going to be all right, honey," she said.

"What's going to happen?" I asked Martha.

"Don't know for sure. Two no-account white trash like them get gunned down in their trailer with drugs everywhere... probably nothing. No one will care, not even their kin. It'll be days before anyone even notices anyhow. I'm toying with the idea of setting their trailer on fire later tonight. Anyway, I'll take care of Emily, and we'll figure it out. Gonna take it one day at a time for now."

Kelly embraced Martha.

"You take care of yourself, Kelly. And you, too, Mr. Eyetalian man. Oh, and before I forget. Here's your driver's license back."

I took it and gave her a warm hug. "Thank you for everything, Martha. You're a diamond in the rough."

She chuckled. "Don't you be trying to sweet talk an old woman, Mr. Eyetalian man. I'm happily married."

Gary dropped us off in front of the Reluctant Panther, and we thanked him. In our room, we stripped off the awkwardly fitting clothing and lay on the bed exhausted, holding each other tightly.

Kelly was trembling. "Well, that was pretty fucked up."

"I'm so sorry you had to go through that, Kel. Are you sure you're okay?"

"I don't know yet. How about you? Your knuckles look awful." They were swollen with abrasions and dried blood on them. They hurt.

"Nothing I won't get over."

She hesitated. "Are we in trouble?"

"You mean the McNealy brothers?"

"Yes, of course that's what I mean. They're dead."

"Well, you are definitely not in trouble. You're the victim. However, I would have a lot of explaining to do if it ever came down to it, but I don't think it will. If only to protect Emily, no one up here's ever going to talk about it again. I'm sure I'll be fine."

"Why should you be in trouble? You were just trying to rescue me. That's not a crime."

"No, but there's that whole excessive force thing. You know, above and beyond what was necessary. Plus, I brought a weapon to the party, which could be interpreted as premeditation. That kind of crap. Of course, there are the extenuating circumstances of the pretty girl being held captive, but then again, they didn't actually kidnap you, did they? You voluntarily went with them, and I even helped you get in the truck. When I arrived at the trailer, I don't recall asking if you were truly being assaulted or just having fun. See what I mean, Kel? This could get ugly real fast in a courtroom. Add that to my, shall we say, checkered past, and a real nice judge might only give me five to ten."

Kelly was depressed. "That seems so wrong."

"What does?"

"That you risked your life to save me from those animals, and it sounds like you're the one who committed the crime."

"Moral ambiguity is always like that, Kel. It's the old, damned-if-you-do and damned–if-you-don't, paradox."

"So how do you know what the right thing to do is in situations like that?"

"You don't, not always. You use your instinct, and basically, you do what feels right."

She stared at me uncomfortably.

"What did I do now?"

"So beating someone half to death with your bare fists felt right to you?"

"At the time, yeah, although I realize that intellectualizing about it now makes it sound a little primitive."

She thought it over, sighed, and rolled on top of me. Naked chest pressed naked chest as she eyed me suspiciously.

"Can I help you?" I asked playfully.

"I'm just trying to figure out how your brain works, Cesari."

"Try not to hurt yourself, all right?"

"You're a funny guy. Did you know that?"

"Funny? Like a clown, funny?"

She chuckled. "Exactly."

"Not to change the subject, but what do you want to do?" I asked seriously.

"What do you mean?"

"We could just check out now and leave. I don't know about you, but I've already had enough fun for one weekend."

She sighed again. "I know what you mean. On the other hand, how much worse can it get? I mean, really?"

"Well, those two guys from the mountain are still out there some-where, and God only knows what they're up to."

"Who were those guys, anyway? You said you recognized them."

"Yes, I think they're the ones from Manhattan. The ones who chased us down the fire escape from Ed Talbot's apartment. I saw them again at The Blue Danube that night we were there, and from Avi and Hesh's description, I think they're the Gestapo men that gave them the black eyes. They must be after the diamonds."

"So, they're not with the goons the police arrested here last night? The ones from the OK Corral?"

"I don't think so."

"How do all these people know where we are, Cesari?"

"I don't know. But if these guys today were at The Blue Danube that night, they might have overheard us talking about our weekend plans with Reg. Maybe they shared the information. Cheryl said someone called that guy, Boom Boom, in Little Italy to tip him off. He might have sent his own crew up. He's got his own reasons for trying to find me."

"It's creepy, thinking that there are so many people watching our movements. Do you think they've been following us around all weekend?"

"I can't be sure of anything right now, Kel. Those guys on the mountain today might have just gotten lucky and spotted us walking into the park. The opportunity presented itself to get us alone, so they took it. That would explain why they weren't dressed for hiking. On the other hand, I can't swear to you that they're not staking out the B&B as we speak. Now that I think about it, it might be a good idea to stay somewhere else tonight."

"I don't know, John. I kind of like it here. Right now, I'm going to shower. We can talk it over during dinner. Either way, I want to stay the night here in Woodstock. I'm too exhausted to drive all the way back to Manhattan. Are you going to ask Cheryl to have dinner with us again? Honestly, I'd prefer not. And why did she stay another night anyway? I don't get it."

"I have no idea why she decided to stay, and no, I wasn't going to ask her to join us. If you're up for it, we could try again to have that romantic night out I promised you."

"That would be nice. I could certainly use a drink right now. That's for sure."

At seven, we left the room and headed over to the Woodstock Inn and Resort for cocktails and dinner. We bumped into Avi and Hesh in the hallway on the way out.

"What are you guys up to?" I asked.

Hesh said, "We are going to have dinner in our room with Hilda. She made a pot roast for us. What a lovely lady. She works so hard, you know. It is not easy running a bed and breakfast. She's been telling us all about it. Right now, she is out getting us some more firewood. Hilda says there is nothing more romantic than dining with a roaring fire in the background, even in the summer. I think she has a crush on Avi. Well, have a good night."

Avi blushed, listening to his brother talk.

"Unbelievable," I said under my breath as we walked out the front door.

"Should you have said anything to them about those guys?"

"What would be the point? They're not going out, and they have company. They should be fine. You look great, by the way." She was wearing a light blue summer dress with sandals and gold hoop earrings.

"Thank you."

I wore jeans, loafers, and a yellow cotton shirt.

"No jacket tonight?" she asked.

"Do you think I'll need one?"

"Only if you want to make me happy."

I hesitated, sighed, and went back to the room to get my blazer.

When I returned I posed for her. "Happy now?"

"I'm always happy when you do what I tell you to do." She slipped her arm through mine and whispered, "If you make me happy, then I'll make you happy. How's that for a deal?"

"Considering the day you've just had, I'd say that was very generous of you."

"I hope you don't think that I'm some sort of shrinking violet, Cesari. I'm a lot tougher than I look."

"I can see that."

R̽ 30

THE Woodstock Inn and Resort was an impressive two hundred year old hotel just off the village green. It was only a ten minute walk from the Reluctant Panther, and we arrived before seven-thirty. There was a massive fireplace in the lobby containing a log the size of a tree trunk. Oversized chairs and a comfortable looking sofa were positioned around the hearth. People milled about the lobby, and some kid snuggled on the sofa, reading a book. A massive set of moose antlers adorned the wall above the mantle.

"Wow," Kelly said, looking around. "This is pretty amazing."

"Yes. It is."

The restaurant was off to the right, so we walked over and requested a table for two. There was a well-dressed woman standing at a podium, greeting the customers.

"Do you have reservations?" She asked politely.

"No, I'm afraid not." I replied.

"I am sorry. We are all booked for the evening, but if you like, you can dine in the pub. It's just down the hall."

I looked at Kelly. She was disappointed. "What do you think?"

She asked the girl, "Is it the same menu?"

"No, they have their own menu. Usually lighter fare and typical pub items, but if you want you can request something from the main restaurant. People do that all the time."

Kelly nodded, satisfied. "Thank you. I think we'll try it."

We walked into the dark pub and noticed that it was three quarters filled. We found two empty leather chairs toward the back and sat down. There was a small wood table between us. Several couples and families were having dinner and drinks. The small bar had six stools, and there was a flat screen television behind the bar. There was a preseason football game on.

We ordered a couple of cocktails and studied the menus. As we did, two men entered and sat at the bar, backs towards us. One of them was limping. The assholes from the mountain. Goddamn, they were persistent. Did they kill Ed Talbot, and what were they planning to do to us? I didn't want to find out.

Our drinks came, and Kelly told the waitress that we needed a few more minutes to study the menu. I took a swallow of my Manhattan while I thought through the problem at hand. They were armed and obviously not having too much trouble keeping an eye on us.

"Interesting menu for a pub," Kelly said, sipping her Chardonnay.

I finally looked down at mine and agreed. "Oysters Rockefeller and escargot with garlic and butter. You don't see that offered very often in pubs. Everything looks great."

"Yeah, and look at the bottom. Tenderloin of venison with cherry compote. Oh my God, and this is just the pub. Can you imagine dining in the main restaurant?" She was very happy. She was pretty tough, after all. I hated the idea that I was going to have to burst her bubble.

"Kelly, excuse me a minute. I have to use the men's room. You can order for me if you want. I'll have the Oysters Rockefeller to start."

"Okay. Are you sure you don't want to see the main restaurant menu first?"

"Yeah, I'm sure. This menu is fine with me. I'll be right back."

I stood and walked out past the guys at the bar. Out of the corner of my eye, I saw them track my movement. I had no doubt that one of them would soon follow. Out in the main lobby, I walked by the fireplace. There was no one around but that kid reading his book, waiting for his parents to finish checking in. I discreetly picked up the poker next to the hearth. No one seemed to notice. I glanced over my shoulder. No one in sight. The guy was giving me some space and hadn't made it to the lobby yet. I walked casually to the men's room on the other side of the lobby, the poker hidden from view as well as possible along the length of my arm.

In the men's room, I quickly ducked into the middle of the three stalls, sat down and waited. I was alone, but that could change in a hurry, so I would have to act quickly and decisively. As if they understood, my bruised knuckles throbbed their disapproval at the thought of any more physical violence. Sorry, boys.

Soon, the door opened and I heard footsteps. I had left the stall door purposefully unlocked and sat there, holding the poker with both hands like a spear ready to thrust forward. What if it wasn't him but some unsuspecting hotel guest? Maybe the kid's dad? Shit.

I waited. The urinal flushed and water started running in the sink. Then I listened as quiet footsteps closed in slowly, cautiously, on my stall.

I leaned back so the door wouldn't hit me and clenched the steel poker. He was in front of me now.

Hesitation and then decision. He kicked the door open violently, expecting to meet resistance from the lock. There was none, and it flew inward, banging against the side wall, trapped there by my knee. He stood there, surprised by the sight of the poker pointing at him. Probably expected to see me with pants down, reading a magazine. The small revolver in his hand still pointed upward. As he recovered and brought the weapon down, I lunged forward with the pointed edge of the poker aimed directly at his chest. The full force of the thrust landed directly in the center of his sternum and he gasped with pain, dropping the pistol. The wind knocked out of him, he staggered backwards into the wall as the gun clattered loudly on the tiled floor. He was lucky the poker had caught his sport coat or it might have gone right through him.

Breathless, he slumped to his knees, and I smashed him viciously with the poker across his shoulder and back. He moaned in pain as I stepped behind him, placing the poker under his chin and against his neck. With both hands, I pulled backward, choking him. He struggled mightily, clawing at me, but it was too late. I eased up immediately when I felt him go limp because I didn't want to kill him. He was just an errand boy, and aside from annoying me, hadn't really done anything yet to deserve the death penalty. A badly bruised sternum, clavicle, and larynx would suffice for now as his punishment.

I searched him quickly and retrieved his wallet, cell phone and car keys. I picked up the gun and placed it in my pocket. It was a Smith & Wesson snub-nosed .38, just like the one I had in New York. I dragged him into a stall, closed the door and left. I opened his wallet and read his driver's license: Colin Murphy from New York City. There was an NYPD badge in the wallet. Great. I returned the poker to its holder by the fireplace and tossed the wallet and cellphone into the nearest trash can as I walked outside to the parking lot.

It was dark outside as I searched the crowded lot. I found three cars with New York plates; one was a red Corolla with a baby seat in the back, another was a Bronco with a bike rack and three bikes attached. The last one, a black Crown Victoria, screamed police all over it.

I looked around and found myself alone. Using his keys, I let myself in and examined the car. There was a police radio and the usual accoutrements of a police vehicle, including a loaded pistol grip shotgun in the back.

In the glove compartment, I found two NYPD ID's attached to lanyards. One belonged to my boy, Colin Murphy, the guy in the bathroom, and the other to a Rick McGrath, who I assumed was the other guy in the bar. I popped the hood of the car and inspected the engine. I pulled as many wires, hoses, and nozzles free as I could, and then opened the trunk. Using the tire iron and jack I found there, I quickly hoisted the rear of the car up and removed one of the tires, which I simply rolled underneath a large bush. I took the jack and shotgun and threw them into a small dumpster I found off to the side of the inn.

Returning briskly to the pub, I saw an exasperated Kelly. My oysters sat on a plate, and she had started on her salad. The guy at the bar looked at me casually, barely raising his head. He wasn't yet concerned. Kelly said, "What took you so long? I was starting to worry. A jazz band is going to start playing. This is going to be fun."

"I'm sorry, Kel but I think we should leave now." I ate one of the oysters and sipped my Manhattan. "Man, this is good."

"Why?"

"Do you see that guy at the bar hunched over his beer?" I nodded in his direction, and she discreetly turned her gaze to the bar. She let out a deep breath as she spotted him.

"Let me guess. One of the guys from the mountain?"

"Yes."

"Damn. Where's the other one?"

"He's unconscious in the men's room and is going to be really pissed off when he wakes up."

I signaled the waitress, apologized, and paid the bill, sucking down one more oyster as I stood to leave.

We walked nonchalantly toward the exit, but as soon as we were outside the building, I grabbed Kelly, and we ran to the side, hiding from view behind a large evergreen. Seconds later, we heard the guy come out the front door, and I could just make out his silhouette as he scanned unsuccessfully for us. Without his partner, he seemed uncertain how to proceed, so he took out his cellphone and called his friend. After several failed attempts, he put the phone away in frustration and returned to the inn to regroup.

"Now what?" Kelly asked.

"I don't know, but we probably shouldn't go back to the B&B."

"What are we going to do? Our car's at the B&B, along with our stuff."

"We could stay here. If they have a room that is."

As we stood in the shadows, we heard two men come out onto the front porch, talking. I signaled Kelly to silence, and we instinctively crouched, huddling beneath the bush. Apparently, the guy in the bathroom had come around a lot faster than I'd hoped.

"They must have gone back to the B&B to get their car, Murph."

The other guy's voice was hoarse. "Yeah, they're going to try to skip out for sure. Let's get over there quick. Goddamn, my chest hurts. That fuck is going to pay for this."

They hustled to their car, and about a minute later, we heard them cursing in the distance, which made me chuckle.

"What's so funny, and what are they angry about now?" Kelly asked.

"Angry white men, who knows? Could be anything."

She shoved me. "What did you do?"

"I sort of disabled their car. By the way, they're cops. Come with me, and let's see if there's a rear entrance to this place."

We cautiously crept out from our hiding space, and staying in the shadows, followed a narrow garden path to the rear of the inn. There was another, smaller parking lot in the back and an employee entrance. We used this to enter the building and passed uneventfully through the kitchen in search of the front desk. The girl there was friendly and found us a room for the night, so I gave her my credit card and filled out the paper work.

"What about our stuff at the B&B?" Kelly asked.

"I'll go over to the Reluctant Panther later and get everything. I want to talk to Cheryl about these guys. She's been concerned about some cops on the take, and these might be them. She should be made aware."

"But what if these guys go over there looking for us? I don't know if that's such a good idea."

We entered our room. It was spacious and clean with a queen-sized bed. No fireplace. Not quite as cozy and romantic as the Reluctant Panther but nice.

"I'll be careful, Kel. It's dark out, and I have a slight edge at the moment. I know where they are, and they don't have any transportation. Besides, we need to get our car before they recover. The window to our room is unlocked. I'll sneak in that way."

She did not like my plan, but acquiesced. "I know, but I'm worried. How long will you be?"

"An hour maybe." I looked at my watch. It was 9 p.m.

"Are you sure you don't want me to come along?"

"I'm very sure. You're tough, but you've been through enough for one day. I would feel better if you just stayed here, all right? And please don't leave the room."

"Fine, but hurry up, and keep your cellphone on. I'll wait for you to come back before I order anything to eat from room service."

We kissed goodbye.

R̵X 31

I left through the rear of the inn and walked around to the front. A tow truck with flashing lights was pulling into the parking lot to rescue the Crown Vic. My two cop friends were busy looking under the hood of their car and didn't notice me slinking clandestinely off to the side. I was about a hundred feet away, obscured by the shadows of large oaks and maples, and they had other things on their minds. Like where the fuck was their shotgun and rear tire.

I walked quickly down the main street the half mile to the Reluctant Panther and let myself in through the main entrance. As long as I knew where those guys were, I didn't see any reason to climb in through the window. I threw all our stuff messily into the small suitcase that we brought and went down the hall to see if Cheryl was in. She wasn't, so I tried her on the cellphone, but it went to voicemail. I left her a message to call me and then went to Avi's room. I knocked and waited for a response.

He stuck his head out. "Can I help you, young man?"

"May I come in, Avi?"

"The room is a little untidy. I am sorry. How about I come out there? Give me one second." About thirty seconds later, he came into the hallway wearing a guest robe and what seemed like nothing else. I looked at his bare chest and feet.

"Where's Hesh?" I asked. "I'd like to speak to you both."

"He's in his room reading the Torah. What can I do for you?"

"I just wanted to give you a warning. I think those guys who beat you up are here in Woodstock. I ran into them twice today, and they seemed to fit the description you gave me. I think they know I'm staying here, so I'm pulling out. I think it might be a wise idea if you guys moved to a different location, too."

"Oy vey. That is bad news."

"Avi, is everything all right? The strudel is getting cold." Hilda called out from behind the door.

Avi turned eight shades of red in embarrassment. He smiled, shrugged his shoulders and I stared in disbelief.

"Heh, heh. Well, I will certainly give it some thought, young man, but right now I am a little busy. I hope you understand."

I smiled despite my apprehension. "I do understand, and I know that I have no right to tell you what to do, but I felt I should warn you. We've decided to move to a different B&B tonight, and then we'll be on our way tomorrow morning."

"Thank you, young man, and I appreciate your concern. But at my age, I don't get so many opportunities like this that I can afford to look a gift horse in the mouth."

"I understand perfectly. Well, I guess I won't have to go find Hilda. Maybe I'll just leave a little note for her somewhere. Well, good luck, Avi, and I hope those guys don't show up. I'll see you back in New York."

"Thank you again and good night."

Jesus Christ. What's going to happen next? Kelly's going to die when she hears this.

I wrote a note to Hilda thanking her for her hospitality and authorizing her to charge my credit card for the remainder of our bill. I left it for her on the reception desk. As I walked toward the front door, I ran into Cheryl, arm in arm with Pascal, from the Prince and The Pauper. Now I knew why she'd stayed up here another night. It was ten o'clock, and love was in the air.

"Well hello, Cesari. You remember Pascal?"

We shook hands, and I smiled. "Very well, actually."

"Hallo, Jean."

"Hello, Pascal."

"Cheryl, I was just trying to reach you. Could I have a minute with you in private about something related to our conversation last night?"

"Sure, would you excuse us a moment, Pascal?" She handed him the key to her room. "I'm staying in room number 4, The Panther's Womb. It's at the end of the hallway. I'll only be a minute."

"I wait eagerly for the return of your divine presence," he said. "Au revoir, Jean."

"Good night, Pascal."

He walked away.

I turned to Cheryl and chuckled. "Should I warn him about your temper?"

She punched me in the arm.

"Shut up and tell me what's on your mind."

"I was followed up here by two New York City cops. It's possible that they were the ones who blew me in to Boom Boom."

"How do you know that they followed you up here?"

"It's complicated, but I think they've been looking for me all week. At any rate, they followed Kelly and me up Mount Tom this afternoon, and tonight they were at the Woodstock Inn watching us while we ate dinner."

"Have they done anything to you? Like threatened you verbally, or physically harmed you?"

"Not exactly, but I definitely feel intimidated by them." I didn't want to tell her that I just assaulted one of them and stole his gun.

"Have you spoken with them?"

"No. We never had the opportunity."

"You're not giving me much to go on here, Cesari."

"Yeah, I know, but let me give you their names anyway. You might find out something interesting."

"All right, write them down on a piece of paper." We walked over to Hilda's desk, and I wrote their names down for her as well as the license plate of the Crown Vic. As I did that, Cheryl noticed the ugly bruising on my knuckles.

"What happened to your hands? They look awful."

"Oh, that. I had no idea how dangerous mountain climbing could be."

"Well, be more careful next time, and you'd better get those looked at."

"Thanks," I said, smiling. "And don't make too much noise with Pascal. The walls are paper thin."

"Shut up, Cesari."

R̸ 32

IN the rear of the B&B, I put our suitcase in the trunk of the Camry. It was ten-thirty, and I had taken just over an hour from the time I left Kelly. As I closed the trunk, a car with its brights on pulled into the driveway way too fast. I turned towards it, shielding my eyes from the blinding light. The car slowed, and I waited for the asshole to pull into a parking space. Instead, he came to an abrupt stop directly in front of me, and someone flung open the passenger side door. I didn't remember anything else.

Sometime later I woke, my chest hurt, and I was sore all over. A throbbing pain in the back of my head told me I wasn't in Kansas anymore. I reached back, and felt a lump the size of a golf ball there. They had probably tasered me, and maybe kicked me a few times as payback for all the trouble I had caused them. I needed to pee.

Assholes.

I was bouncing around in the trunk of a large car, probably the Crown Vic. They must have found the tire or were riding on the spare. I guess I wasn't as good at disabling cars as I thought I was. Why didn't they restrain my hands? Good question. Maybe it was because they'd snatched me from a public place and wanted me out of sight quickly before one of the other guests saw. If they were in that much of a rush, then perhaps they hadn't bothered to search me either. I reached down into my pockets and felt both my cellphone and the .38 still there. How stupid could these guys be?

The phone said it was after midnight, and I had only missed five calls and seven texts from Kelly. I remembered it was ten-thirty when I was packing the Camry, so I was still only about an hour or two tops from Woodstock. If I called Kelly on the cellphone now, they might hear, but she was doubtlessly starting to panic. I compromised and sent her a text saying that I was okay, but delayed. I then powered off the phone.

The ride was bumpy and uncomfortable, and I hoped we weren't going too much further. We were doing around fifty, and from the way the car shifted, slowed, and accelerated, I guessed we were probably on a winding country road. I could unload the .38 into the car blindly, hoping to nail them, but that was fraught with risk. The vehicle might swerve uncontrollably and we might all die. Plus, the .38 was a small caliber weapon, and by the time they passed through front and rear seats, the rounds might lose too much kinetic energy to even hurt them. I decided to sit tight and bide my time.

Thirty minutes later, the car braked hard on a gravel surface, and the momentum caused me to slide forward in the trunk. Both sides of the car opened, and men got out. I decided to play possum and use surprise to my advantage when they came for me. The .38 was nestled firmly in my hand, pointing at the trunk lid. As it opened, their torsos would be the easiest targets, but what if they wore vests? A head shot then? Lying in an awkward position in poor lighting, I doubted my chances of making two head shots with a snub-nose revolver. The more I thought it over, the less I liked my odds.

I heard them talking as they walked toward the rear of the car, pausing by the trunk.

"What do you think, Rick? Should we check on him?" I noticed his voice was very raspy from when I had strangled him.

"Nah, he'll be out cold for the rest of the night. I'm sure of that. I unloaded the Taser into him good, and that kick to the head you gave him should've sealed that deal, if it didn't kill him, that is. Jesus, Murph, you got to learn to take it easy. We need this guy alive, at least until he tells us where the diamonds are."

"I know, but this asshole has really pissed me off. I can't remember the last time anyone made me this angry, but you're right, I can't afford to lose it like that when I'm on a job. All right, let's go get our shit from the motel and get the fuck out of this God-forsaken hole. Where are we going now anyway?"

"My uncle has a country home in a remote, wooded area, maybe an hour from here. We can take our time there and interrogate him properly. As soon as we find out what we need to know, you can express your displeasure with him to your heart's content."

"What are we going to do with the body when we're done?"

"That's a good question, Murph. Do bears eat human flesh? I know there are a lot of bears in the woods around here. We could cut him up and leave pieces here and there for them. We'll talk it over later. C'mon let's check out of this fleabag."

Finished, they walked away, leaving me there. They obviously weren't worried about me regaining consciousness and yelling for help. Maybe the last time they'd tasered someone and kicked him in the head, the guy had remained unconscious for several days, but not tonight. My mother always told me I had a hard head, and I'm glad she was right about that. As I got older, I'd started to realize she was right about a lot of things.

I waited patiently in case they changed their mind and decided to check on me. Still, I didn't want to wait too long. After five minutes, I felt it was safe to move around. First order of business was to see if the car had an emergency trunk release mechanism. They were required by law in all cars, and were usually by the trunk latch. I felt around, but didn't find anything. They might have disabled it. That wouldn't be too hard to do.

Okay. Most cars also had trunk release cables that allowed the driver to pop the trunk open by pulling on a lever by the driver's seat. The cable usually ran along the floor, from the front of the car to the trunk, underneath the carpet. I crawled around with difficulty and began pulling up the matting in the trunk. There it was. I felt the metal cable in the dark, and forcefully yanked on it. The trunk latched clicked open, and the lid rose upward an inch or two. I peeked through the opening to check out my surroundings. I was in a poorly-lit, deserted parking lot and heard a train rumbling in the distance. The cool night air filled my lungs, rejuvenating me and clearing my head.

About a hundred yards away there was a small, seedy-looking motel, with a blinking, red neon sign overhead, missing several of its letters. I climbed out of the trunk, stretched and looked around some more. I was stiff and had a headache, but nothing was broken. A factory of some type stood several hundred yards to my left and a rail yard directly behind me. I could see multiple crisscrossing train tracks and several dormant train cars.

I couldn't be more than two and a half hours from Woodstock, at the most. On the other hand, I could be just five minutes away for all I really knew. It was one thirty in the morning, I was in the middle of fucking nowhere and I didn't have a fucking clue how I was going to get out of here. These guys were morons, but could they have been dumb enough to leave the keys in the ignition, too? I walked quickly to the driver's side door, opened it and checked. No keys. As I toyed with idea of hot-wiring the engine, time ran out.

Shouting from the motel doorway in the distance, Rick and Murph had spotted me and taken off at a full charge. They dropped their luggage, retrieving handguns from holsters. Instinctively, I turned and fled in the opposite direction toward the rail yard, sprinting the fifty yards to the tracks as a southbound freight train approached at about thirty miles an hour. I leaped over the rails seconds before the train reached my location, placing it between me and the bad guys.

I paused to get my bearings and catch my breath. The wind turbulence and noise caused by the passing train was both unsettling and thrilling. There were many box cars, and the train didn't appear to be stopping. Behind me was nothing but the blackness of a Vermont forest. Tough decision.

An approaching box car with its door open beckoned me, and I decided to hop a ride. I started running alongside the train, and when the car was in position, I grabbed the side of the door and jumped on. I didn't quite make it all the way, and was dragged, half in and half out, wiggling my way on board. A pair of hands reached out from the darkness and hoisted me upward.

"Thank you," I said breathlessly. I had no way of knowing how many others there were. What light there was from the moon did little to illuminate the inside of the car. No one responded. It was noisy, but not that noisy, so I said "thank you" again. I heard people moving around and sitting down.

"Everybody's tired, so shut up," a voice called out.

"I just wanted to thank whoever it was that helped me."

Quiet.

Finally someone said, "Listen, pal, the road is dangerous, and people are suspicious of strangers."

Fair enough.

"I understand. My name is John. Can someone tell me where we are and where we're heading? I'm totally disoriented."

"If you don't know where you are or where you're heading, why did you get on in the first place?"

"I was kidnapped and thrown into the trunk of a car. I managed to escape and the kidnappers were trying to throw me back in the trunk of the car when the train came along."

"Why were they trying to kidnap you?" A different voice asked. "Are you important?"

"I'm not important."

"Women get kidnapped for sex. Men get kidnapped because they're important. You must be important."

"I'd really like to know where we're going. Is that too much to ask?" I persisted.

"Everybody here minds their own business. It's best that way. You follow the rules and we'll get along."

"What are the rules?"

"No talking after midnight is rule number one. Now shut up and go to sleep, asshole," said a third voice angrily.

The first voice said, "We're somewhere in Vermont, heading south. That's all any of us knows. Any more noise and we throw you overboard."

I turned on my cell phone and saw another four texts and calls from Kelly, each one more frantic than the last. I texted her that I was okay, and that I would call her as soon as possible. I should have called, but that might have pushed my new friends over the edge.

I dozed uncomfortably for a couple of hours and woke up when I felt the train slowing to a stop. It was 4 a.m. Nobody else seemed to care. I saw the lights of a city ahead and decided to get off. Without saying goodbye, I jumped out of the box car, started walking towards the lights and called Kelly.

"John, what happened? I've been worried sick. I haven't been able to sleep. Are you okay? Where are you?"

"I'm okay, Kel. Just a little sore. I don't know where I am at the moment. I'll know better in about ten minutes. I'm at the outskirts of some town."

"What happened?"

"Those guys from last night caught me in the back of the B&B and threw me into the trunk of their car. I managed to get out and hopped on a passing freight train. I just got off."

"Oh my God. What should I do?"

"Try to get a few hours sleep while you can, Kel. You have a long ride ahead of you. I'm willing to bet the Camry is still in the parking lot of the Reluctant Panther with the suitcase in the trunk, and you have the other set of keys. I already settled up with Hilda. I'll call you back in a couple of hours when I figure out where I am, okay? Try not to worry. I'm fine."

"John..."

"Yeah?"

"I love you."

I didn't respond.

"You don't have to say anything."

"Kel, c'mon. I don't need anymore stress."

"You just got kidnapped, are in the middle of nowhere and the words *I love you* make you feel stressed? Okay, I'm sorry. Forget I said anything. Call me when you find out where you are, okay?"

"I will. I promise. Now get some rest. You're going to need it. I'll call you back soon. Bye."

"Bye."

Why do women always have to do that? You got guys trying to kill you every which way you turn, and all they can think about are their feelings? What about my feelings? I don't even know where I am, and now I have to deal with all this extra pressure. *I love you?* What does that even mean? I was very hungry and on the verge of getting cranky.

I tramped into town like that.

℞ 33

FIFTEEN minutes at a brisk pace brought me to the center of the town. It was pretty dead, with just a few homeless people sleeping in a litter-filled park. It looked like any other small city in America. The core had died out years ago, leaving empty store fronts and rundown apartment buildings. Most of the businesses had probably moved to strip malls on the periphery.

It was four-thirty and even the saloons were closed. The rumbling engine of an old, black Camaro that needed a new muffler caught my attention, and I watched as the lone car turned onto my street, pulling alongside me. The windows were tinted, and I couldn't see inside. The vehicle came to a stop, and the driver side window rolled down. A young Hispanic male, maybe twenty, not a day over, grinned in my direction.

"Hey, Chico, looking for a party?"

I approached warily, and looking past him, I could see two others, a male of similar age in the passenger seat and a younger girl in the back. She couldn't have been more than seventeen. Clouds of marijuana smoke billowed out the window.

"What kind of a party?"

"Whatever kind you want, Chico. You ain't no cop, are you?"

"No, I'm not a cop."

"Well then, I got grass, ludes, acid. If you want, Maria will blow you like a trombone. Hell, for the right price, I'll blow you like a trombone, too." Everyone in the car roared in laughter.

"Very tempting, but no thanks. However, I could really use some information. Like what's the name of this town?"

"Do I look like the fucking yellow pages to you, bro? I'm a business man, and now you're wasting my fucking time."

I took out my wallet and handed him a twenty.

"Where are we?"

He took the twenty. "Man, you are fucked up. You're in Brattleboro, dude. You stoned or what?"

The girl in the back seat said, "Maybe he's a spaceman, Carlos, ask him." They all thought that was funny, too.

Carlos had other things on his mind, however, as he eyed my wallet. "How many more twenties you got in there, bro?"

"Why?"

He smiled. "I'm selling raffle tickets for my church. Maybe you'd like to buy some? Let me show you." He reached over and opened the glove compartment without waiting for my reply. Before he could take the handgun from its hiding place, I quickly pulled my .38 out, reached inside the car, and pressed it firmly against the side of his head, cocking the trigger loudly. Things got suddenly very quiet.

Carlos was leaning awkwardly towards his companion with his right hand still in the glove compartment. I glanced quickly at the girl in the rear. She was cute, and I was wrong. She wasn't a day over sixteen, and was wide-eyed with fright. No threat there. The guy in the passenger seat looked paralyzed as well. They were all young and very high, and this wasn't how they'd planned on ending the night, with Carlos getting them all killed.

I said, "Don't do anything stupid, amigo."

To emphasize the point, I jammed the tip of the barrel hard into his temple, eliciting a grunt. I reached over him with my free hand, pushed the gear shift into park, and turned the ignition off, taking the key.

"That's better. Now slowly, very slowly, with just your thumb and index finger, remove the gun from the glove compartment, and hand it to me gently. Keep in mind that I'm seriously pissed off. Do we understand each other, Chico?"

"Do what he tells you, Carlos." Maria said nervously. "We don't want any trouble, mister."

Carlos nodded his head anxiously. "Take it easy, bro. I didn't mean no harm."

He gingerly passed me the weapon, and I breathed a sigh of relief. It was a 9mm Glock, the safety on. I stood up, removed the clip, emptied the chamber and tossed it to the street while they watched.

Carlos asked. "Can I sit up?"

"No, stay leaning over your friend for now. It's easier for me to keep an eye on you while we talk."

I leaned back into the car that was now filled with frightened kids sobering up and realizing that they were up to their eyeballs in shit.

"Look, guys. I wasn't looking for any trouble tonight, but now we have a situation. But I think I see a way out."

"And what's that?" Carlos asked.

"You said you were a business man, right? So how about we do some business? I'll give you fifty bucks if you drive me to the nearest diner and don't do anything stupid on the way."

Carlos replied, "You're kidding?"

"No, I'm not. I'm starving. Well?"

"That's it? You're not going to shoot us?"

"No, why would I do that? Anymore guns in the car, by the way?"

"No, that was it."

"You sure?"

"Swear on my mother's grave. Besides, I've had enough for tonight."

"We got a deal, Carlos?"

He thought it over for a few seconds. "Yeah, c'mon in." He turned to his friend in the passenger seat. "Yo, Angel, get in the back seat. Maria, put out the joint."

I walked around the car, got in and buckled up. I laid a fifty down on the center console and handed Carlos his keys. I kept the .38 in plain sight for insurance. He rolled down all the windows to air out the marijuana smoke, and we drove in silence. Minutes later, he let me out in front of an old fashioned diner in a slightly better part of town. I stepped out, pocketed the handgun and thanked him for not doing anything stupid.

He asked, "What's your story, man? Walking around in the middle of the night. Don't even know where you are?"

"You wouldn't believe it if I told you, Carlos. Have a good night and thanks for the ride."

"Peace, bro."

"Adios, Señor Spaceman, and thank you for not killing us," Maria added as I walked away.

They drove off, and I walked into a fifties style diner called The Rockin' Robin. There was a long, well-worn, formica counter lined by round, swivel stools and a row of booths with tables. There were two guys in flannel shirts hunched over their coffees at the counter and an exhausted, forty-year-old waitress, waiting for her shift to end.

I took a seat in a booth, and ordered scrambled eggs, home fries, toast and coffee. It was just after 5 a.m., and the light of the coming dawn was peeking through the night sky. I figured that I would let Kelly sleep another hour and then give her a wake-up call. The question right now was how much longer I was going to make it before I passed out from exhaustion. The waitress poured my coffee while I watched the sun rise.

"How far are we from Woodstock?" I asked.

"Not far, maybe an hour, straight up Route 91."

"Are you sure that's all?"

"Definitely. I go there all the time. Why?"

"Seems like it took me all night to get here from there."

"Maybe you drive like an old lady, but the real question is why would anyone want to get here in the first place?"

"Not much to do here, huh?"

"Let's put it this way, handsome." She leaned over, revealing cleavage. "Wait for my shift to end, and I'll go wherever it is you're going and do whatever it is you want. Just promise not to bring me back."

I chuckled. "Well, I'm glad we cleared the air about that."

"I'll go check on your breakfast, hon." She turned and walked toward the kitchen.

I didn't quite get it. It seemed like I should have been a lot farther away than I was. Where was I when I got on the train? Good question, but one that I wasn't going to get any answers to tonight.

Ten minutes later, she returned with my breakfast, and I started eating ravenously.

At six, I called Kelly and woke her up.

"Sorry to wake you, Kel. How'd you sleep?"

"Not well. I'm exhausted. So, where are you?"

"I'm in a place called Brattleboro, a small city about an hour south of Woodstock. Right now, I just finished breakfast at a diner on Rte. 5. Just take 91 South to the Brattleboro exit, and make a right onto Rte. 5. It's five minutes from there, on the left side of the road. You can't miss it."

The waitress chimed in as she refilled my coffee. "Just tell her to take a right at K-Mart when she gets off the highway."

"Did you hear that?"

"Yes. Right at K-Mart off the highway. Who was that?"

"The waitress."

"The name's Erma."

"Her name's Erma. I'll be the guy sleeping in one of the booths. And Kel..."

"What?"

"I'm sorry about...you know, the love thing. I kind of overreacted."

"Forget it. I already have."

"Thanks."

She didn't forget anything. I was a dead man walking.

It was closer to two hours later when Kelly picked me up. We got right back on 91 and settled in for the three hour or so ride back to Manhattan. As we drove, I gave her the short version of last night's events. She took a deep breath and let it out.

"How are you?" I asked.

She yawned, "Pretty tired. I couldn't sleep at all worrying about you." We were both wearing the same clothes from the night before. At least she was clean. "Why do you smell like pot?" She asked.

"It's a long story." I reclined back fully in the passenger seat and watched the trees go by. "Suffice it to say that there's a lot more going on in Vermont than flannel shirts and apple pie."

"Any new ideas about the diamonds?" she asked, making conversation.

"To be honest, Kel, so much has happened since we last discussed it that I really haven't given it much thought. Clearly there are people out there who not only want their diamonds back, but are willing to kill for them. They know us, and that's not good. The question is, who are they and can we negotiate with them? That's a big question mark, and now there are New York City cops involved, although I'm convinced they are just hired guns. Then there is the issue of Ed Talbot, Reg and Gina. I can't for the life of me see how they're all related. I don't know if I mentioned this to you, but Gina used to date Ed Talbot."

"You're kidding?" She seemed as astonished as I was when I heard.

"At least that's what one of the anesthesiologists told me. That would definitely complicate things."

"How so?"

"Well, it could certainly explain why Ed had such an interest in what was going on late at night in the OR. Maybe he was stalking Gina? Maybe he was still in love with her and became obsessed with everything she did and who she did it with? You know how guys get? Perhaps he stole the diamonds to give to her to prove how much he loved her in order to win her back?"

She thought that one over. "Fair enough, but it still doesn't explain where the diamonds came from in the first place or how Ed came to be in possession of them. Nor does it explain why Reg does so many colonoscopies at night with Gina." She hesitated. "You don't think that has anything to do with the diamonds, do you?"

I chuckled. "What are you implying? That Reg is a diamond smuggler? Now that would be funny. No, I really don't think so. He probably earns close to half a million dollars a year as the chief of gastroenterology at St. Matt's. Throw in another quarter of a million in lectures, books, research grants and medical product endorsements and you have a guy who is doing pretty darn well for himself. It is also widely known in the hospital that his wife is loaded. Why would he take the risk of getting involved in such an overtly dangerous criminal activity?"

"I don't know. I'm just thinking out loud."

"Besides, do you have any idea the kind of testicles you would have to have to get in bed with the Russian mob? I just don't think Reg has it in him."

"Okay, Cesari, I was just asking a question."

"Well you asked a good question, but I think there's something else going on at night in that hospital that doesn't meet the eye, and I intend on finding out. As soon as I get back, I'm going to go to medical records and dig a little deeper. I suppose I could just ask Reg directly about his call cases, but telling the boss that I've been spying on him would be political suicide. And what if he doesn't have a good answer? No, the best way to approach this is to find out who else was in the OR those nights Reg was there and discreetly ask them what they know. There are always gaggles of people around for these types of cases: at least two endoscopy nurses, a recovery room nurse, an anesthesiologist, ER docs, transport people, etc. I'll start with Gina. Her name stands out in all of this like a beacon in the night."

"Gina?! You better stay away from her, Cesari. She's a man-eater and has a bad reputation in that hospital. There are more than a few rumors floating around about her."

A man-eater? What did she ever do to you?"

"She breathes."

I laughed and then yawned. "Mind if I take a nap?"

"No, go ahead. Just don't dream about Gina."

"You're the only girl I ever dream about."

R͓X 34

GODDAMN," I said.

We stood in the middle of our ransacked, Greenwich Village apartment, assessing the damage. The smell of rotting food from the overturned refrigerator was almost as disgusting as watching the flies feast on it. We were both exhausted from the ride and didn't need to deal with any more shit like this. I opened a window for some ventilation.

"Good thing I put the diamonds in a safe deposit box before we left," I commented.

"Can't we just give them away, Cesari? I mean, to anybody?"

"That won't stop these guys, Kel. Don't you see? As long as they think we have the diamonds, they're going to keep coming, and I'm afraid it's becoming very personal for them."

"What do you mean?"

"We made fools of them in Vermont, Kel, and I assaulted one of them at the Woodstock Inn. Hell, I even stole his gun... No, there's no way they're going to let go of this even if I giftwrap the damn diamonds and mail them back with an apology card."

"Great."

"Look, we'll have to stay at a hotel for a few days while we get this mess cleaned up. I'll call a cleaning company and let the landlord know what happened. Then I guess we'll go shopping for new furniture and stuff."

"Why would someone destroy our appliances?" It looked like someone had tried to rip the back paneling off the refrigerator with a crowbar, and the microwave had been smashed on the floor repetitively, its door now lying several feet from the main compartment.

"I don't know, Kel. I just don't know. Maybe they were angry because they couldn't find what they were looking for. They could have saved themselves some trouble by using a screwdriver."

We packed some clothes and made a reservation for the St. Mark's Hotel a couple of blocks away from the apartment. It was very close to Saint Matthew's Hospital and would be convenient for work. We walked there in silence, wondering what new unpleasantness would be heading our way. The receptionist was knowledgeable and very friendly. She handed me back my credit card and directed us to our room.

"I know it's not the fanciest place in Manhattan, Kel, but it's only a block away from the hospital, and the price was right."

The elevator doors opened and we entered, Kelly pressing the button.

"It's fine," she said. "It's only going to be for a week at the most. I can handle it." The room was functional, but on the small side. We were on the tenth floor, and had a decent view of the city. Most importantly, it was clean, and the staff were polite and enthusiastic.

"Where are you going to keep the guns?" Kelly asked, referring to the two .38's that I now had in my possession. There was the one I'd taken from the cop, Murphy, in Vermont, and the one from my apartment. Whoever had torn apart the flat hadn't noticed the false bottom in the lower drawer of the armoire in the bedroom. I kept the lockbox with the .38 and ammo there. I was very careful about hiding my gun when I wasn't around. Handguns were illegal across the board in New York City, and I was paranoid about my landlord accidentally coming across it.

"I'll keep them in the hotel safe. It's in the closet by the bathroom. They should be okay there. Although, I was toying with the idea of carrying one now that things are starting to get dicey. What do you think?"

"I think that's a very bad idea, Cesari, so get it out of your head. Guys who carry guns make bad decisions. Besides, this is New York City. If you get caught with it, there's mandatory sentencing. No ifs, ands, or buts, and I'm too young to wait for you."

I was silent while I thought about it. She was right, of course. On the other hand, I'd carried the .38 before without her knowing it.

I was hurt, though. "You wouldn't wait for me?"

"No."

"Really?"

"Really."

"But I thought you said you loved me."

Bad play, Cesari. She glared and then threw a pillow at me. "I can't believe you have the nerve to bring that up."

* * * * * * *

"So tell me again what happened, Rick?"

"We went up to Woodstock to interrogate Cesari, like we talked about, Uncle Reg. Two of Boom Boom's guys got there ahead of us and had already checked into the Reluctant Panther. I didn't think it would be a smart move for two of New York's finest to be sharing a boarding house with known hit men from Little Italy. So we kept our distance and moved to a motel just a few miles away in a place called White River Junction."

"Stop there just a minute. That's the part I'm having trouble with, Rick. Why were Boom Boom's guys up there in the first place?"

"Well, once we identified the guy, I did a routine background check on him. I searched his name in our databases just to see what would come up."

"And what came up?"

"That he's a real asshole. Has a rap sheet as long as my arm from when he was a kid. Mostly petty stuff and nothing ever stuck. He was suspected of being a leg breaker in the Bronx, and possibly worse, but then, just like that, nothing. He goes off the grid for ten years until last year when all of a sudden his name is tied to the Barazza case."

"Big Lou Barazza? What does he have to do with this?"

"That's just it. I don't know because the file is restricted, and I don't have clearance to access it without having all the wrong people crawling up my ass. So I did the next best thing and called Boom Boom to ask him what he knew about the guy because I knew Boom Boom used to work for Barazza. I figured he might know something but he didn't."

"Rick, how many times have I told you to stay away from the guineas? They're bad news. If they hear about our business, we'll be working for them, too. It's bad enough I got that asshole, Sergei, breathing down my neck. He calls me every fucking night like I'm his bitch."

"I got it under control, Uncle Reg. Boom Boom's a friend. We went to City College together, and we've been through this kind of shit before. Anyway, Boom Boom never heard of the guy, although he was interested because of his association with Barazza. Next thing I know, two of his guys are up there getting pinched for a stolen car. Unbelievable. The local cops filled us in. It was a big night in Mayberry R.F.D."

"I'll bet. Okay, then what?"

"Not much to tell. We had him in the trunk and were heading to your cabin to slice and dice him. We drove back to our motel to get our gear, and when we came out of the motel we saw him standing outside the car like nothing had happened with the trunk door wide open. I have no fucking idea how he did it. I disabled the safety release myself a long time ago. It must have malfunctioned somehow. Anyway, he disappeared into the woods and we haven't seen him since."

"All right, Rick, stake out the apartment and hospital again. I'll check his schedule to see when he's working and get back to you. It's time to take the gloves off with this guy, and I mean it. If it has to get messy, then so be it. Sergei will be here Friday, and we'd better have those diamonds.

"Understood."

R͟X 35

MONDAY morning came, I went to work as usual, and Kelly went shopping. She was off until Wednesday. I grabbed my usual cup of coffee from the Starbucks in the lobby and went to the locker room to change. Kirk, the anesthesiologist, was there.

"Hey, Kirk, how's it going?" I placed the charts I had to return to medical records to one side and opened my locker.

He turned toward me. "Not bad, Cesari, and you?"

"Really good. You know I took your advice and spent the weekend in Woodstock with Kelly. We had a great time."

"That's great to hear. I'm really glad you enjoyed it. People are really different up there, aren't they? Like a breath of fresh air."

"Definitely. Say, Kirk, can I pick your brain about something?"

I hung my shirt and pants in the locker and closed it.

"Sure. What's on your mind?"

"I've been doing some peer review for the department of medicine, and I came across something that caught my attention. Nothing major. Just something that seemed different."

"So spit it out, Cesari."

"Well, I noticed that Dr. Griffin does all his scheduled colonoscopies with an anesthesiologist, but his last five call cases were done late at night without anesthesia. He administered the sedation himself. Why would he do that?"

Kirk put one foot up on the changing bench and watched me as I slipped surgical booties over my shoes. He thought over my question for a minute. "I don't really know. He is a big proponent of anesthesia, and like you said, uses it with almost all of his outpatients. Of course, it's his prerogative if he wants anesthesia or not. There are no rules about it, but there are some clear-cut advantages to having an anesthesiologist present. Speed and efficiency is the big one. We can knock the patients out faster and deeper than you can, and then it's our job to recover them so you can move on to the next patient. Safety is the next big advantage. If there is an adverse reaction, we can manage the airway while you focus on the procedure. The only real downside to anesthesia is that it increases the overall cost of the procedure."

"So if he were doing a case in the middle of the night, it really wouldn't make any sense to sedate the patient himself. It would take him much longer to get out of here, and if something went wrong, he'd be here all by himself, dealing with complications."

"You're right, it wouldn't make any sense at all. Especially since we're here all the time anyway. Why stick around recovering a patient at two in the morning when we can do it for you? Not that we like to, but that's our job."

"Thanks, Kirk."

"No problem. Look, I got to run. See you."

"One more thing, Kirk, before you leave."

"Sure, but make it quick. I'm already running a little late for my first case."

"Do bears eat human flesh?"

He laughed. "Fucking Cesari. I don't know. I grew up in a house, not a log cabin. Why do you want to know?"

"Just curious is all."

"Well, I'm sorry I can't help. Bye."

"Bye."

I performed three colonoscopies in a row and had nothing else scheduled. They were pretty routine: a couple of polyps here, a couple of polyps there. It was another slow day and I was glad I was salaried. If they wanted to pay me to do nothing, I wasn't going to complain. If I'd been in private practice and business was this slow, I'd already have a For Sale sign on my house. The only problem with being an employee of the hospital was that someone could walk up to me at any time and tell me to get my shit and get out.

At eleven, Kelly called.

"Hi, Babe."

"Cut it out. I don't like to be called Babe."

"Okay, Babe."

"Cesari..."

"Just teasing. How's your day going?"

"Good. I'm at Macy's. It's a beautiful day out. I wish you could be here with me."

"Me too, but one of the unfortunate side effects of being an employee is that they spell out clearly when and where I'm supposed to be all day. And I'm supposed to be here until five p.m., even if I have nothing to do."

"I know. I was just saying..."

"Saying or whining?" I laughed.

"Both, maybe. Do you think we could meet for lunch?"

"Sure, how about we meet at Aladdin's, the gyro place down the block from the hospital? I don't think anyone will mind if I walk a hundred feet from the main entrance. I'll meet you there at one. That'll give you plenty of time to finish your shopping."

"Finish my shopping? Babe, I'm just warming up."

"I don't like to be called 'Babe', Kel."

"See you at one, Babe."

Kelly hung up before I could say anything. She was starting to come out of her shell and I wasn't sure if that was a good thing for me.

Down in medical records, I returned the charts I'd borrowed. Lori was there filing, saw me and smiled. I gave her a little wave hello. There was a private room nearby with computers and a dictation machine for doctors to use, so I went in. Sitting at one of the desks in the small room, I accessed the hospital's medical records and thought about how best to form my query. Might as well start by doing a more thorough, line by line review of those five charts and colonoscopy reports.

When I finished that, I queried the records for all of Dr. Griffin's on-call cases for the last year and then changed the query to search his on-call activity going back two years. After an hour of studying the records, I sat back and contemplated the information. Very interesting, I thought. This sudden need to do cases late at night without anesthesia had begun about one year ago. Before that, he couldn't be caught dead in the hospital after 5 p.m. In fact, not counting this year, I had to go back at least three years before I could even find his name on a single night-call case. Curious, but so what? And why did the very dead Ed Talbot care? Maybe there was something else about these records that interested him. I went through them again and again. And then I saw it, or thought I did. My cell phone rang. It was Kelly.

"It's a quarter past one. You're late."

I looked at my watch. "Sorry. I'm on the way. Order me a gyro, extra tzatziki sauce and a Pepsi. I'll be there in five. Kisses. Bye."

I jumped up to leave and heard someone enter the room.

"Hi, Lori." She was leaning back against the door and the top three buttons of her blouse were open.

"Hello, John." She stared at me.

John?

"Lori, I wish I could stay and talk, but my *girlfriend* is waiting to have lunch with me. Now, if you could just step aside."

"Kiss me."

Uh oh!

"That would not be a good idea, Lori," I said softly. I was frozen in place, afraid to move.

"Kiss me just once, please," she pleaded. Her eyes were big and her voice throaty.

Not good.

"Lori, I think there has been a terrible misunderstanding and I'm very..."

"If you don't kiss me, I'll scream. I swear it, and then I'll tell everybody that you attacked me."

Oh God. She's crazy.

"You won't do that."

"How do you know?"

"Because you're a nice girl, and if you do that then we can never be friends."

Well played, Cesari.

She screamed—loudly.

I was starting to get nauseated and felt panic sweep over me. Any decision would be the wrong one. I was the deer in the headlights, so she'd made the decision for me. Sensing my paralysis, she stepped forward quickly and threw her arms around my neck. She pulled my head down to her, and on tiptoes, planted a big wet one on my lips. Her momentum carried me into the wall behind me. I wanted to push her away, but was afraid to touch her. Her tongue wiggled its way into my mouth, and I was finally working up my resolve to act like a man when the door opened.

Reginald Griffin III cleared his throat. "Are you all right, Lori? I thought I heard someone yell."

She let go of my neck and smiled contentedly. "Yes, Dr. Griffin. That was me. I saw a mouse and got scared. That's all. I was just thanking Dr. Cesari for protecting me."

"I see," Reg said, but clearly didn't.

"Well, I'd better get back to work. Thanks again, Dr. Cesari. I'm sorry for being such a scaredy-cat." Lori walked past Reg into the file room.

I hemmed and hawed. "It's not what you think, Reg."

"Really. Then why don't you tell me what I'm thinking."

"She's got a little crush on me, that's all, and got carried away."

"Do you have any idea how old she is?"

"I don't know, twenty-four, twenty-five…?"

"Her nineteenth birthday is next week. She's a friend of my daughter."

I gulped and felt beads of sweat form on my forehead. "I know it's hard to believe, but I didn't do anything."

"Cesari, let me give you some words advice, if I may. Having spent a few decades longer on planet Earth than you, I have seen many brilliant careers crash and burn precipitously because of a similar lack of impulse control. Maybe you're one of those guys who just can't keep it in his pants, I don't know. Sexual addiction is one of those illnesses that we are finding out is much more common than previously believed. I would suggest therapy, early and aggressively, before it gets out of hand or before your girlfriend finds out. I'll have my secretary book you an appointment for a licensed therapist before you become an embarrassment to the department and the hospital. There's no need to thank me, nor for me to remind you that St. Matt's Gastroenterology division has a top notch reputation throughout the city, and I won't allow one rogue buck to tarnish its reputation. Now I need to ask you something seriously and I want a straight answer."

"Yes, sir."

"Are you sure you're not a homosexual?" he asked, deadpan.

I was bewildered and didn't even understand the question. "Pretty sure, why?"

"Because I have seen this kind of behavior before in pretty guys like you who are in denial about themselves. They get the pretty girlfriend or trophy wife and then massively overcompensate sexually to the point of almost predatory behavior, trying to prove to everyone and themselves that they're something they're really not. I would much rather you face the truth and come out of the closet. At least then we could use it to the advantage of the department. It would look good in our brochure to list you as the first openly gay gastroenterologist at St. Matt's. They'd love it in the Village. Think about it."

"I will."

"Okay, then. I think we understand each other. Now, on a more pleasant note. I had a wonderful time with you and Kelly the other night. She's a very charming young woman, and I hope to see more of you both socially. As long as you can get your house in order, if you know what I mean. Hmm?"

"Yes, I will, and thank you."

"All right. Have a nice day. I must be getting back to work."

I flew out of the file room so fast that I forgot to log off the computer.

℞ 36

KELLY was pissed. By the time I got to the lunch place, it was almost two. She had already finished her lunch by the time I sat down across from her.

"Sorry I'm late. I ran into Reg as I was leaving to meet you, and he wanted to chat." There was a gyro with chips and a pickle on a paper plate waiting for me.

"I could have spent an extra hour in Macy's, and why are you still wearing hospital scrubs?"

"I'm sorry about Macy's, and I didn't want to waste any more time by going to the locker room to change."

"You should have at least worn a lab coat, don't you think?"

I scanned the room and saw many casually dressed customers. "I look fine. So I see you're having a productive day," I said, taking a bite of my sandwich and noting the two big Macy's bags at her side.

That brought her around. "They had some great sales today. Their fall wardrobe is out, and all the summer stuff was marked to go. It was a madhouse in there."

"So what did you get?" I continued playing my trump card.

She smiled. "You mean what didn't I get: tops, jeans, shorts, shoes, a bathing suit, and lots more. All the cosmetics and jewelry were twenty percent off, too."

"Jesus."

"He was there, too, getting new sandals."

"That's blasphemy, Kel. You're going to burn."

She rolled her eyes. "Oh, spare me."

"Only the Lord can do that."

"Shut up and eat."

I took another bite and sipped from a soda can. "Man, this is so good. By the way, do we have anything left in the bank after today?"

"No," she laughed. "You're going to have to work extra hard to pay off this bill. So how's your day going? How was Reg?"

"He's fine. He said he had a great time with us and thinks you're great."

"Any new information? I was thinking it over and think that maybe you should just come out and ask Reg about those cases."

I glanced around furtively, which made Kelly chuckle. The place was crowded, but I didn't recognize anyone.

She said, "You love this spy stuff, don't you? Are you going to eat that pickle or not?"

I slid my plate over to her. "Help yourself. This is serious stuff, and I don't want the whole world knowing what I'm doing."

"So, go on."

I lowered my voice. "First of all, as I said once before, I don't think it would be a good idea to let Reg know that I've been spying on him. In fact, I know that it would be a very bad idea. He is my boss and would definitely not appreciate that. Anyway, I reviewed those files again more thoroughly and found out some interesting things. It turns out that all twelve times he was on call this past year, Reg came in to do a colonoscopy at around midnight. Not just five times. Before this year, no one ever saw the guy when he was on call. That's amazing, but there's more. All the patients were perfectly fine, never dropped their blood counts, and all were discharged right after the procedure. He did all the cases by himself without anesthesia, which means that he had to stay even later to recover the patients himself. What's unusual there is that he does all his cases during the day with anesthesia so he can move faster. Which begs the question, why would he not use anesthesia at night?"

I could see from her facial expression that she was starting to get into it with me. "Agreed. That's seems pretty odd, but what's that got to do with Ed Talbot or the diamonds?"

"Nothing as far as I can tell, but there's something fishy about all of this. There's one more thing. All those cases he did late at night. I only saw one other signature on the op-record—Gina's."

"We already knew that. You told me that she was on call with him all the time."

"Yes, but I didn't realize until today that she was the *only* nurse with him. Usually, there are two nurses on call to assist with the colonoscopy and a third to help recover the patient."

She thought about that. "So what you're saying is Reg and Gina are always alone when they do call cases. What do you think that means?"

"I'm not sure."

"Maybe Reg thinks Gina's got a great ass. I know that's what you think."

"I resent and deny that emphatically," I said. She rolled her eyes, and I continued. "It can't be just a coincidence that every time he's on call she's on call, too, and every time they have to do a case, they never bother to call in other nurses or anesthesia."

"Oh my God," Kelly said, suddenly smiling. "Do you thing Reg and Gina are having an affair? That's too funny."

I looked at her. "No, that's not what I was thinking, but now that you mention it... Geez, it didn't even occur to me. He's so much older than her."

"Cesari, you don't have a clue. That's why they schedule themselves on call together. He probably calls the ER, and tells them to call him for anything no matter how trivial so he'll have an excuse to tell his wife. She calls the other OR nurses on call and says she can handle it by herself, so go back to sleep. He doesn't want anesthesia there because he wants to be alone with Gina and have an excuse to stay even later. It's perfect except for one thing. You figured it out, and now they're busted."

She was very pleased with herself, and I was suddenly confused. Everything she said made sense. Reg was married, and it really was the perfect excuse to get out of the house late at night, but why not go to a hotel or his office? Maybe they did that, too.

I finished my lunch. "The food here is great, by the way. Best gyro in the city as far as I'm concerned. I have to tell you, Kel, I'm more than a little bummed right now."

She laughed. "Why, because there's no great conspiracy going on or because Reg is banging Gina and you're not?"

"Wow, did you get up on the wrong side of the bed this morning or what? That was a terrible thing to say, and I demand an apology at once. I'm bummed because I thought I was starting to hone in on what's going on here, and now I realize I've been barking up the wrong tree. Still, there's got to be something about those charts that Ed Talbot thought was important unless he was just stalking Gina like I mentioned the other day."

"He was a crackhead, Cesari. Who knows what he was thinking... and I'm sorry. I was just joking about Gina. I know you would never go for some big-boobed, skanky wop like that."

I just shook my head. "You are so bad. The ACLU probably has a whole department keeping an eye on you, but I accept your apology."

We both laughed.

"Just remember who you belong to, Cesari."

"Hey, wait a minute," I said snapping my fingers. "Gina and Ed Talbot used to date, right?"

"I remember. You said the anesthesiologist told you. So, she has poor taste in men. Who doesn't?"

I let that one slide. "Yes, and he also implied that she was a druggie, too, although that kind of surprised me because she didn't seem like one."

"Where are you heading with this?"

"Don't you see? If Gina and Ed were involved and using drugs, it would change her motivation for being with Reg. Maybe she was milking him for money to support her or Ed's habit. Maybe she was trading sexual favors for cash. That would seem to fit better than her actually being attracted to a guy twice her age."

She narrowed her eyes suspiciously. "Why does it bother you that she might be attracted to Reg? Lots of women like older men. Are you jealous, Cesari?"

"God, no." I said defensively. "I just don't buy it, that's all. Besides, if it's true, then Reg is such a hypocrite. He had the nerve to lecture me about inappropriate sexual behavior today."

She sat back and folded her arms.

Uh oh.

"And why did Reg feel it necessary to lecture you about inappropriate sexual behavior?"

Okay, go with the truth.

I took a sip of my soda, trying to be casual. "It was nothing..."

"I'm waiting."

"There's this girl in medical records."

"What's the name of this girl in medical records?"

"Lori, I think. I'm not sure. It begins with an L." I looked around and saw the lunch shop was starting to empty out. I was hoping someone would come by and ask us to leave.

"Hmm, so how old is this girl in medical records?"

"I don't really know."

She was starting to frown as dark clouds moved in. "Try a guess."

I cleared my throat. "I don't know. I'm terrible at guessing people's ages, Kel. Maybe in her early twenties— or just a tad younger."

"Is she in her twenties or not, Cesari?"

"Maybe she's nineteen—almost."

"Are you kidding me?"

"No, it was all innocent. I swear."

"Scale of 1-10?"

"What?"

She was starting to look pissed, and her frown had turned into a scowl. "You heard me."

"Four, maybe a five, seven-and-a-half, tops."

"Go on. Finish the story." She reached for her bottled water. "So what happened between you and this nineteen year old, seven-and-a-half, girl? I'm just dying of curiosity."

"She's got like a teenage crush on me, you know?"

"And?"

"She kind of gave me a kiss."

"A kiss? Cesari, I can't believe you. She gave you a kiss?"

"Yeah, a little one."

"Where?"

"You know. Where you usually get kisses."

"The forehead, the cheek, your penis? Where?"

"The lips." I was sinking faster than the Titanic.

"And what were you doing while this nineteen-year-old girl was giving you a kiss on the lips?"

"I was trying to get away. I really was. She caught me by surprise, and then Reg walked in by accident. He spent a half an hour lecturing me about morality. Don't you see how hypocritical that is considering his own behavior?"

She wasn't impressed by my closing argument. "I wonder what Reg would have walked in on if he had just waited another five minutes."

"Kel, please. Nothing is going on, okay? This girl is just a little confused is all. I think she understands that I'm happily in a monogamous relationship."

"Maybe she'll understand better if I go down there and stab her in the heart."

"Whoa. Take it easy, OJ. You might be getting just a little carried away. I swear there is nothing going on."

"If she so much as breathes in your direction again, I want to know about it, got that?"

"Got it."

"And don't compare me again to an insanely jealous murderer."

"Why would I do that?"

She picked up her Macy's bags. "I'm going back to the hotel. Call me when you're on the way home, and we'll figure out something for dinner."

We walked outside together and kissed goodbye. I exhaled slowly, watching her disappear into the crowded sidewalk.

Next time, lie.

R͓x 37

RETURNING to the hospital around 3 p.m., I changed back into civilian clothing and, from there, headed over to the OR lounge to kill some time before going home. It was a fairly large room with a ten foot long table, a flat screen television, a sink, a refrigerator and several reclining chairs. There was a view of a centrally located outdoor courtyard with flowering trees and shrubs. The intent of the small garden was to help the staff forget they worked in Manhattan, the mother of all concrete jungles.

Gina sat at the table sipping a cup of coffee, her long dark hair sweeping down around to one side and well over her shoulder. Kelly's warning about her echoed in my mind, but she didn't seem all that dangerous at the moment. It was time for a little cat and mouse.

"Hello, Gina," I said, taking a chair opposite her. Man, she was adorable. Great lips. I had a hard time picturing her with Ed Talbot—or Reg—but who was I to judge matters of the heart?

"Hi, Cesari." She looked up, and I could see she was upset about something.

"Everything okay? You look a little down."

"Yeah, I guess. I don't know. No, not really."

"What happened?"

"A friend of mine is missing. It's been a whole week now, and no one's heard from him or knows where he is. He doesn't answer his phone or anything."

"I'm sorry to hear that, Gina. Have you called the police?"

She nodded. "Yeah, but they took one look at his apartment and gave up. It was a disaster, and there was crack everywhere. The police can be very judgmental once they know drugs are involved. Maybe they're right, but I knew him before he became an addict, and that's the way I'll always remember him. You might have met him. He's worked here as an orderly. His name is Ed Talbot."

Was it possible that word still hadn't gotten out yet about his untimely demise?

"Doesn't sound familiar," I lied. "I'm truly sorry, Gina. I wish I could help. If there's anything I can do…"

"I'm not sure there's anything anyone can do."

"Well, you know what I mean. I'm here for you."

She hesitated. "Do you mean that?"

My cell phone rang, and I fished it out of my pocket. "Excuse me a minute, Gina. Hello, Cesari."

"Hello, Dr. Cesari, this is Marsha from Dr. Griffin's office. He asked me to make you an appointment for sexual addiction counseling."

Oh shit, I forgot. "Yes, thank you, Marsha."

"I made your appointment for tomorrow, Tuesday, at six p.m. It's on the tenth floor of the Givelber building in the NYU complex. It's easy to get there from here. All you have to do…"

I sighed loudly into the phone. "I know where it is, Marsha."

"The doctor's name is Pamela Gottlieb."

"Thank you, Marsha." I bowed my head and hung up.

"Everything okay, Cesari?" Gina asked.

"Yeah, everything's just great. I'm sorry, Gina. I didn't mean to interrupt you."

"Did you mean it when you said you wanted to help?" Her big brown eyes got even bigger.

"Sure."

"Can I tell you something in strictest confidence?"

"Of course."

"You can't tell a soul."

"I understand, Gina."

She glanced around the empty room and lowered her voice. "Very few people know this, but a while back, Ed and I used to date before he became an addict. I broke it off because I didn't do drugs, but we stayed friends and I even tried to help him. I got him into rehab, but it didn't work. He just wasn't committed to it."

"Wait a minute, you said his name was Ed Talbot, right?" I interrupted, feigning sudden recognition.

"Yes.

"I think I remember him now. He was a skinny guy, looked kind of malnourished. He worked here in the OR sometimes, right?

"Yes, that's him, or was. Who knows?"

"Well, what can I do to help, Gina?"

She took a deep breath. "Well, he had something valuable of mine, and I think he may have placed it in his locker for safe-keeping. I'm not certain. Today, I asked the hospital administration if they would let me in to get it back, but they said no because there's been no official decision yet as to what to do about Ed. Since he's only been missing a week, he's just considered AWOL. They said that until they reach a final determination, or a body shows up, that's his personal stuff, and no one can touch it but him."

"Hmm. Interesting problem, but you're not sure if what you're looking for is really there. Okay, what is it you think I can do?"

"You can get me into the men's locker room so I can search his locker. I have the combination to his lock."

Obviously she didn't know there wasn't any lock on Ed's locker since I'd never bothered to replace it after I'd broken in last week, so I kept up the pretense. "Why don't you give me the combination, and I'll check the locker for you? I mean, why take the risk of getting caught if you're not sure he put it there in the first place?"

She hesitated, choosing her words carefully. "It's complicated. What he has of mine is extremely personal and sensitive, and I don't feel comfortable allowing anyone else to see it. It's not that I don't trust you."

A tear formed in the corner of one of those big eyes.

I was curious about what she was looking for that might be in the locker. Did she know about the diamonds? That thought hadn't entered my mind until just now. On the other hand, she had known

Ed on a personal level and there could be any number of reasons for her concern. Who knows, maybe Ed had taken naughty pictures of her when they were dating, and now that that he's missing, she's worried they might suddenly surface.

"I understand, Gina. So you want me to sneak you into the men's locker room, and then what? I just stand guard outside while you rummage through Ed's locker, looking for something that may not even be there?"

"That sums it up, unless you think it's too risky."

I thought about it. "There's no question that we'll both get in a boatload of trouble if we're caught. Who else knows about this besides the administration?"

She shook her head. "No one. I haven't discussed this with anyone until now. I've been unwilling to accept that he's not coming back."

That made sense. I looked at the wall clock. "I see, and when exactly did you want to do this?"

"As soon as possible. We can come back later tonight. I mean like around eleven when we can be sure no one else is around. It'll be safer then. It will only take me a minute, I promise. I would be so grateful."

"There's a slight problem here, Gina. I live with my girlfriend and we're very happy. I can't just disappear at night without some explanation, and I'm certain I don't want to tell her that I'm meeting a sexy nurse in the men's locker room. That might not go over well."

"You think I'm sexy?"

"Yes, I do, and so does Kelly."

"Kelly?"

"My girlfriend. She's an ER nurse. I think you may have met her once or twice."

"Kelly—black girl with the beautiful green eyes?"

"That's her, although I see her as the most beautiful girl I've ever known— who happens to have green eyes."

She smiled. "That's sweet. I had no idea about you two. You think she would feel threatened by me?"

"I think most of the women in Manhattan would feel threatened by you."

She let out a deep breath and looked distraught. "Then I don't know what I'm going to do."

I groaned silently. "Okay, okay. Let me think about how best to do this."

Kelly would kill me if she found out, especially after the fiasco in medical records today, but I was interested in seeing Gina's reaction to finding nothing in Ed's locker. Then there was the subject of what she was doing all alone with Reg every time they were on call. Helping her with this might help break the ice on that topic. I just couldn't believe she was having an affair with Reg.

She said, "I have an idea. Tell Kelly you switched call with one of the other doctors, and that you're covering the ER tonight. I'll page you later and you tell her that you have a case."

"That would work, but what do I tell her when I return ten minutes later?"

"That's easy. Just tell her that the case was cancelled for some reason or the patient refused... I got it. Tell her that somebody got a piece of food stuck in their esophagus, and by the time you got here, it had passed spontaneously so the procedure was cancelled."

I took a deep breath. Any woman that could lie that well was way over my pay grade. Every inch of me screamed to get as far away from her as possible. She was trouble, from her beautiful brown eyes right down to what I was sure were beautiful little toes. Unfortunately, she was my only lead and I needed to follow it. The fact that she was easy on the eyes had nothing to do with it.

"Sounds like a decent plan, Gina."

R̸ 38

IN the hotel room, I brought Kelly up to speed on my chance encounter with Gina.

She was resolute. "No, absolutely not."

"But Kel, this is the best lead we've had since this whole thing began. Think about it. Gina's the first person who's shown any interest in the contents of Ed Talbot's locker who hasn't tried to kill us."

"I don't care. I am not allowing you to be alone with that creature and that's final. I told you already what I think of her. She will chew you up and spit you out, and I am not letting her get her claws into you. You can't be that stupid, Cesari! She bats her eyes and wiggles her butt, and you're ready to do anything she wants, even if it means losing your job."

We were sitting on the edge of the bed arguing. It was almost 10 p.m., and Gina was going to have me paged soon.

"But Kel, don't you see? It's important to find out if she knows anything about the diamonds, or if her interest in the locker is completely unrelated."

"You said she didn't mention anything about the diamonds."

"No, she didn't mention the diamonds, but I wouldn't have expected her to. According to Avi and Hesh, the diamonds are flawless and easily worth five million dollars, possibly more. If Gina knew, for a fact, Ed Talbot had a fortune like that hidden in his locker, don't you think she's going to be a little upset when she finds out they're gone? Of course she will be. She'll never be able to hide that kind of disappointment. If it's the diamonds she's looking for, she'll have a heart attack when she finds out they're missing. That's why I want to be right there to see her reaction."

"Won't she be just as disappointed not finding the nudie pics Ed took of her while they were dating?" Kelly asked sarcastically.

"No, because she said she wasn't certain where Ed had saved whatever it is she's looking for. In other words, if she's telling the truth, she'll be frustrated, yes, but more puzzled than anything else because she wasn't sure it was there in the first place. Get it?"

"Yeah, I get it. You're setting a trap for her. If she freaks when she finds the locker empty, then it means she knew exactly what was in it."

"Yes, aren't I clever?"

"You're a regular Perry Mason. I just don't want her to start feeling too comfortable around you."

"C'mon, Kel. She doesn't do anything for me."

She softened up and put her arms around me. "And she better not start doing anything for you. You know, Cesari, I was just starting to feel like maybe I overreacted this afternoon about that Lori girl in medical records and now you spring this on me." "Think about it, Kel. This is a real solid connection. We can't let it slip away."

She sat there brooding.

My pager went off, and I looked down at it. "It's Gina."

She stood up. "C'mon, let's go. I'll wait in the ER lounge and stay out of sight. I'll give you fifteen minutes, then I'm coming up to get you, and she better be in her cage."

"That's the spirit. Let's go."

As we walked toward the hospital, Kelly started to warm up. "Okay, so tell me again what you were doing instead of coming straight home to me after work."

She was referring to the fact that I'd arrived home two hours later than she had expected me.

"I picked up a replacement lock for Ed's locker and a cheap pair of chain cutters at a small hardware store in the Village. Then I returned to the OR, placed the lock on Ed's locker, and hid the chain cutter in the locker room. Gina will find that she can't open the lock with the combination she has. The plan's a little shaky here, but I'm hoping she'll get frustrated and come to me for help. I'll fortuitously discover the chain cutters, and we'll open the locker together. I want to study her face at the moment she opens the locker. She won't have time to conceal her true emotions."

"You don't think finding a chain cutter in the locker room will seem a little suspicious?"

"Every plan has flaws, Kel. Yes, it will seem odd, for sure, but I'll explain it away by telling her that the maintenance guys were up there earlier in the day working on the bathroom plumbing, and must have forgotten it. I placed it under one of the bathroom sinks, and I think she'll be so relieved that she won't give it too much thought."

"Why didn't you leave the locker as it was, without a lock?"

"Two reasons for that. One, I felt I would have lost the element of surprise if she thought the locker had been tampered with before she looked in. And two, I need a reason to come into the locker room with her. She didn't want me to see what was in the locker, so I was going to wait outside, but that will change if she requires my help. The fact that her combination doesn't work could easily be explained if, for some reason, Ed decided to change the lock himself without her knowledge. I'll plant that idea in her head when she asks me for help."

We entered the main entrance to the hospital together and waved to the security guard. I walked Kelly over to the ER lounge and hung out for a few minutes. At 11 p.m., I kissed her and went upstairs to the OR. It was deserted and dark. I found Gina waiting for me in the lounge. I had never seen her in civilian clothes or made up. Better not let Kelly see her like this. Could jeans get any tighter? She'd brought a big Coach bag with her.

"Hi, Gina, ready to go to work?"

"Yes, and thanks for coming, Cesari. I wasn't sure if you'd chicken out."

"The thought crossed my mind, but a promise is a promise. Let me check out the locker room first, and you come by a minute or two later. If anybody is in the hallway with me, keep walking to the female locker room like you forgot something there."

The men's locker room was about twenty-five yards from the lounge. The hall was dim, but not too difficult to see along, so I stepped out of the lounge, looked both ways, and proceeded directly toward my destination. The locker room could only be accessed by entering a numeric code, followed by pressing my thumb into a scanner. Once I did that, the light turned green and the lock clicked open. Thirty seconds later, I reemerged, signaling Gina the coast was clear. She approached anxiously, the scent of her perfume filling the hallway.

I held the door open for her. "All clear, Gina. Good luck. I'll wait out here. Come get me if you run into any problems."

"Thanks, Cesari, I'll be quick."

I glanced up and down the hallway impatiently. The only thing that could go wrong now would be if somebody came along just as she came out. That would be hard to explain, and by morning the rumor mill would be working overtime.

Several minutes later, I was starting to get edgy. C'mon, Gina, you're not going to open the lock, so give it up. I thought about going in after her, but decided that would defeat the purpose of trust-building. Five minutes later, she came out with a big smile on her face.

"How did it go?" I asked, surprised by her satisfied look.

"Terrific, how can I ever thank you?" She was beaming and put her arms around me. I stepped back, uncomfortable and confused. She wasn't insulted. I had this image of Kelly coming down the hallway at just the wrong moment.

"I just wanted to thank you," she explained.

"That won't be necessary, Gina, and you're very welcome. So, no problems in there?" I was puzzled to say the least.

"No, everything went well. Okay, let's go."

I hesitated. "You leave first, okay? I'll follow a few minutes later. It might not look good if we're both seen leaving together. No point in helping the gossip mongers. They seem to do just fine on their own."

"You're right, that's a good idea. Well, good night, and thank you again."

I watched her walk to the elevators, and after she disappeared from sight, I went back into the locker room. Ed Talbot's locker still had the replacement lock on it, and I opened it with the combination I had. It was empty, just as I had left it. A careful inspection of the rest of the locker room didn't reveal anything unusual. I checked the trash cans and the bathroom. The chain cutter was still in its hiding place under the sink. Nothing was amiss. What the fuck? I sat on the changing bench and scratched my head.

There was a gentle knock on the door. My heart stopped. Gina? I opened it and was surprised.

"Kelly? What are you doing up here? I was about to come downstairs to find you."

"I told you I'd come up in fifteen minutes. Where is she?"

"She left already. Come on in. You can help me think through a problem."

I filled her in as we sat on a bench and stared at the empty locker.

She asked. "She found what she was looking for?"

"Apparently."

"How can that be?"

"I don't know, but from the look on her face I believed her. She was real happy."

"Then whatever it was she was looking for wasn't in Ed's locker, so she couldn't have been looking for the diamonds."

"True, but what was it then? Even more puzzling, where was it, and why did she tell me that cock-n-bull story of needing to get into Ed's locker?"

Kelly thought about that. "I don't know, unless she needed to get into one of these other lockers here and didn't want you to know which one."

"That would make sense, but which one? None of them look disturbed, so she must have known the combination."

"John, which one is Reg's locker?"

I pointed to a locker about five feet away with a combination lock on it. We walked over to it. It looked undisturbed. I looked at Kel, and she looked at me.

"I hope you're not suggesting I break into the boss's locker, Kel."

"I'm not suggesting anything, but if she has some sort of special relationship with Reg, then she may have known his locker combination, and as long as we're here and dying to find out what's going on.... Besides, maybe we've been thinking of this all wrong. Maybe Ed Talbot isn't the missing piece of the puzzle. What if it's Reg?"

"Reg? I don't know, Kel. Part of me thinks we're about to break into Reg's locker just to find some lurid evidence of his relationship with Gina. If it doesn't have anything to do with the diamonds, I should mind my own business."

She nodded. "I agree, but we won't know for sure standing around like this, will we?"

I sighed. "Okay, you win. We look in Reg's locker, but if we find love-letters or sex toys, we high-tail it out of here, understood?"

"Agreed, but wouldn't that be fun?"

I went to the sink and retrieved the chain cutters. In front of Reg's locker, I took a deep breath and cut the lock. At the bottom of the locker was an unsealed envelope and nothing else. Kelly reached down and picked it up.

"Go ahead," I said. "Can't hurt now."

She opened it. There was a plain white piece of paper with a short note typed on it.

I have your diamonds and I know what you did to Ed Talbot.

Gina talks in her sleep, but you already knew that. I'm willing

to keep my mouth shut for a price.

Cesari

"Holy shit," I said in surprise.

"Wow."

"I guess I was wrong about Reg being a diamond smuggler, and Gina's up to her eyeballs in this. She just threw me under the bus, but why?"

"Bitch. I knew it."

"And she tried to kiss me."

"She did what? And when were you going to tell me that, Cesari? I can't let you out of my sight for five minutes."

"Kel?"

"What?"

"I said she tried to kiss me. I didn't let her."

"I'm not sure that makes me feel any better."

"It might be a good idea to leave now." I put the note in my pocket and closed the locker.

"What about the lock?"

"We'll take it outside and toss it in a trashcan. There's no point in leaving finger prints. Shit, I just thought of something."

"What?"

"That's why Gina wanted me to let her into the locker room. The electronic code and finger print scanner will keep a record of who entered the locker room tonight when no one was around. If Reg found that note tomorrow, I couldn't deny it because he could easily prove I was here late at night without a good reason.

"Well, it's a good thing that he's not going to find that note."

"Yeah."

R͓x 39

IT was midnight, and we strolled toward the St. Mark's Hotel with our arms around each other. "I'm sorry for getting so jealous, John. I don't know what's been coming over me lately."

"No need to apologize, Kel. I can't say that I blame you. There's been a lot of circumstantial evidence. Plus, there are so many unattached females running around this city, I think it would drive any woman a little crazy. My mother used to have a saying for situations like this."

"And what was that?" She looked up at me, smiling again.

I chuckled, recalling the sweet way my mother used to drive home her lessons on life. "She used to say that if you had a room full of women, they might all be great friends until a man walked in, and then all hell would break loose. Only she would say it like this, with a thick Italian accent. *Now that'sa the prescription fora the disaster.*"

Kelly laughed. "She was a smart woman."

"Yes, she was."

"So, you don't think I'm crazy?"

"I think all women are crazy. Ouch." She'd punched me.

"I thought you said it was just white women who were crazy."

"That's true, actually."

"So then what do you think my problem is?"

"I don't think you have a problem. If you're feeling a little inse-
cure and vulnerable lately, then it's probably my fault to some degree.
Maybe I haven't been paying you enough attention, I don't know. If it is
my fault, then I'm sorry and I'll try to fix it. How's that for reasonable?
But you don't have to feel insecure about me. You're the only woman
I'm interested in, okay? You rock my world, Kelly."

We stopped and kissed under a street light.

She studied me carefully. "So you don't think it has anything to do
with the fact that I'm late?"

"Late for what?"

She smiled. "I thought you were a doctor?"

Silence.

Comprehension.

"You're kidding?"

"No. Just a couple of days. Nothing to panic about." She rested her
head against my chest, and I held her tightly.

"Then why am I panicking? I don't understand. Did you forget...?"

"Birth control isn't foolproof, Cesari."

"Hmm, I see."

"Are you okay?"

"Couldn't be better."

"You're an okay guy, Cesari. You know that?"

"Yeah, I know."

"If it doesn't happen by tomorrow, I'll make an appointment with
my gynecologist. But it's probably just stress, all that's been going on."

Taking deep, cleansing breaths, we stood there quietly, and eventually returned to the room, lost in thought. A lot was happening.

"Gina, Gina, Gina," I said, lying in bed, staring at the ceiling.
"What are you up to?"

"Bitch. I told you."

I laughed again. "That's not very helpful."

"I'm not trying to be helpful. I want to stab her in the heart."

"Oh my God. Who are you, Jack the Ripper? Enough with the
stabbing in the heart stuff."

She flung a pillow at me.

"Okay, let's review what we know." I took out the note and read it aloud again. "According to this, the diamonds belong to Reg, and he is to blame for Ed's death."

"Right, and she also made it clear that you two are sleeping together. Probably wishful thinking on her part, but from the tone of the note, I'd guess she was trying to make him angry or jealous."

"I agree, but why would she send Reg a note making him think I'm blackmailing him?"

"I haven't the slightest idea. How would she even know you have the diamonds?"

"I don't know."

Kelly rolled onto her side, looking at me. "This is all a little hard to believe. Do you really think Reg is capable of murder?"

"Facts are stubborn things, Kel, and there's no other way of interpreting this note. Somehow, Reg got a hold of stolen Russian diamonds, which made their way into Ed Talbot's hands and now mine. Ed died because of them, and we're next on the list."

"If Reg had Ed Talbot killed, does that mean he's the one who sent those guys to Vermont looking for us?"

"Good question. Certainly a possibility, but doubtless there are probably multiple people looking for those rocks. The guys in Vermont were New York City cops, and I can't believe they would take orders from Reg. Unfortunately, the only thing that's clear at the moment is if Reg didn't know about my involvement before, Gina is planning on bringing him up to speed on the subject real quick and not to my advantage. Why, I don't know."

"Maybe or maybe not. She may have been taking a shot in the dark. As a woman, I see that note in a totally different light. Look, she's young and beautiful, and he's much older and paunchy. For whatever reason, they're in a relationship and something happened to rock the boat. She decides to get his attention by making him think she's throwing him overboard for a much younger, good-looking guy. She throws in the diamonds and Ed Talbot for good measure to let him know she's serious. It's as if she were saying to him, through you, 'I got you by the balls, old man, how hard do you want me to squeeze?'"

"Hmm, that's interesting. So maybe she doesn't really know I'm involved at all, and she's just trying to piss Reg off? Maybe he dumped her or something? Or perhaps she still has feelings for Ed and got upset when she found out what happened... but this a very dangerous way of venting her anger."

"Which part of 'I told you she was a bitch' didn't you understand? Women don't play by the same rules men do, Cesari. I can't believe you haven't figured that out by now. When women get angry, they don't throw a few punches, buy each other beer and make up. They go for the jugular. They want you dead, no survivors, get it?"

I looked at her, shocked by this apparent revelation on the female condition. "You paint a grim picture of the weaker sex, Kel."

She looked at me sympathetically. "Let me explain this better. Most women have more anger and aggression in the tip of their pinky than most men do in their entire body. When a man gets angry, he explodes like a firecracker. You walk away, have a sip of wine, and a few minutes later, you're fine. The next day he will have forgotten all about it. When a woman gets angry, it's like a nuclear explosion that destroys everything in its path, and for years afterward, you have to deal with the fall out."

"Okay, well I'm glad we cleared that up. So for reasons unknown, possibly because she's pissed off at Reg, she decides to send him a blackmail note from me. Why— to make him angry or feel threatened?"

"Neither, I think the main purpose of the note was to make him jealous, but to just come out and say what was on her mind would have been too straightforward. Women are never that direct."

"God, how passive aggressive do you have to be to do something like this? And what was she going to say if Reg decided to kill me in a jealous rage?"

Kelly laughed. "Mission accomplished."

"Okay, so what you're saying is, she writes the note, and he gets all riled up, but he calms down and sees it for what it really is, a message from his girlfriend telling him she's upset. Instead of coming after me, he goes crawling back to her, begging forgiveness for whatever it is he's done. She never expected anyone but Reg to read the note, so no harm no foul, and you think this is standard operating procedure for most women."

"Exactly."

I chuckled. "Well, I don't know if I buy all of this, but there's one thing for sure, and that's that Gina knows a whole lot more about what's going on than we do."

"Great. So now you're going to start spending more time with her. That's not going to help my insecurity."

"Gina and Reg obviously know all about the diamonds, and she thinks she's my friend now. We can use that."

"I don't want her to be your friend. It irritates me that she even wrote that about you and her, and I don't care why she did it."

"Hey, I just had an idea."

"What's that?"

I called the hospital switchboard. "Could you tell me the next time Dr. Griffin is on call for gastroenterology? Yes, I can hold."

Waiting.

I put my hand on the receiver. "That's a cute night shirt, by the way." It was pink with a big picture of Minnie Mouse on the front.

"Thanks."

I returned to the call. "Yes, I'm still here. Tomorrow? Thank you. Bye."

"What are you thinking, Cesari?"

"I want to know what goes on when those two are on call."

****

"Sorry it took so long to get back in town, Uncle Reg. The Woodstock police found our shotgun, and we had to go all the way back to claim it. Explaining why we didn't report it missing was pretty embarrassing, but we took care of it."

"Cesari must know more than he's letting on, Rick. I caught him snooping through my charts down in medical records. The asshole forgot to log off of the website after he ran a search of my records. Damn. And Sergei called again last night. He wanted to know if we got the diamonds back. That fucking commie is starting to feel like a 400 lb. gorilla on my back"

"What did you tell him?"

"I told him everything's fine, of course, and that we'll have them by the time he returns to the U.S. on Friday. There's another shipment of diamonds coming tomorrow. Look, I know exactly where you can find Cesari. I made an appointment for him at six p.m. in the Givelber building at NYU with a Dr. Pam Gottlieb on the tenth floor. I made it clear to him that he better show up, too. I want this kept as far from the hospital and me as possible. Take him down and don't worry about Gottlieb; she's expendable. Just in case, I have my girl, Gina, working on a backup plan, but I'm hoping I don't have to use it."

R_X 40

THE next morning, I woke up early and left for work while Kelly and the city still slept. I had a plan in mind and felt energized. Things were starting to make a little more sense, and I was taking steps to control rather than react to events. *Reg and Gina, Gina and Reg, New York City cops, diamonds, Russians, Boom Boom, Barazza.* I was standing on the corner of 3rd Avenue and E. 9th St. deep in thought, waiting for the light to change, when a Lincoln Towncar with tinted windows squealed to a sudden stop in front of me, causing me to step back instinctively. Doors opened and large men got out, grabbing me roughly by the arms.

"Get in the car, asshole."

They shoved me roughly into the back seat where I found myself sandwiched between the two guineas from Vermont, Boom Boom's guys. Great. The car took off with a lurch, and another New Yorker disappeared in plain sight never to be seen or heard from again. The guy on my right looked at me briefly, and then punched me viciously in the jaw.

A burlap hood over my head and the taste of blood in my mouth, I regained consciousness some time later. I was hot, and my face was swollen and painful. One of my lower teeth jiggled loosely. The car stopped, the doors opened and I was dragged out, hood still on, and marched up a flight of stairs. At the top, another door opened, and I was shoved, stumbling, into a room where someone punched me in the stomach and flung me backward onto a sofa.

Coughing and wheezing, I sucked air through the hood. Eventually it was yanked off, and I found myself sitting on a leather couch in a familiar setting. This was Big Lou Barazza's place in Little Italy on Mulberry Street. He was the asshole from last year who ran the drug ring upstate and tried to kill Kelly and me. The same asshole that I put in a coma with a crowbar when he admitted to murdering my father. This was definitely that apartment, and I was about to meet the new tenants.

On either side of me were the two goons from Vermont, and directly in front of me, leaning back on a desk, was a swarthy bull of a man with hair cut high and tight. He was maybe six feet one inch tall, 250 lbs., no neck, wearing dress pants, shoes and a black turtleneck. In his right hand was the largest handgun I had ever seen, the Colt .44 magnum, the Anaconda. His close-set, beady eyes bore into my soul. This had to be Boom Boom.

I said, "I think there has been a misunderstanding."

He didn't say anything.

There was a mug of coffee on the desk next to him, which he picked up with his ham hock-sized free hand. Taking a sip, he contemplated me. He was trying to get under my skin, and succeeding.

I repeated myself, "I really do believe there has been a misunderstanding."

He put the mug down. "I heard you the first time, asshole. So who—the fuck— are you?" he said, slowly and deliberately in a raspy, rumbling baritone.

"My name is John Cesari and I'm a doctor at St. Matt's Hospital. I'm a gastroenterologist."

"What's a gastroenterologist?"

"I specialize in diseases of the intestines."

He nodded.

"Do you know who I am?"

"No," I lied.

"My name is Salvatore Moretti, and you have something of mine."

"Mr. Moretti, I wish to reassure you that I have no idea what you are referring to. Like I said, I'm just a doctor."

"Did you know Big Lou Barazza or his pal Vito Gianelli?"

Better not lie to this one.

"Yes." I looked around the second floor apartment which was located above The Café Napoli, a busy trattoria serving traditional southern Italian cuisine. We were on Mulberry Street in Little Italy. The apartment hadn't changed much since the last time I'd been there.

"So tell me, how well did you know them?"

"Well, I grew up with Vito in the Bronx. Before I went to medical school, he and I were collectors for Frank Dellatesta," I said truthfully.

They all found this amusing, including Boom Boom, who bellowed in laughter. "Are you trying to be funny, Doc? You used to break legs for Frankie D. in the Bronx?"

"Yes. You can check it out. I was arrested twice for assault when I was twenty trying to make collections. They couldn't make either charge stick. Vito and I were in a major car accident on Pelham Parkway in the Bronx ten years ago. It's all part of the public record."

I could see they were starting to change their opinion of me. Boom Boom eyed me carefully, sizing me up.

"Where in the Bronx you from, Doc?"

"Allerton Avenue."

"I'm from Morris Park Avenue." Another well-known Italian enclave in the Bronx.

"I know that neighborhood well. I used to date a girl from Williamsbridge Road."

He nodded. "So why is your name all over an FBI file with Lou Barazza's and Vito Gianelli's?"

"Well, last year, and unbeknownst to me, Vito and Lou were running a prescription drug ring out of the hospital I worked at. When the feds came and broke it up, they thought I was involved because of my past relationship with Vito, but I wasn't. I didn't know anything about it, but the FBI are a cynical bunch to say the least, and although they let me off the hook, they insisted on putting an asterisk next to my name. That's probably why it's attached to that file you mentioned."

Boom Boom mulled that over and put the Colt down on the desk behind him. "Bobby, get the doc a cup of coffee and a wet towel to clean the blood off his face. Sorry about that, Doc." Bobby quickly disappeared into the kitchen.

"No problem. I would have done the same thing."

Boom Boom nodded approvingly at that, and the one called Bobby returned, handing me a towel and a cup of black coffee.

"Thanks. So what is it that you think I can help you with?" I wiped my face and took a sip of the coffee.

"Ten million dollars of my money went missing last year, and I want it back. Vito put Big Lou in a coma, stole the money, and left for parts unknown. We don't know if he's dead or in hiding, and so far, you're the only name we have."

"Vito put big Lou in a coma?"

Actually, Vito watched while *I* put Big Lou in a coma and took the loot, but this wasn't the time to set the record straight.

"That's the word on the street, and we think he's got the money. The question is, where do you fit in, and why is a New York City cop checking you out? That's how I found out about you in the first place. The cop in question found your name on that FBI file we're talking about, so he called me, thinking I might know you."

My curiosity got the better of me. "Why would a cop call you to find out something like that?"

"I'm asking the questions here, Doc, and don't make me say that again."

"I already told you how I fit in. The FBI mistakenly thought I was involved with Vito and Lou and wouldn't let go of it. You know how they can be. That cop who called you wouldn't be someone named Colin Murphy or Rick McGrath would he?" I suddenly had a stroke of genius.

He looked at me and then at his men. "You know those assholes?"

"Not personally, but they've been chasing after me for the last week."

"Why is that?"

I took another sip of coffee. Nice and strong. The way I liked it. "I accidentally came into possession of a large quantity of diamonds, and for some reason, those guys believe they belong to them. So instead of just asking me for them nicely, they've been taking pot shots at me all week and otherwise making my life miserable. Plus, they're such assholes. I went to Vermont last weekend for a little R&R, you know? They followed me up there and had two innocent guys arrested for no reason at the bed and breakfast where I was staying, just so they could get their rooms."

The two gorillas looked at each other and then at Boom Boom. Silence in the room.

"Tell me about these diamonds. How'd you come across them?"

"Believe it or not, some guy in an alley handed them to me literally seconds before one of those assholes put a bullet between his eyes. Then they tried to shoot me, too. That's all I know, I swear. I've been trying to stay alive ever since. I don't even want the damn diamonds. I really don't."

"Where are the diamonds now and how much are we talking about, Doc?"

"I have them in a safe deposit box. They haven't been formally appraised but my guess is they're worth close to five million dollars, and I also suspect there's probably more where they came from."

"And you don't want these diamonds?"

I shook my head, "I really don't. I wish to God that I had never come into contact with them. They've been causing me nothing but grief ever since I laid eyes on them. I just want to get rid of them and get these guys off my back."

"So where did they come from?"

"Not clear, but I have friends in the diamond business who say that there have been rumors of Russian diamonds being smuggled over here, but I'm not certain about that. Like I said, the guy who handed them to me had his brains blown out before he could tell me much."

He thought that one over.

"Doc, meet Bobby and Giorgio."

"Hi guys."

They nodded.

"Have you had breakfast yet?"

"No."

"Good. Then you'll eat with us while I check out your story with my guys in the Bronx." He put his hand out. "They call me Boom Boom."

R̫ 41

BOOM Boom clicked off the phone and looked at me. We were in his kitchen eating warm croissants with jam, thinly sliced imported prosciutto di Parma and freshly brewed espresso. Some of the benefits of living directly over the Café Napoli. Boom Boom had let me call my secretary to cancel my patients.

"Okay, Doc, your story checks out. There are still enough people around in the Bronx that remember you. They said you were pretty good, too."

"Thanks."

"Well, don't thank me just yet. There was also a rumor that you deliberately tried to kill Vito in a staged car accident years ago just before you suddenly disappeared to attend medical school. Care to elaborate on that?"

"There's not much to say other than it's total bullshit. Vito and I were pals. We were coming home from dinner late one night, and some drunk hit us while we were stopped at a light. Unfortunately, Vito didn't have his seat belt on. He didn't hold it against me, so I don't see why anyone else should."

I had tried my best to kill the prick, but the best I could do was a six month stay in the head trauma unit at Jacobi Hospital in the Bronx.

Boom Boom quietly studied me before coming to a decision. "Okay, Doc, it's ancient history. So what are we going to do about those diamonds?"

"They're yours if you want them. I just want to be left alone."

"Just like that? You don't want anything in return?"

"A finder's fee might be nice."

"I think I can help you with that." Bobby and Giorgio were stuffing their faces and slurping coffee. "How about five percent?"

"How about ten percent?"

"How about I throw you down a flight of stairs while we negotiate?" He sipped casually from his cup.

"Five will be fine, but I can't get them until Friday."

"Why not?"

"Like I said, the diamonds are in a safety deposit box, and as a security measure in case someone ever searched my apartment for the key, I sent it to the law firm of Keith, O'Malley & Goldfarb in Ohio. I'll call them and have them mail it to me. It'll take a couple of days to get through the paperwork."

The key was actually in the safe at the St. Mark's Hotel, but he didn't need to know that, and I needed some time to think.

"Fair enough, let's say Friday, then."

I agreed. "Friday, it is. I'll get the ball rolling with the key today. Can you keep me alive until then?"

"Don't worry, Doc. Bobby and Giorgio are going to be your guardian angels. You may not always see them, but they'll be right behind you. They're protecting my diamonds now."

"That's right," I said. Looking at Bobby and Giorgio, I had trouble picturing them blending discreetly into the background. They were both well over six feet tall and clearly ate too much red meat. Their slicked back hair and massive chests would make them hard to miss in a crowd.

"What about the rest of the diamonds? You said there might be more."

"That's the problem, Boom Boom. I don't know yet how many more diamonds there are or how they've been bringing them in. I just latched onto a lead and was going to launch my own investigation when your guys snatched me off the street."

Boom Boom reached out and slapped Bobby in the back of the head.

Bobby winced. "I'm sorry about that, Doc. It was a misunderstanding."

"It's okay, Bobby. I understand. Let's put it behind us."

"How can I help?" Boom Boom asked.

"I think having your guys covering my back will help a lot. But watch out for those cops, they're pretty tough guys."

Everybody at the table laughed. Boom Boom most of all. "I think we can handle them. Besides, we have a bone to pick with those guys anyway. It was Bobby and Giorgio they had arrested at the B&B last weekend."

"That was you guys?" I said incredulously. "What were you doing up there?"

Boom Boom was still chuckling. "They were looking for you, and I guess those fucks didn't want us to find out about the diamonds. They're going to pay for that one. I had to post $100,000 bail for each, which I'm never going to see again because they're not going back."

"Well, I'm glad we're on the same side, Boom Boom. May I call you Boom Boom?"

"Sure. Why not?"

"Thanks. Maybe I should be heading back now."

"Bobby, Giorgio, drive the Doc back and stay with him, okay? Don't let him out of your sight. You both know Rick and Murph, so it shouldn't be too hard to keep them away from the Doc. Let's exchange phone numbers, Doc, in case we get separated."

Bobby and Giorgio dropped me off at the entrance to the hospital at noon. We agreed that inside the hospital was probably safe for me, and that it would be smarter if they waited outside. I would call them when I came back out. I had to admit, I did feel safer already.

Up in the OR lounge, I ran into a gaggle of nurses waiting for their next case to start.

"Hi, Cesari."

I turned. "Oh, hi, Gina." She was wearing a big smile and blue surgical scrubs that barely contained her voluptuous body. Unlike every other guy in the room, I tried not to notice. Well, maybe not as hard as I could have.

She asked, "Do you have any cases today, and what happened to your lip?" I guess it was starting to swell pretty good.

"No cases today, Gina. Business isn't picking up as quickly as I had hoped. I hurt my lip playing basketball at the Y.M.C.A. this morning. It was just a pickup game. I've been trying to stay in shape and got an elbow in the face instead."

"I'm sorry. Well, in terms of business, you just have to be patient. There are plenty of people out there who need a colonoscopy. Things will pick up, I'm sure. I was just going down to the cafeteria to have lunch. Care to join me?"

She was cool. I had to give her that. You'd never know she'd just tried to sabotage my life. "I'd love to, Gina. I had a late breakfast, but I'm always in the mood for coffee."

In the cafeteria, she grabbed lunch and I got a coffee. We sat ourselves at a corner table in the very busy lunch room.

"Did everything go okay last night with Kelly?" she asked.

"What do you mean?"

"Did she suspect anything?"

I had forgotten about our little cover story. "No, everything's fine. All's well on the home front."

She was eating a Cobb salad, and it looked good. My coffee was nice and fresh, too, although nothing compared to the freshly brewed espresso from the Café Napoli.

I watched her facial expression carefully for signs of complicity, and found none. "What about you, Gina? Everything better today?"

"Yes, thanks to you."

"Well, I'm glad I could help. Do you have a busy schedule in the OR?"

"It's not too bad, but I'm on call with Reg tonight, and he has had such bad luck lately with night call. It seems like he always gets called in."

"Well, that's just luck of the draw I guess. Call cases can be unpredictable like that."

"Yeah, I know," she said, stretching like a cat, her breasts rising in the air and pointing straight at me. She spotted my gaze and smiled. "It's funny, but no one's seen Reg today. He didn't have any cases scheduled, but he likes to come in and check on the worker bees, if you know what I mean."

"Well, I'm sure he'll show up. He always does."

My cellphone rang. It was Cheryl. "Excuse me, Gina. I have to answer this." I stood up and walked to a more private area.

"Hi, Cheryl."

"Hello, Cesari."

"How'd your weekend go?"

"Actually, it turned out quite nice. Pascal and I hit it off pretty well, and he'll be coming down to the city this weekend to visit me."

"I think that's great."

"But that's not why I'm calling, Cesari."

"I'm listening."

"I did a little research on those cops you told me about, and they are definitely on Santa's naughty list. Even worse for you is that one of them, the Rick McGrath character, went to school with none other than Boom Boom Moretti himself. They spent a year together at City College before both dropped out. McGrath fancies himself a bit of a wiseguy, so doubtless, he was the one who called Moretti asking about you. But that's not the best part. Rick McGrath is the son of the late city Comptroller, Isabelle McGrath, who had a brother by the name of—are you ready for this?"

I was captivated. "Yes, who?"

"Reginald Griffin III."

"You're kidding?"

"I wish I was, Cesari. So watch out. They got eyes on you. Look, I've got to go. I hope that helps."

"It does, and thanks. Bye."

So Rick McGrath was Reg's nephew. Now that was interesting. This was getting more complicated by the minute. What the hell was going on here? I returned to the table, and Gina was almost finished with her lunch.

"Sorry about that, Gina."

"Everything okay?" she asked pleasantly.

"Everything's fine."

"You know, Cesari, I wish there was something more I could do to thank you for your help last night." She glanced at me seductively, and

I felt my knees get weak. Jesus, I'm a grown man, and I could barely defend myself against her.

"You've already thanked me enough, Gina. You don't owe me anything."

"Are you sure?" she said, running her tongue slowly along her upper lip.

Man, she was a piece of work, but I decided to play along.

I cleared my throat nervously and smiled back, my eyes lingering on her cleavage just a little too long. "Yeah, I'm sure. Look, I really don't want to get in trouble, Gina. Kelly's the jealous type. If you know what I mean?"

She smiled again, sensing weakness. I was in her jungle now and she knew it.

She lowered her voice, never taking her eyes off of me. "I understand perfectly, and I would be very discreet."

I hesitated. "I don't know, Gina."

She looked at the wall clock. "I have to go back to work now. Can I call you later?" She stood slowly, allowing me a full view.

"Sure, I'll be around all day."

She leaned across the table and touched my hand. "I meant much later— like after work."

I took a deep breath and felt my pulse quicken. "Sure."

I watched her backside as she walked away and exhaled slowly. Damn, women like that should be outlawed. I told myself to stay focused. What was she up to, and where was Reg? I finished my coffee, thinking things through. My cell phone went off again.

"Hi Kel, how's it going?"

"I'm exhausted. I'm going straight to bed tonight, so don't get any ideas. By the way, everything's okay today. You're not going to be a father, so you can start breathing again."

"Thanks for letting me know. Well, I'm sorry you're having a bad day. Don't forget I have that appointment with the sex addiction counselor tonight."

"I did forget. That's so ridiculous that you have to do that."

"I know, but I have to play ball. Despite our suspicions, we have no real proof yet of any wrongdoing, and Reg is still my boss, so I have to do what he says."

"Okay, well I'll see you afterwards unless I'm asleep. In which case, please don't wake me up. Bye."

"Bye."

I killed the rest of the afternoon reading journals and doing on-line medical education activities. At five-thirty, I headed out and let my bodyguards know where I was going. They trailed a short distance behind.

I arrived at the Givelber building and hopped on an elevator to the tenth floor, where I found Pam Gottlieb's office. I was spending way too much time up here. The door was open, so I took a seat in the waiting room and flipped through a magazine. A short time later, she came out wearing a big smile and another short skirt. She must have a closet full of them.

"Hello, John, welcome back."

"Hi, Pam."

"Well, come on in, and we'll get started. I must say, I was pretty excited when I heard you were on the schedule for additional counseling."

I walked past her. "Shut up, Pam."

The circle of chairs was gone, stacked off to one side of the room. There was now a long sofa and a plush lazy boy chair next to it. "You've got to be kidding," I said. Her desk was in the same place with a high-top, black leather chair behind it.

"You can sit or lie down. That's your decision, but the important thing is to relax during these sessions. Tension is our enemy, and we want to get to the bottom of your problem."

I sat down on the sofa. "I don't have a problem."

"Let's talk about that. So, why do you think you're here tonight then?" Sitting down next to me on the lazy boy chair, she crossed her legs. She had great calves that looked even better in the nylons she wore. I tried not to look. There was a legal pad on her lap, and she took notes with a Mont Blanc fountain pen.

"I'm here because some girl in medical records has a crush on me and decided to act on it just as the chairman of the department walked in. He's terrified over any possibility of a scandal, and so here I am."

"So, it's not your fault that you're here."

"Exactly."

"Hmm, I see. John, I need to ask you a few background questions. It's just a formality. Is that okay?"

"Fire away, Doc."

"Did you ever accidentally walk in on your parents having sex?"

I raised my eyebrows in surprise. "I'm not answering that."

"Do you masturbate?"

"I'm not answering that, either. I didn't do anything and I'm not a sex addict."

"Hmm."

"Will you stop saying that? And while we're at it, have you ever asked yourself why you always wear short skirts and high heels? Maybe you're the one with the problem."

"Very hostile today. Why is that?"

I grunted and lay down on the sofa, hands behind my head, legs crossed at the ankles. "I'm not having a great day."

"I can see that. What happened to your face?"

"I got punched."

"Really?"

"Really."

"What happened?"

"Some guy didn't like my face. It's okay. We're friends now."

"Really?" She looked astonished as she scribbled furiously on her note pad.

"Really."

"So tell me about this girl."

"There's nothing to tell. She's a girl. She likes me. She got carried away and I got detention."

"Do you always blame others for your problems?"

I stared at the drop ceiling overhead and started counting the tiles in my head. "Only if it's true, Pam. Only if it's true."

"Why don't you like the way I dress?"

"I didn't say that."

"You find it threatening."

"No—maybe a little."

"Why?"

"I don't know. It's distracting."

"You feel like you might lose self-control and that bothers you?"

"I don't lose self-control, so no."

"How old were you when you lost your virginity?"

"Thirteen."

"Really?"

"Really, and where are we going with this?"

"Was it with a family member?"

"That's disgusting."

There was a knock on the door. She looked up and then at her watch. It was only six-thirty. We weren't supposed to finish until seven.

"Next appointment, Pam?"

"I don't have a next appointment. Let me go see who it is. I do apologize." She left into the outer room. The sound of gruff voices arguing with her could be heard through the closed door, and a minute later she returned with two men, Colin Murphy and Rick McGrath, weapons drawn.

"Don't move, asshole," Rick growled, pointing his .45 at me.

"Is that really necessary, officers?" Pam asked, becoming visibly alarmed at the sight of firearms. "Please don't resist, John."

"Listen to the doctor, Cesari, and you won't get hurt. Now get on your knees, hands behind your head."

"Okay, but please don't hurt her, all right? She's got nothing to do with this and doesn't know anything."

"Why would they hurt me?" Pam asked, bewildered.

Once in position, Murph got behind me, slapping handcuffs tightly on my wrists. He then grabbed me roughly by the arm, dragged me to my feet and punched me in the stomach. I coughed, wheezed and doubled over in pain.

"That's for the little stunt you pulled in Vermont."

Rick came over and slapped me in the face with the side of his gun. I winced, spit blood and saw stars.

Pam was indignant. "You can't do that! That's police brutality. Aren't you even going to tell him why he's under arrest?"

"Sure," he said, and slapped me again. "You're under arrest for murder."

"Who did he murder?" Pam persisted. "And please stop hitting him!"

Murph reached down his leg and pulled out a second weapon from an ankle holster: a small revolver, maybe a .32, what the police liked to call a throw-away.

"Run, Pam. Run!" I yelled.

"Run? Why should I run? I didn't do anything, and who did he murder?" She was frightened now. There was an ominous vibe in the room.

"You." Murph turned toward her with an evil grin, aiming the revolver at her heart. He was only inches away, and she froze, wide-eyed as he cocked the trigger.

A loud voice boomed from the doorway. "Drop it, Murph."

Bobby and Giorgio had burst into the room. Bobby held small cannons in each hand; they looked like .45's, and Giorgio, a sawed-off shotgun. They didn't look like they were in a good mood. Murph and Rick were out of position, outgunned and facing the wrong way. Murph held the little gun, still pointing at Pam, and Rick had holstered his piece. The .32 would do little more than irritate guys as big as Bobby and Giorgio, assuming he even got a shot off. Of course, Pam and I would get caught in the crossfire in the event of a shootout, but that's not what happened.

After a brief moment of hesitation, Murph uncocked his weapon and gently laid it on the floor as they both slowly turned to face the newcomers.

"This is police business, Bobby," Rick said, recognizing Boom Boom's boy.

Bobby wasn't impressed. "Hands in the air, assholes, now."

Rick, Murph, and Pam put their hands up.

"Not you, Pam," I said. She looked at Bobby, who nodded, and then she collapsed onto the floor, sobbing.

"On your bellies, hands behind your heads," Giorgio shouted.

"We're NYPD; you can't do this." For his effort, Murph got slammed in the face with the stock of Giorgio's shotgun.

When they were lying face down, Giorgio frisked and disarmed them. Bobby took a running start and kicked Rick as hard as he could in his side. Two or three ribs cracked loudly, and he gasped in pain.

Giorgio wasn't quite as sophisticated as Bobby. He lifted Pam's lazy boy chair high over his head and brought it crashing down onto Murph's back. I didn't hear anything break, but from the way Murphy groaned, he was going to have to seek immediate medical attention.

"That's for all the aggravation you caused us over the weekend," Bobby said.

Rick hissed through clenched teeth, "What the fuck are you talking about?"

"Shut up." And he kicked him again, only this time in the face. "Giorgio, uncuff the doc and let's get out of here."

"What are we going to do with these scumbags, Bobby?"

"Not my problem, Giorgio."

Giorgio released me from the restraints, and I rubbed my wrists where the cuffs had bit into them. "Thanks for the rescue, guys, but it wouldn't be fair to Dr. Gottlieb to leave them here. How is she going to explain this to anyone?"

Bobby scratched his head in thought. "I guess you got a point. Hey, I got an idea. Let's bring them down to the basement."

Pam was catatonic and hyperventilating. I put my arm around her and held her close to me. "You're going to be all right, Pam. Take a deep breath and let it out slowly. There you go, just like that. I want you to come with me. Okay? We'll take you home."

She was trembling uncontrollably. "He was going to kill me."

"Yes, he was, but he didn't, and now you're okay."

"But why?" She buried her face in my chest, crying.

"It's a long story, and I can't explain it right now."

Bobby was busy dragging Rick by the hair. "C'mon, Doc, we can't stay here all night. The cleaning people are bound to show up."

"Who is he?" Pam asked, nodding at Bobby.

"He's the one who didn't like my face."

She turned suddenly and threw up on the floor.

R̂x 42

WE took a cab and dropped Pam off at her apartment on Charles Street in the West Village. She had collected herself by then, but remained very quiet. Stunned by the day's events, she decided to take the rest of the week off. I went with her up to the fifth floor apartment.

"Are you going to be okay, Pam?" I asked gently as we reached her door.

She nodded and fumbled for her keys. "I don't know. I need a drink desperately. Would you like to have one with me? I'd really like that."

"I'll have to take a rain check, Pam. I'm sorry. I hate to leave you alone after what just happened, but those guys are waiting for me in the cab downstairs and we have unfinished business."

"I understand. What were those men going to do to you?"

"Nothing good, Pam. Nothing good. I really can't go into it. Look, I have to go. You have my number. Call me for anything, okay?"

She nodded, unlocked her door and stood on the threshold looking at me. "Thank you, John. I feel like I may have misjudged you"

"Not to worry, Pam. Do you mind if I call you tomorrow just to see how you're doing?"

"No, I don't mind at all. In fact, I'd appreciate that. What's going to happen to them? Were they real cops?"

"They were real, all right, and I don't know what's going to happen. They're missing their badges and weapons now and no easy way to explain it. That kind of stuff doesn't go over well with the NYPD. My guess is they'll make up some ridiculous story. Anything but the truth. The good news is they're both injured pretty badly, so we won't have to worry about them bothering us for a while."

"My God, Cesari. Who are you?"

"Just a guy in counseling."

"Yeah, right."

"I'll call you tomorrow, Pam."

I went outside to where Bobby and Giorgio were waiting.

"She okay, Doc?" Bobby asked.

"I think so. She's pretty tough. A couple of drinks, a good night's rest and everything will seem different in the morning."

It was after eight o'clock when the boys dropped me off at my apartment.

"Thanks for everything guys, and have a great night."

"We called Boom Boom, and he said we should come back tomorrow. Just letting you know."

"Then I would do whatever Boom Boom says."

"That's the way we figured it."

I went inside the hotel and up to the room. Kelly was already sound asleep. She really was tired. I left a note on her night table telling her that I'd gone out for a walk.

Out on Third Avenue, I found a coffee shop and sat down. The waitress poured me a cup of black coffee, and I thought about what had just transpired. Bobby had wanted to finish those guys off, but I was able to talk him out of it. That might have been a mistake on my part, but only time would tell. So we'd compromised, and brought them down to the basement where we cuffed them buck naked to pipes in the boiler room. While I was with Pam, Bobby called EMS and had an ambulance dispatched to pick them up. Rick was wheezing terribly from broken ribs, and Murph might have a broken spine. They hadn't looked too good.

I looked around the coffee shop, people watching. Couples talking about the day's events. Kids hanging out with laptops, I-Pads, and

Kindles. Baristas proudly making their lattes. The counter was filled with pastries, cookies and pre-made sandwiches. I liked places like this. They were full of life. I had a ham and cheese sandwich on ciabatta for dinner, read a newspaper and passed the time away. I was wound up pretty good.

I started to yawn when my cell phone went off. It was Gina. I had almost forgotten that she was going to call. It was 10 p.m.

"Hi, Gina."

"Hi, Cesari."

"It's kind of late, Gina, don't you think?"

"I'm sorry. You said I could call you. Can you talk?"

"I am talking." I signaled the waitress for my bill.

"Where's Kelly?"

"She's sleeping. We've had some pretty late nights recently, and she's exhausted. I was just thinking about hitting the sack myself. So, what's up?"

"Can I see you? It's important."

I hesitated, but dove in head first. "Where are you?"

"I'm in the OR lounge. Where are you?"

"I'm just down the block in a coffee shop. Give me five minutes."

"Okay, see you."

I left cash on the table and walked the short distance to the hospital. Maybe ten minutes later, I was standing in the OR lounge with Gina.

"What's up, Gina?" She looked great, and kept batting those big eyes at me. I had always been a sucker for big eyes. I wondered why that was. There must have been some evolutionary reason for it.

I walked around the table and sat down in a chair opposite her. She followed me around and sat on the edge of the table next to me. She was in blue surgical scrubs, so she'd either never went home or had gotten called back in. She faced me and was close enough that her calf brushed my thigh.

I looked at her. "So, what's going on?"

"It's complicated, Cesari."

"I'm a pretty smart guy. I can handle it. Besides, I have time. Like I said, Kelly's sound asleep."

"Is she? Good."

"Why's that good?"

"This way she won't worry about you."

"Why would she worry about me?"

"You know..." She smiled and batted her eyes again.

"Is this a booty call, Gina?"

She liked that, and said coyly, "Do you want it to be?"

"I haven't made up mind yet about that."

"Well, that's not exactly why I called," she explained, shifting gears. "I'm worried about Reg. No one's heard from him since early this morning. He came in briefly to see patients, but that's it. He fell off the radar."

"I remember you mentioning that at lunch. Maybe he's sick and just keeping a low profile."

She looked concerned. "I don't think so. He's on call tonight and I've been trying to reach him for hours. I've called him over and over on his cellphone, paged him and I've even called the manager of his apartment building on the Upper East Side. He went up personally and knocked on his door. This is not like him. He's definitely not around. The manager told me Reg checked his car out of the garage this morning and hasn't been seen since."

I thought about that. "Okay, fair enough. He's AWOL, but what's that got to do with me?"

"He's upset."

"About what?"

She looked away, embarrassed.

"C'mon, Gina, it's late."

"He was upset because I told him I couldn't see him anymore."

I studied her carefully. I wasn't expecting that kind of an admission. Nor did I fully believe it. Reg was a big boy and was married. I found it hard to accept that he would go over the deep end like that because of a girl thirty years his junior. And if she dumped him, why did she write that note trying to make him jealous? Trying to figure out women was becoming a full time job for me. Nonetheless, stranger things have happened. I had to admit my curiosity was getting the better of me. I didn't just want to know what was going on. I needed to know. Besides, hanging around Gina wasn't exactly the most unpleasant experience I had ever had. The endorphin rush was pretty intense. Was she really a man-eater like Kelly said? If she was, I bet those guys went to their deaths willingly.

I took a deep breath and let it out slowly, feigning surprise. "I see. I didn't know you two were—friends."

She sighed. "Hardly anyone knew. We were very careful because he's married. Look, it was a mistake. I know that now, so please don't judge me, all right? Anyway, it was time to move on, and he didn't handle it well."

"I don't judge people, Gina. He just needs some time. He's a grown man. He'll be okay."

"Maybe, but I don't want his career to suffer because of me."

"What do you mean?"

"Like I said, he's on call for the ER tonight, and if he doesn't show up to do his cases then he'll be accused of dereliction of duty."

She was right about that. Agreeing to be on call was a serious obligation. Shirking that responsibility would have serious ramifications both locally and on the state level.

"What do you want me to do? Try to find him? I wouldn't even know where to begin."

She glanced around furtively. "No, I don't think you'll find him if I can't. I thought maybe you could take call for him tonight so he won't get in trouble. I'm hoping that he'll come to his senses by morning."

"I see now. You want me to cover the ER for him. You could've just said so on the phone, Gina. Well, consider it done. I've got his back. I'll tell the ER that they should call me the rest of the night and not Reg. Well, if that's all. That's no big deal."

I stood up to leave, and she placed a hand firmly on my shoulder. I sat back down, but she didn't take her hand off me. In fact, she used the opportunity to slide over, and was now sitting more or less in front of me, her legs slightly parted, pressing against me.

"There's more," she said and exhaled slowly. "One of his patients came into the ER earlier today, and before he disappeared, Reg gave orders to prep him for a colonoscopy tonight. The guy's perfectly stable, but has been waiting all day and is expecting to go home if everything turns out okay. Reg usually likes to finish office hours and then go have dinner with his wife before coming back to do cases like this. He doesn't like to let work interfere with his personal life, even if he has to do the case late at night. The problem now is that if he doesn't show up to perform the procedure, he's going to be in hot water, and I feel responsible for putting him in this frame of mind."

"What are you getting at, Gina?"

"I want you to do the colonoscopy for Reg."

I hesitated but quickly recovered. "I see, but if the guy is stable like you say, can't Reg just do it tomorrow? I mean, he's bound to show up eventually, and it's his patient after all. He might get upset if I just waltz in and take over."

"Don't you see, Cesari? Waiting until tomorrow would be even worse. By morning, administrators, case management and social workers are going to be crawling over this case trying to figure out why this guy has been hanging out in our ER all night. The ER staff is going to be wild about it, too, and what if Reg still doesn't show up? Cesari, you have to help me out here. I'm just trying to do some damage control for Reg. I'm sure he would be very grateful, and I know I will."

With that, she slid off the table and onto my lap in one smooth move. Her lips were inches from mine, and her hands rested on my chest. I should have pushed her away, but I couldn't. We had just crossed that line you're not supposed to cross, and we both knew it. I was starting to tingle all over.

I sighed deeply. This wasn't what I'd expected. I was trying to figure out what Reg did late at night with Gina, not what I did late at night with Gina. Furthermore, I didn't like the idea of scoping one of the boss's patients without his direct permission, but she was right about how much trouble Reg would be in if he didn't show up for a planned procedure. This was a clear-cut case of patient abandonment and could get his license suspended. The problem was that I suspected him of much worse crimes, but had not one shred of evidence other than Gina's note, which didn't prove anything except that I might be an extortionist. Alternatively, he might not be guilty of anything other than letting the little head make decisions for the big head, but who hasn't gone down that road once or twice?

"Give me a second to think, Gina."

She watched as I took my cellphone out and dialed Reg. Up close, she smelled nice. She made no move to get off my lap, and I made no move to get her off. I was already guilty of something. The call went directly to voicemail.

I looked at her some more as I thought it over, and she wrapped her arms around my neck to encourage me. There was me, Gina and a table. As if reading my mind, she mouthed the words "Bad Boy" at me. If I wanted to find out what was going on, this might be a good start. For whatever reason, she desperately wanted me to do this case. My whole life, I had wondered how Adam could have fallen for that trick with the apple, and now I knew.

"Okay, Gina, let's get a move on. I don't want to be here all night. What's the guy's name?"

She jumped up. "Alexander Raskolnikov. He's forty-two years old and has had rectal bleeding for two days. His blood counts are stable and I'll do all the paper work. Okay?"

"Does he know I'll be doing the colonoscopy and not Reg?"

"I'll explain everything to him and get the consent. He'll be fine."

I nodded. "I'll change into scrubs. Should we call in another nurse?"

"That won't be necessary. There's no point in bothering someone else at this hour. I can handle it."

"All right then, let's get this show on the road."

R̽ 43

❝OKAY, Gina, you can turn the lights down. He looks pretty comfortable." The patient lay on his left side, facing away from me with his legs curled up. We called this the left lateral decubitus position. It wasn't really the fetal position, although most people thought of it like that. He was gently snoring from the effects of the sedation I had given him through his IV line. The video monitor was directly across from me, and Gina stood on my left.

"Are you sure that we don't need another nurse?" I asked again. I had never done a colonoscopy with only one nurse before and felt a little uneasy.

"Relax, Cesari. We'll be fine. Reg and I have done many cases like this. Besides, do you really want to wait another hour for someone to get here? It's almost midnight."

"No, not particularly. All right, let's start."

Turning around, I picked the colonoscope off of the cart and checked all the dials and operational buttons. Once powered up, the light source glowed brightly in the dark room. I hoisted the scope over my shoulder and turned back to the patient.

"Okay, here we go. Reg owes me big time for this."

"I do, too," Gina said, playfully tapping my foot with hers.

Ignoring her flirtation, I lubricated the tip of the colonoscope and inserted it gently, focusing my full attention on the video monitor as I gradually advanced the scope through the colon.

"At least he's nice and cleaned out," Gina commented.

"You're right about that." There's nothing more annoying than struggling your way through a poorly prepped colon in the middle of the night, but he was a young guy, and it was an easy exam. Within ten minutes, I had reached the cecum, the proximal end of the colon where the large intestine met the small bowel. He slept comfortably throughout the whole thing.

"What the hell is that?" I commented, as an odd-looking object suddenly appeared in view. It was not a tumor or anything natural to the colon and was stained with fecal matter. It looked enormous on the screen, magnified greatly by the optics, but was probably no more than two inches wide and three inches long. I pushed on it with the tip of the colonoscope to see if I could move it, but couldn't. It seemed to be firmly attached to the colon wall. My first thought was that he had swallowed something and it had gotten stuck there for some reason.

"Is the cleaning apparatus set up, Gina? I need to wash this off to get a better view." She was awfully quiet for some reason.

"Yes, it is. The peddle is right by your left foot."

I glanced downward, stepped on it, and watched water spray out from the tip of the colonoscope, rinsing the object clean. It was a brown leather pouch with a drawstring, and I could see now that it had been clipped to the colon wall with metal surgical clips, the type that we used all the time in endoscopic procedures.

"What do you think it is, Gina?"

"I don't know. Drugs, maybe?"

"Could be, although drugs are usually packaged in plastic bags and not leather pouches with drawstrings. I've never encountered anything like this before. I can't just leave it there. He might develop an obstruction or perforation, but I'm not sure how to get it out either. Those clips look like they're in there pretty tight. Any ideas?"

"How many clips are there?" she asked.

I pushed and prodded the pouch with the scope to see around it as best I could. "Looks like there are three of them."

"Don't they normally fall off after a few days?"

"Actually, they can last up to a week, but yeah, generally they just slough off with time. Why?"

"Maybe you should leave it alone. You know, let nature take its course. It'll probably just pass on its own in a few days."

I thought about that. "I don't know if I like that option, Gina. If anything happens to this guy, everyone will blame me for not doing something when I had the chance. You know how that is. I mean, what if it's filled with a toxic substance and it leaks out? He could die."

She nodded sympathetically at my dilemma. "Good point. Well, if the clips just fall off with time, doesn't that mean that they're not buried too deeply into the bowel wall? Maybe you could yank them off without too much difficulty." She sounded very reasonable and her logic made sense.

"I see what you mean, and you're right. He might bleed a little, though. They don't seem that shallow to me. Whoever put them there buried them in good, but still, they should come out relatively easily. They're not meant to be permanent."

She looked at me supportively. "If he starts bleeding, we can fix it with more clips. I also have epinephrine and the heater probe set up on the cart behind us."

"You're prepared for everything, aren't you?"

"This ain't my first rodeo, Cesari."

I chuckled. "Okay then, Gina, why don't you hand me the snare and I'll give it a whirl? By the way, he's not on any anticoagulants, is he?"

"No, he's a healthy guy on no medications. I checked."

She handed me the long plastic sheath that covered the metal snare, and I inserted it into one of the ports at the proximal end of the colonoscope. I fed it through the length of the instrument until I saw it emerge on the video monitor.

I relaxed and sized up the situation, trying to decide on the best approach. "Let the snare out slowly, Gina."

She advanced the snare out as I instructed, and the metal loop emerged slowly from its plastic sheath. When it was fully deployed, the snare was slightly wider than the width of the leather pouch. Once in position around the small bag, I had Gina close the snare, grasping it tightly where the metal clips held it in place to the colon wall.

I looked at Gina. "Are you ready?" I took a deep breath and let it out.

She nodded, and sensed my tension. "Relax, Cesari. Everything will be fine."

Tugging on my end of the snare, I watched it pull against the leather pouch. I tugged harder, and watched the colon wall stretch towards me. It took a few more test pulls before I was sure how much force was going to be necessary. I looked at Gina one last time and turned back to the screen.

This was what I'd come for, so let's do it. I pulled and twisted the colonoscope forcefully towards me. At first there was resistance, but it gave way. In my effort, I had pulled so hard that when the pouch detached from the colon wall, the scope recoiled like a spring, rapidly retreating from its original position. The pouch was firmly in the grasp of the snare, but its proximity to the tip of the scope impaired my field of view so I decided to withdraw the scope all the way rather than risk losing the bag. It was an easy matter to pull the scope out of the guy, and I deposited the pouch onto the scope cart behind us.

I heard Gina breathe a sigh of relief. "Want to open it, Gina?"

"I don't think we should, Cesari. What if there are drugs in it? We could get in trouble. We could be accused of tampering with evidence."

"Open it, Gina. I'll take full responsibility."

There was a drawstring at the top of the pouch, and she gently pulled on it, spilling a dozen or so large diamonds into a specimen container. So, that's how they did it.

"Wow," I said.

She agreed.

"C'mon, Gina, let's finish up here and then you and I have a lot to talk about." I turned around to reinsert the colonoscope while she placed a cover on the container with the diamonds. Once the scope was reinserted, I realized I was in trouble. There was blood everywhere.

"Shit."

I advanced the scope through the colon as best I could, but the going was a lot slower this time around because of the blood obscuring visibility. It was kind of like driving at night in dense fog. The patient groaned in discomfort as the effects of the sedation wore off.

"Give him another two milligrams of Versed, Gina. I need him quiet."

"I'll have to get some from the medication cart in the other room. I didn't bring extra. Give me one second, and I'll be right back."

"Okay, but hurry up. This looks serious." She dashed off while I struggled, trying to advance the scope to the site of hemorrhage.

Holy shit. Look at this. He's already going to need a transfusion, and I didn't even know if there was any blood on hold for him in the blood bank. Continuously washing and aspirating in a frustrating effort to clean my field of view, I rapidly used up the scope's water reservoir and watched as the last few drops sputtered out.

According to the monitor, his heart rate was creeping up and his blood pressure was dropping from blood loss. Not good. Several minutes later, I was still waiting for Gina. Where the fuck was she?

I called out anxiously. "Gina?"

No response.

With great difficulty, I finally reached the site in the colon where I had ripped the clips off, and saw an artery pumping blood fast across the screen. It was a fairly large caliber vessel, and the stream of blood was thick and bright red. I needed water to clean the field in front of me. I needed epinephrine to slow the bleeding. I needed clips to clamp the vessel. I needed a drink to calm my nerves.

"Gina! Hurry up," I shouted, panic etched in my voice.

I placed the scope down on the stretcher behind the patient, and leaned over him so I could increase the flow rate of his IV fluids. I turned around and searched the cart for the epinephrine and clips. I glanced back at the screen and saw nothing but red. The white sheet he was lying on was turning crimson as blood oozed out from him around the scope still in his rectum. There was no epinephrine or clips on the cart as Gina had said, and the heater probe wasn't set up either. Damn. She had said everything was ready to go.

"Gina! Forget the goddamned Versed and get back here. I need you!" I was starting to lose it. I needed help.

The monitor wailed its warnings at me as his blood pressure reached critically low values and still no Gina. As I scanned the room, looking for anything that might help me, I noticed something amiss. He wasn't moaning anymore. I grabbed him by the shoulder and shook him. "Hey, are you okay?"

Nothing, so I rolled him over onto his back. He wasn't breathing. I looked at his heart monitor and saw nothing but disordered activity. He was in full cardiac arrest.

Shit.

Blood splattered everywhere as I yanked the colonoscope out with one big pull. I ran to the phone on the wall and called in a cardiac arrest in the OR and began one man CPR, but I knew that without blood or surgery he was gone.

Fucking Gina.

I performed mouth-to-mouth breathing and pumped on his chest furiously to the point of exhaustion. By the time the hospital emergency response team arrived, I was ready to have my own heart attack. They took over, and I sat on a stool panting, covered in perspiration. Someone called for blood.

I watched them intubate him, put in more IV lines, and then shock him multiple times. His chest heaved from the artificial respirations of an ambu-bag. It wouldn't work. He needed blood. It was on the way, but would take time. After thirty minutes, the leader of the code team, Art, declared it over.

"Okay, everybody. That's it. There's nothing more we can do here. I'm pronouncing him dead at 12:51 a.m. Everybody okay with that?"

Two seconds later, a nurse came flying into the room holding two units of blood in her hands. "Am I too late?"

Art said, "Thank you, Mary, but he's gone. Sometimes it's just not meant to be."

He came over to me and sat down while the nurses prepared the body for the morgue. "Want to tell me what happened here, Cesari?"

I was in shock. "I don't know what happened, Art. I was doing a call case. He was a young guy with a lower GI bleed, and I found a foreign object in his colon. I removed it, and he started bleeding like stink. I've never seen anything like it before. The nurse who was assisting me left the room to get more Versed because the guy was getting uncomfortable, and she never returned. I was here all alone trying to stop the bleeding, and the next thing I know, he's not breathing. I felt like the little Dutch boy with his finger in the dike."

"How come he doesn't have an ID bracelet, Cesari?"

"Who?"

"The dead guy."

"I don't know. I didn't notice. He's an ER patient."

Art looked at me, puzzled. "Who is?"

"The dead guy. C'mon, Art, what's with the third degree? Can't you see I'm a little upset? His name is Alexander Raskolnikov. He's been in the ER all day."

"The hell he has, Cesari, and stop yanking my chain. I've been in charge of the ER for the last twelve hours, and I've never seen or heard of this guy. I was just finishing up my shift when they called the code."

I looked at him for a long time before answering. I stammered, "I don't know what to say to that. That's what Gina, my nurse, told me when she admitted him for the procedure."

"That's another thing. There doesn't seem to be any paperwork on this guy. I mean *nothing*, and where is this nurse, Gina? No one's seen her either."

"I don't know where she is. Like I said before, she disappeared in the middle of the case and never returned." I was getting a sinking feeling in the pit of my stomach.

"Look, Cesari, I don't know you that well, but I have to tell you something. Come morning, you had better have some answers that make sense about what happened here. Right now, this is looking a little fishy."

I nodded. "I know it does, and thanks for the advice." As we talked, the stretcher with the body rolled past, and we angled away to let it pass. I let out a deep breath.

"Okay, Cesari, try to get some rest and we'll straighten this out tomorrow."

"Good night, Art."

He left with the nurses, and I sat there quietly by myself, contemplating what had just happened. I was shaken to the core as I gazed at the mess. Housekeeping would be here in a few minutes to cleanup. There was blood all over the floor, along with gauzes, dirty towels, needles and used IV bags. There was nothing messier in all of medicine than watching a guy exsanguinate before your eyes.

I walked around the room in a trance with no particular purpose in mind. I didn't see the little leather bag or the diamonds, but they could easily have been misplaced or tossed in the trash in all the chaos.

234

I searched the floor and saw nothing. The trash can was overflowing with debris, and I rummaged around in it, but didn't find anything. I turned it over and spilled its contents onto the floor. Several bottles tinkled onto the tiled surface, but no brown pouch or diamonds. Had Gina taken them? Well, of course she had, but what was the point of leaving me in the lurch like that?

I looked at the small bottles on the floor. Several had been used during the code, including epinephrine, atropine, and vasopressin. There was a bottle of Versed from the colonoscopy, and lastly, there was an empty bottle of Heparin which I picked up to study. Heparin was a potent, rapidly acting anticoagulant. No one in their right mind would inject a patient with a full bottle of heparin right before a surgical procedure or during a code. Where had it come from?

The realization of just how badly I had been fucked slowly dawned on me. Gina, what did you do? That's what I get for thinking I could outsmart a girl with large breasts.

I ran over to the phone and called the lab. "Hi, this is Dr. Cesari."

"Yes, Dr. Cesari."

"There was a code up in the operating room a little while ago. Did you get any blood work on the guy?"

"Yes. we did. Five tubes of blood came down on a John Doe. We heard the code ended unsuccessfully and were going to discard them. Why?"

"Could you do me a favor?"

"Sure, what do you need, Doctor?"

"Please run an activated partial prothrombin time on one of the tubes, and do you have the ability to test for the presence of heparin?" The partial prothrombin time or PTT was a simple blood test which would tell me just how badly off his ability to clot had been.

"We most certainly can do both. The partial prothrombin time will take about an hour, and the other one will probably take the rest of the night. I'm sure by morning I'll be able to give you an answer."

"Thanks."

R̶x 44

IT was 3 a.m. when I arrived at the Saint Mark's hotel and passed out on the bed next to Kelly. My last thought as I drifted off was that she was going to kill me when she found out what had happened.

The next morning, I woke late, and Kelly was already gone. I jumped in the shower, dressed and ran to work. I got to the OR at eleven and was dressed and ready to work by eleven-fifteen. I was only forty-five minutes late for my first case. For some surgeons, that was still fifteen minutes early.

I walked into the pre-op area, greeted my ten o'clock patient and apologized for my tardiness. I whipped through his and four other colonoscopies in record time and by one-thirty found myself ready to pass out from hunger. I had choked down a cup of coffee and some crackers in between cases, but was ready for a meal. I hadn't seen Gina all morning and wasn't quite sure how I was going to approach her when I did. Yesterday, I had been concerned about whether Reg was capable of murder, but now it was Gina I was worried about.

As I headed toward the cafeteria, the lab called me and confirmed my suspicion that the John Doe, or Alex Raskolnikov, or whoever he really had been, had been injected with a high dose of heparin, a potent blood thinner just prior to the procedure. His coagulation studies were off the chart, and he would've been at high risk to bleed to death no matter what I did. When I yanked those clips out of him, I'd inadvertently facilitated the process. Basically, he sprung a leak, and couldn't clot it off.

Fucking Gina.

My cell phone went off. It was Reg. I guess he was over whatever it was he'd needed to get over.

"Could you meet me in my office, Cesari?"

"Sure. When?"

"Now."

"I'm on the way."

His office was one floor up from the OR, and I arrived there five minutes later. I had grabbed a couple of leftover donut holes from the lounge and chugged them down on the elevator.

I knocked on his door and he beckoned me to enter. He sat in a leather chair behind his large mahogany desk, the top of which was cluttered with charts, papers and a laptop.

"Hi. Reg."

He sat back in his chair. "Sit down, Cesari, and enough with the bullshit. All right?"

There were two comfortable consultation chairs in front of his desk, and I plopped down in one of them. I looked around casually. It was a nice big office with plush carpeting. Pictures of his family adorned his desk and walls.

"You're going to have to be a little more specific, Reg. I've had a rough night taking call for you."

Reg wasn't in a good mood. "Okay, you want me to spell it out, asshole. Then I will. You have my diamonds and I have your balls. You give me what belongs to me, and I might—might—give you what belongs to you."

"I think there's been a misunderstanding. Gina took the diamonds last night. I don't have them."

"Don't be a wise guy, Cesari. Gina already brought me those. I'm talking about the diamonds you got from Ed Talbot last week."

"Oh, those diamonds. You know, Reg, if you had just asked nicely for them the first time around, we might have spared ourselves a lot of anxiety and unpleasantness."

"Be that as it may, here we are. As I said, those are my diamonds, and I want them back. And if you want your freedom, you'll do exactly as I say."

"How do you figure?"

He smiled. "Do you know what they call that little adventure of yours last night?"

"An accident?"

"Keep making jokes, Cesari. You took a human being up to the OR last night without his permission or any justification that has been documented, and he died as a result. You weren't even on call, and therefore had no business even being in the hospital at all last night. You starting to understand now?"

"Oh, please. You know I was set up by Gina as well as I do. She injected him with heparin right before the procedure, knowing he would bleed to death the minute I touched him. Yeah, that's right, I figured it out already."

"Well, isn't that a sad story? Too bad you can't prove any of it, and your only witness, Gina, wasn't even on call last night. Furthermore, she will swear under oath that she has no idea what you're talking about, and I sincerely doubt that she's going to admit to giving anything to anybody. Right now, it looks like you grabbed some schmuck off the street for your own sadistic purpose and butchered him like a calf. The press will be calling you the new barber of Fleet Street."

"I have malpractice for this kind of thing."

He laughed.

"This is way beyond malpractice, Cesari. This is at a minimum gross misconduct, and at the worst, cold blooded murder. The hospital board is convening an emergency session at five tonight to discuss what to do about you, and I'm your only hope. They wanted me to suspend you today pending an investigation, but I asked them for a little time to hear your side of it before rushing to judgment. If I go in there tonight pissed off, then I'm going to recommend not only your immediate suspension, but aggressive criminal investigation. You'll be in cuffs by tomorrow morning, and don't bother looking for Gina either. She's taken a leave of absence until things blow over."

Fuck. He had his ducks in a row.

He tossed a manila folder across the desk at me. "You might want to look at this. If you don't play ball, it'll be sent anonymously to the press, the board and, needless to say, the police."

I opened the folder and saw my mug shot from years ago along with detailed arrest records and psychiatric evaluations. He smirked.

"You forgot to mention this on your application for appointment here at Saint Matt's. No matter how you slice this, you're going to be one very unhappy wop by the time I'm through with you. Capisci, greaseball?"

He was even less attractive now than when I'd watched him do the Salsa with Kelly. "It seems that you're holding all the cards, Reg. Nicely played, but tell me something. What was that little stunt with Gina and the lockers all about?"

"Did you like that? That was her idea. We thought it would suck you in deeper, make you curious, deepen the mystery, and it did. Gina's something else, isn't she? She's a great lay, too. I knew you'd get a hard-on for her. Okay. What's your answer, Cesari? Are you going to play ball or not?"

"Doesn't sound like I have a choice."

"No, you don't. It's your own fault. What the fuck were you doing in the alley with that scumbag Ed Talbot anyway?"

"I was being mugged."

He chuckled. "You're kidding?"

"No, seriously."

"Well, that's too bad. Look, I want those diamonds on my desk before five tonight or I tell the board that you are clearly an unbalanced murderer with a criminal record and that we should call the police immediately."

"What do I get in return for being cooperative?"

He relaxed a little and sat back in his chair. "That's better, Cesari. I don't mind negotiating. First of all, I sweep everything under the rug. All the paperwork and proper consent forms with that guy's signatures on them miraculously reappear. Gina suddenly remembers what happened last night, including that you did everything you could to help the poor bastard. At the worst, you'll get a slap on the wrist for not calling in a second nurse to help out. You're young and we all make mistakes, but your heart was in the right place. We put it behind us and start over. Two months later, when the dust settles, you decide to move to another city for a better paying job. I give you a recommendation and everybody cries when you leave. I got the board wrapped around my finger, and they'll do whatever I recommend."

"And this folder with my police record?"

"I hang on to that for safe-keeping in case you try to break our deal."

"What about the dead guy?"

"Fuck him. He's Russian. Last I heard there were several hundred million more of them."

"Out of curiosity, Reg, how did you know he was going to bleed like a stuck pig?"

"Because they always bleed like stuck pigs, even without heparin on board. I usually have to inject them multiple times with epineph-rine and put two or three clips on them to stop the bleeding just so I can get them out of there."

"You're a real compassionate guy, Reg. You know that? Gina, too. She practically dared me to rip the clips out. What a sweet girl."

"Fuck you, Cesari. Next time, think with your head and not your dick. Besides, I heard what you did to my nephew last night, so don't expect any sympathy from me. Yes or no, are you going to bring me the diamonds or should I just call the police now?"

"I can't get them till Friday morning."

"Why not?"

"Because they're in a safe deposit box and I don't have the key. It's being held by a law firm in Ohio, but I can get it by Friday."

"Very smart." He thought it over. "Okay, I'll recommend a post-ponement of any decision on the Cesari problem until Friday at noon. Those diamonds had better be on my desk before then. I'm giving you the rest of the week off to think about your sins. Now get out. I've got work to do. You've been a real pain in my ass."

"Care to tell me what's been going on, Reg? The big picture, I mean."

"Get the fuck out of my office before I change my mind."

R℞ 45

BEFORE I left the hospital, I stopped at the operator's desk and asked them who'd been on call the night before for endoscopy. The gray-haired woman who had worked there since the Jurassic Era fumbled through a stack of papers and eventually found what she was looking for. She thumbed down the list of names.

"Here it is. Dr. Griffin was the doctor on call, and the two endoscopy nurses were Linda Campbell and Maureen Hanlon."

"Are you sure about the nurses?" She looked again.

"Yes, want to see for yourself?"

"No, that's okay. Thank you."

"Is there a problem?"

"No. Thank you again."

Shit. Gina hadn't even been on call last night. I'd told the operator that I was covering Reg, but he'd deny it. And Gina wasn't on the schedule. I'd been covering a guy who didn't ask me to cover him with a nurse who wasn't on call and now couldn't be found. My story looked like shit no matter how you cut it.

I left through the main entrance without going to see Kelly at work in the ER. Bobby and Giorgio were down the block, maybe a hundred feet away, watching me. Reg thought he had me by the balls, and maybe he did, but I had a bigger problem now. I had promised the diamonds to Boom Boom and that was a promise I wasn't about to break. On the other hand, last night's death in the OR would certainly end my career, brief as it was. Could I really go to jail for that? Probably. He had a point. Without Gina, there was no proof that the guy went up to the OR voluntarily or even that he had a problem that warranted medical intervention. They would paint me as some sort of deranged psycho.

I called Kelly. "Hi, hon. How's your day going?"

"Good, I slept well last night. How's your day?"

"Great. How about Italian tonight?"

"Sounds good. Where?"

"I was thinking about John's Pizzeria over on Bleecker Street. Nothing fancy."

"Okay, that would be fine. I'm sorry I didn't say goodbye this morning. It's just that you were sleeping so soundly."

"That's okay. I appreciated it. I was tired."

"We haven't talked since yesterday afternoon. I assume you have a lot to fill me in on."

"I will tonight over dinner, okay?"

"Okay. John..."

"Yeah?"

"I love you."

"Kel..."

"I don't care. That's how I feel and I'm going to say it. Bye."

"Bye."

It was close to two on a Wednesday, and 3rd Avenue was jammed with people and cars. Late summer in the city. The sights, sounds and smells were exhilarating. I had approximately forty-eight hours to come up with a solution. Plenty of time for a clever guy like me. That thought made me chuckle. After what had just happened, you'd think I'd be just a teeny bit humbled. My mother was right. She had warned me about girls.

I needed to think things through. I needed quiet time. But I also needed someone else to act as a sounding board. I needed Kelly. She was my best friend and she was smart. I walked over to our apartment in the Village to see what the status of the cleanup was. It was Wednesday and they should have been close to finishing up. We didn't have any appliances, but maybe we could move back in anyway. The bed frame had been broken and the mattress was all cut up, but it would still work.

I passed by Avi and Hesh's jewelry store and stopped in.

"Hey guys."

They greeted me from behind the counter. Their shiners had greatly improved.

"Hello, young man. We were wondering when we would see you again."

They inspected my fat lip. "I hope the Gestapo men didn't pay you a visit?"

"Actually, they did, but somebody else did this to me," I said pointing to my face. "Anyway, I just wanted to say hello and let you know there have been some changes in the status of those diamonds. I may have to return them to the owner."

"You found the owner? But I thought there was no owner," Avi said.

"No, but there are people out there who feel very strongly that the diamonds belong to them."

They both nodded knowingly. Hesh said, "Diamonds make people feel that way all the time. Well, you know where we are if you need us."

As we talked, I heard a woman's voice humming "Edelweis." Avi and Hesh acted like they hadn't heard anything. I looked past them toward a back room.

I asked, "Is there someone else here?"

Before either could answer, Hilda appeared in the doorway and called to them.

"Avi, Hesh, the strudel is ready." She returned to the back room without acknowledging me. I guessed she didn't recognize me or was still mad about World War II.

I stared hard at the little guys and then laughed. "You guys are doing all right."

They smiled, shrugged and went into the back room for strudel and God knows what else. Unbelievable! I was going to have to bring this up with Kelly. Octogenarians getting laid more than me was simply unacceptable. She was slacking off.

Leaving the jewelry store, I hiked over to my apartment, and before entering, waved to Bobby and Giorgio. I took the elevator up and found the door to my apartment ajar, so I walked in. The windows were wide open and there were two large standing fans blowing at high speed. The smell of ammonia was strong in the room. There were two women working hard, red-faced and sweating, mopping the floors. Everything had been cleared out. It looked even emptier than the day we'd moved in. The hardwood floors looked very clean.

One of the ladies stopped what she was doing and looked at me. She was forty and round, her hair bunned up in a red kerchief. She said in broken English, "Your house?"

Several of her front teeth were made of gold. Her accent was unusual, and I guessed she was Albanian. I nodded. "Yes."

She smiled. "Ready tomorrow."

"Thank you."

She went back to work. Kelly and I needed to buy a few things, starting with a refrigerator and some dishes. I left the women to their work and went downstairs to find Bobby and Giorgio.

"Hey, Doc."

"Hey, guys. Where's your car?"

"We left it in the hospital parking lot," Bobby answered. "Why?"

"I feel like going to the library."

"The big one on Fifth Avenue in mid-town?"

"Yeah, that's the one."

"Let's just take a cab, Doc. It'll be easier than fighting with traffic."

"You guys got library cards?"

They laughed.

We hopped a cab on Sixth Avenue, and after five harrowing minutes and two near-miss accidents later, we stood in front of the New York Public Library. Bobby reprimanded the driver as he paid him. "We told you we weren't in a rush, asshole."

The Indian driver smiled broadly. "Thank you, sir. You are too kind." I guessed that was the extent of his English. We grabbed a couple of Sabrett hot dogs off a corner truck and had a late lunch.

I said, "Okay, you guys don't have to come in if you don't want. I need about an hour at the most. Just hang around here and I'll find you when I'm done."

They breathed a sigh of relief, as if entering a place with a lot of books might sap them of their strength. I walked up the steps to the entrance, admiring the architecture and found my way to the main reading room. I requested the books I needed and took a seat at one of the many desks. It was a big room and was filled with people. I read for about an hour from the reference books on gemology and eventually realized that I was barking up the wrong tree. Then an idea came to me.

I went out and found my bodyguards. "C'mon. Let's go to the Gemological Institute on Madison Avenue. It's not that far from here." I looked at my watch. It was four-thirty. It was only a few blocks away and we were there in less than ten minutes.

"Wait out here. It's on the second floor. I shouldn't take too long. I just have a question or two."

"Take your time, Doc. Me and Giorgio could use the exercise. Besides, I see another hot dog stand over there. Are you in, Giorgio?"

Giorgio rubbed his stomach. "Always, Bobby."

R̲X̲ 46

❝THANK you for meeting with me on such short notice, Dr. Lipincott.❞

"It's my pleasure, Dr. Cesari. It's not often that a gastroenterologist shows this kind of interest in gems. How may I help you?"

I was in the office of the Curator of the Gemology Institute and Museum on Madison Avenue. His name was Alvin Lipincott PhD, professor of gemology, and he was considered the world's foremost expert on diamonds. He was a little guy of about forty-five years with a closely cropped beard and gold rimmed spectacles wearing a double breasted gray suit and red tie. I guessed he didn't get out much.

"I just had a few questions about diamonds, Dr. Lipincott. I'm doing a little research for a journal club I belong to."

"Fire away." He leaned back in a leather chair and crossed his legs. His office was spacious and overlooked Madison Avenue.

"Have you ever heard of the Alrosa diamond mine in Russia?"

"Of course I have. In my field, the Alrosa diamond mine is roughly the equivalent, in terms of importance, of the Harvard or Columbia medical schools in yours."

"Actually, I went to the State University at Buffalo School of Medicine. I thought it was pretty good."

He cleared his throat. "Hmm. I see. I hope you didn't have to do much remedial work after graduation in order to pass your boards."

"No, not too much. They were very understanding. So, what can you tell me about the Alrosa diamond mine, Dr. Lipincott?"

"Did you have anything specific in mind or just in general?"

"Just in general."

"Well, the Alrosa diamond company is located in the Yakutsk region of Russia, which is on its eastern-most border about a thousand miles from nowhere. The Russians currently produce more diamonds than any other country in the world, and Alrosa accounts for ninety-five percent of that. Their net revenue last year was close to five billion dollars."

"That's a lot of diamonds. I had no idea."

"Thirty-three million carats to be exact, and hardly anybody knows that."

"Wow. Thirty-three million carats. So, if a few diamonds were missing here and there, they might not be noticed."

"Certainly, but if you're talking about stealing from the Russians, that's not a game I would want to play. Security there is tighter than at Fort Knox, and there are rumors that the Russian Mafia really runs the mines. That means if you get caught pilfering diamonds, no one's ever going to see or hear from you again. Do you mind if I smoke, Dr. Cesari?"

"Not at all. What can you tell me about synthetic diamonds?"

He shook out a cigarette from a pack of Parliaments and lit it up with an expensive-looking table lighter that caught my eye because of the symbol on it. "Is that the Lamborghini symbol on the lighter?" I asked.

"Yes, in addition to making very expensive cars, they also make very expensive lighters. This one cost $500, but they make others that cost more than a thousand."

He took a long drag on his cigarette and blew it out the side of his mouth, away from me. "Anyway, back to your question. Synthetic diamonds, or man-made diamonds, are a fascinating subject for gemologists. Synthetic diamonds, also known as laboratory-created diamonds, are produced by an artificial process as opposed to naturally occurring or mined diamonds, which are created by natural geological processes. Synthetic diamonds are also widely known as HPHT diamonds or CVD diamonds after the two most common production methods. How much detail are you interested in, Dr. Cesari?"

"I'd prefer you keep it simple. Remember, I didn't go to Harvard."

He chuckled. "Okay, well, simply put, HPHT refers to the process of applying very high temperatures and pressures to a substrate to produce diamonds, in effect mimicking mother nature. CVD, or Chemical Vapor Deposition, creates a carbon plasma over a substrate onto which the carbon atoms deposit to form a diamond. There are other methods, but those two are the most common."

"Are these diamonds considered real?"

"Absolutely, they're indistinguishable from mined diamonds."

"Are you saying that if I walked into a jewelry store, I could buy a fake diamond made in a factory?"

"I'm not saying that at all. First off, let's be clear. Man-made diamonds are not fake. They are as are real as you get, just made in a factory, not mined from the ground. They are not cubic zirconia. But you won't find many for commercial sale in jewelry stores. Most man-made diamonds are used as abrasives in cutting and polishing tools, and not for ladies wear."

"Why is that?" This was starting to fascinate me.

"That is an excellent question, Dr. Cesari, and one which cannot be answered easily without sounding overtly sexist."

"Sexist? Please explain. I assure you, I don't represent the thought police."

He chuckled again and I was almost starting to like the guy.

"I appreciate the disclaimer, Dr. Cesari. This is Manhattan, and political correctness is a fanatical religion here. Well, here goes. Women are, by far and away, the major driving force behind diamond purchases, but if they're not dug out of the ground, women don't want them, no matter how real they are."

"I don't understand."

"A flawless white, one carat diamond dug out of some hole in the Congo that has made its way here over the blood and corpses of God knows how many people, is worth about five thousand dollars, maybe more. A similar diamond, one hundred percent indistinguishable, made in a factory in Indiana, will cost about two or three hundred dollars."

"But if the diamonds are indistinguishable, I don't get it."

"Well, De Beers, which is one of the largest diamond distributing cartels in the world, claims there is a difference. In fact, they claim to have developed a spectroscopy device that can distinguish between mined and factory-made diamonds, but most people believe they are blowing smoke. It doesn't matter because they have handily won the PR campaign. The fact is, if you buy your loved one a diamond, and tell her that you saved a fortune because it was made in a factory, she will probably throw you out of the house. Beauty is in the eye of the beholder, Dr. Cesari. Have you ever thought about why precious gems and metals are precious in the first place?"

"No, not really. Why?" I sat back, perplexed.

He took another drag on his cigarette. "Because they are shiny and pretty and girls desire them. There is nothing intrinsically special about gold or diamonds. The more they sparkle in the light, the more girls want them. That's all. If something is rare, of course it adds to the value, but I have never heard of a woman wanting a gem that didn't sparkle in the light. This has been true for thousands of years, by the way. Jewelry, diamonds in particular, symbolize our love for one another. The idea behind the gift of an expensive diamond is that you are making a statement that no price or sacrifice is too great for the woman you love, so you had better not cheap out. When a man gives a woman a diamond, he is telling her, and more importantly, all her friends, that she means more to him than all his worldly possessions."

This was great. "Very interesting. So, Dr. Lipincott, if I bought a man-made diamond and went to a jewelry store to sell it, would the jeweler be able to tell the difference?"

He thought about that. "Probably not, would be my guess. There are not that many of them floating around, so the jeweler's suspicions would be low, and most small jewelers probably would not have an expensive spectroscopy machine, even if it really did work. And that's a very big if."

"Where could I get ahold of some man-made diamonds in a hurry, if I wanted to?"

"Lots of places. Just Google it up."

"Really? The internet? It's that easy?"

"Sure. You can get anything you want on the internet, even a mail-order bride."

Hmm, I let that one slide. "Well thank you for your time, Dr. Lipincott. I really appreciate it, but I must be going now. This was very helpful."

"You're welcome, Dr. Cesari. It was a pleasure meeting you."

I stood to leave.

"Um, Dr. Cesari, can I ask you something personal?"

"Sure, go ahead."

He hesitated and looked embarrassed. "I have sort of a problem, and I think I might need a gastroenterologist. It's nothing major, mind you. I was wondering…"

I reached into my pocket for one of my business cards.

"Is there anybody good in Manhattan you would recommend? You know, with an Ivy league education."

I returned the card to its resting place. "Well, there are a lot of charlatans out there, so you have to be careful, but I think I can help you. Can I borrow a pen and a piece of paper?"

I wrote down the address to the gay bar across the street from my apartment in the village. "This is where all the Harvard trained gastroenterologists hang out at night, so it's a great place to network and make connections. I'm sure you'll meet someone there. Just make sure you wear a pink shirt. That's Harvard's color."

He seemed puzzled. "I thought crimson was Harvard's color."

"Yes, the undergraduate is, but I was talking about the medical school."

"Oh. Well, thank you. That's a good tip."

We stood up and shook hands. I left the Gemology Institute and found Bobby and Giorgio leaning against the side of the building. It was five-thirty.

"Sorry, guys. It took a little longer than I anticipated. Let's grab a cab and head back down to the hospital."

In the car, I called Pam to see how she was doing. "Hi, Pam."

"Hello, John. Thank you for calling."

"Are you having a good day, Pam?"

"Not really. That was quite a fright yesterday. I'm still pretty shaken up over it. What happened to those guys? I watched the news all day and didn't hear anything."

"We called EMS anonymously last night and told them where they were. I'm sure they're being taken care of properly."

"So, that's it? A firefight takes place in the middle of my office in Manhattan and that's it?"

"Happens every day, Pam."

"They should go to prison. They're evil."

"In a perfect world, they would. But that's not the world we live in. So my guess is that nothing will happen to them."

"I know, and that stinks."

"It does. I agree. Do you need anything?"

"No, thank you. It's kind of weird. I didn't sleep at all last night and haven't gone out at all today. The thought of it kind of frightens me."

"That's very normal, Pam. That was a terrible experience you went through. You'll be okay. You just need a couple of days."

She laughed. "You should have been a psychiatrist."

"Well, I've seen enough of them. Look, I just called to say hi and let you know that I was thinking about you. Like I said, if you need anything, please let me know. It would be no trouble or bother at all. I feel kind of responsible."

"Please don't feel that way, John. I don't look at it that way at all, but what about you? How are you handling what happened? It was you they really wanted to hurt."

"I'm fine. Thank you. I'm used to people hating me. I'm a doctor. If you saw what I charged for an office visit, you'd hate me, too."

She chuckled again. "You're good for my morale, John. I need to laugh right now, and I don't believe anyone hates you. You know, I kept thinking about you all night. I almost called you several times."

"You should have."

"I will next time."

"When are you going to go back to work?" I asked.

"I took the next few days off, but will probably go in tomorrow and do some paperwork if I feel up to it. I cancelled a lot of patients today and am going to have a lot of catchup next week."

"Yeah, that's the way it is. Anyway Pam, I have to run. It was nice talking to you and I'm glad you're feeling a little better. I guess I'll see you next week at counseling." The taxi pulled to a stop in front of the hospital.

"Are you still going to come to the sessions? You don't have to. I'll let you out of it." She sounded surprised—and happy.

"Sure, I'll come. I mean, why not? I thought we were making some real progress with my problems."

She chortled. "Whatever you want, Dr. Cesari. So, I'll see you then, unless you would like to get together for lunch or coffee beforehand?"

"I never turn down coffee."

"Will you call me tomorrow?"

"Sure. I got to run now. Bye."

"Bye."

R̲ₓ 47

THE boys dropped me off at the hospital, and I went over to the ER lounge to wait for Kelly. Her shift ended at seven, so I had about an hour to kill. There was a computer in the lounge, and I googled man-made diamonds. Multiple hits popped up, and I scrolled through a bunch. Prices ranged, but were ridiculously low considering that the average jeweler couldn't tell whether they were mined or factory-made. I ordered a couple of dozen to be shipped overnight to the hotel and then closed my eyes for a short nap.

"Hey, sleepy head, I'm sorry I'm a little late. I missed lunch, so let's go before I pass out from hunger." I rubbed my eyes, yawned and looked at my watch. It was a few minutes after seven.

"Beautiful evening, isn't it, Kel?" We strolled over to Bleecker Street hand in hand, and I filled her in on my activities. Bobby and Giorgio hung back about fifty feet behind.

Fifteen minutes later, we were seated at one of the ancient wooden tables in John's Pizzeria, an iconic joint in the village. We had a great view of the old wood-fired pizza oven and ordered a thin crust pepperoni pizza with a carafe of the house chianti. The place was packed to capacity as always. This was one of the coolest places to eat in one of the coolest neighborhoods in the coolest city on Earth.

"Okay, Cesari, apparently I missed a lot since yesterday morning. Tell me again. Who are the two behemoths standing outside the restaurant watching us?"

"They're my bodyguards, Bobby and Giorgio, and they're not watching us so much as watching over us. I promised Boom Boom the diamonds, and he just wants to protect me until I deliver them."

"I see, and the bigger one is the guy that gave you the fat lip?"

"Yeah, but that was just a misunderstanding. Boom Boom and I straightened things out."

"Boom Boom and you are pals now?"

"Not exactly pals, Kel."

"Hmm. So, what exactly then? Partners? Associates?"

"People with mutual interests."

She nodded her head. "Okay, so you promised Boom Boom the diamonds, but you also promised Reg the diamonds?"

"Yes, or he'll destroy my career and send me to jail."

"And what will Boom Boom do to you if you don't give him the diamonds?"

"I'd rather not think about that."

She paused and I could see she was starting to get all worked up. "Tell me about this patient you killed last night because of Gina?"

"I didn't kill him purposely, but he died as a result of my actions, so yes, I'm responsible. There's no doubt about that, but if Gina hadn't anticoagulated him just before I started, things wouldn't have turned out the way they did."

"But you can't prove that Gina did anything."

"No, I can't."

"Didn't I tell you to stay away from her," she scolded. "What didn't you understand?"

"You're right. I'm not arguing. She suckered me in good. I admit it." I sat there meekly, letting her cool off.

The waitress poured our chianti. "Your pizza will be out soon."

I said, "Thank you," and took a sip of wine. "Not bad."

Kelly sighed. "So where do we stand now?"

"I have a plan that should buy us some time. I purchased a couple of dozen man-made diamonds online, and they'll be delivered to the hotel tomorrow. I'll give half to Reg and the other half to Boom Boom."

"And they won't know the difference?"

"Not according to the gemologist I spoke with today at the GIA."

"The GIA?"

"The Gemology Institute of America. It's on Madison Avenue. It's a museum, and I spoke to the curator there. The head gem guy. He says man-made diamonds are indistinguishable from mined diamonds, except through some type of exotic testing not generally available."

"Why not just give Boom Boom and Reg the diamonds you have and be done with them?"

"There aren't enough of them for starters. Reg knows how many there should be, and I told Boom Boom how many to expect. I can't show up with half of what I promised. I figured if I was going to give phonies to one, I might as well give phonies to the other. Besides, I was thinking of having the real ones made into a necklace for you."

She smiled and shook her head. "You won't be happy until we're both floating at the bottom of the East river with cinder blocks tied to our ankles, will you?"

"Are you sure you're not part Italian, Kel? That was very Italian, what you just said."

"I'm sure. So what if Reg doesn't hold up his end of the bargain?"

Our pizza came and we started eating.

"Why wouldn't he hold up his end of the bargain?" I asked.

"Because he's an asshole and probably a murderer. He might just think it's a good idea to have you out of the way regardless of whether you return the diamonds."

"Fair enough. You're right, maybe I should take out some insurance."

"What kind of insurance?"

"Something to convince Reg that it would be a mistake to double-cross me. I'll need to think about it. This pizza's pretty good."

She held a piece in her hand gingerly, trying not to let sauce or cheese spill onto her. "Yes, it is. Tell me again about the diamonds you found during the colonoscopy last night."

"The diamonds were in a small leather bag that had been clipped into the colon wall. There were about twelve, maybe fourteen very large diamonds, just like the ones I found in Ed Talbot's locker. I didn't have time to count them. Gina took them when she ran out on me and gave them to Reg."

"What do you think?" she asked.

"I think that somewhere, halfway around the globe, somebody is stealing diamonds from the Alrosa diamond company. They arrange to have them sewn into some guy's colon. Those guys hop a plane over here, and when they arrive, Reg arranges to have them come into the ER on nights he's on call. He does the colonoscopy late at night when no one's around. Gina's in on it, too because he needs an assistant and someone to corroborate the false record keeping. They pocket the diamonds and the guy goes home. How's that sound?"

"Sounds good, but what about that guy last night? You said he never went to the ER."

"Last night was different. They set me up in order to blackmail me into returning the diamonds I have in my possession. I think normally Reg would have called the guy to let him know where and when to show up. Last night they simply bypassed the ER and had the guy meet Gina directly up in the OR. The guy wouldn't have known the difference or cared. The poor bastard was probably in the endoscopy room the whole time Gina was working on me to do the case, and Reg was probably having a cocktail somewhere, laughing his ass off."

"What a pair those two are."

I nodded. "Premeditated murder. That's what it was, and they used me as the instrument of death."

"So who was he?"

"I don't know. I assume he was just some schmuck they recruited for the job over in mother Russia. He may not even have known what he was carrying."

"How do you think something like this works?"

"Well, I can't be sure of anything, but I've been doing some research, and the Alrosa diamond mine is enormous with thousands of people working there. It must be self-contained like a small city and probably has its own medical facilities. My guess is that they have a gastroenterologist on their payroll over there to do the procedures. They probably recruit some low level worker making peanuts and offer him what must seem a like a fortune to have two colonoscopies: one there to plant the diamonds and one here to have them removed.

As a bonus, he gets a vacation in Manhattan, all expenses paid. Not a bad deal, actually."

"That seems like a reasonable theory, except now he's dead."

"Except now he's dead."

"Won't somebody miss him?"

"Sure, but I guess Reg figured it was worth the risk to have me over a barrel like this. I mean, there are multiple witnesses that will testify to what they saw last night. It's all part of the official record now and looks pretty bad for me."

Kelly thought it over for a minute. "Okay, it all sounds plausible, but it also makes me very concerned."

"About what?"

"Sooner or later, whoever it is that has been smuggling these diamonds out of Russia is bound to show up to claim his property. What do you think will happen if he were to find out who you are and what you've been up to?"

I sat quietly, pondering this and saw exactly what she was hinting at. "You think Reg might tell him?"

"Like I said before, once Reg gets the diamonds, he might think of you as—an inconvenience."

"Then I think I definitely need some form of insurance against Reg."

We sat there thinking about that while we finished the pizza and wine.

She said, "And then there's your pal, Boom Boom."

"What about him?"

"He's not going to be your pal for long when he finds out you gave him phony diamonds. It may not be today, or tomorrow, or even the next day, but sooner or later he is definitely going to find out the truth. I think you have to assume that."

I finished my wine and looked at her long and hard. Finally, I said, "You're no fun at all."

"I'm just trying to keep you alive, Cesari. I like having you around. You amuse me."

"I amuse you?"

"Yes, you do."

257

"So you keep me around because I entertain you, like a court jester. Is that it?"

"That's it exactly."

"Well, okay then. I just wanted to clarify that."

"Is it clear now?"

"Yes."

"Good."

R̥ 48

GLANCING over my shoulder, I spotted Bobby and Giorgio half a block back as we walked past the portico to Washington Square Park toward the hotel. It was nine-thirty and the park was thronged with people, as usual.

"Kel, I need to speak to Cheryl. I hope you don't mind. I'll be quick."

She had her arm around my waist. "Go ahead, but I'm going to start calling old boyfriends, too."

I chuckled as I dialed the number.

"Hi Cheryl. Cesari here."

"Hi. What's up?"

"I need to ask a favor."

"You mean another favor."

"Yes, I need another favor. I have to find Vito."

"Vito who?"

"Vito Gianelli."

"You can't be serious?"

"I am."

"I can't help you do that, Cesari."

"Officially, you mean."

"I mean, I would lose my job if I divulged the location of someone in witness protection. Technically, I'm not even supposed to know that information."

"That's my point. If, technically, you don't know the information, then technically, you could not have divulged it to anyone."

"Are you trying to be funny? Because technically, you're not."

"I'm very serious about finding him, Cheryl. Hey, I have an idea... Is it possible for you to give him a message to call or contact me? Then he can make his own decision."

"That would be even worse. I cannot go anywhere near that guy or contact him in any way. If he subsequently winds up dead, it will be on my head if anyone finds out. What do you need to talk to him about anyway, or don't I want to know?"

"I can't tell you, other than it's important."

"That's what I figured. He's afraid of you. Did you know that?"

"Really? Well, we sort of left off on a bad note." Kelly and I crossed over to E. 8th Street and were approaching St. Mark's Place. "That's one of the reasons I need to talk to him. I feel kind of bad over the way things ended."

Uh, oh. Poor phrasing.

Suddenly and unexpectedly, she yelled into the phone. "You feel bad over the way things ended with one of your gangster friends? You didn't feel bad over the way things ended with me and we were sleeping together. Why should I risk my career for you? You heartless guinea bastard."

I hadn't expected that and stepped quickly away from Kelly, cupping my hand over the receiver. I whispered, "Whoa. Calm down, Cheryl. I thought you didn't hate me anymore. I told you how sorry I am about all of that."

Silence as she collected herself and sighed deeply into the phone. "I don't know what just came over me. I'm tired and work has been very stressful lately. I feel bad now. I didn't mean that. Let me think it over and I'll get back to you tomorrow. You have no intention of killing him, right?"

"Absolutely not, and thanks."

"Bye."

Jesus.

I closed my phone and put it in my pocket. Damn. They never forget, they never forgive and—they never apologize. I wish someone had taught me all this stuff when I was a kid. It might have saved me some aggravation.

"What was that all about? Was she yelling at you?" Kelly asked, sensing something amiss.

"No, I had trouble hearing because of the background noise. She was in the subway."

"Is she going to help you?"

"She has a lot on her plate right now, but she's going to think about it."

Kelly put her arm in mine and said, "Okay, how about paying some attention to me now? All we've done all night is talk about other women."

"Really?"

"Really."

"We're just going to have to fix that. Aren't we?"

"We had better, Cesari."

I put my arm around her waist and we walked into the St. Mark's Hotel. I waved to Bobby and Giorgio and they waved back. We went up to our room and they went home.

"The apartment will be ready for us to move back in tomorrow," I said. "I went by today to take a look. It's nice and clean."

"Good. We've been so busy this week, we haven't gone shopping for appliances and a bed frame. Maybe we should do that tomorrow. We're both off."

"Sounds like a good idea."

"So why do you want to talk to that creep, Gianelli? He tried to kill us."

"You can't afford to hold grudges in this business, Kelly. He might be a changed man. If he is, he may be able to help me. I have to consider all my options."

"I don't know if I like this idea, and why would he come out of hiding? Aren't there people trying to kill him?"

"Yes, there are lots of people trying to kill him. He turned state's evidence and ratted out his former pals. But you don't understand what it's like for a guy like him to be in witness protection. He's probably bored out of his mind. This is a guy that's used to wearing $5,000 hand-tailored suits and alligator shoes. He used to be able to get out of bed whenever he wanted and do whatever he wanted every day of the year. Now, he's probably bagging groceries or mowing lawns in some small town in Kansas. His head must be about ready to explode. I think he would jump at the chance to do something—anything different."

"Yes, but would he help you? You're the reason he's in witness protection in the first place."

"He, most of all, would understand. Shifting alliances is standard operating practice for the mob, Kel. Yeah, he may blame me for his current problems, and I have to admit I was pretty mad at him for trying to kill us, but that was then and this is now. No reason we can't put it behind us as long as we each have something the other wants."

"Do you ever listen to yourself, Cesari? You think a dangerous mobster is going to come out of hiding to do a good deed for you just because he's bored?"

"I think he would consider it for the right price. Besides, it was your idea."

She was indignant. "What do you mean it was my idea?"

"You asked me how I could be sure that Reg would live up to his side of the bargain once I handed him the diamonds. Well, Vito is going to be my insurance against such a betrayal. I'm going to introduce the two of them so Reg gets a clear picture of who he's going to have to deal with should he double-cross me, or if I should happen to disappear one day because he ratted me out to some Russian mobster." Vito was six-foot-three, two hundred and forty pounds of pure mean. Piercing gray eyes, jet black hair, he oozed danger from every pore, and I had no doubt Reg would get the message.

"And in your mind, this was my idea?"

"Sort of."

"What if Reg isn't impressed when he meets Vito?"

"That would be his second big mistake."

"What was his first?

"Thinking he could flirt with my girlfriend and get away with it. That's right, I saw you two dancing at The Blue Danube." I laughed.

"Oh, stop it."

I grabbed her around the waist and kissed her passionately. "Did I tell you that I'm very upset with you about something else, too?"

She smiled, a little breathless, and held me tightly. "What did I do now?"

"It's what you haven't been doing. I know a couple of little old Jewish guys over on E.9ᵗʰ St. who get more booty than I do."

She giggled and we kissed again, more gently. "Well, that is totally unacceptable. I agree. So, are you going to do something about it, or are you going to let those old guys keep making a fool of you?"

Rx 49

THURSDAY morning, we took a cab over to a place called Appliance World and ordered a refrigerator, microwave and television to be delivered next week. We then went shopping for a new bedframe, mattress, pillows and lamps at Macy's. I called Bobby to let him know that I had the day off and would be wandering around Manhattan, and that I would catch up with him later. He and Giorgio had been sitting outside the hospital for the last few hours wondering what had happened to me. He wasn't thrilled because Boom Boom had told him not to let me out of his sight until I delivered the diamonds, and I promised him I wouldn't tell a soul. After several hours of shopping with Kelly, I was starting to get fatigued, so we stopped in Eataly on Fifth Avenue for a panini. It was eleven-thirty and we had to fight through mobs of people to find a seat.

I had mortadella with provolone on freshly baked Italian bread, and Kelly had a roasted eggplant, red pepper and goat cheese sandwich splashed liberally with extra virgin olive oil and balsamic vinegar. They were delicious. Top that off with freshly brewed black coffee, and I was in a very good mood.

Kelly beamed. "I think we had a very good day shopping." She was very happy. Women always seemed to get an endorphin rush when they were spending money.

"I agree. I really enjoy shopping for sheets and pillows."

"Stop, you're having fun with me and you know it. By the way, how will we know when the phony diamonds arrive?"

"We won't, but I paid extra to have them delivered before noon. I asked the hotel manager to put them in the safe for me, and please stop calling them phony. They're very real."

She rolled her eyes. "Take it easy. What time are you going to meet with him tomorrow? Reg, I mean."

I took a sip of coffee.

"The meeting about me with the board is at noon. I figured I'll go to his office at about eleven-thirty. Might as well make him sweat a little, too."

"And Boom Boom?"

"I'll give his boys the diamonds first thing in the morning to get rid of them. I can't have them hanging around while I give a second set of diamonds away."

My cell phone rang.

"Hi, Cheryl."

"Hi. Look, before I begin, Cesari, I just wanted to say again how badly I feel for snapping at you like that last night. I'm embarrassed and would appreciate it if we just put it behind us."

For a girl, that was pretty darn close to an apology. "It's already ancient history. Besides, I can't even remember what I had for breakfast, so forget about it."

"Thanks. Where are you?"

"I'm at Eataly on Fifth Avenue and 23rd Street having lunch with Kelly."

"Oh, good. I'm just around the corner at the Supreme Court Appellate Division on Madison Avenue. Finish your lunch and meet me in fifteen minutes in Madison Square Park by the fountain. I have something for you." She hung up.

"What was that about?" Kelly asked.

"It was Cheryl. She has something for me, but didn't say what it was. She said she wants to meet in the park across the street."

"She really didn't say what she wants to meet you about?"

"No."

"I'm getting tired of all this spy stuff."

"Let's go over there and find out what's going on. It's only a five minute walk from here and it's another beautiful day in the city."

We finished our paninis and headed over to the park. It was just across Fifth Avenue from where we were. The park was crowded with people enjoying the last days of summer, and I spotted Cheryl already there, sitting on a bench. Hungry pigeons surrounded her, waiting for crumbs from the pretzel she was eating. As we approached, she stood and greeted us. Her dark blue business suit screamed lawyer from a mile away.

"Hi, guys. Look, I don't have much time," she said. "I have to get back to work." She handed me an envelope. "This is the information you asked for. Sorry for the cloak and dagger routine, but I don't feel comfortable talking about stuff like this on the phone. Just remember, you didn't get it from me. I wasn't going to do this, but I felt bad about last night. So here it is. Now, I have to go. By the way Cesari, do you know why last night's sexual harassment meeting was cancelled? Not that I care. I just want to get it over with."

"Not sure. I heard Pam was a little under the weather."

"Okay. Well, goodbye and good luck."

She walked away quickly.

"What happened last night? She seemed a little embarrassed."

"Nothing, really. She was just a little cranky on the phone is all. I think she's getting nervous. Pascal is coming down from Vermont to spend the weekend with her."

"Really? Wow."

I opened the envelope and there was an index card inside with an address; nothing else, no name, no phone number. I read it to her, "143 Hackett Blvd., Albany, New York."

"Gianelli?" she asked.

I looked at my watch. It was twelve-thirty. "I can get there by four."

We walked quickly back to the hotel. "Let's get the diamonds from the hotel safe and bring them up to our room," I said.

We found the hotel manager and he retrieved the FedEx package for us, which had arrived at ten sharp. Kelly and I went up to our room and spread the diamonds out on the bed. There were two dozen absolutely beautiful factory-made diamonds. They ranged in size from three to five carats and were perfect. Kelly smiled. Girls always smiled at the sight of diamonds. It was a cross-cultural, cross-ethnic, cross-racial phenomenon.

"They look pretty good."

"I'll say." She eyed them hungrily.

"Easy girl. Remember they're phonies." I joked.

"They look pretty real to me now."

"They really do, don't they?"

I found the biggest one and put it into my pocket. The rest I put back into the brown package they'd come in.

"What are you going to do with that one?"

"A peace offering for Gianelli."

She thought that was funny. "A fake diamond as a peace offering? You're such an asshole, Cesari. No wonder he wanted to kill you."

"If a jeweler wouldn't know the difference, then neither will Vito."

"You better not try to give me one of these. I want the real thing. It's got to cost a lot to mean anything."

I looked at her and thought about what the gemologist had said about women and the price of diamonds. "I'll keep that in mind. Meanwhile, I'll put the rest of these in the safe, and then I have to move fast. I have a long ride ahead of me."

The safe was built into the wall of the closet next to the bathroom. It was a big closet and I was hidden from Kelly's view while I put the diamonds away. I looked at the two Smith and Wesson's and discreetly pocketed my .38 loaded with the five hollow-point bullets. I closed the safe and made ready to leave.

Kelly put her arms around me. "You don't mind traveling alone? I have to do the night shift tonight and I can't get out of it."

"I'll be fine. I just hope Vito gives me a chance to talk before he starts swinging his fists."

"He'll be fine. He'll probably be in shock when he sees you."

"No doubt about that. He'll probably think that I came to finish the job."

"Just be careful and try to smile. It will disarm him."

"I'll try."

"Practice for me. C'mon, give mama a big smile."

I smiled for her. "How's that?"

"He's definitely going to start swinging," she laughed.

We kissed goodbye and I went to get my car from the parking garage.

R͟X 50

I arrived in Albany at four-thirty and got off of the thruway onto Route 9, which turned into Delaware Avenue, eventually meandering onto Hackett Blvd. He lived in a small red ranch in a nondescript lower middle class neighborhood. There was a beat-up green Impala sitting in the driveway of an attached garage and the lawn needed mowing. The thought of Vito Gianelli pushing a lawn mower made me chuckle.

About half a block away from his house, I parked my car and watched. The last time I'd seen Vito, he had begged for his life and I had granted it. He'd turned against the mob and was now in permanent hiding as part of the Federal Witness Protection program.

Nothing happened for about half an hour, so I decided to get a closer look. I got out of the Camry and walked casually down the quiet street, wearing sunglasses and a Yankees cap. At house number 143, I paused and checked the .38 in my front pocket. It was still there, so I went up to the front door and rang the bell. No answer. I tried looking through the windows but didn't see anything.

Around back, there was a small yard, and I laughed quietly as I observed the mess; weeds, cracked cement, a rusted grill and a shed in disrepair. Poor Vito. He had no idea how to maintain a home. The gutters were probably clogged and he didn't even know it.

The back door, which had a window-paned top half, was locked. Looking around, I observed homes on either side of his, but tall bushes and trees gave him a fair amount of privacy. The home on my left was a two-story wood-framed house. If someone were upstairs, they might be able to see me, but all the shades were drawn, so I took a chance. Using the butt-end of the .38, I broke one of the small glass panes near the handle, allowing me to reach in and unlock the door.

There was no alarm system, and I entered his kitchen uneventfully, observing that it was just as messy as his backyard. A sink full of unwashed dishes highlighted an unremarkable and extremely ordinary room. I performed a quick walkthrough of the small house, searching unsuccessfully for anything interesting. The place reeked from the stench of cigarettes and I nearly gagged from it.

Standing in the middle of his living room, I scratched my head. Now, where would I keep it if I were Vito? I searched the bedroom again and found nothing. The kitchen drawers and cabinets were equally disappointing. I opened the refrigerator and helped myself to a can of Bud Light from the otherwise empty refrigerator and was just about to close it when I noticed something odd. The beer in my hand wasn't cold. In fact, the refrigerator wasn't even remotely cool. Since the light was on, I surmised it was plugged in, but for some reason the cooling mechanism wasn't working. That would explain its lack of contents. Poor Vito, he was barely surviving in this wilderness that was Albany, and I was starting to feel sorry for him.

The freezer door was slightly ajar so I opened it, discovering a loaded .45 caliber Ruger. I think I understood now. He had deliberately disabled the cooling elements to the refrigerator in order to keep the gun at room temperature. I assumed he was trying to minimize the chance of accidental malfunction in case of an emergency, or maybe he was worried about the long term effects of the low temperature. This was his worst case scenario weapon. If somebody he didn't like ever came to visit him, he would offer them a beer or something cold and retrieve the .45. Of course, possessing a handgun was a violation of his agreement with the feds, but I guess self-preservation comes before honor. I felt better now. It was unlikely that he would be armed when he came home.

I took the clip out of the gun and emptied the round from the chamber. The bullets from the clip went into my pocket, the clip back into the gun and the .45 back into its hiding place in the freezer. Now I was ready. I went into the living room and sat on the couch, drinking his warm beer. Dr. Phil was on television, and I amused myself watching while I waited. Some guy had cheated on his girlfriend, so she'd gotten her revenge by sleeping with his best friend. Now she was nine months pregnant and not sure who the father was. They were sitting around on the set yelling at each other. This was great stuff.

At six, I heard a vehicle pull up outside, so I turned off the television and went to the window to peek through the blinds. A UPS truck had stopped in front of the house, and a large man in brown got out of the passenger side. It was Vito, and he looked ridiculous in those brown shorts, although judging by his muscularity, he appeared to still be in great shape. He said goodbye to the driver and walked up to his front door. This was too funny. He had put more guys in hospitals, morgues and various parts of the New Jersey wetlands than anyone I had ever heard of and now he was delivering for UPS.

I pulled out the .38 and hid to one side of the door, listening as the key engaged the lock. The door swung casually inward and he entered, unsuspecting. His back was toward me and I stepped out of the shadow fast, pressing the barrel of the .38 hard into the base of his head.

"Relax and close the door gently, Vito. No sudden movements, all right? I'm a little nervous."

He closed the door slowly and stood perfectly still. "Who is it?" He asked in that deep, raspy cigarette voice that I remembered well.

"We'll get to that in due time. Now get on your knees and put your hands behind your head. Don't be stupid either. I'm loaded with hollow points that will make a hole in your head the size of a grapefruit."

He got on his knees, facing away. "Good. Now, all the way down on your face. Nice tan, Vito."

"Cesari? Is that you?"

Keeping the gun in its lethal position the whole time, I patted him down quickly. He was unarmed. "Yeah, it's me. Unbuckle your belt and take it off and remember to move very slowly." I gave him some room to perform the operation, but pressed the .38 even more firmly into the base of his skull. I wanted him to know that any sudden movement would result in instantaneous death.

"Did you come to kill me, Cesari? Because if you did, then I have to warn you, you'll be doing me a favor. I can't take another minute of this nine-to-five shit."

He handed me his belt.

"Now cross your wrists behind your back, and no, I didn't come to kill you. If I did, we wouldn't be talking about it because you'd already be dead, but if you do something stupid, that could all change." I tied his arms tightly together with the belt, just above the elbows. It looked very uncomfortable. When I was satisfied with my work, I stepped away from him.

"Okay Vito, up and on the couch. Nice and slow. That's it." It was difficult without hands for support, but he eventually maneuvered clumsily to his knees and then stood up and walked over to the sofa.

"What do you want, Cesari? Haven't you made my life miserable enough already?"

He was sitting in the middle of the couch, and I stood in front of the television facing him, a healthy distance away with the gun trained on his face. If he charged me, I would empty all five rounds into him. He was a big guy, but five rounds at close range would definitely take him down. He read my mind and sat perfectly still.

"You shouldn't have tried to kill me and Kelly, Vito. Besides, you got off easy. After the things you've done, you don't have the right to expect any sympathy from me or anyone else. You got more than most people in your position could expect or deserve: a house, a job, people watching over you, but most importantly, you got a clean slate and a chance to start over."

"Yeah, I got it great," he replied sarcastically. "I'm making ten bucks an hour driving a UPS truck. I have an eight o'clock curfew. I can't drive beyond the city limits, and I have to meet with the feds every week. If I break any of their freaking rules, they'll let every hit man in New York know where they can find me." He was like an animal in the zoo that had beaten itself against the iron bars of its cage until exhaustion, and then finally, realizing the futility of it, resigned itself to its fate.

"Cry me a fucking river, Vito. It's better than Sing Sing. Now stop your whining. I'm here to make you a business proposition and a way out, at least temporarily. Think of it as a day pass from hell. How would you like to wear a hand-tailored suit again?"

He looked up interested, although somewhat suspicious. "Of course I would. What kind of proposition and what do I have to do?"

"I need your help."

He started laughing. "You're too funny, Cesari. You have a peculiar way of asking favors, tying me up and shoving a gun in my face."

"Look at it from my point of view. I know I'm not exactly your favorite person, and I wanted to make sure you would let me talk without going nuts, but we're talking business now, so let's put the personal stuff behind us."

"If it's just business, then why don't you untie me?"

I hesitated as I thought about it. Even if I let him loose, I still had the gun. In the end, I decided that trust building trumped safety at the moment. "All right, Vito. Kneel down in front of the couch."

After I freed his hands and tossed the belt onto the floor, I watched him rub his arms and sit back down. His body language was relaxed as I returned to my position across from him.

"So, tell me about this proposition of yours, Cesari."

I took the five carat factory diamond out of my pocket and tossed it to him, watching him greedily examine it, his eyes growing wide. "Is it real?"

"As you or me."

"Okay, so tell me about it."

"It's five carats and flawless. It's worth about five hundred thousand dollars, and it's yours. A peace offering from me to you."

He stared at it. "How do I know it's not fake?"

"You don't, but why would I come all the way up here to palm off a fake diamond on you?"

"Where'd you get it?"

"That's my business."

"What do I have to do for it?"

"You can start by acting like a man."

"Fuck you, Cesari. You're the one who did this to me."

"Fair enough, but now I'm giving you a chance to be your old self again. I need a bodyguard."

He laughed even louder this time. "You're a riot, Cesari. You know that? All I ever do is dream about killing you myself."

"Well, now you can start dreaming about keeping me alive. Consider that diamond a retainer, and there's more where that came from."

"Who's trying to kill you?"

"Lots of people. Some who want to kill you, too."

He nodded. "And you think you can trust me?"

"Sure. Do you want to spend the rest of your life delivering packages from Amazon and living in this shithole?"

"No, I don't," he answered truthfully. His voice and facial expressions were sincere.

"I'm offering you a chance back in. Do you want it or not?"

"Of course, I do."

"Okay, then stop your jawing and go pack a bag. I'll fill you in on the details while we drive and we'll eat on the road."

"For Christ's sake, Cesari, I just walked in the door. I worked all day in the freaking hot sun. At least let me grab a beer."

I looked at my watch. It was almost seven. "Sure, but hurry up. It's a long ride and we've got to get you some real clothes. The situation I'm in is time sensitive. I checked your closet and you might want to donate that wardrobe of yours to the Salvation Army." He stepped into the kitchen and I stood there anxiously. Vito was about take his final exam in trust building 101.

I heard the refrigerator door open and a can of beer pop.

Quiet.

After a minute passed, he returned to the living room, holding a Bud Light in one hand and the .45 in the other. I tensed and waited. He took a long pull from the beer can and awkwardly shoved the pistol into his waistband. I let out a deep breath.

"Give me five minutes to change my clothes and pack a few things, all right?" he asked.

"Sure, no problem."

℞ 51

"I can't believe I'm doing this, Cesari. I hate you. You ruined my life."

"You sound like one of my ex-girlfriends, Vito. Get over it. I'm going to make you a rich man."

We were in my Camry, an hour north of Manhattan on the thruway.

"So I heard Big Lou is still in a coma," he said.

"You heard right."

"Who took his place?"

"A guy named Salvatore Moretti. They call him Boom Boom. Ever heard of him?"

"Yeah, I heard of him. He's a total asshole, like you."

"Yeah, well, he promised the bosses your head on a platter."

"Yeah, I heard that too, and you're driving me right smack into the belly of the beast."

"Can't be helped, Vito. There's a guy down there giving me grief and I need to convince him to stop."

"Why can't you convince him yourself? You didn't have any trouble convincing me to back off. Why so shy all of a sudden?"

"This situation requires a little more subtlety. It's complicated, but he has me over a barrel, and if he pulls the trigger, I'm a goner. He set me up real good. I need him to understand that if anything happens to me that there's going be somebody waiting to bury him, too. I don't want to push him too hard, though. He's not a pro and might over-react."

"Okay, I got it. You want me to break a few bones or just smack him around?"

"I don't want you to do anything. Just stand next to me and look mean. I'll do all the talking, and you go with the flow. Act like I'm your boss, and that if I give you the word, you'll rip his head off."

"For five hundred thousand dollars, I will rip his head off."

"I know, but I don't want that. He's out of line and I just want him to get back in line. That's all."

"What about Boom Boom? Is he involved, too?"

"Unfortunately, yes, it was unavoidable. He won't be there tomor-row, but he's on the horizon. Separate problem."

"For you maybe. He's my main problem."

"We'll work on that next, I promise. If you help me with this, I'll help you with that. By the way, you're totally out of shape. I took the bullets out of your gun, and you didn't even notice. They're in my pocket."

He chuckled. "You cocksucker. You found the .45 in the freezer? Damn. You always were good, Cesari. Too bad you went to medical school; you could have made a name for yourself."

I turned onto the West Side Drive and glanced over at him.

I said, "Yeah, too bad."

He took out a pack of unfiltered Pall Malls and lit one up without asking.

"It's okay, Vito. I don't mind if you smoke." I gave him a sarcastic look.

He opened his window a crack to appease me.

"I have to admit it, Cesari. It feels good to be doing something again. I was going crazy up there."

"You never told me what your cover identity was, Vito."

He laughed and blew a puff of smoke out the window.

"I'm Michael Di Marco, single white male, never married, no kids, family on the west coast. I moved here because of a girl. She dumps me and I'm left holding the bag. I don't know how the feds expect these stories to last long. Sooner or later, people start asking questions. Even worse, the people you work with want to get to know you, and if you don't go out with them, they start to suspect something's not right. I've already had a bunch of women ask me out, but I've had to put them off. You know, I'm too heartbroken and that kind of stuff, but eventually, they start to wonder if you're a homo or maybe a pedophile."

"I never thought about it like that, Vito. I guess it would be a little strange for a single guy not wanting to socialize with his coworkers, but why can't you go out on dates?"

"C'mon, Cesari, you're a smart guy. You know how nosy women are. How long do you think it would take for some broad to figure out I'm not who I say I am? Even the hookers start asking questions after a while."

I laughed. "Good point, but I didn't know hookers got that personal." I had never been with one.

"Of course they do. They're just like other women, no different. Maybe they don't pry the first time round, but if you start showing up on a regular basis and treat them nice, then the gloves come off."

I glanced over at him. "They're just like other women? Are you kidding?"

"Don't be stupid, Cesari. Of course they are. Hookers are your sister, your mother, your cousin, your daughter and your next door neighbor. No girl grows up thinking she's going to turn tricks for a living, but shit happens and they fall into it. Usually, it's drugs. I think it's why they call them hookers in the first place because so many are doing it to support their habit. But deep down, they're just girls, and want somebody to be nice to them."

"And you're nice to prostitutes?" This was a side of Vito I didn't know existed.

"Yeah, sometimes—most of the time."

"I had never thought it through like that. So, you got a soft spot for these girls?"

"Let me tell you something, Cesari, They're a lot easier to deal with than some of the chicks I work with. Those broads at UPS are as hard as nails. It's either their way or the highway, if you know what I mean. There's one dame there I went out with twice. She started getting all personal and asking questions I didn't have answers to, so I told her I couldn't see her anymore. I've been ignoring her and won't return her calls, so now she's pissed and telling everyone I'm some sort of whacko who's up to no good. She's spreading rumors all over town about me, and there ain't a goddamn thing I can do about it."

I chuckled. "That's pretty funny, actually, but what can she do?"

"A lot, that's what. Once people up here decide you're a weirdo, everybody starts to do their own little investigations, internet searches, keeping an eye on you, that kind of stuff. They don't even pretend to be subtle. They aim their phones right at you and start snapping pictures. I don't need the feds watching me. I got half of Albany spying on me. So, it was just a matter of time before my cover was blown anyway, and they were going to have to move me. I talked with one of the agents, and he said it was always like this. To be honest, it was a good thing, you coming along when you did."

"That's too bad about witness protection, Vito. It almost sounds like you would've had more freedom in prison."

"Yeah. Too bad they don't tell you what it's really like before you rat on all your friends and have guys coming after you in your sleep. They make it sound like you're going to have a happy little life. Go fishing on the weekends. Maybe take up golf. Heh, can you picture me in golf clothes?"

I laughed. "No, that would be a bit of a stretch. Fishing maybe."

"So what's your story, Cesari? How'd you wind up in Manhattan?"

"Well, Kelly and I couldn't see working at that hospital in upstate after what happened last year. There were too many bad memories. Besides, I had my license suspended for six months because of that little episode, so we decided to move to Manhattan and start over. I figured I had a better chance of finding work there."

"Kelly? The black chick? You still with her?"

"Yeah, but let me give you a word of advice, girls don't like to be called chicks, and I'm pretty sure 'broad' and 'dame' are off limits too. You may want to practice that before we get there, and it's African-American now, not black."

"Fucking Cesari, when did you become so politically correct?"

"I'm not, but the chicks make all the rules, so if you want to get laid, you follow the chicks' rules."

We both laughed. "You're a real pisser, Cesari, you know that?"

"By the way, you had better be nice and contrite when you see Kelly or the deal's off. She voted against me coming to get you."

"I will. It was nothing personal against her, you know that. So are you going to tell me exactly what this guy has on you or do I have to stay in the dark?"

I pulled into a garage and parked in the first open space.

"Let's get some coffee." It was just after 11 p.m.

We walked to a coffee shop on the corner of Christopher and Gay in the Village and sat at a small table. There were a handful of other people sitting around, listening to a guy strumming a guitar and softly singing folk tunes. We ordered espressos and I slid his bullets across the table to him, which he pocketed.

"Feels like old times, doesn't it, Cesari?"

"Yeah, it does, Vito. I admit it. I can feel my adrenaline pumping."

"So we wipe the slate clean and move on. Is that it?" He asked.

"Can you do that, Vito? I know it's asking quite a bit. There's a lot of water under that bridge between us. You did some nasty things to me, but I admit that I did some nasty things to you, too. Let's just call it even."

"What about you, Cesari? Can you really just put it all behind you?"

"I already have."

He sipped his coffee and thought it over. "Then I'll try, too."

"Well you have five hundred thousand reasons to try real hard, okay?"

"That's true. So tell me what's going on."

I gave him a synopsis of my problems, including the death in the OR, but I left out the part about the factory-made diamonds.

He thought about it. "So this guy, Reg, wants his diamonds back or he turns you over to the cops and destroys your medical career? And you're afraid that even if you give him the diamonds, he's going to double-cross you?"

"Yeah, it's a distinct possibility."

"And Boom Boom wants his cut?"

I nodded. "I had to offer him something."

"Okay, so we know how they're bringing the diamonds in, but we don't know exactly where they came from or how many more are on the way?"

"The rumor mill is churning that they're being smuggled out of some Russian mob-controlled diamond company halfway around the planet. The Russian mob steals them first from the diamond mine, and presumably, someone inside the mob steals them after that. I'm not sure exactly how they're making the diamonds disappear, but eventually they're put in little bags and sewn into colons for delivery here."

"So this doctor pal of yours, who's threatening to make your life miserable, is just a technician. His job is just to retrieve the diamonds and pass them along to someone higher up the food chain."

"Well, I haven't really pieced it all together yet, and he wasn't forthcoming, but my guess is you're right. I mean this is Russian mob stuff, and I don't see how Reg could possibly be anything more than just a cog in the machine. How he got involved is anybody's guess right now. Why? What are you thinking?" I could see the wheels spinning.

"Technically, he's nobody then."

"What are you getting at, Vito?"

"What I'm getting at is, why don't we just eliminate this guy, Reg, and take over his end of the business?" A leopard can't change its spots.

I chuckled. "That's a problem for several reasons, Vito. Number one, I don't know who his contacts are and what his relationship is to them. They might not take kindly to his being eliminated. Number two is that I am a board certified gastroenterologist now. This is my chosen profession, and I gave up *eliminating people* a long time ago and don't really want to go back. I just want to be left alone to take care of my patients."

He rolled his eyes. "Give me a break, Cesari. You mean to tell me that you don't miss the life we had?"

I thought about that. "Well, I have to admit, it was exciting."

"Johnny, we were like lions roaming free on the plains of the Serengeti. We were on top of the food chain. Came and went as we pleased. Did whatever we wanted."

I smiled. "Yeah, it was exactly like that. The only thing we had to worry about was if one of the other lions snuck up behind us and put a bullet in our brains." That was a great analogy or metaphor. I was never sure what the difference was. "But those days are behind me now."

"Cesari, can't you see that you were cut out for this life? Yeah, I get it. You're a doctor now and you wear a white coat, but that's not who you are. You got the drop on me without even breaking into a sweat, and I'm not exactly a slouch. I live every day looking over my shoulder. There's something about your genes that make you a natural at this stuff. You should embrace who you really are and stop fighting it. We could make a fortune if we worked together."

"Maybe, but that's not going to happen, so shut up already." I was getting irritated because he was making a lot of sense and saying things I didn't want to hear. He was starting to appeal to a side of me that I didn't want to acknowledge existed.

"Okay, it was just a thought. You're legit now. I got it."

"While we're at it," I said. "We should hammer out a few ground rules. Rule number one is, I make all the rules. Understood?"

He nodded. "Got it. It's your show, fine and rule number two?"

"Same as rule number one. Just keep saying that over and over to yourself."

"Fine, but I think we're missing a golden opportunity here."

"I heard you the first time, and an opportunity to get involved with the Russian mob is something I don't mind missing. I got enough problems with the guys who live just a few blocks away in Little Italy. Let's just do this job together and go our separate ways. Okay, we need to wrap this up, I'm tired. I got you a room at the hotel where I'm staying. I want to be at Macy's when it opens tomorrow to get you some decent looking clothing so you can look the part."

I reached into my pocket and came out with a wad of fifties and a credit card. "Here's five hundred bucks walking around money and my Visa card. Don't break the bank, all right? Besides clothes, get yourself a cellphone. I still can't believe you don't have one. Who on earth doesn't have a cell phone?"

"Guys who don't want to be found, that's who."

"All right, let's pay the bill and go."

R⅄ 52

FRIDAY morning, I called Bobby and told him to meet me at the entrance to the hospital at nine-thirty sharp. The banks didn't open until nine, and I had to pretend that I needed time to get to my safety deposit box. I told Vito to meet me in the men's department of Macy's at ten sharp.

Kelly was astonished. "He really agreed to help you? I find that so hard to believe." She sat on the edge of the bed, lacing up a pair of sneakers.

"Don't sound so surprised, Kel. I can be very persuasive. After all, I convinced you that I'm not such a bad guy."

She laughed. "Yeah, you're right about that. You tricked me good. So, if all goes well, when will I see you?"

"I should be free by noon. I'll call you and we'll have lunch together, okay?"

"Sounds good. I'm going to head uptown to the Museum of Modern Art for a few hours. It doesn't open until ten thirty. Figure at least two hours looking around, take a cab back—how does one thirtyish or two sound to you for lunch? Or do you want to meet me up there?"

"Sounds like I'll need a snack to hold me, but sure, either way will be fine. I'll call you when I'm done."

I took the diamonds out of the safe and divided them into two piles. I placed each pile into a small leather bag with a drawstring that I'd purchased at a dollar store.

"Okay, I'm off, Kel. See you later."

I gave her a quick kiss and went to find Bobby, who was standing outside the entrance to St. Matt's with Giorgio. I looked at my watch. It was nine-thirty on the dot.

"Good morning, guys."

"Good morning, Doc."

We walked down the block to get away from the bustling hospital foot traffic. I didn't waste any time, and fished one of the little bags out of my pocket, handing it to Bobby.

"Do I need to look in, Doc?"

"No, but I want you to anyway. I don't want any misunderstandings."

He nodded and peeked inside the pouch, his appearance changing to that of pure amazement. "Damn, you weren't kidding, were you? How much are they worth, Doc?"

"Not sure, maybe five or six million, give or take. Well, say hello to Boom Boom for me and thanks for your help the other night."

"Our pleasure, Doc. See you around."

I watched them walk away and then grabbed a cab to Macy's, where I met Vito in the men's department, modeling a black, two-piece suit. He spun around in front of a full-length mirror, eyeing himself up and down.

"I don't know if can wear stuff like this, Cesari. I'm used to much better quality."

"It's just for today, Vito. We don't have time to get you a hand-tailored suit. I looked at my watch. "Let's take the black one. You look good in it."

"What about a shirt and tie?"

"I think a black turtleneck will be more effective for what I have in mind. It's the image I'm looking for. Don't forget a belt and shoes, and for God's sake, hurry."

"Take it easy, Cesari. I'm the one who has to wear these things all day."

He changed while I paid the bill, leaving his old clothes in the dressing room. We caught a cab and were back at the entrance to St. Matt's at eleven-fifteen. I paid the driver and we hustled into the hospital, walking through the main lobby in silence toward the elevators.

At Reg's door, we paused and I looked at Vito. He looked perfect for the part, like a big slab of hired muscle. He reminded me of that old joke: *You're so ugly that when you were born, the doctor slapped your mother.* The black suit and turtleneck were a great idea, too. Anybody with a television would have that image of a bad guy imprinted in their minds.

I whispered, "Just stand behind me and stare at him. Don't say anything, all right?"

He nodded. "I got it, Cesari."

I knocked, but no one answered.

We waited.

I looked at my watch and knocked again.

No response.

I glanced at Vito. He returned my gaze and shrugged. Maybe Reg got hung up in the operating room with a patient. He was the chief of the department after all, not just a diamond smuggler.

"What do you think, Vito?"

"The meeting's at noon, right?"

"Yes, and it's only eleven-thirty."

Shit. Did I push the envelope too far or did the meeting start early for some reason? Is Reg there right now telling them to fuck me over? But why not wait a few more minutes?

While I dithered, Vito opened the door and entered with me right behind.

"Holy shit," he said in surprise, stopping abruptly. "Is that him?"

"Damn." I took a deep breath and quickly closed the door behind me, locking it. Reg sat in his chair with his head arched backwards at an unnatural angle. Blood covered him and was still oozing from his slit throat. The macabre smile from the ear-to-ear wound mocked us and his lifeless eyes stared at the ceiling. On the desk in front of him lay his right ear.

"Yeah, that was him," I said.

"What happened here, Cesari?"

"How the fuck would I know? But we need to get the hell out of here, and I mean now."

Close by, a revolver cocked and we spun around toward Reg's private bathroom. Two men burst out, one holding a .357 magnum revolver and the other an Uzi. They were both about six feet, muscular and fair-skinned with shaved, tattooed heads. The one with the revolver was missing his right ear and had a brutal-looking, jagged scar running down the left side of his face. I dreaded to think how he'd gotten that. The one with the Uzi circled quickly around back of us, cutting off the exit.

The guy with the revolver was smart, and stood off to one side so that he would be out of the line of fire should the guy behind us get trigger happy. "Where are diamonds?" He asked in a thick Russian accent.

I didn't think this would be a good time to challenge his intelligence. "I have them in my pocket. May I ask who you are?"

These guys were obviously very serious about their work, so we froze in place. Neither Vito nor I were armed because our purpose was to intimidate Reg only, and I'd figured there was no point in getting arrested on a weapons charge.

"Give diamonds now, yes?" He said, ignoring my question.

"They're in my pocket."

"Slowly. I watch." He aimed the large revolver directly at my chest while I retrieved the pouch with the diamonds and held them up.

"Put on desk and hands in air."

I did as I was told, moving very slowly. Vito stood motionless. He knew the drill. The guy with the magnum motioned us away from the desk and we took a step back while he picked up the small bag and emptied its contents onto Reg's desk for inspection. It was then that I noticed a foul odor emanating from the bathroom. I glanced at Vito, who had picked it up as well.

The man with one ear seemed satisfied. "Who are you?"

"I'm a doctor here at the hospital. My name is Cesari. I found the diamonds accidentally and I thought they belonged to him, so I came to return them." I explained and nodded in the direction of Reg's corpse.

He thought about that for a second. "My name Sergei. Diamonds belong me, not him. He tell me someone bring."

"Why did you kill him if you knew you'd get the diamonds?"

"Sergei no kill for diamonds. Sergei kill for Alex."

"Who is Alex?" I asked, curiosity getting the better of me.

"Alex my brother. He die in operating room other night because of fool's incompetence." He spit on Reg's body.

Vito and I looked at each other apprehensively.

"I think I heard about that," I said. "I'm very sorry about your brother, Sergei. Well, now that you have your diamonds, I guess we'll be on our way. It was nice meeting you, it really was." We didn't move.

He stared at me, trying to understand. "Ah yes, nice of you to meet me. But no move, yes? Keep hands in air." He waved the gun at us and we raised our hands higher.

"Now what I should do?" he asked, grinning. Were those wooden teeth?

"Sergei, we don't know anything. We'll just leave and you'll never see or hear from us again."

He nodded. "But now you know Sergei. Is shame, no?" I heard a switch blade click out of its sheath and glanced over my shoulder. The guy with the Uzi in one hand had produced a five-inch blade in the other, still covered with Reg's blood.

"Don't kill us, Sergei. We can help you," Vito said suddenly and with great confidence. I looked at him, bewildered.

Sergei was curious, and took the gun off me, aiming it at Vito. "How help Sergei?"

"He's a doctor," Vito said, nodding at me. "Just like that dead guy over there. He can get the diamonds for you just like he was doing. Your operation doesn't have to skip a beat."

Sergei was puzzled. "What mean, not skip a beat?"

I said, "It means everything can continue as usual."

Sergei was quiet for a minute, and then asked Vito, "Who are you?"

"My name is Vito. Me and him, we're business partners." He nodded in my direction again.

"Empty pockets on desk," Sergei ordered.

I put my wallet and cellphone on the desk. Vito put his wallet down. Sergei picked up my wallet and opened it. "John Cesari, M.D." He had trouble pronouncing my name. He flipped through the wallet and found a picture of Kelly and took it out. He held it up for me to see. "Your woman?"

I nodded. "Yes."

"What name?"

I thought about lying, but remembered that she had signed the back of it.

"Kelly."

He studied the picture carefully. "She has nice ears."

Vito and I looked at each other. I was starting to get nervous. The stench from the bathroom was growing.

He put the picture in his pocket. "I keep." I felt my heart sink. I didn't like the way this was going.

He picked up Vito's wallet and inspected it. "Michael Di Marco? I thought name Vito?"

"My friends call me Vito. It's sort of a nickname." Good thinking, Vito.

"Why Sergei trust you?"

"Why did you trust him?" Vito asked referring to Reg.

"Because he greedy. I understand that."

"We're greedy, too. Even greedier than him."

Sergei seemed amused. "I think, and you two go in bathroom now. I take wallets but leave cell phone. I call in fifteen minutes. You answer. If no answer, I come find you. Not good." He picked up my cell phone and dialed his own number to record mine in his contact list.

"We'll answer," I promised.

They ushered us into the bathroom where we discovered the source of the awful smell. Curled up in a ball on the floor was Reg's secretary, Betty. I hadn't known her well, but she'd seemed nice enough, and certainly hadn't deserved to die like this. There was no blood, but I could see red bruises on her neck from where they'd strangled her. She had become incontinent in death and the smell was horrific in the small room. They shut the door and propped a chair up against it.

They left in a hurry and we had to get out of there, too. We turned the knob and shoved with no result. So we took a deep breath, slammed our full weights against the door, which gave way, and we tumbled out into the office, gagging.

"Jesus Christ, Cesari, was that the ugliest guy you ever saw or what?"

"After you, yes. Let's get the fuck out of here while we still can and we'll talk outside."

I picked up my cell phone from the desk, and we raced from Reg's office, desperately hoping we weren't noticed. Thank God it was lunch time and there was no one around. Outside on 3rd Avenue, we let the adrenaline surge come down, and I called Kelly.

"Hi, Kel, look, something's come up. Things didn't go quite as planned, and I'll need you to stay uptown for now. I'll explain later. Just stay away from the hospital and the apartment until you hear from me."

"What happened?" she asked nervously.

"The Russians are here and they killed Reg."

"Oh my God. Why? You gave them their diamonds, didn't you?"

"Yeah, but that guy who died the other night in the OR was the head guy's brother. He assumed it was Reg who did it, so he killed him. He thinks it was old-fashioned incompetence. I can't wait to see how he's going to react when he finds out who really did it."

"I knew this was going to happen, Cesari. Where are you now?"

"Vito and I just left the hospital. We're waiting for the Russian to call us. He wants to talk."

"You can't be serious?"

"Unfortunately, I am. He's got my wallet and all my ID. He can find me any time he wants."

Vito and I walked with no particular destination in mind.

"Stay there, Cesari. I'm coming right now."

"No, Kel. I'm serious. These guys are real assholes. Just sit tight for now and I'll call you later. Promise me, please."

Silence as she thought it over. "I'll hang out here at the museum. Call me in exactly one hour."

"I will."

I'd no sooner hung up then the phone rang again. "Go corner of 3rd Avenue and 12th Street. There is green Suburban. Get in. We are watching." He hung up.

"Do we have any options, Vito?"

"Not good ones. Especially you. I don't have anything to lose, but he knows who you are and where you work. Even worse, he knows who Kelly is."

"Fuck, and thanks for offering my services to him."

"I saved your life, Cesari. You can thank me any time you want. If I didn't make a play we'd already be dead, and we might even make a buck or two out of this if we're smart. Let's talk to him. If he was going to kill us, he would have done so already."

"He could always change his mind."

We hurried down to 12th Street as police sirens raced by us towards the hospital. Somebody must have discovered the bodies. There was a green Suburban with tinted windows double-parked at the corner, and a door opened as we approached, so we got into the back seat. There were two guys in the front and another two behind us in the third row. The driver and passenger were both bulky guys with crew cuts. The one in the passenger seat was pointing some type of submachine gun at us. Sergei and the other guy from Reg's office sat behind us, and I felt the Uzi in the back of my head. Hoods were placed roughly over our heads, the doors locked and the driver sped off. We drove in silence for about thirty minutes, eventually coming to a screeching halt.

Sergei started it. "Tell Sergei again why he shouldn't kill you both?"

I had thought about it during the drive. "Because we can help you, Sergei. We already know about the diamonds and how you're getting them into the country." I was having trouble talking through the hood and was getting very warm in there.

I took a deep breath and continued. "Dr. Griffin told me every-thing. I'm a gastroenterologist just like him and I can continue per-forming the procedures. This way, there will be no interruption in the flow of diamonds. In fact, I'm even better than he was. What hap-pened the other night to your brother would never have happened with me. Just think about it. You won't have to go through the trouble of recruiting anybody else or changing your methods, which have worked well so far."

He thought that over. "And what is price?"

"Whatever you were paying him will be fine for me."

Vito added in a muffled voice. "Plus ten percent of course. After what happened today, the risk just went up."

Sergei sat back in his seat and said something in Russian to his friends, and they all started laughing. I turned slightly and asked, "Ev-erything okay?"

"Everything okay," he said, chuckling. "Sorry for laugh, but think funny that we hold guns and friend try negotiate."

"Oh yeah. My friend is very funny like that."

There was silence as he mulled it over. Suddenly, and just as roughly, they removed the hoods from our heads. We both took a deep breath and noted that we were in some type of parking garage. I heard the sound of jet engines roaring close by and surmised that we were either at LaGuardia or JFK Airport. The garage was nearly empty and I saw construction signs off to one side prohibiting vehicular traffic, but I guessed that didn't mean us.

Sergei looked pensive. "Okay, Sergei give test. More diamonds arrive tomorrow. I pay one hundred thousand dollars. Excuse, one hundred and ten thousand dollars. Ten percent extra for added risk," he chuckled.

"But I'm not on call tomorrow, Sergei. I can't just go into the OR and perform colonoscopies any time I want."

The other guy poked me in the back of the head with the Uzi, and Sergei said, "No disappoint Sergei, yes?"

Vito jumped in and I shut up. "Don't worry, Sergei. We won't disappoint you. We'll make it happen."

"Good. I call let know who is patient and how reach. We see. Maybe I keep big friend for insurance."

"I need him, Sergei. He's my bodyguard. This is a very dangerous city. That's why Dr. Griffin lost the diamonds in the first place. He was robbed right on a city street." I didn't know that for sure, but it sounded good.

Sergei was quiet. "All right, big man is bodyguard. Now everybody out. I call later."

Vito and I got out of the Suburban in the deserted garage. Sergei threw our wallets out the window at us and they sped off.

"God damn, Cesari. How long does it take you to do a colonoscopy?"

"About fifteen minutes."

"That's one hundred and ten thousand dollars for fifteen minutes work. That's not bad scratch."

"Not bad at all, as long as we don't get our throats slit."

"Yeah, that was pretty nasty, and it was you that killed his brother. Man, he's going to go nuts if he ever finds out, and what's with all this stuff about ears?"

"Fuck if I know, Vito, and did you hear that comment he made about Kelly's ears? This guy is crazy for sure, and we just became his junior partners. God damn it. How am I going to do this? There's more to doing a colonoscopy than just dragging a patient up to the OR. I need nursing support and there's going to be a paper trail."

"Just do what your predecessor did. Send the guy to the ER and then call over and tell them you'll be right in to take care of him."

"Yeah, but Reg was chief of the department. He could do stuff like that without being questioned and who am I going to use as my nurse assistant?"

"Isn't your girl, Kelly, a nurse?"

Great.

"You're forgetting that I might be fired or suspended when I get back, and that's assuming no one spotted us leaving Reg's office. In which case, I'll be the number one suspect in yet another murder."

"Yeah, I did forget about that. How long will it be before you know what happened at the meeting?"

"Not sure. They were all waiting to see where Reg was going to fall on the issue."

We walked to the garage's stairwell and went down to street level. My cell phone rang. It was Boom Boom.

"Hello."

"Where are my diamonds, asshole?" I signaled Vito who it was.

"What do you mean? I gave them to Bobby."

"Yeah well, Bobby and Giorgio are missing, and I haven't heard from them since this morning when they were on their way to see you."

I looked at my watch. It was close to three. "I have no idea where they are. I gave Bobby the diamonds at nine-thirty sharp and both he and Giorgio said goodbye. That's all I know."

"Well, I haven't heard from either one all day. You better not have double-crossed me, Cesari, and what the fuck is going on at your hospital? It's been all over the news: a double homicide, a doctor and his secretary. Shit, this city isn't safe anymore."

"Why would I double-cross you? I'd have to be crazy to do something as stupid as that. Maybe Bobby and Giorgio decided to have a long lunch or something, and I have no idea what's going on at the hospital. I had the day off and have been shopping in midtown."

"Well, I had better hear from them soon or you're going to be in hot water. I hope we understand each other, Cesari."

He hung up.

Shit. What happened to those guys?

"What the fuck did that asshole want?" Vito asked.

"Two of his guys went AWOL with the diamonds I gave them this morning and he thinks I may have double-crossed him."

"Looks like we both got a Boom Boom problem now, Cesari. You better start coming up with some ideas on how to fix it."

"Yeah, well, first things first. C'mon, let's get out of here."

Once at street level, we discovered that we were at LaGuardia Airport in Queens, and hopped a quick cab back to Manhattan. I called Kelly on the way.

"Hi, Kel. How's the museum?"

"I left about an hour ago. I've been doing a little window shopping and trying to keep myself calm. It's been all over the news about Reg and his secretary. One of the nurses from the ER called me. Apparently, it's a zoo down there with all the police and reporters."

"Yeah, I bet. Why don't you meet me back at the hotel and we'll grab a bite somewhere? I'll fill you in on what's going on. I should be there by five. I'm going to head over to the hospital now. I want to find out what decision, if any, was made about me at the board meeting this afternoon."

"Okay, I'll see you later, and good luck."

R℘ 53

THE cab dropped us off in front of the hospital and I went in, hoping to find a friendly face. Vito went to buy himself a cell phone. There was a large crowd of people outside the ER where the bodies of Reg and his secretary were being processed, awaiting transfer to the morgue. Upstairs in Reg's office, hordes of police photographers and forensics people were salivating with excitement as they recorded the scene and searched for clues. I wondered how many fingerprints of mine they would find in Reg's office. Nothing I could do about it now, but I was sure they would find many other fingerprints besides mine. Reg was an important guy in the hospital and routinely had other physicians and administrators in his office. I hadn't touched either of the bodies, so DNA analysis should clear me if it ever came to that.

I saw my friend, Kirk, the anesthesiologist, standing around gawking in disbelief like everyone else. I went up to him. "Hey, Kirk."

"Hey, Cesari, unbelievable, isn't it?"

"Yeah."

"Apparently, his wife doesn't even know yet. No one has been able to reach her. They have a second home in Martha's Vineyard, and they think she may be up there. Talk about fucked up, and poor Betty, his secretary. Her husband is in the trauma room being sedated, he's so upset."

"Terrible thing, Kirk. What's the word on what happened? Any theories yet?" I asked.

"None that make any sense. Reg had quite the reputation as the ladies' man, though. There could be dozens of husbands or boyfriends out there who might have decided it was time to fix his ass. But why kill Betty? And why cut off Reg's ear? Did you hear about that? That's the part that doesn't fit. Right now it's anyone's guess, although I heard one just a few minutes ago that almost knocked me off my feet." He hesitated and looked around to make sure no one could hear him.

"Go ahead, Kirk. I'm listening."

"Someone suggested that it might have been his wife who hired hit men to take him out. Two big ugly guys were seen up on the fourth floor earlier today. One of them was missing an ear. That would explain the ear thing and maybe why no one can find the wife. She might have skipped out to have an alibi."

"But why did they kill his secretary?"

"Who knows, Cesari, maybe she was just in the way, or maybe Reg was having an affair with her too, and his wife decided enough was enough and had them both killed. Betty wasn't much to look at, but since when did that ever stop a horny guy?"

While we were talking, Art, the ER attending, came up to us. "You have got to be the luckiest son of a bitch on the planet, Cesari."

I turned in surprise. "How do you figure that one, Art? I lost a patient in the OR the other night, I'm on the verge of losing my job, possibly my license, maybe my freedom and my boss just got murdered. I'm surprised that I'm not the prime suspect."

He laughed. "Reg getting murdered was the best thing that could have happened to you. I was at that board meeting today. They asked me to come by to tell them what happened from my point of view since I was an eye witness. When Reg didn't show, they decided to adjourn until Monday. Everybody knows Reg owns the board, so they didn't want to make a decision without him. An hour later, all hell breaks loose when they find the bodies in his office. Now the board is in total freefall. I just got off the phone with one of the board members and he said they're most likely going to drop the Cesari thing all together. They're concerned about all the bad publicity that the hospital is getting right now and don't want to add to it by suggesting that a staff physician, you, may have murdered somebody during a colonoscopy. The fact that no one can find Gina has also raised some concern about her role. They're going to continue to let you work while they investigate further, and that could take weeks, maybe months, maybe forever, if you get my point. Personally, I think that they're just going to let it drift away. You're lucky that no one has come forward so far to make a stink about the dead guy, though."

"What about you, Art? Do you believe my story? You were pretty skeptical the other night."

"Yeah, well, that's how I get at one in the morning after I've put in a long day. The more I thought about it, the less sense it made. What possible reason could you have had to drag a guy up to the OR in the middle of the night, other than to do what you said you were doing? And if you were going to kill him then why would you call a code? If you called the code just to cover your tracks, then it was the sorriest cover up story in the history of recorded crime. You looked pathetic sitting there crying about how your nurse abandoned you. Then there's Gina. I personally have been trying to find her all week to corroborate your story and can't. That girl has flown the coop, and rather unexpectedly at that. The nurses in the OR told me that this little vacation of hers was completely unplanned, and nobody up in the OR knows where she is. Her credibility is starting to take a hit, to say the least. All in all, I decided to postpone judgment on you until I had more facts. I told the board the same thing and they agreed."

"Can they do that? Just forget about it?"

"The board can do whatever it wants. It's their job to do whatever is in the best interest of the hospital. Well, right now, it is in the best interest of the hospital to pretend the other night never happened, and not to have one of its physicians hauled out of here in handcuffs. Do you have any idea how much revenue the gastroenterology department brings in every year to St. Matt's?"

I shook my head. "No."

"Tens of millions, Cesari. And that's just the revenue from endoscopic procedures. It's a whole lot more when you factor in referrals, lab tests, and x-rays. No, they decided this thing with Reg is bad enough. They don't want another public black eye. At least that's the way I presented it when they asked my opinion. Besides, I don't know what really happened that night, but I don't believe that you set out to kill anyone, so don't prove me wrong."

"Thanks, Art. I won't. I owe you one."

"No problem, Cesari. Look, I've got to get back to work. See you later. You too, Kirk."

"See you later."

"Congratulations, Cesari," Kirk said. "You're off the hook, at least for now."

"Thanks. I assume the rumor mill has been churning fast and furious about my little misadventure the other night."

"Oh yeah. The whole hospital has been buzzing about it. Real hot stuff. This is how legends are made, Cesari. I didn't want to bring it up unless you did first, but personally, I think Gina fucked you over good. I told you about her. She's probably all strung out somewhere. She may have been stoned that night in the OR and didn't want anyone to catch her like that when the shit hit the fan, so she ran and now she's hiding."

"Yeah, well I'm sure all will be revealed in time, as they say. She's bound to show up sooner or later. I'm not going to worry about it. Okay, well, I've got to get going. Nice talking to you, Kirk."

"Take care, Cesari."

I looked at my watch and saw it was almost five. My phone buzzed in my pocket.

"Hi, John."

"Hi, Pam. How are you?"

"Not great. I'm not sleeping well and every time I think I'm putting it all behind me, I suddenly feel like something bad is going to happen. I feel ridiculous for being so scared."

"It's perfectly normal to feel that way. I was very scared, too."

"Well, thanks for saying that, although I don't believe you. You didn't look the least bit scared. I didn't hear from you yesterday—"

"You mean about having coffee?"

"Yeah, I was kind of looking forward to it."

"I'm sorry, Pam, I was pretty tied up. I went to Albany to visit a friend, and today has been pretty chaotic. I don't know if you heard what happened at the hospital."

"It's okay, and I did hear. It's been all over the news. That's so awful. Unfortunately, that news has increased my sense of dread exponentially."

"Yeah well, it was pretty bad for everyone. That's for sure."

"What do you think happened?"

"I really don't know. Right now, all bets are off as to what's going on."

"John, please don't think I'm crazy, but I feel like I'm being watched. Do you think we could meet somewhere just to talk? I would feel better if I saw you."

"I don't know, Pam. There's a lot going on. I was about to have dinner with my girlfriend."

"There's a Starbucks just down the block from my apartment... but I'm not sure I want to leave my apartment right now. God, this is a terrible feeling. Am I losing my mind?" I could feel the stress in her voice and was starting to worry about her.

"You're not losing your mind, Pam. Somebody really did try to kill you the other day. You may be developing a little post-traumatic stress, though. Look, why don't you stay put. I'll come over later after dinner to check in on you. Is there anything you need?"

"I don't need anything and thank you. When can I expect you?"

"How about nine?"

"That would be great. See you then."

Rx 54

I picked up Kelly and we met Vito at McSorley's for burgers and a round of Guinness. As he sat down, and before anyone spoke, Vito said, "Look Kelly, before anything else, I want to say how sorry I am for everything that happened last year. I want you to know how deeply I regret my actions, and I hope that you'll give me the chance to make it up to you."

Not bad, Vito. It was just as we had rehearsed and very sincere. Girls liked it when guys groveled. When in doubt, always throw yourself on the ground and beg for mercy. It had something to do with the nurturing instinct.

Kelly looked at him sharply. "I'll do my best to get past it, but I won't make any promises other than I'll be watching you closely, and if anything happens to Cesari, I will hold you personally responsible."

Not quite what I had hoped for, but at least she didn't stab him with a fork.

"Okay," I said. "Now that we're all friends, let's eat." We all ordered cheeseburgers, fries and Guinness.

Kelly turned to me. "So fill me in. What's the deal with this Sergei character, the guy with one ear?"

"He's obviously some type of Russian mobster. How high up is difficult to know. My guess is he's just an enforcer type, not the main guy pulling the strings. There's no question, however, that he feels comfortable with the use of lethal force and judging by his appearance and demeanor, I suspect that trying to intimidate him into backing off would be a mistake. He looks like he could take a punch and a whole lot more. His ear wasn't just missing, Kel. It looked like it had been ripped off."

"Or bitten off," offered Vito sipping his Guinness. "He looked like a real asshole, if you ask me."

Kelly absorbed the information. "Great. And you just offered to take Reg's place in delivering the diamonds to him."

"That was a tactical decision made under great duress, Kel. It was looking very much like we might wind up like Reg, so we offered the guy something we thought he would want."

"So now what?" she asked.

"Sergei's going to call us to let us know who the next guy is and how to reach him. Then we're supposed to make the arrangements for him to have his colonoscopy."

I cleared my throat. "There's one more thing I think I should mention, Kel."

Vito kept his eyes down. Kelly looked at me suspiciously. "And what would that be, Cesari?"

"Well, I really can't do a colonoscopy by myself. I'm going to need a nurse to assist me."

She glared at me. "Are you out of your mind? I can't just waltz on up to the OR and do a colonoscopy with you. I'm an ER nurse now. I'll get fired or lose my license."

We waited as the waitress served us our meals.

"Yes, that's a possibility, of course, but you used to be an OR nurse and a very good one at that."

"Cut the bullshit because I'm not doing it."

I pleaded. "Kelly, I really don't have anyone else I can ask to do this and we don't have a whole lot of time."

"Cesari, what are you getting us into? Have either one of you thought one step ahead? What happens after this case? What if Sergei decides that he's just going to keep on bringing in more diamonds? Then what? Is smuggling diamonds going to be your new career?"

"We'll have to cross that bridge when we come to it, Kel. Right now, we agreed to do this to buy ourselves some time. If we back out now, then we better head right for the airport and disappear because this Sergei guy doesn't look like the understanding type."

Vito agreed. "He definitely won't be sympathetic, Kel, that's for sure. He's a real asshole. I know the type."

Kelly looked at him crossly. "Did I ask for your opinion? I was speaking to my boyfriend." Vito took the rebuke well, looked down at his plate and stuffed a pile of fries in his mouth.

She turned her attention back to me. "Do you have any idea what you're asking me to do? I'm not the secret agent type. I get nervous when I'm late making a payment on my credit card."

"I know, but it's not like I'm asking you to do something you haven't done hundreds of times before. It's a simple colonoscopy, and if we don't do this, we're all going to be in big trouble. Even if I could find someone else to assist me, once they see the diamonds, word would spread like wildfire what I've been up to."

She ate in silence, and Vito finally worked up the courage to speak again. "Kelly, this guy wants to pay us a hundred-and-ten thousand dollars cash to do one colonoscopy. I don't know what you make, but I just left a $10 an hour job. I can't sneeze at this kind of dough."

She looked at him the way you would a small child who didn't understand why you shouldn't play with matches. "I don't think you understand, Mr. Gianelli. John has put the gangster stuff behind him, and we want to move forward together and have a normal life. This is dragging us backwards, and I don't like the idea of going backwards."

He was quiet.

I said, "I know what you're saying, Kel, and I have no intention of making this a permanent habit. Unfortunately, this guy Sergei not only can find me whenever he wants, but there's another, even more important, reason why it might be a bad idea to disappoint him."

"And what's that?"

"He knows who you are too, Kel. There was a picture of you in my wallet and he asked about it. There was no point in lying since you signed it, and wrote 'I love you' on the back. He kept the picture, and there's only one reason why he would do that."

"And what is that?"

"It was a not so subtle threat that anybody I care about is in grave danger."

Vito cleared his throat. "I have to agree with Cesari on that one. This guy is definitely not subtle. He's a real asshole."

Kelly looked disgusted. "Will you stop saying that already?"

Vito said, "I'm sorry."

I agreed, "I'm sorry, too."

"Will the both of you shut up? I'm trying to think." She looked depressed.

I looked at Vito. "We've been under a lot of stress."

He nodded. "I see that."

Kelly finally came to some sort of conclusion. She took a deep breath and let it out. "What are we supposed to do with the diamonds after we retrieve them from the guy's colon?"

"We don't know yet. Sergei was going to call me, and fill me in on the particulars. I assume we don't give them to the patient because he's sedated and may lose them. In addition, he may not even know what he's carrying, so there must be some sort of drop-off plan he'll tell me about."

"And what am I supposed to do exactly?" Kelly asked.

"I'll switch call duties with the gastroenterologist on call tomorrow night and let the ER know. Once Sergei gives me the guy's contact information, I'll send the patient to the ER and tell the doctor to keep an eye on him for me, and that I plan on scoping him later in the evening when I'm free, just like Reg would've done. You set up the endoscopy room and get things ready for me. Then I'll go down to the ER and get the patient while you stay in the OR. No one will even need to see you."

Kelly was puzzled. "Why not just have him come to the OR directly, like Gina did?"

"Because that will raise too many eyebrows if we're caught. Everybody knows what happened the other night in the OR, and if it suddenly happened again, it would make me look guilty as sin. The board would be forced to act against me. I need to leave an appropriate paper trail this time so it looks like just another on-call case, no different from what Reg had been doing. So, the guy goes to the ER, and tells them that he's bleeding and I'm his doctor. The ER will do the rest."

We finished our meals and paid the bill.

"Do you mind taking a walk with us, Vito?"

"Sure, where are we going?"

"My sexual addiction counselor is having a bad go of it and needs some company."

Vito looked at me and then started laughing. "Good one, Johnny."

"I'm serious. Her name's Pam Gottlieb. She's very nice, but hasn't been doing well since we were attacked the other night. I told you about that. The cop who is the nephew of my dead boss threatened to kill her and would have, too, if Boom Boom's guys hadn't shown up. She's having anxiety right now, which is understandable, but she may be getting a little paranoid. She thinks she's being watched. I'm starting to get a little worried about her."

"I remember you telling me about the dirty cops, but I don't remember the part about sexual addiction. That's great." He was enjoying himself.

"It must have slipped my mind. Put it behind you, and remember, this isn't funny to her."

Ten minutes later, we arrived at Pam's apartment building in the West Village. When she opened the door, we were shocked by her appearance. She was disheveled, wearing a terry cloth robe, and I suspected she hadn't bathed in several days. Her eyes were puffy from crying, and she nearly collapsed in my arms when she saw me.

"Pam, are you okay?"

"No, I'm losing it, John. I keep thinking people can see me through the walls. I'm afraid to go outside. I don't even want to go downstairs to get my mail." Kelly and I walked her over to her sofa and sat beside her. It was a very nice apartment with a big living room and nice-sized kitchen. Vito closed the door and sat down on a chair, watching us.

"Pam, this is Kelly and Vito. They're friends of mine."

"Hi, I'm Pam."

I looked at her sympathetically. "Pam, I think you may need professional help at this point. The symptoms you're having are much more severe than I would have expected given the circumstances. I have a friend who's a psychiatrist. Would you mind if I called him for you? He's a great guy."

Pam nodded and started weeping into Kelly's shoulder. In between sobs, she said, "I was watching a movie today, and I thought the guy on the television was laughing at me. I knew that couldn't be, but I couldn't stop feeling that way."

Shit. Those fucks had destroyed her emotionally.

Kelly placed an arm around her and gave her a hug. "It's going to be all right, honey. We're going to stay with you until we get you help."

"Thank you."

I took out my cell phone and called Mark.

"Hello, Cesari, how have you been?"

"I'm very well, Dr. Greenberg. How's my favorite psychiatrist?"

"Disappointed that I haven't heard from you in months."

"Sorry about that, Mark. Look, I have a friend who's having some sort of acute anxiety attack. She's falling apart fast and needs real help."

"What happened?"

I stepped away from Pam and walked into her kitchen for privacy.

"Several nights ago, a couple of guys came into her office and threatened to kill her."

"Oh my God. Why?"

"It's complicated, but they were trying to frame me for her murder."

"You? Once again, why?"

"Does it really matter?"

"No, I suppose not. So what happened?"

I opened the refrigerator while we talked, looking for something to drink and found some bottled water. "Two other guys rescued us in the nick of time."

"Us? You were there when this happened?"

"Yeah, I'm her patient."

"She's a doctor?"

"She's a psychologist."

"I thought I was your shrink."

"You are. I was forced to see her by the chair of my department at St. Matt's."

"Wait a minute. Was that the guy I saw on TV this afternoon? The one who was murdered in his office?"

I sipped from the water bottle and peeked in the living room to check on the others. "Yeah, that was him."

"Holy shit. Why did he make you see a psychologist?"

Silence.

"I'm waiting."

"It was very unfair."

"That's not an answer."

"He thought I might have sexual addiction."

He started laughing. "Finally out of the closet, huh? Is that why you killed him?"

"I didn't kill him."

"So why is he is dead?"

"It's complicated, but he was an asshole."

"If every asshole on the planet deserved to get murdered, and did, there wouldn't be any doctors left."

I laughed this time. "You're right about that. Look, I really can't go into it right now, Mark. Suffice it to say that when it came to my late boss, there was a lot more than meets the eye. Can you help my friend?"

"Of course I can help your friend. She's not suicidal, is she?"

"I didn't ask, but I will."

"Well, as long as she's no immediate threat to herself or others, then just keep an eye on her tonight, and I'll see her first thing tomorrow morning. Can you bring her up to my office on the West Side? Do you remember where it is?"

"Yeah, I remember where it is. What time?"

"8 a.m. sharp, and Cesari, when can I start spending that money I got in the Caymans?"

"Not yet. Things are still very hot, and there are a lot of people looking for that money. I'm sure they have people down there monitoring for any unusual transactions. I'm just sitting on mine for now and you should do the same. Consider it a nest egg for when you're forced into early retirement because of this affordable care bullshit."

"Understood. See you at eight."

"Thanks, Mark. Bye."

R͓x 55

BACK in the living room, I saw Pam holding onto Kelly for dear life. Vito was off to one side, silently watching and clearly uncomfortable. They all looked up at me as I entered the room.

Kelly asked, "What did Mark have to say?"

"He'd like to see Pam first thing in the morning, if that's all right with you, Pam?"

She nodded. "Who is he?"

"His name is Mark Greenberg and he's a psychiatrist on the upper west side. He's on the faculty at Columbia and is a good friend of mine. I've known him for practically my whole life. He'll take good care of you."

"Thank you."

"He suggested we stay with you tonight to keep you company. Would that be okay with you?"

"Sure, but I don't think I have enough room. It's only a one bedroom," she said, gazing around the apartment. It was a nice apartment, but four, even three people, would be a bit much.

Kelly agreed, "I'll stay with Pam. You two go back to the hotel. What time is the appointment tomorrow?"

"It's at eight in his office on the west side. You were there with me a couple of times. We probably should leave here about seven."

"I remember it well. Look, it's only ten. Why don't you run over to the hotel and get me a few things I'll need, like a change of clothes? In the meanwhile, Pam and I will get to know each other."

"Sure thing. C'mon Vito. Let's go."

We took a cab back to the Saint Mark's Hotel and went up to our rooms. Vito's was on the fifth floor. When the elevator stopped, I said, "I'll meet you at six-thirty downstairs in the lobby. We'll grab coffee and head over to pick up the girls."

"Why do I have to go to the shrink's office with you?"

"I think we should stay together, don't you? Besides, we've got a lot to talk about."

He thought about that. "Yeah, maybe you're right."

"I always am, Vito. Get some sleep. We're going to be up late tomorrow night."

I went to my room on the tenth floor and packed a few things for Kelly in a duffel bag. Downstairs, the cab was still waiting for me, as I had asked. The driver smiled and nodded toward the back seat. Entering the rear of the taxi, I was surprised to see that I wasn't alone.

"Gina, what the fuck are you doing here?"

She didn't look so good, and appeared very stressed. She had been crying, and wasn't wearing make-up.

"I don't want to die, Cesari. Please help me. I don't want to die."

I was very angry. "What are you talking about, and why should I give a shit about anything that happens to you?"

She bowed her head, and I instructed the driver to take us back to Pam's apartment.

She started sobbing. "You're right to feel that way, and I'm sorry about what happened. The heparin was Reg's idea. We didn't think the guy would die, just bleed a little and maybe require a transfusion at the worst. He just wanted to get you in enough trouble so that you would cooperate with him and return the diamonds. We were both shocked when we heard that he died. You have to believe me. I'm not a murderer, and I'll never believe Reg would have put me in that position on purpose."

"Yeah, well, Reg didn't seem shocked or that he even gave a shit that somebody had died. Besides, is that supposed to make me feel better? I feel like smacking you right now."

"Go ahead. I deserve it." She lifted her head up and closed her eyes just in case I took her up on it.

"Stop it," I snapped . "I don't hit girls, but don't tempt me again. You really fucked up my life. Half the hospital thinks I'm some sort of maniac. So why did you come out of hiding? To apologize?"

"I heard what happened to Reg and I'm scared. The Russians killed him, I know it. They know who I am, and if they killed him, they certainly will want to kill me, too."

"Why would they want to kill you, Gina?"

"Because I know who they are. I've met the one in charge, a guy called Sergei, several times. He considered Reg and me a team."

I was getting curious again. "Really? Because I met Sergei and he didn't mention you."

"You met Sergei?"

"Not only met him, but thanks to you, I'm now working for him."

"You're taking Reg's place?"

"Not because I want to, but yes, at least temporarily. Do you know why he killed Reg?"

"I just assumed it was over the missing diamonds."

"Even better, Gina. That guy you injected with heparin was Sergei's brother, and he was kind of pissed. So, now that I think about it, he will most certainly want to kill you if he ever finds out what you did."

She turned pale right in front of me, and I thought she might pass out. She sat back, staring at the roof of the car. "Oh my God."

"So Gina, you didn't say how it is I'm supposed to help you."

"I don't know. I'm scared, and I don't know who I can turn to who would understand what's going on. I really am sorry about the position I put you in. Reg could be very persuasive when he wanted to."

The cab pulled to the curb outside of Pam's building and I paid the driver.

"Come with me, Gina."

"Where are we going?"

"A friend's apartment. Don't ask questions, all right?"

"All right."

We went up to Pam's, and I knocked on the door. Kelly opened it and her mouth dropped in surprise when she saw Gina. "What is this bitch doing here?" she said angrily.

Gina wisely didn't say anything.

"She needs a place to stay, Kel."

"Here? You've got to be kidding."

"I suppose I could bring her back to the hotel with me." Kelly looked at me with daggers in her eyes. This was no time for jokes.

"Why can't she just sleep on the street with the other whores? There's a comfortable looking dumpster next to the building."

Gina spoke up softly, her voice cracking. "I deserve that, Kelly. I'm sorry about all the aggravation I've caused you both, but I got caught up in everything that was happening. The hole just kept getting deeper and deeper, and I didn't know how to get out. I know it sounds lame, but it really is the truth. I had no idea things were going to spiral so far out of control."

Why don't we come in and talk this over?" I asked. We stood there waiting for Kelly to make up her mind. She sighed deeply and stepped aside, allowing us entry.

She said, "Keep it down. Pam's sleeping in the bedroom." I saw the sofa had been made up with a sheet and a pillow. "You get the floor, Gina."

"That's fine with me. Whose apartment is it?"

"A friend of mine," I replied. "She's a psychologist. That's all you need to know right now, okay? We'll clear it with her in the morning." I was getting a little edgy and besides, we weren't friends. I looked at my watch. It was past eleven. "Gina, the price for staying here is full disclosure, so I think it's time to tell us all about you and Reg. It's getting late and I'd like to go to sleep. No more bullshit."

We all sat down, Kelly next to Gina on the sofa and me on the lone chair in the room.

Gina looked at us, confused. "You already know everything. What more can I tell you?"

"How did you get mixed up in all of this in the first place?" I asked.

Kelly wasn't that subtle. "Were you fucking Reg or not?"

Gina sighed. "Yes, but there's not that much more to tell. We had this on and off again thing, but mostly, we were just friends. He could be a lot of fun when he wanted. It was nothing serious. He was married, but I don't think his wife cared. She did her thing and he did his. What can I say?"

She shrugged her shoulders. "Anyway, about a year ago, Reg comes up to me and asks if I'd like to make an extra ten-thousand tax free dollars a month. All I would have to do is one, maybe two colonoscopies with him per month and not ask any questions. It was very tempting. Living in this city is very expensive, as you know. There didn't seem to be any harm in it, although it was obvious that what we were doing was illegal. I figured that if we ever got caught, all I would have to say was that I was simply doing what the doctor told me to. At first, I never looked in the little bags, but eventually, I got curious."

"Someone else got curious, too, didn't he?" I asked.

"You mean Ed Talbot?"

"Yeah, Ed."

"Yeah. He worked the night shift and had to clean up the OR after we did our cases. He began to notice the pattern of Reg and I always working together late at night. Pretty amazing considering he was strung out most of the time. He started to keep tabs on us and eventually even started spying on us. He even placed a small video camera in the endoscopy room, and actually recorded us one night. That's how he found out about the diamonds for sure. Then one night he made his move and waited for Reg and me as we left the hospital at two in the morning. He caught us off guard and had a gun. We were tired and in complete shock. Reg handed him all the diamonds and you know the rest. It was pretty stupid of Ed, but what do you want? He was a crackhead."

"So you never dated him?"

"That part was true. Years ago, before he got into drugs."

"Where have you been the last few days, Gina?"

"I've been staying at Reg's apartment on the East Side. His wife's been at their summer home in Martha's Vineyard. When I saw what happened on the news, I knew immediately who did it and that I'd better get moving. Either the Russians or the police would be coming there. I was afraid to go to my apartment and started looking for you out of desperation. Your landlord told me you were staying at Saint Mark's, so I sat and waited in the coffee shop across the street. I saw you get out of the cab with the big guy. The cab driver didn't go anywhere, so I asked him, and he told me that you were coming back down. Twenty bucks and he let me wait in the car for you."

It was almost midnight and Kelly gave her a stern look. "It's time to go to bed."

Gina said, "Thank you, and I really am sorry."

"Don't forget who the alpha female is."

"I won't."

Kelly looked at me just as sternly. "Go, I'm tired."

R_X 56

I decided to walk back to the hotel rather than take a cab. It was no more than a fifteen minute stroll, and I needed some fresh air and time to think. That Gina was a piece of work for sure. I hoped that they didn't kill each other by the time I returned in the morning. Three intense women in one little apartment might be pushing Mother Nature to the limit. Definitely a prescription for disaster.

Walking down E. 8th Street, I was about to cross over to St. Mark's Place when something I didn't like caught my eye. Rather than go into the hotel, I ducked into the diner across the street and sat by a window. Peeking around the curtain, I spied a Lincoln Towncar with tinted windows parked in front of the hotel with its engine running. I had seen it a few blocks back parked by the entrance to Washington Square Park as I walked by, and then again as I crossed Broadway. I was lost in thought and didn't notice it at first, but now it was obvious that it had followed me. I couldn't make out the driver, but I had a bad feeling about it.

The two cops? They drove an unmarked Crown Vic. Besides, I doubted they were in any shape to be players after the beating Bobby and Giorgio gave them. The Russians? They drove a Suburban, but they could have another car. Why would they be following me? Maybe they were keeping an eye on me to protect their investment. I ordered a cup of coffee and watched the car while I thought it over. Was I letting my imagination run away with me? I didn't want to go into the hotel where I might be trapped or ambushed while I slept. It wouldn't take a genius to find out which room I was in. Just flash cash at the kid minding the desk. Goddamn, I was getting tired and I didn't have my .38.

I took out my cell phone and dialed Vito. One ring, two rings, three rings. It went to voicemail. I called the front desk at the hotel.

"Hello, Saint Mark's Hotel. How may I help you?"

"Yes, hi. Could you put me through to room 509?"

"I'm sorry, sir, but that will not be possible. The hotel has a strict policy of not disturbing its guests after midnight unless specifically requested to do so by the guest."

"But it's an emergency. Both he and I would be very grateful."

Silence.

"How grateful?" He asked.

"Twenty bucks grateful."

"I'm sorry, sir, but the hotel has a strict policy of not disturbing its guests after midnight."

"I'm sorry. I meant fifty bucks grateful."

"How can I be sure of that?"

Cynical little prick, wasn't he. "I have a friend who works at the diner across the street from where you are. I'll call her and she'll bring it over to you. I'll call you back after that, okay?"

"I'm not going anywhere, and I also won't be holding my breath."

I signaled the waitress. Her name tag said Lisa. "Lisa, how would you like to make a quick fifty bucks?"

She smiled and looked around. "I don't get off for another hour, but I could meet you in the men's room. It's pretty quiet right now."

Jesus!

"That's not what I meant, Lisa. I'd like you to do me a favor and go over to the Saint Mark's Hotel across the street. I want you to deliver a note to the guy at the desk and then I'd like you to go up to room 509 and wake up a friend of mine. Tell him to call me on my cell phone, but don't be afraid of him when you see him. He looks kind of mean, but he won't hurt you. It shouldn't take you more than ten minutes, and I'll give you the fifty bucks right now." I took out my wallet and handed her a fifty.

"That's all you want me to do? Wake him up?"

"Yes, that's all."

"Can I ask why you can't go over there yourself?"

"You can ask, but don't expect an answer."

She laughed. "Okay, I was bored anyway. Need a pen?"

"Yes, thank you."

I wrote a short note on a paper napkin while she watched. *"Fuck you, asshole."* I folded the napkin and handed it to her. "Give this to the kid at the front desk."

She turned around, told the other waitress that she was going to step out for a quick cigarette, and I watched her cross the street toward the hotel. Ten minutes later, my cell phone rang as I watched her return to the diner. The Lincoln hadn't moved.

"Vito."

"Cesari, what's with the cloak and dagger? I almost dragged that poor girl in here for a little R&R if you know what I mean."

"Why would you do that?"

"I thought you sent a hooker to my room dressed as a waitress. You know, like the old days."

I took a deep breath. "Well, sorry about the confusion. Look, there's a Lincoln towncar sitting outside the hotel and I think it's been following me. I'm in the diner across the street."

"What do you want me to do?"

"First of all, make sure your .45 is loaded and meet me down here in the diner in five minutes. Walk well behind the Lincoln so they don't get a good look at you."

"I'm on the way."

He emerged from the front entrance of the hotel and walked discreetly past the towncar, crossing the street at the corner light. He took a seat opposite me and the waitress poured him a cup of coffee. He smiled at her. "Hey, honey, once again, I'm sorry about the misunderstanding."

"No problem, handsome. Maybe some other time. It's a good thing your friend warned me about you."

They both giggled and Vito stared at her as she walked away.

I snapped my fingers in front of him to get his attention. "Okay, let's come up with a plan quick. It's getting late," I said.

He took a sip of coffee and thought it over. "Why can't we just walk up to the car and ask them who they are and what they want?"

"Vito, you can't be that rusty at this stuff. Look at the car. See the tinted windows? There could be one guy in there or five. For all we know they might have submachine guns. What if they get nervous?"

He nodded. "I see what you mean. So we have to get them to come out of the car."

"Or get the drop on them. We have at least one advantage in that they don't know that there are two of us."

"We could go wait in your hotel room and see if they come charging in?"

"I thought about that. But what if they don't? Are we going to stay up all night waiting for something that's not going to happen? No, we have to make something happen."

We sat there looking at each other, sipping our coffees and looking around. It seemed like an okay diner. I spotted an apple pie under a plastic cover.

"Hey, Lisa, could you come over here? I want to ask you something." I waited as she walked over from behind the counter.

"What's up?"

"How would you and your girlfriend each like to make fifty bucks?"

"Another fifty bucks? What is it this time? Tony's going to get mad if I leave the diner again." She looked over at a burly looking guy flipping burgers behind a griddle. "He's the night manager."

There were three waitresses. If two left for a minute, there would still be one left to mind the customers. "Tell Tony there's fifty bucks in it for him, too."

"That should do it. So what is it?"

"I need you and one of the other waitresses to take a pot of hot coffee, some cups, and a couple of pieces of pie out to that Lincoln parked in front of the Saint Mark's Hotel. You walked by it before. One of you goes on each side of the car and knock on the windows. Tell them that the pie and coffee they ordered has arrived and that they owe you what? Ten bucks?"

"Close enough."

"I don't know how many guys are in the car. When they roll down their windows, take a quick look in the back. If anyone is in the back seat, apologize for the misunderstanding and come straight back. If there's only the driver and a passenger, then when they tell you to fuck off, make a big stink about it like you're really pissed that you're getting stiffed. I wouldn't object to you dumping the hot coffee in their laps if you got the gumption."

"Oh, we got the gumption, all right. Do it all the time. Really calms down the excitable ones fast, but what if they get nasty? Tony's got a baseball bat and a sawed off shotgun behind the counter in case of trouble, but we'll be way out there all alone."

"Tony's got a sawed off and a bat?"

Vito grinned. "I knew I liked her."

She grinned back. "You're cute, too."

I said, "Tell Tony I'll give him a hundred dollars if he lets me borrow the shotgun for ten minutes. It doesn't have to be loaded and you won't be alone because Vito and I are coming with you. The minute the guys get agitated or look like they're going to get out of the car, you and your friend high-tail it back to the diner."

I handed her two hundred bucks, fifty for her and her friend and a hundred for Tony. She returned with a girl named Gabriella, a couple of large cups of coffee and two slices of apple pie. Tony stood right behind them, holding the shotgun and baseball bat.

"Who are you guys?"

"Two law abiding citizens being harassed by the guys in that car over there." I pointed to the Lincoln.

He looked through the curtain and nodded. "The one with the tinted windows?"

"Yeah."

"Look, I can't give you any shells. Too risky, but you can have the gun for show. Nothing better happen to the girls. Lisa, Gabriella, I'll wait by the door with the baseball bat. Anything happens, move your asses." They nodded.

I said, "Thanks, Tony, I appreciate your help and your trust."

He wiped his hand on his dirty apron. "Who said anything about trust? I want both your driver's licenses to hold while you do whatever it is you're doing. I'll give 'em back when you return the shotgun."

We dumped our licenses onto the table, and he snatched them up, handing me the sawed-off wrapped in a white towel.

"Vito, you go out there first. Walk down the block a little before crossing over, and come up behind them. We can see you easily from here. When you're in position, I'll send the girls out with the pie. Once they start talking to them, I'll come out casually like nothing's going on and walk right in front of them in full view. Vito, don't do anything until the girls are out of the way, and girls, I mean it. You say what you got to say and then clear out. The element of surprise won't last long. Vito, I take the driver and you get the guy on the passenger side, all right?"

Vito said, "What if there are more than two guys in the car?"

"We abort and regroup back here for further discussion."

I threw a twenty on the table for our coffees. Vito went outside and strolled nonchalantly down our side of the street for a couple of hundred feet before crossing over and doubling back. As he approached the car from the rear, he slowly maneuvered onto the street directly behind it and crouched low when he reached the trunk. If anybody in the car saw him, they weren't letting on. Hell, it was after one in the morning and they were probably tired, too.

The two waitresses approached the car from either side and knocked on their respective windows. They were holding large Styrofoam cups with hot coffee and small plates with apple pie. I watched as the windows opened and the girls went into their routines. I'd never seen the driver before, couldn't see the passenger and had no idea what might be going on in the back seat.

I walked out of the diner and headed over to the driver's side, cradling the shotgun still in the towel. I was directly behind Lisa, who blocked his view of me. I heard the waitresses arguing on both sides of the car. I was halfway across the street when the girls simultaneously dumped the hot coffee and pies onto their laps. The men started cursing, and both girls took off like rabbits back to the diner where Tony was waiting for them. Vito came charging around to the passenger side, thrusting his .45 into his guy's face. I rushed the few remaining feet to the driver's side, uncovered the shotgun and shoved it into the side of the driver's head, cocking the trigger so there would be no misunderstanding. I glanced quickly toward the back seat, confirming there were no others.

"Don't move, assholes." I reached in quickly and grabbed a nine millimeter Glock from his shoulder holster while Vito disarmed the other guy who was similarly armed.

We jumped into the backseat and I shouted, "Drive, motherfucker, now."

"Wait—wait," Tony was running across the street, waving at us.

"Hold on," I ordered the driver, poking him hard with his Glock.

Tony reached the car, short of breath. I passed him his shotgun and he handed me our driver's licenses. "Thanks, Tony."

We pulled away down Third Avenue with the nine millimeters pressed against the backs of their heads.

"Where are we going?" the driver asked.

"Shut up and turn right down 12th Street. Head over to the FDR drive and pull over under the overpass." Five minutes later, the car came to a stop in a deserted section of terrain beneath the highway; the sounds of traffic could be heard overhead. He put the car in park.

"Cut the engine, hand me the keys and put both hands on the steering wheel." I turned to the passenger. "Lean forward and put your hands on the dashboard where I can see them, and don't do anything stupid. Okay, now who the fuck are you two before I blow your heads off?" They were both young and seemed inexperienced.

The driver spoke first. "Boom Boom sent us." Vito and I glanced at each other.

"Sent you to do what?"

"To pick you up and bring you down to his place in Little Italy."

"Why is that?"

"I guess he wanted to talk to you."

I smacked him in the back of the head with the gun.

"Oww. Fuck. That's all I know. He gave us your name, and said 'go get him and bring him to me.'"

"Nice and slow. Reach into your pockets and hand me your wallets and cell phones. Don't twitch. I got nothing against you guys, but it wouldn't bother me one bit to leave you here permanently."

They did as they were told and passed me the items I'd requested.

"Any other weapons? If you lie, you will regret it. Believe me."

They nodded. The one on the passenger side said, "I have a .32 in an ankle holster on the right."

"Reach down slowly with your left hand and with your index finger and thumb, grab it by the handle and slowly pass it to my friend." He did as he was told and Vito relieved him of his backup weapon.

I opened the driver's wallet. Michael D'Alessio, twenty-five years old. He had credit cards, about two hundred dollars in twenties and a recent picture of me. It looked like it had been taken when I was sitting on Boom Boom's couch. He must have a hidden camera in his apartment, I thought.

"Do you mind if I borrow the cash? I'm a little low."

"Go ahead," he said.

The other guy's driver's license said that his name was Roberto Valentino, age twenty-six. He had another hundred dollars, which I borrowed.

"So how was this supposed to go down, Mike?"

"No set plan. When it looked like we could snatch you without too much commotion, we were to bring you down to the apartment in Little Italy. He said that you were a doctor and that it shouldn't be much of a problem bringing you in. We have plastic restraints in the glove compartment in case you gave us a hard time."

"How long have you worked for Boom Boom?"

"About a year. Mostly just guarding the doorway to his apartment, running errands and backup stuff. This was supposed to be a lightweight job, a no-brainer."

"What about you?" I asked Roberto.

"I just started. I haven't even met Boom Boom yet. Mikey cleared my being here with him. This was supposed to be my chance to prove myself. I'm trying to get in on a more permanent basis."

"Why didn't you pick me up down by Washington Square Park? I walked right by you."

Mikey said, "I wasn't sure if it was you. It was dark out. No offense, but you look like a million other guys."

Vito chuckled at the, *you look a million other guys comment.* I said, "No offense taken, but you've been following me around for hours. How'd you find me?"

"We knew about the woman doctor from Bobby, so we staked out her apartment. I saw you come out of the building, but like I said I wasn't certain it was you, and didn't want to bring the wrong guy in. I knew you were staying at the Saint Mark's from your landlord, so I figured we'd pick you up there. We weren't in any rush."

"Pop the trunk, Mikey. Roberto, get the wrist restraints out of the glove compartment. The trunk clicked open and Roberto leaned forward to open the glove compartment. He moved a little too quickly, and my mind raced back to Carlos in Vermont and the handgun in the glove compartment. It was dark in the car, but I thought I caught the glint of metal out of the corner of my eye, and yelled, "Gun!"

Vito fired twice into the guy's back, and Roberto slumped forward, dead. The roar of the pistol in the close quarters of the car was deafening and the smell of gunpowder filled the air. As the smoke cleared, the open glove compartment revealed nothing more than the plastic restraints and a small, silver, metal inhaler for his asthma.

Mikey cringed and I think he wet himself. "Fuck, he didn't do anything."

"Damn," Vito added.

I was pissed at myself. "Mikey, pop the trunk and get out of the fucking car. Keep your hands behind your head. Vito, throw Roberto into the trunk and leave room for Mikey."

His voice trembling with fear, Mikey asked, "Are you going to kill me, too?"

"Shut up, asshole, that was an accident, but he should have picked a different career. Now move to the back of the car."

I watched Vito pick up the body and hoist it into the large trunk. He pushed the body in as far as he could, tucking Roberto's limp legs and arms under him. I restrained Mikey with his own plastic handcuffs and then squished him into the trunk beside his friend. Looking down on him, I shook my head and let out a slow, deep breath. He didn't say anything. I brought the butt of the Glock down on his head hard, and he went out for the night.

R 57

"WELL, that really sucked, Cesari."

"Yeah, I know." I was very upset. "I'm sorry about that, Vito."

"Don't feel too bad, though, I would have done the same thing. It's better to be safe than sorry. What do the cops say? Better to face twelve guys on a jury than six pallbearers."

"I'm pretty sure that has nothing to do with this, but thanks anyway. I know what you're trying to say."

It was 2 a.m. and we were in the Towncar with the two guys in the trunk, driving towards Little Italy. Vito and I had a long talk as we drove, concerning the future and how hard it was to escape the past. He convinced me that it might be easier to contain certain undesirable elements in my life by taking a more proactive role rather than just playing defense, an effort that had been largely unsuccessful for me so far. For better or for worse, I found him making a lot of sense.

I said, "Well, we might as well take care of the Boom Boom problem while we got momentum and surprise on our side. You up for it, Vito?"

"Oh yeah. I just hope that guy Roberto was serious when he said he never met Boom Boom before."

"I think he was. Okay, so let's go over it again. You pretend to be Roberto, and I'll be me. You bring me up to the apartment with my hands cuffed behind me, only they won't be cuffed. I'll just keep them crossed behind my back as if they were, and you stay close behind me so no one gets a good look. Mikey's Glock will be tucked in the small of my back underneath my shirt and you have your .45. If we catch everybody by surprise, we should be okay. You're sure you never met Boom Boom before, Vito?"

"I've heard of him, but never had the pleasure. I make it a point never to be photographed either, but we can't be sure that he hasn't seen an old mug shot of me. Still, he won't be expecting me to walk in through the front door."

"And what happened to Mikey again?"

"He was a casualty. You caught him by surprise with a bat, and now he's on his way to the hospital."

I parked on Hester Street just off of Mulberry and looked at Vito. "Go ahead and make the call. Try to sound nervous. Remember, this was your first firefight and things went sideways." He took out Roberto's phone and dialed Boom Boom.

I could hear Boom Boom snarl on the other end. "Who's this?"

"It's, Roberto, Mikey D'Alessio's friend. I went with him to snatch the doc."

"Yeah, I remember. How'd it go and where's Mikey?"

"Mikey got hurt pretty bad. The doc surprised him with a baseball bat to the head. He's down at Bellevue getting treated. He was still unconscious when I left him."

"Shit. Where are you now?"

"I'm driving toward Mulberry Street with the doc handcuffed in the trunk of the Towncar. I'm almost there."

"Good work, Roberto. Good work. Fuck, the doc got moxie. I didn't expect that."

"What should I do? You want me to babysit him 'til morning? I know it's late."

"No, bring him here now. You know where my apartment is?"

"Yes, up above the Café Napoli."

"That's right. I'll let the guard know you're coming."

"I'll be there in a few minutes."

Vito hung up and turned to me.

"Nicely done, Vito."

"Of course. I'm telling you, Cesari, we make a great team. We always did. You're not going to regret this, partner."

"Yeah, right. Famous last words. Besides, I'm already regretting this, and it's 'managing partner.' Don't forget that."

"Look, Cesari, we give it whirl for a year and see what happens. If you're not happy, I'll buy you out and no hard feelings."

"Let's see if we survive the night first. There are a lot of ifs we have to get past first. C'mon, let's go. We're wasting time."

As we approached on foot, we noticed Mulberry Street was pretty quiet and all the restaurants were closed. I kept my hands crossed behind my back, pressed against the Glock. Vito stood slightly behind me with one hand on my shoulder, and every so often, he would shove me roughly to fuel the illusion I was a captive. Boom Boom's sentry stood a hundred feet away, observing us suspiciously. He was about Vito's size, a little younger, clean-shaven and with a gold earring. Ten feet away, he put one hand up and opened his windbreaker so we could see the handgun in his waistband. I kept my head bowed submissively.

"That's close enough," he said. "Are you Roberto?"

Vito nodded. "Close enough for what?"

"Shut up and look at the camera, asshole." He rested his hand on the pistol.

We looked up at the security camera above the door. A minute later, the guard's phone rang and he answered.

"Sure thing, Boom Boom." He hung up and motioned for us to come forward. He unlocked the door and opened it without uttering a word. We stepped past him and he slammed the door shut behind us. There was an old wood staircase in front of us and we marched up with me in front. At the top, another door opened and we found ourselves staring down the barrel of .12 gauge shotgun. Another one of Boom Boom's bodyguards waved at us to enter, which we did, I meekly, hands crossed behind my back.

He asked Vito, "Is he armed?"

"No, I frisked him already. He's just a fucking doctor anyway."

The guy relaxed a little. "Boom Boom's waiting for you two in the living room." He pointed towards a hallway leading into the living room. It was a very big apartment. As big as most homes and encompassing the entire second floor of the building. Close to five thousand square feet, I guessed. We walked in silence with Boom Boom's guy pulling up the rear. Vito kept pushing me for effect and to impress upon the others how helpless I was.

Boom Boom sat at a large desk drinking from a scotch glass when we entered. Scanning the room, I didn't see any other guards. Boom Boom stood up, chuckling. "Welcome back, Doc. Have a seat on the couch."

I sat down awkwardly in the center of the sofa. As I did so, I slipped my hand underneath my shirt and wrapped it around the Glock. He turned to Vito. "You must be Roberto."

"Yeah, nice to meet you Mr. Moretti, and thank you for the opportunity to prove myself." He extended his hand to Boom Boom, who took it.

"Good work, Roberto. I'm impressed. I didn't think the doc was going to give you guys such a hard time. I feel bad about Mikey. He gonna be okay?"

"Too soon to tell. The medics were talking about swelling on the brain or something. Yeah, the prick took poor Mikey by surprise. He was acting like he was going to surrender, you know. Said he just wanted to get a jacket from his closet and then comes out swinging a bat. Total asshole."

"Unbelievable." Boom Boom hesitated as he looked funny at Vito. "Have we met before, Roberto?"

"I don't think so," Vito said.

Boom Boom turned to his man, "Nunzio, pour Roberto a scotch. You know, Roberto, when Mikey told me about you, I got the impression that you were a much younger guy, just a kid."

Vito chuckled. "Maybe it's because I act young. Mikey's always so serious, you know?"

Boom Boom smiled. "Yeah, maybe that's what it was. Well, let's hope Mikey pulls through okay. He's a good kid."

"I hope so, too. I was going to check on him when I was through here."

Boom Boom nodded approvingly and turned to me. "So Doc, we seem to have a little problem. First of all, I don't like it when my guys get hit with baseball bats." He walked up to me and suddenly slapped me hard with the back of his hand. I rocked to the side from the impact, but thankfully didn't move my hands. I straightened up, my face stinging from pain. Boom Boom leaned back against his desk. "But then there's the other problem, the one I'm really upset about."

"What's that, Boom Boom?" I asked.

"Giorgio turned up dead in a dumpster behind one of the restaurants in Times Square a couple of hours ago, no one knows where Bobby is and I still don't have my diamonds. Maybe you would like to shed some light on what the fuck is going on."

"I'm sorry to hear that about Giorgio, but I told you everything I know on the phone this afternoon. I gave the diamonds to Bobby at nine-thirty this morning. He and Giorgio looked fine then. Maybe they got mugged."

"Mugged? Two of the biggest guys on the planet armed with Berettas and they got mugged? You're a pretty funny guy, Doc. I hope you're still laughing when I'm done."

Vito took his scotch from Nunzio and perused the room defensively. The place was very large and I had warned him to check it out as best he could before we made our move. There could be other guys.

"May I use the bathroom?" Vito asked politely.

Boom Boom glanced at him. "Yeah sure, it's down the hall and to the right. Don't take too long, though. I'm going to start interrogating the doc for real as soon as I finish my drink. You'll want to watch the master at work. Nunzio, take a walk with Roberto so he don't get lost and bring me back some towels. We'll need them to clean up the mess we're about to make and don't forget to wash your hands, Roberto. We're not animals."

I said calmly, "Have you given any thought to the possibility that maybe Bobby killed Giorgio and took off with the diamonds?"

"The thought crossed my mind for half a second, sure. Except where the fuck would he go that I wouldn't find him? Bobby has worked for me for ten years. He knows that if he betrayed me, I wouldn't rest until I saw him hanging from a meat hook. You, on the other hand, don't know me at all and might be under the impression that I'm a nice guy."

"I assure you that I was definitely not under that impression. But I don't think it makes sense that I would kill Bobby and Giorgio and steal five million dollars' worth of diamonds that I promised to give to you in the first place. I hope you're not under the impression that I'm that stupid."

"Money brings out the worst in people, Cesari. That's a cold hard fact that I learned a long time ago. But it don't matter, by the time I'm done with you tonight, I'll know the truth for sure. Hey Nunzio, hurry up with the towels. I'm ready to start," he called out and downed the last drop of scotch. "I'm sorry about the delay, Doc. It's just that blood stains are very hard to clean." Boom Boom sat down behind his desk, opened one of the drawers and pulled out a pair of wire-cutters, holding them up for me to see. I wiggled my fingers instinctively, wondering what it would be like to miss a few.

"I really don't think that will be necessary, Boom Boom."

Before he could respond, a gunshot rang out loudly down the hall. Boom Boom leapt to attention, turning in the direction of the sound and I jumped up, pulling the 9mm out from my back. A second shot echoed through the apartment.

"Step away from the desk, Boom Boom," I ordered. He froze, staring at me, eyes wide in surprise and disbelief. Vito burst into the room seconds later, his .45 aimed straight at Boom Boom.

Boom Boom exclaimed, "Roberto, what the fuck is going on here? What happened to Nunzio?"

Vito walked closer, looking extremely dangerous. "Nunzio was on the wrong side of history, asshole, as was the other guy down the hall watching your video cameras. Now sit down, slide your chair away from the desk and try to relax," Vito said calmly. Boom Boom sat down in his high-back leather chair and rolled it away from the desk. "Put your hands in your pockets and keep them there."

I took a step closer to the desk. "Vito, I know he has a .44 magnum in one of the drawers. Why don't you check that out before we talk?" As Vito searched, I kept the Glock trained on Boom Boom's face.

"Vito?" Boom Boom said. "You're not, Roberto?"

Vito chuckled. "You're a pretty smart guy, Boom Boom. You're gonna go far in this business." Boom Boom's features clouded over in thought and comprehension.

"You're that fucking rat, Gianelli. Damn, I thought there was something familiar about you. You're a dead man, asshole. I hope you know that."

"That's what we're here to talk about, Boom Boom."

"I don't make deals with rats," he blustered.

Vito opened the desk drawers one at a time while Boom Boom threatened him and eventually pulled out the .44 magnum. He weighed it in his hands and checked to see if it was loaded.

"Nice piece, Boom Boom. Good balance. I never liked the .44, though. Too heavy."

"Fuck you, dead man." As he cursed at Vito, his cell phone rang. Vito pressed the muzzle of the .44 up against the side of his head. "Who is it?"

Boom Boom took his cell phone out of his pocket and looked at it. "It's Alfonse, the sentry downstairs. He must have heard the shots."

"Answer it and be careful what you say." To reinforce his authority, Vito tapped the back of Boom Boom's head with the heavy gun hard enough to cause him to wince.

"Yeah Al, what do you need?"

He listened.

"I was just giving the doc a little demonstration. Everything's okay."

He hung up.

Vito grinned. "That's a good boy. Now leave the cell phone on the desk and very slowly stand up and walk over to the sofa. Remember who's holding all the guns. That's it. Nice and slow. Now sit on the floor and lean back against the edge of the couch. Lean back just a little more. That's enough. Hands back in the pockets. That's good. Okay then, let's talk."

He was sitting at a very awkward angle, and couldn't make any sudden movements like reaching for a hidden weapon. Vito took a chair in front him and just beyond his reach. I went to the desk to rummage around for anything that might be useful to us.

"What do you guys want?" Boom Boom asked. "You can't be serious, making a move like this."

"Who's your boss, Boom Boom?" Vito asked.

"I don't have one."

"Everybody's got one, Boom Boom. Don't be difficult, all right?"

"Fuck you. I don't talk to dead people."

Vito shook his head and reached into his pocket for his beloved Pall Malls. He lit one up and took a long drag, blowing smoke deliberately at Boom Boom, who looked at him with disgust. Vito just sat there for a few minutes in silence, thinking and smoking. Then I guess he came to some sort of conclusion because he picked up a sofa pillow and placed it over Boom Boom's left thigh. Boom Boom didn't have time to react as Vito quickly pressed the muzzle of the .44 into the pillow to muffle the sound and pulled the trigger. The explosion from the discharge of the large weapon shook the room, filling it with smoke. Boom Boom screamed as the cartridge shattered his thigh bone, ripping through muscle and tendon. The bullet exited from his leg and crashed into the floor board beneath, splintering it.

Vito sat back in his chair, watching Boom Boom writhe in pain as his blood oozed onto the hardwood floor. He took his hands out of his pockets to clutch his wounded leg, but we forgave him for that. I hoped Vito hadn't hit the femoral artery because then it would all be over in a minute or two, and we might not have enough time to get our questions answered. Boom Boom was already starting to look a little shaky from the trauma.

"I asked you who your boss was," Vito repeated coolly.

"Domenico Gribaldi, he's in Brooklyn." Boom Boom hissed through clenched teeth.

Vito nodded. "Yeah, I know him."

"I got his number right here, Vito," I said, scrolling through the contact list in Boom Boom's cell phone.

"Besides promising to kill me, what were your other responsibilities?"

"What do you think? The usual things. I run the sharks, drugs and girls in Little Italy and lower Manhattan for Domenico." He was sweating profusely now and had laid himself down flat on the floor, staring at the ceiling. His color wasn't looking too good, and I thought he might lose consciousness soon. The .44 magnum was a very large caliber pistol, and at that range, the wound would be horrific.

"Was Bobby your number two man?"

He nodded. "Yeah."

"What about the guy downstairs? Does he know your contact people?"

"He don't know anything. He's just a kid," he gasped. "Don't hurt him. He's an okay guy."

"I want the names, Boom Boom, now." Vito pressed the muzzle of the .44 into the leg wound and ground it in hard, causing Boom Boom to moan in agony.

"They're in the cell phone." His voice was getting progressively weaker and his eyes began to flutter. There was now a large pool of bright red blood under him and spreading fast. Vito had hit the artery.

"Vito, I found them. You're not going to believe this. He's got them listed under B for bag men, S for sharks, D for drugs, and G for girls. Can you believe that?"

Vito made his decision. "I guess we're all done here, Cesari. Sorry, Boom Boom."

"Fuck you, Gianelli," he whispered back, barely audible. His lips were gray and his eyes glassy. It wouldn't be long.

Vito knelt down by Boom Boom's head, covering the dying man's mouth with his left hand and pinching his nose with his right. Boom Boom barely struggled as his life drifted away. The Colt .44 was a very nasty weapon.

It was 3 a.m.

R︎X 58

"LET'S hit the road, Cesari."

"What about the guard downstairs?"

"What about him?"

"We're just going to walk right past him?"

"No, I'm going to bring him up here. I need to talk to him. Give me Boom Boom's cell phone."

I handed him the phone and he called Alfonse, the guard downstairs, just by redialing the last phone call.

"Yeah, Al, look, you better get up here fast. Boom Boom collapsed, and I think he's having a heart attack. He was smacking the doc around and then he just keeled over."

Silence as he listened.

"Nunzio can't talk. He's doing CPR on Boom Boom. Look, I got to go help. I already called an ambulance, and it's on the way." He partially covered the phone and called out. "I'll be right there, Nunzio. I gotta go, Al. Hurry up." He hung up.

I said, "That was pretty good, Vito. Very convincing. Have you ever thought about acting lessons?"

"Giving them or taking them?"

We walked over to the entrance to the apartment, guns drawn. We didn't have to wait long. Alfonse came charging up the staircase, bursting through the door. Vito and I grabbed him, using his momen-

328

tum to fling him to the floor. In seconds, we disarmed and seated him on the living room sofa in full view of his late boss. Alfonse was maybe thirty years old, if that, and was completely stunned.

Vito sat next to Alphonse with the cocked .44 pointing in the direction of Al's groin, and I leaned back against Boom Boom's desk just as he had before when I was on the couch.

Vito cleared his throat and said, "Al, as you can see, there's been a slight change in management. Are you okay with that?"

Alfonse looked around wide-eyed and nodded. He looked like he was afraid to breathe.

"Good. My name's Vito Gianelli. Have you ever heard of me?"

He nodded. "Everybody has. You're the rat."

To Vito's credit, he didn't overreact.

"I'm going to let that pass, Al, but don't ever let me hear you say that again, all right?"

The guy nodded. "I'm sorry."

"Besides, I'm not a rat. I was framed by this asshole lying on the floor in front of you, but you work for me now, understood?" Alfonse nodded. It wasn't true about his being framed, but he might as well start circulating the story on the streets. It was always the same thing. The king is dead, long live the new king.

"First order of business, Al, is that your pay just got doubled. Now, I want you to get Mikey and explain to him that his pay just got doubled, too. He's locked in the trunk of a Lincoln Towncar around the corner from here with Roberto, who's dead."

He handed Alfonse the keys to the Lincoln. "I want you two to clean up this apartment tonight. There are three dead bodies here and Roberto in the trunk. Pack them all in the Towncar and bring them out to JFK long-term parking. Find a remote spot and leave the car there, but first wipe it down as well as you can. If they don't all fit in the trunk, put one or two in the back seat, but cover them up good. That will buy us some time until I can figure out a long-term solution."

"How do we get back from the airport?"

"You go out there in two cars or take a cab, Al. C'mon, start thinking on your feet."

"Then what?"

"I want to meet you and Mikey here in the kitchen at ten a.m. sharp. I want a pot of espresso waiting for me and when I walk in the door, you guys had better be sitting at the table with both hands where I can see them. Do we have an understanding, Al?"

"Yes."

"If anything at all is out of place or if you haven't done exactly what I told you, I'll do a whole lot worse to you than what I just did to these guys. You can run, but I warn you now that there is no place you'll be able to hide. Well, what are you waiting for? Go get Mikey and start cleaning up."

Alfonse jumped off the couch and made a beeline for the exit. He was in such a rush, he forgot to say goodbye.

Vito and I left the apartment and walked to the Saint Mark's Hotel. It wasn't that far and we needed to clear our heads and discuss the future.

"You'd do that for me, Cesari?"

"Yeah, it's only money."

"It's ten million dollars' worth of money, but if you lend it to me so I can pay off Domenico as a peace offering, I might be able to pull this off. It sure as hell would help smooth things over when he finds out what happened here tonight. Plus, if I can convince him that business won't miss a beat down here, he may decide to let me back in rather than risk a war to fill the vacuum."

"I can have the cash wired to you from the Caymans on Monday, Vito. I also have some friends in the diamond business who can unload the diamonds for me. It might take a week, and I promised them a fifteen percent cut, but that should still leave us with at least the ten million you need."

"And as soon as we're done with these Russians tomorrow night, I'll start meeting with the guys on the street and get them in line before anybody gets any ideas. I've been gone less than a year and most everyone will still remember me. I'll start with the drug guys because they're generally the biggest assholes."

"No drugs, Vito, at least nothing stronger than pot. If the dealers don't like it, they can fuck themselves. I'm giving them one week and then they have to disappear."

"Cesari, you can't be serious. We're going to lose a lot of money that way."

"Vito, we'll talk about these things more when I've had some sleep, but that is one point I'm not going to negotiate on if we're going to be partners. We can make plenty of money without selling crack and heroin to kids. Drug dealers are scumbags by nature anyway, haven't you noticed that? I want them out of my neighborhoods. I have to be able to sleep at night."

"Okay. What about girls. You got a problem with that, too, Mother Theresa?"

"Not at all. Sex is good. If more people were having sex, we'd have fewer wars. But if the girls are doing it because they're hooked on drugs, then yes, I do have a problem. If they got a drug habit, they go to rehab. If they still want in when they're done, we can talk. Women can do whatever they want with their bodies, but I want them indoors, not on the streets. They get yearly medical exams, two weeks paid vacation like everybody else in the country, and nobody works on Columbus Day."

"Hey, Cesari, when did you become fucking Santa Claus? The pimps are going to go nuts. We're not running a whore daycare center down here."

I turned to him. "That's another thing. The next time I hear that a pimp hits one of the girls who didn't hit him first, I'm going to beat him with a crowbar. In fact, we should beat one or two publicly just to get the message across."

Vito shook his head. "That would definitely work."

"I want everybody to know who's in charge down here by the end of the week. We're going to be very hands-on." I felt my blood pumping.

"What about the sharks, chop shops, floating poker games, restaurant supplies, protection?"

I yawned. "Enough for tonight, Vito. I need some shuteye. For Christ's sake, it's almost four. You call Domenico in the morning and present the deal. Boom Boom's out and from now on it's you running Little Italy and lower Manhattan with me as your silent partner. Also, promise him that despite some of the minor changes we plan on making, we guarantee him ten percent over whatever Boom Boom was paying him in tribute if he supports us."

"What if he tells me to fuck myself?"

"Then I'd high-tail it back to Albany as fast as you can, but he won't. He's a businessman, and like they say, there's no point in crying over spilled milk. But don't say anything about the Russians or the diamonds. That'll be our business. We split that fifty-fifty like everything else from now on, and another thing…"

I looked at him seriously.

"What?"

"If Kelly hears about any of this, I will most definitely kill you."

"She won't hear anything from me—ever. I swear." He had a huge smile on his face, and looked like a kid opening his presents on Christmas morning.

So I asked him, "What's with the grin?"

"It feels great to be back, Cesari."

"You just killed four guys and you feel great?"

"All in the line of duty, Cesari. All in the line of duty."

We walked into the Saint Mark's Hotel and I went up to my room, collapsing onto the bed fully clothed. I stared at the ceiling and took a deep breath. Fucking A, Kelly was going to go nuts if she ever found out.

R_{X} 59

I woke up late Saturday morning at ten a.m. and saw three missed calls from Kelly.

Shit. Pam's appointment was at eight with Mark. I called Kelly.

"Cesari, where are you?"

"I just woke up. I'm sorry, Kel. How'd it go?"

"How'd it go? Let me see. Pam woke up at two in the morning screaming from night terrors and then spent the next two hours crying on the couch. Gina woke up and started crying because she thinks it's all her fault. I've been up the whole night trying to console two white women crying at me in stereo. I'm exhausted and then you didn't show up to help me."

"I'm sorry, Kel. Vito and I got in late and I overslept."

I heard her take a deep breath. "Well, we took a cab up to Mark's office on the west side this morning. Gina came with us because she didn't want to be left alone. She was a mess, too. Mark took one look at her and decided he'd better put them both on tranquilizers. We just returned and I dropped them off at Pam's apartment. I'm at the pharmacy now picking up their meds. I can't believe this."

"I'll be right over to help out, Kel. You're a saint."

"I don't want to be a saint."

"Why not?"

"Saints don't get laid."

I chuckled. "I'm glad you still have your famous sense of humor. I'll be right over."

"You'd better be."

I hung up and dialed Vito.

"Cesari, what do you want? I'm conducting a business meeting with Mikey and Alfonse."

"I was just checking to see if you're still alive."

He laughed. "Everything's fine. Al makes a great pot of coffee. I'll talk to you later."

The real test was going to be in convincing Domenico that Boom Boom had somehow framed Vito and stolen the ten million himself. That was going to be a tough sell. Whether or not he actually believed Vito was somewhat irrelevant because he would want the ten million dollars back no matter what. There was almost nothing in this business that money couldn't fix. So, we figured he would make himself believe it and convince others of the same. Besides, Boom Boom was dead anyway, and nothing was going to bring him back. The ease with which Vito and I cleaned house would only serve to convince Domenico that Boom Boom wasn't the right man for the job anyway.

I showered quickly and hopped a cab over to Pam's apartment, grabbing a cup of coffee at a Starbucks on the way. Kelly looked totally exhausted. I didn't see Pam or Gina.

"Where are the girls?" I asked.

"They're sleeping together in the bedroom. Pam has a king-sized bed. I gave them both a hefty dose of Xanax. Mark said to only give them one, but I gave them both four pills each with a shot of Brandy. I needed them quiet so I could get some rest."

I laughed quietly. "I hope you didn't kill them."

"I doubt it. The first three pills barely touched them, they were so wired."

I nodded knowingly. I had seen people in the middle of anxiety attacks before. It was impressive how much sedation they required just to bring them down to normal, let alone put them to sleep.

I hugged Kelly. "What did Mark have to say?"

"He agreed with you—white women are crazy." She yawned. "Now be quiet, I'm going to take a nap on the sofa."

"What should I do? Does she have any food? I'm kind of hungry."

"Yeah, she's got a well-stocked fridge and pantry. Please try to keep it down, all right?" She lay down on the sofa, covering herself with a blanket.

In the kitchen, I opened the refrigerator, found some deli meats, bread, and mustard and made myself a sandwich, washing it down with bottled water. I ate standing by the sink, deep in thought. Returning to the living room, I sat down opposite Kelly who was already gently snoring, and soon I was doing the same, overcome by fatigue. Around noon, my cell phone buzzed in my pocket, waking me. It was Sergei.

I walked into the kitchen so I could talk without disturbing Kelly.

"Cesari, here."

"It is Sergei."

"Yes."

"Patient name, Vladimir Pudnovsky. I text phone number so no mistake. He wait for call. You tell what do. When have diamonds you call Sergei, understood? We watch. Always watch."

He hung up before I could say anything. Asshole. My phone buzzed with a text message from him a few seconds later. It was the guy's phone number I was supposed to call.

I called the hospital switchboard. "Hello, this is Dr. Cesari. Could you tell me who's on call for GI tonight?"

"Dr. Chowdery. Would you like me to put you through to his cell?"

"Yes, please."

Waiting.

"Hello."

"Raj, this is Cesari."

"Hi, Cesari, what's up?"

"Look, I need a favor. It's important that I switch call with you tonight. I'm scheduled to take call next Saturday, but I'm going away and won't be able to do it. Can you help me out?"

"No problem, Cesari, but I'm warning you now, the ER's already a zoo today. I've been called six times in the last hour, for total bullshit, I might add."

"That's the breaks, but thanks for the warning. I'll call the ER to let them know about the switch."

I called Vlad with the number Sergei gave me.

A deep voice answered. "Yes."

"Is this Vladimir Pudnovsky?"

"Yes."

"I am Dr. Cesari. Sergei told you that I would be calling."

"Yes, he tell Vlad."

"I want you to go to the emergency room at Saint Matthew's Hospital on Third Avenue. Do you know where that is?"

"Yes, I have been once before."

That took me by surprise, but that would make sense. Why not use the same couriers more than once?

"Go there at 3 p.m. and tell the doctor who greets you that you have been bleeding from the rectum for three days. Let them take your blood and put an IV in you. Tell them that I am your doctor and that you insist they call me. Later they will bring you some medicine to drink to get you ready for your colonoscopy. Please drink it all. You got all that?"

"Yes."

"Any questions?"

He hung up.

I turned around, and Kelly was standing there looking sleepy. Cute, but very sleepy. "Is that your idea of being quiet, Cesari?" Cranky, too.

"I'm sorry, Kel. Go back to bed. I'll step out."

"Don't bother. I'm awake now. So what's up? Who were you talking to just now?"

"That was Vladimir Pudnovsky, the guy we'll be doing a colonoscopy on tonight. I just told him to go to the ER later and ask for me. Sergei called while you were sleeping and gave me his number."

She yawned. "Do you think we could go out and leave them alone for an hour or two? I'm going a little stir crazy in here."

"Yeah, I don't see why not. Four Xanax isn't going to kill anyone. It's not like they took the whole bottle. We'll check on them before we leave to make sure they're still breathing. Where'd you want to go?"

"Not far. Even the Starbucks down the block would be fine. I just need to get away from the insanity for a bit. You didn't even kiss me when you came in." I did, but didn't see any point in arguing.

"Well, I can fix that." I put my arms around her and pulled her close for a patented Cesari, guaranteed to knock your socks off, wet one.

She pulled back laughing. "I didn't say I wanted your tongue all over me."

"I must have misunderstood."

"Yeah, right. C'mon, let's go."

We grabbed a table and a couple of coffees at the Starbucks and studied each other's tired faces.

"So, what could go wrong?" Kelly asked.

"Everything." I laughed.

"I'm glad we settled that. What time do we pick up this guy from the ER?"

"I'm thinking around eleven would be good. The OR should be dead at that hour, and if things go well, we should be finished around midnight or twelve-thirty. How long do you think you'll need to set up the endoscopy room?"

"Twenty minutes at the most. How long are we going to recover him?"

"That variable is hard to predict because everybody is different in their response to the medications. I'll try to keep him lightly sedated if I can. I'm figuring anywhere from thirty minutes to an hour, but if it looks like he's not waking up on schedule, I can always bring him back down to the ER for them to babysit."

"Is someone going to pick him up or is he just going to be allowed to walk out of the hospital after he wakes up?"

"You know, Kel, I didn't ask, and I'm not sure that I care. He's in Manhattan. He can always take a cab back to wherever he came from. By the time he leaves, he'll be no worse off than if he'd had a couple of beers."

"Yeah, I guess." She looked at the counter with baked goods.

I followed her gaze. "What?"

"Would you get me a cinnamon scone? They look so good."

"Why didn't you get one when we bought the coffees?"

"Really?"

"Okay, I'm sorry. I'll be right back."

"Thanks."

Two minutes later, I returned with a cinnamon scone.

"Thank you."

"You're welcome. Now where was I?"

She said, "I'll have the endoscopy room set up for a colonoscopy, rain or shine, by eleven p.m., and who cares how the guy leaves the hospital after we're done. If he passes out on the sidewalk, fuck him. As long as it's outside the hospital, it's not our problem. Did I summarize that well?"

"The hospital's legal team couldn't have said it better."

"Oh my God. This is so good." She swallowed a bite of her scone.

It really did look good.

"Can I have a bite?" I asked.

"Why didn't you just get your own while you were up there?"

"Really?"

She laughed and broke off a teeny-tiny piece to hand me.

I looked at the crumb she offered me. "Could you possibly have given me a smaller piece?" She laughed again and broke off a bigger piece.

"All right," I said. "What about Pam and Gina? What does Mark want to do with them?"

"He wants them on the Xanax once a day to start, for anxiety. He thinks it's just an acute reaction from all the stress they've been under. Mostly, they need a good night's sleep. He's a little more worried about Pam and wants to see her again in one week. If she hasn't come around by then, he may start her on something stronger like Cymbalta. His main advice was that they need to reduce the stress in their lives. He specifically told me to keep them as far from you as possible."

"He didn't say that, did he?"

"No, that was my suggestion, but he agreed."

"You're pretty funny for someone who's got bed head."

"Someone's got thin skin, doesn't he? Back to the colonoscopy tonight. After the case, what are you supposed to do with the diamonds?"

"I don't know yet. Sergei told me to call him when I'm done. I presume he'll tell me where to bring them."

"What about your friend, Vito? Is he going to go back to Albany?"

"Not clear. He hasn't been in the city in almost a year. He's kind of enjoying himself. I'm certain he'll stick around until we finish this thing with Sergei, and I would feel better if he did. You know what I mean?"

"Yeah, I know. I just don't like you hanging around with gangsters or ex-gangsters, although I have to admit, he seems like a totally different person than the nasty Vito we met last year."

"Yeah, ain't that something."

My cell phone rang. "It's the ER, Kel. It's show time."

"Okay, take the call. I really should be getting back to the apartment anyway to keep an eye on those two. Give me a kiss." She stood to leave.

I answered the phone. "Cesari here."

"Hello, Dr. Cesari, this is Nadine in the ER, can you hold for Dr. Khalid?"

"Sure." I stood up and kissed Kelly goodbye. "I'll call you later, all right?"

She nodded. "Okay, bye."

I watched Kelly leave the Starbucks.

"Cesari, it's Ramses Khalid, in the ER. You're on call, right?"

"Hi, Ramses. Yeah, I'm on call. I see they finally let you out of Guantanamo."

"You can suck my dick, Cesari."

"You'd like that, wouldn't you? I've heard about you Egyptian guys."

He chuckled. "I'm going to enjoy torturing you tonight, you racist, homophobic guinea. There are already six patients down here screaming for a GI consult, and I might just decide to hang on to them until midnight before calling you in."

"In that case, please allow me to apologize for any of the aforementioned offensive comments. What can I do for you, Ramses?"

"That's better. Did that guy Chowdery sign anything out to you?'"

"Not specifically, but he mentioned that you guys had called him several times."

"Well, there's a seventy-year-old female down here who came in this morning with severe abdominal pain and vomiting. She really looked awful and was writhing about on the stretcher for a few hours. Her white count is up a little, no fever, urine's clean and her labs are more or less normal, although her potassium was a little on the high side. Past medical history includes atrial fibrillation, high blood pressure and adult onset diabetes. Well, I talked to Chowdery about her earlier in the day, and he recommended a CAT scan of the abdomen. She just got back and it was normal. We're not sure what to do with her."

"You didn't mention her abdominal exam, or whether she had her appendix out."

"Her appendix is out and her exam is benign. I mean really benign. She looks great now and says the pain is gone. By the way, she's not on any anticoagulants for her atrial fibrillation."

I thought it over. "I think you had better call a surgeon, Ramses. It sounds as if she may have mesenteric ischemia. I would consider getting an angiogram on her if I were you."

"Really? I mean, she looks great now."

"They always do. It's the calm before the storm. What you described is a classic presentation of intestinal ischemia; severe symptoms, and almost no or minimal physical findings. I certainly wouldn't let her go home. At the very least, she should be admitted for observation, but with this disease, there is a very narrow window in which to act between the onset of symptoms and a subsequent catastrophic vascular accident and death."

"Holy shit, Cesari. You're scaring me. I've never taken care of a patient like this before. Are you coming in?"

"Certainly, but do me a favor and call the surgeon now. You might as well set her up for an emergency angiogram and an ICU bed. Make sure you plug some big lines in her and give her some antibiotics. What's her name, by the way?"

"Gutiérrez, Evelyn Gutiérrez."

I finished my coffee leisurely. There was no point in rushing. The wheels of medical care, unfortunately, turned slowly. It would take at least an hour to get the patient the angiogram I requested. Eventually, I got up to leave, and as I walked by the baked goods, I noticed a solitary cinnamon scone. It was the last one and looked pathetic sitting there all by itself, as if it had no friends. The girl behind the counter smiled, and I hesitated.

"I'll take that one."

R℞ 60

THE ER was a madhouse of activity and noise when I entered at three p.m. Every room was occupied and patients were lined up in the hallway on stretchers, waiting to be seen. The overcrowded waiting room teemed with exhausted, anxious family members. There were four ER physicians on duty, four physician's assistants and twice that many nurses running around. Constructed as a giant oval, the forty patient rooms surrounding the central nursing station bustled with activity.

Video monitors providing live feed from all the patient rooms as well as continuous heart rate and blood pressure monitoring dominated everyone's attention. I said hello to several of the nurses and asked them which room my patient was in. Ramses, the ER doc I had spoken with, was tied up with a patient and I didn't want to bother him.

I was told she was in room number eight, so I negotiated my way over there through the controlled chaos. Her nurse Sally, a middle-aged blonde, was in the process of pushing a syringe with something in it into the lady's IV. Mrs. Gutierrez was a tiny, seventy-year-old Hispanic woman in obvious distress.

"Hi, Sally. What's going on?"

She turned to me. "Oh, hey there, Cesari. I was just giving her some Zofran for nausea. The poor thing started vomiting again." The old woman didn't look too good. She was sweating profusely and holding an emesis basin in her lap.

"Hi, Mrs. Gutiérrez. I'm doctor Cesari. I'm a gastroenterologist..." She started vomiting bilious green material violently into the emesis basin. When she was done, she took a deep breath and lay back in the bed, exhausted. Her heart rate monitor screamed at us its distress signal.

"When is her angiogram?" I asked Sally.

"I don't really know. The radiologist didn't seem to think it was that urgent. Dr. Khalid spoke to him twice."

I looked at Mrs. Gutiérrez. "Are you in any pain?"

She nodded. "Yes, terrible dolor del stomaco. Terrible." She could barely speak from the pain. She rubbed her hand over her entire abdomen. She was very petite, maybe five feet tall and 100 lbs. dripping wet.

"When did the pain come back?" I asked Sally.

"Maybe fifteen minutes ago. She was fine before that."

"Have you given her anything for it?"

"Just the Zofran. Dr. Khalid wanted you to see her before we gave her any narcotics. What do you want?"

"Go ahead and give her two milligrams of Dilaudid IV right now. I'll go write the order. Turn up her fluids to one-hundred-and-fifty milliliters an hour of normal saline and put some oxygen on her. I want you to get another set of labs as well. A white count, amylase, potassium and a lactate level, and put an oxygen saturation monitor on her. Has the surgeon been around?"

"Not yet. He was notified an hour ago."

"All right, thanks, Sally."

Ramses walked into the room. "Hey, Cesari, thanks for coming so quickly. As you can see, things have changed a little since we spoke." We shook hands and he continued. "The interventional radiologist is being a pain in the ass about doing the angiogram. Doesn't think it needs to be done urgently. I was hoping you would talk to him. The surgeon is stuck in a complicated gallbladder up in the OR, but he knows we have a situation down here and will come as soon as he's free. Right now, it's just me and you."

"All right, Ramses. I'll stick around until we get her settled in. Let's give her plenty of fluids and pain meds, okay? No point in being stingy. I'll call radiology after I've examined her. Would you mind talking to the family and letting them know that this is pretty serious?"

"Sure thing, Cesari." He turned to leave.

"One more thing, Ramses? Can I borrow your stethoscope?"

He took the instrument from around his neck and handed it to me. "Don't lose it or try to pawn it."

I chuckled. "Thanks. I'll bring it right back when I'm done."

I performed a quick, focused history and physical examination on Mrs. Gutierrez. The dilaudid was kicking in and she was starting to feel a little better. After reassuring her that we were going to do everything we could for her, I went back to the nursing station to write my consult note and nursing orders. When I finished, I had the operator put me through to the radiologist on call.

"Brian Zinburg, here. Someone looking for interventional radiology?"

"Hi, Brian, the name's John Cesari, gastroenterology. I don't think we've had the pleasure yet. Hey look, Brian, did the ER call you earlier about doing an emergency angiogram on one of the patients down here?"

"Yeah, I told them that we have her scheduled for first thing tomorrow morning."

"Well, she needs it done sooner than that, like right now."

"Wish I could help you, Bud, but it doesn't work that way. It's Saturday and there's no one around to help me. I'd have to call in nurses from home and they get paid time-and-a-half on the weekends, not to mention I have dinner plans tonight and can't afford to get stuck in a complicated case. Besides, I'm not even sure what the indication is for this angio. They told me her CAT scan was negative."

I took a deep breath, counted to five, and let it out slowly. "The indication is mesenteric ischemia and the CAT scans are usually negative early on in the course, Brian. In case you're not familiar with this disease, mortality approaches seventy to one-hundred percent unless the diagnosis is made promptly. I've examined the patient myself, and if we don't act quickly, we might have a disaster on our hands."

"C'mon, you guys are always pressing the panic button down there in the ER. Call me back after a surgeon sees her, all right? If he says she needs an emergency angiogram then I'll come in and do it.

An emergency angiogram on a Saturday is a big deal. It's a massive inconvenience for everyone. I hope you are aware of that. And another thing, I checked her admission paperwork already and she doesn't even have insurance, which means I have to take this one up the ass. You know, Cesari, we haven't met, but between me, you, and the wall, I don't work for free."

Fuck. He'd managed to insult and offend me at the same time. That wasn't an easy thing to do. "Look, Brian, the surgeon's tied up in the OR and we're not sure when he'll be free. I really don't think this should wait, and I'm qualified to make this decision without him."

"Well, that's the deal, buttercup. I'll be at Daniel's in mid-town having dinner. It's a real nice French place and I had to wait two months for the reservations. I'll have to turn off my beeper when I'm there, so have the surgeon call me directly, and let's just hope that I'm not in the middle of my foie gras when he does because then you'll both be out of luck."

This guy was playing with matches. "What kind of car do you drive, Brian?" I felt smoke billowing out of my ears.

"What?"

"You heard me, Brian," I repeated calmly. "What kind of car do you drive?"

"A Mercedes SLS, GT Coupe, why?" he asked in exasperation.

"That starts at just over two hundred grand, right?"

"What are you getting at, Cesari?"

"What I'm getting at is that I don't like your attitude, and I really don't give a crap about whether you have to take it up the ass once in a while to save somebody's life. You're not on food stamps, and I have a human being in front of me that needs your help. Now let me explain this to you as simply as possible. You're the goddamn angiographer on call and I need a goddamn angiogram right now, not tomorrow, not eight hours from now... now. So either you come in and do your goddamn job or I'm going to come to Daniel's and shove your foie gras up your ass. And another thing, don't ever call me buttercup again."

Silence.

"Who the fuck do you think you are, Cesari? You can't talk to me like that."

"Stop being an asshole and I'll try to be nicer. Look, I'm doing you a favor. You should have been here an hour ago. If this woman dies because there was a delay in her care, I'm going to hold you personally responsible and you don't want that, Brian. You really don't. You're a physician and that means you help people, rain or shine, insurance or no insurance. You took an oath, remember? Save your financial problems for the fifth avenue crowd and not for some poor woman whose life is depending on you. Now get in your GT Coupe and drag your ass down here and I better not hear anymore shit about her insurance. Are you starting to understand a little bit better who I am, buttercup?"

Silence.

"I'll come in, but this isn't over between me and you, Cesari. Got that?" He hissed and hung up.

Ramses saw me on the phone and came over. "How'd it go with that asshole radiologist?"

I looked up as if nothing had happened. "He was very cooperative. He said he'll be right in."

"Really? Damn, Cesari, you're a miracle worker. He gave me such a hard time. Well I hate to keep bothering you, but the place is jumping with GI patients. There's a guy in room fourteen who says you're his doctor. He's a forty-year-old Russian by the name of Vladimir Pudnovsky. He barely speaks English, and says he's had rectal bleeding every day for the last two weeks. We're plugging a line in him and getting some labs. He looks fine, but would you mind saying hello while you're here?"

"Sure. I know him. Nice guy."

I walked over to room fourteen and peeked in. There was a husky looking forty-year-old guy lying on the stretcher and looking like he was waiting for someone to bring him a cocktail. He had hard-looking, weathered features like he'd spent a lot of time outdoors.

"Vladimir?"

"Is I. Who you?"

"I'm Dr. Cesari. We spoke on the phone earlier today."

"Yes. I do what say. How long wait here?"

"You have to stay here several hours, all right?" I looked at my watch. "I just wanted to say hello and see what you looked like. I'll tell the nurses to bring you the medicine I need you to drink to clean out your colon. I'll see you later. Please be patient, and if you have any problems, just ask the nurse to call me."

"Yes, I do what told. See you later."

I went back and found Ramses. "That guy in room fourteen looks okay to me. Give me a call when his labs come back. I think I'll do his colonoscopy tonight. It looks like I'm going to be here anyway. There seems to be a lot of stuff going on and I don't see any point in making him wait. Do you mind babysitting him for me?"

"Well it depends on how long and how busy we are, but in principle, no. Sure you don't want to just admit him to the hospital?"

"I thought about it, but you know, he's pretty young and healthy. If his colonoscopy is negative, I'll send him home tonight. I'd hate to see him get nailed for a big hospital bill if it wasn't necessary."

"Good point, Cesari. You one-percenters really do have a heart." He laughed. "Okay, I'll keep an eye on him. When do you want me to start prepping him for the colonoscopy?"

"I'll take care of all of that, Ramses. I'll talk to his nurse, Sally. You just make sure nothing happens to him, but I doubt that he'll give you any trouble. I'll discharge him right from the OR when I'm done."

"Sure thing, and thanks for your help with that other lady. I'll let you know what the angiogram shows if you're not here."

"Thanks, Ramses, but I think I'll stick around."

R̶ₓ 61

AN hour later, they transported Mrs. Gutierrez to radiology for her angiogram. She had stabilized and looked fine as she passed by the nursing station where I was sitting. I finished writing orders for Vlad's colonoscopy and decided to head over to the angio room and see how things were going with my new friend, Brian, the interventional radiologist. I could be a world class nutbreaker when I wanted to.

On the way there, I called Kelly to let her know that I was going to have dinner in the hospital cafeteria, and that we should just meet in the OR around ten p.m. She didn't answer her phone, so I left a voice message. I saw a missed call from Vito and called him back.

"How's it going, Vito?"

"Mostly pretty smooth. Domenico was pissed at first, of course. That was to be expected. You can't just call up a guy like that, announcing you killed his top guy in Little Italy and expect him to be happy. But once I got him to calm down enough to hear me out, he started to warm up. I told him the story we concocted about how Boom Boom was the one who stole the money and framed me. I also told him that I knew it looked bad, so I went into hiding until I was able to figure out what happened and that I could have his money for him by the end of the week. Basically, he'll hold off on taking any action against me until the end of next week. I have to get him the eleven million by next Friday as a sign of my truthfulness, or he's going to send everybody he can after me. Bottom line is this. If he gets his money, we're in business."

"Eleven million? I thought you only owed him ten?"

"He's charging me an extra ten percent immediately as a penalty for not coming to him first before taking down Boom Boom. What was I supposed to do? Argue with the guy?"

"Jesus Christ, Vito. I don't know if I can get another million."

"Well, we got a whole week to figure it out. Meanwhile, I've spent most of the day rubbing elbows with guys in the neighborhood to let them know I'm back. I'm being well-received so far. It seems Boom Boom was a bit of an asshole, but no surprise there."

"Okay look, why don't you come down to the hospital, and we'll grab a bite to eat while we discuss business, and bring me a weapon."

"I got plenty of those. Boom Boom had a whole room full of them. A real arsenal. It's like he was getting ready to reinvade Vietnam or something. Okay, I'll wrap up what I'm doing and meet you in about an hour. Where?"

"The hospital cafeteria. It's in the basement. Just take the main elevators down one flight and follow the signs."

"Fuck that, Cesari. I'm not eating in any cafeteria. I've been doing that for the last year."

"I'm too busy here at the hospital to leave, Vito."

"How about I bring something there?"

"Like what?"

"I don't know yet, but I'll figure something out. Let's say seven in your cafeteria."

I hung up just as I reached the angio suite and quietly entered the dark room. Mrs. Gutierrez was on the specialized table they used and the procedure was already in progress. There were two nurses assisting the radiologist, and a healthy distance outside the more or less sterile field, was the surgeon. He wore blue surgical scrubs. I joined him to watch the procedure.

"Hi, Carl. How goes it?"

He turned to me. "Hi, Cesari. Busy day for sure. They're just getting started here." He leaned close to me and whispered. "This guy's not in the greatest mood." He nodded in the direction of the radiologist. "I'd keep the chatter to a minimum if I were you."

I nodded. "I wonder what's eating him?"

He shrugged. Carl was fifty years old, black, and very experienced. He had five kids, which explained his gray hair. I couldn't remember ever running into him when he didn't look exhausted. His two oldest were already in college and another on the launch pad for the fall. Working night and day to pay the bills was something he had resigned himself to and it had given him a unique perspective on life. Fortunately for him, he had a great attitude and was one of the few people left in medicine who really cared about what he was doing. If anybody was going to save this woman, it would be him.

I said, "What did you think of her story?"

"I agree with you, Cesari. It definitely sounds like ischemia. I just hope we're not too late. I really don't want to spend the rest of the night removing dead bowel."

The radiologist was a tall guy. He looked like he might be in his thirties and spent some time in the gym. He wore a blue surgical gown, mask and hat, so I couldn't really tell what he looked like. He was focusing hard on snaking a catheter up the patient's femoral artery and hadn't noticed me yet.

I whispered to Carl, "How are the kids?"

"Great. I got two in college here in the city. One's talking about going to medical school and the other's going for her masters in physics. My middle child's starting Tuft's this year. Tuition's only sixty grand a year, and we're not eligible for any financial aid. Can you believe that? Straight A student and valedictorian of her class. They didn't even offer us one fucking dime. Take it or leave it, they said. With all the cutbacks to physician reimbursements, I should be working until I'm eighty-five before I'm done paying for all of their educations."

I chuckled. "No one told you to have five kids, Carl."

He laughed, too. "Yeah, right, like I had any say in the matter. You just wait, Cesari. One day you'll get married and find out who's really in charge. One minute it's love, honor, and obey, and the next thing you know, you're taking out a second mortgage to pay for college. And I don't remember anyone ever asking me if I wanted five kids. Yeah, and no one told me I was going to be working for free the rest of my life either."

I had to control myself from laughing out loud. I almost felt bad for the guy, but I knew how much he loved his wife and kids, and wouldn't change a thing even if he could. He was just belly-aching, and I figured he had a right to. So I went along with him and gave him a sympathetic pat on the back. "You're a prince, Carl. Your kids are very lucky to have a dad like you. So, what's going on here?"

"Shhh, looks like he's in position."

We both turned our full attention to the radiologist, who was speaking to his nurse and staring at the fluoroscopy screen in front of him. "Okay, we're now in the superior mesenteric artery. Start injecting." There was sudden flush of opaque contrast material on the screen as it flowed through her artery.

Carl got excited. "Wow, look at that."

The radiologist said to the room, "Okay, this is pretty classic ischemia. Severe vasoconstriction of the superior mesenteric artery and its branches. I don't see an obvious clot, but it may have broken up already. I'll start infusing vasodilators. Kathy, load up the papaverine and we'll start a continuous drip." He turned to Carl and finally saw me.

"Carl, she's going to need an ICU bed. We'll run the drip for twenty-four hours and I'll image her again tomorrow morning, but we got here in time and I think she'll be all right."

Carl said, "You're a hero, Brian."

Brian studied me and I could see his eyes narrow. "Who are you?"

"The name's Cesari."

He didn't say anything. Just turned back to finish his work.

Asshole.

I walked with Carl outside the angio room. "What was that all about, Cesari? If looks could kill, they'd already be calling the morgue for you."

"Ah, nothing really. We had a minor disagreement over the health benefits of French food. Anyway, he'll get over it. Thanks for taking care of this lady, Carl. I feel a lot better knowing you're on the case."

"No problem. I'm going to be here all night anyway. There's another hot gallbladder and an appendicitis in the ER waiting for me. By the way, you look great, Cesari. You been working out?"

"Yeah, I do lot of deep knee bends in front of the refrigerator looking for leftover pizza."

He laughed. "Anyway, this lady's going to be fine. I'll call you if anything happens."

He headed off to the ER and I went to the cafeteria to meet Vito. When I arrived, he was already sitting at a table waiting for me with two large bags full of food. It was getting late and there weren't too many people there.

"What did you get?" I asked.

"Hope you like Thai food, Cesari."

"Mmm, I love Thai food." He took out several plates to share and we used cafeteria utensils. The smell was wonderful as he laid out skewers of chicken satay with peanut sauce, phat thai noodles with pork, ginger beef, sticky rice and spicy lemon grass shrimp.

I looked at him and smiled. "Fucking Vito, you outdid yourself. This is great. You think there's enough?" I asked sarcastically. There was enough for another four or five people.

"Well, we got a lot to celebrate. I had a really good day. I'll be moving into Boom Boom's apartment this week. Domenico owns the building and gave me his approval, pending the payoff, of course."

"You're kidding, right? You're moving into Big Lou's apartment? Excuse me, Boom Boom's apartment."

"You heard me right. Think about it. It makes perfect sense. Domenico didn't believe a word of that cock and bull story about Boom Boom setting me up, but it was plausible enough. He wants the money and for business to continue as usual. He also doesn't want to appear like a fool to the other bosses. So he wants me right where he can find me if he decides he has to throw me under the bus in order to save face"

"And you're okay with that?"

"I've known these guys a long time, Cesari. Money talks and bullshit walks. As long as everybody's rolling in the dough, no one will even care what happened last night. By the way, there's plenty of room there if you need a place to stay."

"Thanks, but I'm okay. Oh my, this is really good." I had just taken a bite of the phat thai.

"Yeah, not bad. Just a little mom and pop place where Chinatown borders Little Italy."

"Where's my gun?"

He pointed to one of the bags. "It's underneath the fried rice. You're going to like the one I brought for you."

I grabbed the bag and pulled it towards me, scanning the cafeteria to see if anyone was watching. Pushing the container of fried rice to one side, I saw it. "What the fuck is that thing?" At the bottom of the bag rested a massive, black handgun.

"It's a Smith and Wesson fifty caliber revolver. Only holds five rounds, but if you need more than that with that baby, you should probably be running."

I lifted the bag off the table. "Fucking Vito, this thing weighs a ton. A little inconvenient, don't you think?"

"Six pounds to be exact. I thought you were a weight lifter. Geez, I thought you'd be happy."

I rolled my eyes in exasperation and exhaled. It never fails. "How am I supposed to carry this thing without anyone noticing? For God's sake, Vito, it's a cannon."

"Just keep it in the bag. Besides, it's only got a four-and-a-half inch barrel. It should fit in your pants."

"What do you got?"

"A Kimber Pro, forty-five caliber, seven round capacity."

"Hand it to me under the table. I want to see it."

He looked around. No one was watching us. He pulled it discreetly out of his pocket and passed it to me under the table. I looked at it in my lap. It was black, semi auto, and weighed less than two pounds.

"Is it chambered?"

"Of course."

"I'll keep this one. You can have the elephant gun."

He laughed. "Fine, for crying out loud. Can we finish eating now?"

Before I could put the Kimber in my pocket, two young women walked into the cafeteria with food trays in their hands. One of them spotted me and smiled. She signaled her friend to come over with her. I left the Kimber in between my legs and pulled my chair a little closer to the table.

"Hi, Dr. Cesari."

"Hi, Lori. What are you doing here so late on a Saturday night?"

Vito looked at the girls and smiled. "Hello, ladies."

They smiled at Vito. "Hello."

"We're visiting a friend of ours. She just had emergency gallbladder surgery today. This is my friend Lucy, Dr. Cesari, and I'm Lori," she said turning back to Vito. "May we join you?" Without waiting for an answer, she sat in the chair next to me and Lucy sat across from her, next to Vito.

"I'm Vito," he said.

Lori looked at our gourmet buffet. They both had cheese burgers. "What are you guys eating?" she asked.

"It's Thai."

Lucy was an adorable brunette, maybe twenty-five years old. She said, "I love chinese food."

Lori added, "Yeah, me too."

Vito chuckled. "Help yourselves, ladies. We've got more than enough."

They both helped themselves to some of the food and started eating, and I couldn't help but smile at them.

Lori glanced at me. "I hope you're not mad about the other day, Dr. Cesari?"

"Forget about it, Lori. It's ancient history. I hope your friend is okay?"

"She's in recovery, but the doctor said she did very well."

Lucy looked at Vito and asked, "Are you a doctor, too?"

He smiled. "No, I'm more of a personal consultant for Dr. Cesari. I'm trying to improve his image with the ladies."

The girls chuckled at that, and I could see Vito starting to shift gears. I looked at my watch. It was getting late. "Well, it was nice to meet you, Lucy. Unfortunately, Vito and I have an important business meeting upstairs in the OR that we have to attend.

"Can't you stay just a few more minutes, please? We'll eat real fast. I promise," Lori pleaded.

Vito said, "Yeah, calm down, Cesari. There's no need to be rude. We've got a minute or two to spare."

I glared at him and felt my sphincter tighten. Lori and Lucy smiled.

Lucy said, "Thank you, Vito."

"So what do you do, Lucy?" he asked.

"Right now I teach Zumba at a place called Mid-Town Fitness, but I'm trying to get into fashion design. I got a degree from F.I.T. I tried modeling for a while, but that business is so unbelievably cutthroat. I couldn't stand it. Everybody from the cab driver who brings you to the shoot to the doorman who lets you in expects you to sleep with them."

"Is that so? I had no idea," Vito said sympathetically. "Well, that's too bad. You're obviously beautiful enough to be a model."

"Thank you, Vito. You're sweet." They were making goo-goo eyes at each other.

I turned to Lori. "What about you, Lori? I know you work in medical records part time, but what are your long term goals?"

"I don't really have any yet. Just kind of looking to have fun right now, if you know what I mean?" She squeezed my thigh under the table while the others were distracted. As she did so, she felt the pistol between my legs and ran her hand over it trying to figure out what it was. I cleared my throat uncomfortably and moved her hand gently back from whence it came. Too late. I could see recognition in her eyes as she realized what the metal object was.

She gave me a sultry smile, her eyes looking directly into mine. "Mmm, I knew you were my kind of guy."

That line caught Lucy and Vito's attention. Vito said, "Hey, what's going on over there?"

"Nothing, but we really have to go now, ladies." I looked crossly at Vito.

"Yeah, I guess." He turned to Lucy. "Maybe I could call you some time?"

"That would be great." She reached into her bag to retrieve her cell phone. "What's your number, Vito? I'll dial it right now so I'll be in your contact list."

While that was taking place, I discreetly maneuvered the Kimber from between my legs and into my pocket. Discreetly being a subjective term since Lori watched me the whole time. I stood up with Vito, who picked up the bag with the other weapon.

I said, "How about we leave the food here for you ladies? As long as you don't mind cleaning up?"

"We don't mind at all, Dr. Cesari," Lori said. "And thank you again."

Lucy gave Vito an awkward little hug and Lori groped me shamelessly. "Hope to see you again soon, Dr. Cesari." I didn't say anything.

"Same here," Lucy said to Vito.

As we walked out of earshot, Vito chided me. "Christ, Cesari. Fuck the diamonds. Let's take them out somewhere. I haven't gotten laid in months."

It's unbelievable how men get when they have a hard-on. "The girls can wait, Vito. I need you to stay focused. Besides, the one that was all over me is the reason I had to go see a sexual addiction counselor."

"No kidding. She didn't look like you were harassing her."

"I didn't say sexual harassment. I said sexual addiction."

"But aren't you going to counseling for sexual harassment, too?"

"Yes, but that was for something else."

"Fucking Cesari, you've got to learn to control yourself."

The irony of having someone who just murdered four people lecture me on self-control was not lost on me. We got on the elevators and went up to the OR. It was eight and I still hadn't heard from Kelly.

R̶x 62

"**DAMN,**" I said in frustration.

"What's the problem, Cesari?" Vito asked while he inspected the large handgun in front of him. We were all alone in the OR lounge. He popped open the cylinder and removed one of the bullets. "Will you look at the size of this thing," he said in amazement. "It's more than two inches long." He stood it up on the table in front of him.

"It's after nine already, Vito, and I still haven't heard from Kelly. Her phone keeps going to voicemail. She's supposed to be here soon to set up the endoscopy room and assist me with the colonoscopy. And would you please put that thing away? They're doing an appendectomy down the hall. Someone might come in here."

"What time was she supposed to get here?" He put the bullet back in the cylinder and the gun back in the bag. It was too heavy and bulky for his pocket or waistband, even he had to agree to that.

"She was supposed to get here at ten to set up and I was going to get the patient at eleven."

"Okay, she's still got time. Don't press the panic button. Besides, a lot of girls turn off their phones when they're having sex, you know what I mean? They don't want to be distracted when they're about to have an orgasm." He laughed as if he had said something really funny.

"You're a regular riot, Vito."

He continued chuckling.

"Relax, Cesari. I'm sure she's only giving the guy head."

"Will you shut up already?" Damn, he was pissing me off. Thankfully, my cellphone rang. It was the ER.

"Cesari here."

"Hello, Dr. Cesari. This is Sally in the ER. I'm taking care of your patient, Vladimir."

"I remember, Sally. How's he doing?"

"Well, he's finished his colonoscopy preparation. He drank it all and has been in the bathroom a lot, so I think he'll be pretty cleaned out. He was very cooperative. No signs of any bleeding and his vital signs have remained stable. I was wondering when you were going to take him up for his procedure."

"I'm just waiting for my nurse to come in, Sally. She should be here any minute. Let me see, it's close to nine-thirty. She needs about thirty minutes to set up... I think between ten thirty and eleven sounds reasonable."

"Okay, I'll let everyone know. Let's say eleven so people don't start getting twitchy down here."

"Sounds good. Anything else?"

"Yes, there was a man down here visiting your patient a short while ago. He said that he was a friend of yours. He left a small, gift-wrapped box for you and asked me to give it to you. I told him that I would call you, but he said he couldn't wait. He just left. Very weird guy. Sounded Russian, like your patient. Wore a hat the whole time he was here and had an ugly scar on his face. Sound familiar?"

"Yes, it does. Just for the record, did he give you his name?"

"Yes, he did. It was Sergei."

What the fuck was he doing here?

"Okay, thanks, Sally. I'll be right down."

I told Vito. "Stay here, all right? I'm going down to the ER and see what this is all about. If anybody asks who you are or what you're doing here, just tell them you're my brother and that I told you to wait here for me."

He looked concerned. "I wonder what that asshole's up to. I don't like it."

"Neither do I."

I hustled down to the ER and found Sally.

"Hi doc. I left the box in the room by the window. You can't miss it. It's got a red bow on it like a Christmas present."

"Thanks again, Sally."

I went into room fourteen and said hello to Vlad, who looked just as puzzled as I did. For some reason, the script had changed. "How's the preparation going, Vlad?" I asked and he rolled his eyes.

"Feel weak."

"I know. It will all be over soon. Did Sergei say anything to you?"

"No, he speak nurse and leave box."

I saw the little box on the window sill. It was wrapped in shiny gold paper and had a ribbon around it tied at the top. It looked very pretty. It was a four inch cube. I picked it up and returned back to the OR lounge. I was quite certain I didn't want to open it up in public.

Vito was still alone and was starting to look a little apprehensive. "What do you think it is?" He asked.

"Haven't the slightest idea."

I placed it on the table and took the ribbon and wrapping paper off. The top lifted off, revealing delicate white tissue paper underneath with specks of red on it. Blood? Inside the tissue paper was a folded piece of paper and an ear. A human ear. A black human ear. I held my breath and my heart skipped a beat. I felt myself getting weak and sat down.

"What is it?" Vito reached across the table, grabbed the box and looked inside. "That fucking commie."

I unfolded the paper. It had one word written on it.

Insurance. I showed it to Vito.

"What an asshole," he said. I couldn't even breathe, let alone speak.

I called Pam. Voicemail.

I called Gina. Voicemail.

Fuck. Maybe they were still out cold from all the sedatives and exhaustion.

I looked at my watch. Almost ten. I felt lightheaded.

I called him. "Sergei?"

"You have diamonds? Is early?"

"Put her on the phone."

"Who?" He chuckled.

"Kelly. Put Kelly on the phone. I want to know that she's okay or you can go fuck yourself."

There was a moment of silence and then a frightened voice.

"Johnny...is that you?"

"Yes, Kel. It's..." I didn't get to finish. Sergei got back on the line.

"Next time call, have diamonds." He hung up and I put my phone down.

"What do you want to do, Cesari?" Vito asked.

I looked at him and didn't say anything. I could feel my blood pressure rising. I was getting angry.

"Cesari, what are you going to do?" He asked again.

"I'm going to cut his fucking heart out and eat it right in front of him."

Vito nodded. "How did he get her?"

"Don't know. He must have been tailing me and seen us together." I looked inside the box again at Kelly's ear and ran over to the refrigerator in the corner of the room. There was a tray of ice in the freezer and I dumped it into a bowl from one of the overhead cabinets. I filled it halfway with water and submerged the ear in it. I didn't know much about this stuff, but figured I had to at least try to save the ear. I covered the bowl with a washcloth that I found underneath the sink and put it in the back of the freezer for safekeeping.

"What now, Cesari?"

"We go through with the plan, Vito. goddamn it. He didn't have to do that."

"I'm sorry."

"Save your sorries for Sergei. When I catch him, he's going to wish he had never left Mother Russia." I was pissed off now for real. "Let's go to the locker room and change into scrubs. I need to think. You're going to have to assist me with the colonoscopy."

"Me? You've got to be kidding," he said incredulously.

"It's not ideal, but if you just listen and do exactly as I say, we might be okay. C'mon, we've got to get started setting things up."

We threw on scrubs and rushed to the endoscopy room to set up my equipment. My nurse usually did this for me. I could do it, but it would take me a little longer and wouldn't be perfect. Vito looked ridiculous in his double extra-large surgical scrubs, stretching at the neck and biceps, but he tried to be as helpful as possible. At least he didn't get in the way as much as I would have guessed. It took me forty-five minutes to set up, twice as long as it would have taken Kelly. Vito and I used the time to discuss strategy.

"I'll go down to the ER and get the patient. Call your guy Mikey and have him meet us with Al at the front of the hospital around midnight. We'll need different weapons than the ones we have, okay? We're going on offense now. For the time being, you stay here in the endoscopy room and don't touch anything."

R⟋ 63

I rolled Vlad on to his left side and had him curl his legs up towards his chest.

"Vlad, you might feel some discomfort during the exam. That's normal. Just take a deep breath in and let it out slowly when that happens. Understand?"

"Yes, understand. But why no sleep? Vlad told he sleep."

"Because I need you awake when we're done. I need your help."

"Sergei no tell Vlad this."

"Yes. Well there has been a slight change in plans. Sergei called me just a few minutes ago and he wants you to cooperate with me. Now I need you to be quiet. You can watch the screen. Don't get nervous if you see blood, okay? You're going to feel something cold now."

I inserted the tip of the lubricated colonoscope into his rectum and he reflexively squeezed and tried to get away. Men always did that for some reason. Big babies. "Please don't move, Vlad, and try to relax. There, that's better. Sorry about that."

I looked at Vito, who was mesmerized by the action on the screen. I distended the colon with a little air and began advancing the scope around the twists and turns. Vlad experienced an occasional cramping sensation, but for the most part tolerated the procedure well. In ten minutes, I found what I was looking for. I had set up the cart behind me with the snare, preloaded syringes of epinephrine and three metal clips. The electro-cautery unit was ready to go as well. All Vito had to do was hand me what I needed when I asked. With a minimum of help, I would be able to muddle through. As long as nothing went wrong, that is. I looked at the little brown bag attached to the guy's colon and washed residual fecal matter off it.

"Interesting," Vlad commented as he watched.

"Yes, very. No more talking, okay? I need to concentrate. Vito, hand me the coiled white plastic tube that's off to the right. That's it. That's the snare. Thanks."

I took the tip from him and loaded it into my end of the colonoscope. I fed it through the scope and it reappeared on the screen. He handed me the handle and I opened the snare wide and grabbed the little brown pouch just as I had the last time. I then gave the handle back to Vito and told him to hang on tight. I pulled as hard as I could and the pouch came free with a gush of blood. I released the pouch into the colon and removed the snare quickly.

"Vito, hand me the catheter with the syringe of epinephrine attached. It's just underneath the snare. Yes, that's it, thanks. Good job. Are you okay?"

He was staring wide-eyed and open-mouthed at the video monitor.

He nodded.

I advanced the catheter with the epinephrine quickly to the site of hemorrhage and injected the area multiple times until the bleeding slowed significantly and eventually stopped. I removed the catheter and then placed a few metal clips on the site to insure success. The last required slightly more input from Vito, but I walked him through it. He was adroit enough to handle it, although I could see beads of perspiration forming on his brow from the tension.

Thank goodness the bleeding wasn't nearly as bad as the other night. It was stressful for me, as well, trying to manipulate the catheters and clips without a skilled nurse assisting me, but I was lucky that nothing went wrong. Once I was satisfied that he wasn't going to bleed to death, I reinserted the snare and removed the brown pouch with the diamonds.

When I was done, Vito finally spoke, "Fucking Cesari, that was the coolest thing I ever saw." I had told him not to talk during the procedure unless absolutely necessary.

Vlad had rolled onto his back and made eye contact with me. "Me, also."

I opened the bag and spilled nearly two dozen large, brilliant diamonds onto a gauze pad.

Vito said, "Damn."

Vlad passed flatus loudly and I looked at him. "You okay?"

"Yes, feel good now."

"I'm glad. Now get dressed quickly. We've got work to do."

I put the diamonds into a plastic specimen container as I watched Vlad.

"What are you supposed to do now?" I asked.

"I go meet Sergei. He pay me. In morning, go back Russia."

"Why doesn't he let me give you the diamonds to bring to him?"

He laughed. "Sergei no trust."

Vito chuckled.

"Where do you meet Sergei?"

"Don't know. Every time different. After exam, I call find out."

"How much does he pay you?"

"Ten thousand American dollars. All expenses paid. First class seat on plane and hotel."

I fished out a large diamond from the bag and showed it to him. "This is probably worth four or five hundred thousand American dollars, Vlad." He studied it greedily. "I'll give it to you and all you have to do is call Sergei and tell me where he is."

"Why want know?"

"That's my business."

"Sergei kill me."

"Sergei's not going to kill anyone ever again after tonight, Vlad, but I need your help. I need to know where he is."

"Why not you call him? Tell that all went well and you bring diamonds."

"No good, Vlad. Then he'll be expecting me and I don't want that. I want the element of surprise on my side, so we have to keep him off balance. Besides, he may not want me to come to him. He may send someone to me to pick up the diamonds. No, we have to convince him that something unexpected happened and that there's been an unavoidable delay. You're going to tell him the colonoscopy was cancelled because of some big emergency here at the hospital and I was in the middle of it all. You tell Sergei that I told you to return tomorrow night and we'll do the colonoscopy then. This will confuse him, and of course, make him suspicious. I'm sure he will insist on seeing you in person because he won't trust you and will want to keep an eye on his diamonds."

"Vlad no understand. Why not I say did job, want money, where come get? Then Vlad tell you where is."

"Because then he'll know I have the diamonds, and if he doesn't hear from me, he'll be pissed and hurt a good friend of mine, or like I said, he might come looking for me himself. I want him to stay put, uncertain of what is happening, but thinking that he is still in control."

He nodded, seeming to understand. "What happen Vlad after make call?"

"We have an apartment you can stay in for a few days. After that, you can go back home or stay here in the U.S. if you want. You'll be illegal, but so what? You'll have five hundred thousand reasons not to care and ten million Mexicans to keep you company."

"If Vlad say no?"

"That is not an option," I said very seriously, and meant it. I couldn't let him run around free now that he knew what I was up to. He was either with us or would soon be with Lenin, Trotsky and all the others.

Vito pulled out the fifty caliber revolver, cocked the trigger and shoved the muzzle into Vlad's abdomen. "I guarantee you a very painful death, Commissar," he said.

Vlad chuckled and looked at us, not in the least bit scared. "Just like Russia. Give me phone— and diamond."

I handed him the rock and he made the call to Sergei. They spoke in Russian for a few minutes and it sounded very much like Sergei was pissed. Vlad clicked off the call and looked at me.

"Sergei at Crowne Plaza in Times Square. Room 1509. I meet him there one hour."

I said, "Thank you, Vlad. Now let's all go down to the main lobby together. Some friends of ours are going to take you to the apartment

I told you about. They'll make sure you're safe. Tomorrow, you can go wherever you want."

"What if no want go apartment?"

"Be cooperative, Vlad. It will be easier all the way around."

"So Vlad prisoner?"

Vito said, "More like a guest, Vlad. Just in case you made a mistake in which hotel Sergei was in or if you warned Sergei we were coming for him. You didn't make a mistake or warn Sergei, did you?"

Vlad was indignant. "Vlad no make mistake. No warn Sergei. Crowne Plaza room 1509."

"Then you have nothing to worry about."

My phone buzzed. It was Sergei. I let it go to voicemail. He called two more times and sent a couple of texts before he got the hint. I figured I'd let him think I was tied up for reasons beyond my control. It was a risky play, but he wasn't sure what was going on and wouldn't overreact, especially since he didn't have the diamonds. He would definitely want to see Vlad with his own eyes.

Vito looked at me. "C'mon, Cesari, let's get out of here."

"Let me get Kelly's ear from the freezer first. I'll meet you and Vlad by the locker and we'll change back into street clothes."

Minutes later, we went outside together where Mikey was waiting with Alfonse to escort Vlad to the apartment in Little Italy. Vito and I took Mikey aside while Alfonse walked with Vlad to the car.

Vito put his arm around Mikey's shoulder. "Be nice to him, but don't let him out of your sight. No phone calls either. Just watch TV and relax. I'll call you when I'm done. If either me or Cesari don't check in with you by morning, it means we're dead and it was probably his fault, so you take care of him. Now, did you bring the stuff I asked for?"

Mikey nodded. "They're in a duffel bag in the car."

I handed Mikey the bowl of ice with Kelly's ear. "Put this in the freezer as soon as you get to the apartment and don't ask questions."

It was after midnight and the front of the hospital was desolate. There were a few pedestrians here and there, but they minded their own business. We walked over to the car and retrieved the duffel bag from the front seat. Alfonse sat in the back with Vlad. In the bag were two silenced Sig Sauer P226 9mm pistols loaded with ten rounds each along with a pair of extra clips and two dark nylon windbreakers. Vito and I donned the windbreakers and tucked the weapons into our waistbands. We zipped up and tossed the other weapons into the duffel bag and handed it back to Mikey, who said, "Everything's loaded and chambered. Safeties are off."

Vito nodded. "Thanks. I'll talk to you guys later."

We pocketed the extra clips and watched Mikey get in the car and drive off. Then we hopped a cab over to Times Square. As always, the area teemed with throngs of people milling about, coming from shows, looking for places to eat and just generally enjoying the nice weather. The silencers made the weapons bulky and uncomfortable, and I squirmed as I walked.

Vito saw and commented, "Cut it out Cesari, and try to act natural for God's sake. This ain't your first rodeo."

We entered the Crowne Plaza and crossed the bustling lobby toward the elevators. Once on the fifteenth floor, we found Sergei's room, 1509. "Now what, Cesari?" Vito asked. We didn't have a firm plan. We stood about ten feet away from the door behind a large potted plant while I thought things through.

"I'm thinking." The hallway was about eight feet wide with thick plush carpeting. I glanced at my watch. "We're about fifteen minutes early, which is good. I guess. I suppose we could just knock or pull the fire alarm on the wall down the hall."

Vito said, "Or we could order room service for them. That'll get them to open the door. Yeah, a nice filet mignon, baked potato, bottle of chianti. When we're done, we could have a snack and send the bill to Moscow."

I checked his face to see if he was serious. He was. "Yeah, but it might also make the waiter a casualty. No, I don't like that idea at all, but I do like the fire alarm idea. They're bound to come out of the room to see what's going on. You got a lighter on you?"

"Yeah, here it is." He handed me his Zippo. Looking around, I found several discarded copies of USA Today outside of guest rooms. I picked them up and crumpled them on the floor in front of room 1509. We looked around furtively and saw there was no one else in the hallway, so I lit the papers as Vito broke the glass case and pulled the fire alarm.

The papers caught with a sudden blaze and burned brightly as the alarm sounded shrilly throughout the hotel. Vito and I stood to either side of the door, guns drawn as pandemonium ensued. The carpet smoldered and flamed up with the newspapers, and smoke filled the corridor, particularly thick in front of Sergei's room.

Sleepy guests entered the hallway. Some saw the fire and screamed. Some saw the guns and screamed. I tossed another newspaper onto the burning carpet, causing it to flare up. Finally, the door to room 1509 opened and a burly thug cursed in Russian when he saw the flames and smoke. He coughed, covered his face and shouted back to someone. As he turned, I shot him in the back of the head with my Sig Sauer. The report was barely audible between the silencer, the fire alarm and all the yelling. He fell back into the room, and I charged over his body. There was another guy in there in the process of getting out of his chair when the round entered his cheekbone, passing through the back of his head and piercing the window behind. He was dead before he even knew why.

Neither one was Sergei, and there was no one else in the room. The bathroom door was closed and I opened it carefully. No one there, either. A thumping sound from the walk-in closet next to the bathroom caught our attention. Opening it, we found Kelly on the floor, wrists tied behind her back with rope and duct tape across her mouth. I quickly untied her and pulled the duct tape off. We hugged briefly and I saw the bloody gauze covering the right side of head where her ear had been.

"We've got to hurry, Kel. We'll talk later, okay?"

She nodded and I helped her to her feet as Vito guarded the door. She was unsteady and clung tightly to me. We put the guns away and hustled into the hallway. The fire had died down, although the carpet was still smoking briskly. People in pajamas stampeded down the stairwells. It was a mass of confusion and noise.

Coughing, I pointed to the crowd. "Let's lose ourselves in the chaos."

We melted into the mob and wound our way slowly down the emergency stairs to the main floor. By the time we reached the bottom, firemen were racing up the stairs past us and the flashing lights of police cars and fire engines lit up 7th Avenue in front of the hotel. The horde of gawkers outside the building was enormous. This was Man-

367

hattan in summertime and there were already thousands of onlookers at the scene. As far as the tourists were concerned, they couldn't have asked for better entertainment. Traffic had come to a standstill, and the police were having difficulty maintaining order and discipline.

Twenty yards away by the curb, I spotted a guy missing an ear staring at the hotel. It was that fuck, Sergei.

I turned quickly to Vito. "Take Kelly to the St. Matt's emergency room and have them look at that wound and don't leave her side for any reason. Have Mikey bring her ear there. If there's going to be any chance of reattaching it, we have to act fast. I see Sergei over there, and I'm going to finish this."

"Cesari, maybe I should stay and help you."

"Just do what I say, Vito, and don't leave her alone, not even for a minute."

"Understood."

Kelly put her arms around me tightly. "I'm not going anywhere without you, even if it means losing my ear."

I hugged her tightly. "Kelly, I can't stop now. He knows who we are and where he can find us."

"Please don't leave me, John, I'm afraid."

"Kelly, look at me." She looked up at my face as tears streamed down hers.

"Yes?" she asked softly.

"I love you, Kelly," I whispered. "I love you more than my own life. Do you understand? I would throw myself in front of a speeding train if I thought it would help you."

She nodded. "I love you, too."

"Now please go with Vito," I said gently, brushing her hair and kissing her.

"Promise me you'll come back, Cesari."

"I promise."

R̲X 64

VITO and Kelly fought through the mass of people, making their way down 7th Avenue, hoping to catch a cab down to Mulberry Street. I kept my eyes peeled on Sergei. I was about thirty feet and a hundred people to his rear. I had the silenced Sig Sauer in my waist band as I bumped into citizens and police alike. After about thirty minutes, the firemen came out of the building and swarms of police went rushing in, and I presumed someone had found the bodies in room 1509. News vans had arrived on the scene by now and were like sharks that had just picked up the scent of blood. An ambulance wailed loudly as it screeched to a halt just behind us.

People were gradually being allowed back into their rooms and I moved forward with the surging crowd, maintaining my distance behind Sergei. To his left was a large guy with a shaved head and I recognized him as the guy who'd been with Sergei in Reg's office the other day. It was an absolute madhouse in the lobby as people were either checking out or furiously trying to find out what had happened. Rumors of terrorism circulated, increasing the already sky-high tension. The area in front of the elevators was jammed with people returning to their rooms. Sergei signaled his companion that he did not want to wait for an elevator and they meandered over to the hotel's bar and lounge area, which had already reopened. The area was packed with guests trying to self-medicate their anxiety and laugh off their fear.

I grabbed a discarded Wall Street Journal to use as camouflage and took a seat at a small table, ordering a bourbon with ice from a waitress walking by. Adrenaline rushed through me as I observed the two Russians sipping vodka from shot glasses at the bar. They and everyone else were engrossed with the news on a large screen TV, trying to figure out what had happened. Sergei made several calls on his cell phone and seemed frustrated. I guessed he was trying to reach his dead friends. Until he returned to the room, he would assume they were wandering somewhere, waiting for the dust to settle. His companion excused himself and walked in the direction of the men's room. This was my chance so I followed him there, a discreet distance behind, and watched him enter. Counting to ten first, I took a deep breath and went in after him. There was another guy inside washing his hands, and I nodded at him while I pretended to use the urinal. He left the room and I scanned underneath the stalls until I saw a pair of large feet. I had to act quickly before someone else came in. I pulled out the silenced pistol, made sure the safety was off and approached the stall door.

I knocked gently.

"Is occupied," responded a gruff Russian accent.

I kicked the door open violently. He barely had time to register surprise when I fired the Sig directly into his chest just over his heart, causing him to propel backwards into the wall. Tile shattered behind him as the bullet exited his back. He didn't die instantly and looked at me in shocked recognition. Clutching his chest at the site of the entry wound, we both watched blood ooze out, staining his shirt. His mouth gaped open as if he wanted to say something but couldn't. I stepped closer and fired the next round more deliberately into his left eye. Brains and blood sprayed against the wall behind him, and he finally slumped forward dead. With the smell of gunpowder in my nostrils, I returned the pistol to my waistband and hurriedly left the bathroom and headed back to my chair. Sergei hadn't moved, and I watched the bartender serve him a second drink as I took my seat. I inhaled deeply and let it out slow, trying to stay calm. My carotids were throbbing in my neck. Soon, there would be bedlam again as some unlucky patron discovered the corpse. Five minutes later, Sergei looked up and around, and I covered my face with the newspaper. He was starting to wonder what was taking his friend so long.

A young man came running out of the bathroom screaming about a murder and everyone in the bar jumped to attention. Everyone but

Sergei, that is. He understood exactly what had happened. He didn't know who, or why, but he didn't need to. Guys like him didn't survive for long without developing instincts for this sort of thing. Without any hesitation, he made a beeline for the exit, weaving through a sea of people as I trailed closely behind.

Outside, men in blue were everywhere, darting back and forth in all directions, setting up a perimeter. A double murder at a five star hotel in Times Square was a big deal, and a triple homicide would definitely rock even New York City. The hotel would definitely be on lockdown now. Sergei headed uptown, hoping to escape the crowds in that direction.

I watched him snake his way along the sidewalk, occasionally glancing over his shoulder. A half block behind, hugging the store fronts, I remained in silent pursuit. He turned right onto 50th Street, crossed over to 6th Avenue and hailed a yellow cab. I was about fifty feet behind and closing rapidly. I started running, picking up speed. The taxi pulled to the curb and as he was entering, I sprinted the few remaining feet, shoving him forcefully the rest of the way in. Pressing the Sig Sauer firmly into his chest, I quickly frisked him, finding only a pearl-handled, five-inch switchblade. He registered neither surprise nor fear on his features and knew better than to resist. I was quite sure that this wasn't the first time he had confronted death.

The Lebanese driver looked confused and a little frightened. I wasn't sure how good his English was so I threw two fifty dollar bills at him and his confidence grew. "The Bronx. I'll give you the address and another hundred when we get there."

"What you want?" Sergei growled.

"I want you to shut up." I wasn't sure if he'd heard me, so I smashed the pistol into the side of his head, stunning him.

It was close to two in the morning and the roads were clear. We sailed up the East Side Drive and onto the Cross Bronx Expressway in a matter of minutes. Sergei knew better than to open his mouth again. Blood trickled down the side of his face from the blow, but he remained stoic and expressionless. We were about the same size, but he looked like he would be comfortable tangling with a Grizzly bear and I intended on taking no chances with him. So I cocked the trigger and he understood that even if we hit a pot hole, he was dead. In twenty minutes, we approached our destination.

"Driver, take the Gun Hill Road exit on the left. Then bear left again onto Allerton Avenue. That's right. Now stop at the next street-light. Thanks."

"Where go?" Sergei asked.

"It's a surprise. Now, get out slowly. Understand?"

"Yes."

I tossed the driver another hundred dollar bill and looked at him sternly. "Now forget you ever saw us."

"Saw who?" I loved these guys. He made a quick U-turn and sped back to the highway.

"Move slowly, Sergei. Do everything very slowly and keep your hands in your pockets at all times." I looked around as we walked. The Bronx wasn't Manhattan. At two a.m., the streets were quiet and desolate. We were two blocks away from our true destination just in case the cab driver decided not to forget us.

"Walk slowly and stay in front of me. I'll tell you when we're there, and remember, the trigger is cocked." I was five paces behind him.

"I thought you doctor? Help people?"

I didn't answer him. Shortly, we reached an abandoned, semi-attached brick row-house, the kind that was built en-masse in the 1950's to accommodate all the soldiers returning home from the war. The windows were boarded up and the small front yard was overgrown with weeds. I looked at the house number—1362. "This is it, asshole. Let's walk around back."

There was a short, narrow alley separating this house from the one next to it. We walked down to the rear of the house, and I directed him down a short cement staircase to the basement door that was old and rusted.

"Stop there and put your hands against the door where I can see them." I was two steps above and behind him. I reached into my pocket and tossed him a set of keys that jingled as they hit the floor.

"It's the one with red tape on it."

He picked them up, opened the door and went in. "Turn the light on," I said. "There's a switch just to the right of the entrance."

I followed him in and locked the door behind me. We were in a small, furnished one room basement apartment. The floor was dusty and made of linoleum.

I pointed to the middle of the sparsely furnished room. "Lay face down on the floor and away from me. Keep your hands in your pockets," I ordered him as I took a seat at the small kitchen table a few feet away. I looked around and memories flooded my consciousness. This was the house I'd grown up in. After my mother passed, I hadn't had the heart to sell it so I kept paying the taxes and continued to perform minimum maintenance. I kept the electricity and gas on, and once a year I would drop by and give it a quick inspection while I strolled down memory lane. Before the linoleum, there was just a cement slab, and I used to roller skate on it when I was a kid.

"What happen Vladimir?" Sergei asked, interrupting my thoughts.

"He's dead like the rest of your friends. Why weren't you in the hotel room?" I'd lied about Vlad, but so what?

"Have drink in bar with Victor."

"Victor? Was that the guy I killed in the bathroom?"

"Yes. What do now?"

"I'm thinking about that. You shouldn't have hurt Kelly. I was going to bring you the diamonds."

He sighed. "Agree. Was mistake. We make deal, yes?"

I laughed. "What kind of deal?"

"You saw diamonds?"

"Yeah, I saw. So what?"

He glanced in my direction. "Many more. Very many more."

"Hmm. Is that so? And where are they?"

"In safe. Brooklyn. I have uncle. Give you all diamonds for me."

I chuckled. "Really?"

"May I sit?"

"If you move anything but your lips, I will shoot you."

"Okay."

"So tell me about your uncle. What's his name?"

"His name Boris Anatolyvich."

"Where's he live? Which section of Brooklyn?"

"Brighton Beach."

I nodded as I thought it over. "Tell me his phone number?"

"Why?"

"I want to see if you're telling the truth."

"(718) 672-8919. Sergei no lie."

I took out my cellphone and dialed the number. One ring, two rings, three rings, four rings. "Da," a sleepy voice said in a thick Russian accent. "Who this?" It was after three a.m.

"Is this Boris Anatolyvich?"

"Yes, who this?"

I hung up.

Interesting.

"What's your uncle Boris got to do with all this?"

"He man in charge. Make all arrangements."

"I thought that was you?"

Now he laughed. "No. I collector. Make sure all go well."

"How did you get Dr. Griffin to work for you?"

"He greedy. Drink too much. Easy convince. I meet in Moscow whorehouse while he visit for vacation. Girl die. He scared. Think spend life in Russian prison."

"How did the girl die?"

"Fall out window."

"A prostitute fell out of a window? What did that have to do with Dr. Griffin?"

"He sleeping in bed when she jump out window."

"Did she fall out the window or jump? There's a difference."

"Yes, she jump—with help."

Finally, I got it. "You mean she was thrown out of the window?"

"He scared. Think go prison."

"You killed a girl just to blackmail him into working for you?"

He was silent as I casually strummed my fingers on the table. I decided that he was an even bigger asshole than I had previously thought.

"So what happened to your ear?" I asked, interested.

"Prison camp, Siberia. Other prisoners try eat Sergei."

"You're kidding?" I almost felt sorry for him—almost.

"No kid."

I took his switch blade out of my pocket and flicked it open. It was five inches long, an inch wide and very sharp. It had a pearl inlaid handle and was quite aesthetically pleasing. Imported, I guessed. Probably Sicilian.

"I had a knife very similar to this one when I was a teenager, Sergei. My mother found it one day when she was cleaning the house. I had hidden it behind some books on a shelf. When I came home, I found it smashed into little pieces and left in a pile on the kitchen table. Neither she nor I ever said anything about it, but I always wondered how angry she must have been to do that."

"Is sad story. Mama no like knives?"

"Mama no like violence. She was a very kind and gentle soul. She could forgive anybody almost anything. She could probably even forgive an asshole like you."

"Sergei understand. Is good to have nice Mama."

"I always wished I had been more like her, but that just wasn't meant to be." I twirled the shiny blade around, enjoying its glimmer in the light. "Is this what you cut her ear off with?"

He didn't answer.

"Hey, I asked you a question."

"Yes."

I inhaled deeply and let it out. "Well, I must say. It has been enlightening talking to you, Sergei."

Standing up, I walked over and knelt down beside him, placing the muzzle of the Sig Sauer firmly against the base of his skull. "Don't move and keep your hands in your pockets."

"What do?"

Without warning, I plunged the large blade viciously up to its hilt, into the approximate location of his right kidney, twisting it clockwise and then jumped away quickly, weapon in hand. He reflexively jerked and squirmed from the pain and surprise. The metal had scraped harshly and audibly over rib bone, and he groaned as I went back to the table and sat down. Watching him reach around instinctively to feel the wound, I hoped I'd hit the renal artery or inferior vena cava, or I would have to go back and do it again. I didn't want to hang out with him all night.

"What you do Sergei? Why? I thought we make deal?"

"No, I'm afraid we are past the deal stage deal, Sergei. You hurt the woman I love and that was your big mistake. I take things like that very personally. But consider yourself lucky. If I had the time, I'd keep you here for days, doing this a lot more slowly."

He had turned around, raising himself to a sitting position and was now leaning against the far wall. Bright red blood leaked out of him fast onto the white flooring, and I hoped he was suffering. Maybe it was wrong, but that's the way I felt. I cleaned the blade on a cloth I found under the sink. He gradually slipped back into a lying position and looked at me with venom in his eyes.

"Bastard," he hissed.

"Yeah, I know."

As his blood pressure started to fall, he became pale and sweaty.

"Finish me. Please," he whispered weakly.

"Can't do that, Sergei. You have to pay for your sins."

"Fuck you."

"I'll tell Uncle Boris you said hello."

It took about ten more minutes, but he gradually lost consciousness. The renal artery was a very large vessel, and by the time he stopped breathing, he had turned a ghastly white. I stood over him, gazing around the small room in a trance, thinking about all the time I had spent here with my mother. I missed her very much, every single minute of every single day. When I snapped out of it, I called Vito.

"Where are you, Cesari? How'd it go with Sergei?"

"He's dead. I'm up in the Bronx at my mother's house. I need you to come up here now and help me clean up the mess. You remember where the house is?"

"I remember it. Allerton Avenue, right? By Eastchester Road?"

"That's right. Where are you, by the way, and how's Kelly? How'd it go in the ER?"

Silence.

Vito cleared his throat. "Kelly's fine, but she wouldn't go to the ER. She's sleeping comfortably."

"What do you mean she wouldn't go? You're three times her size, for God's sake." I was starting to get agitated. "Jesus, Vito."

"Give me some slack, Cesari. She said she was exhausted and just wanted to get some sleep first. She also said that if she was going to need surgery that she wanted you there with her, not me. I tried to convince her otherwise, but she's one strong-willed girl, I'll tell you that. She ain't going to do nothing she don't want to, that's for sure."

I took a deep breath and let it out, trying not to get angry with him. "Okay, meet me up here as soon as you can and bring a mop. How's Vlad?"

"He's sleeping, too. I feel like I'm running a boarding house," he chuckled.

"Okay, we'll talk more when you get here, but tell Mikey and Alphonse that Vlad's under house arrest. I'm going to need someone who speaks Russian."

"Always scheming, Cesari. All right, here I come."

"Also bring something to wrap the body in."

"Okay, Cesari, you don't got to keep repeating yourself. I'm the one who taught you, remember?"

Vito arrived a half an hour later and backed a Cadillac into the driveway. We wrapped Sergei in an all-purpose tarp and carried him out to the trunk. It was almost five, and dawn was still about an hour away. We went back into the basement and mopped the floor with bleach. Mop, buckets, and empty bleach containers all went into the Caddie's trunk, and we drove off into the night.

"Nice ride, Vito. Whose car?"

"It's Al's. They left Mikey's Towncar at JFK with the bodies in it. So, where to, Cesari?" "Let's go to City Island where all the seafood restaurants are. It's only a few minutes away and we'll find an empty dumpster there. There won't be anybody around for a while." Fifteen minutes later, we hoisted Sergei's corpse into a large metal dumpster behind one of my favorite restaurants.

"Do you remember this place, Vito?"

"Sure I do. We ate here a thousand times. Best lobster ravioli in the city."

"Damn right about that."

By six we were back in Little Italy. I went into the apartment, nodded at Mikey and Al, found Kelly sleeping in one of the bedrooms and crashed down next to her, asleep before my head hit the pillow.

℞ 65

SUNDAY morning arrived, and I woke up late to an empty bed and the smell of espresso. I found the bathroom and was just stepping out of the shower when Kelly opened the door and came in.

"There's some fresh clothes on the bed. Vito sent one of his guys to the hotel to get our stuff this morning. We can check out formally later. That's your toothbrush and razor there on the sink."

I looked at her as I wrapped a towel around my waist. She had showered and her hair was still damp. There was fresh gauze on the side of her face and I hugged her. "Good morning, Kel. How'd you sleep?"

"Not too well. My ear or what's left of it hurt like hell."

I decided it wouldn't be a good idea to criticize her decision not to go to the ER. "I'll get dressed quick and we'll go to the hospital together. You really need someone to look at that."

"I know. Hurry up, it's almost eleven. There's a fresh pot of coffee and bagels in the kitchen. Everybody slept in."

I turned to the sink and started brushing my teeth, but noticed she was still staring at me. I rinsed out and looked back at her. "Everything okay?" I asked.

"Did you mean what you said last night or were you just trying to humor me?"

Hmm. She was smarter than the average bear. I put my arms around her again and kissed her long and slow. "Want me to say it again?"

She hugged me tightly. "Yes."

"I love you." My towel fell to the floor and she giggled.

I attempted to pick it up, but she wouldn't let go of me. She said, "Vito is in the kitchen waiting to talk to you about something."

"Tell him I'll be right there."

As she turned to leave, I bent down to pick up the towel and heard a laugh from the doorway. "Nice butt, Cesari."

A short time later, I poured myself an espresso and sat at the table across from Vlad. Kelly had left us alone to talk.

The Russian spoke first. "Why Vlad cannot leave?"

I said, "You can leave anytime you want, Vlad, but I'd like to make a proposal to you first."

He looked at Vito, who was spreading cream cheese on a bagel. "What mean proposal?"

Vito said, "A proposal means a business deal."

"What kind of deal?" He asked, eyeing me suspiciously.

"How well did you know Sergei?"

"I know Sergei many years."

"Do you know his Uncle Boris?"

"I meet once, maybe twice. Bad man. Worse than Sergei."

Vito and I looked at each other. I said, "Okay he's bad, but did he seem like a reasonable man to you?"

"He seemed like greedy man."

"That's a good thing, Vlad."

"What happen Sergei?"

I sipped my espresso. "He left Manhattan and won't be returning. My friend Vito and I were wondering if you would like to have his job."

Vlad sat back in his chair and smiled. "Maybe I have cup coffee while talk."

Vito chuckled. "Help yourself."

He poured himself a cup, took a sip and thought it over. "So what plan?"

"You call Uncle Boris and tell him something bad has happened to Sergei. He got into a dispute with Dr. Griffin who was helping to bring the diamonds into the country. The argument was over money.

He killed Dr. Griffin, but Dr. Griffin's friends found out and killed Sergei for revenge. You're the only one left who knows how things run. You tell him that you know another doctor, me, who's willing to do the job for him. If he wants, the operation could continue running smoothly with you acting as the supervisor, so to speak."

Vlad's brow furrowed and he scowled. "Uncle Boris no like. Probably kill Vlad."

I nodded. "Probably, but if he goes for it, then just think about how rich you'll be, and you'll never have to go back to Russia. This is how capitalism works, Vlad. One seizes the opportunity as it arises, and takes big risks for big gains. With socialism there are no risks, just a lot of poor people."

He was silent for about a minute, thinking it over. "I make call."

"Good. If Uncle Boris seems receptive, we'll set up a meeting somewhere to hammer out the details."

After we finished talking, Kelly and I went to the St. Matt's ER and had her wound examined. They gave her a tetanus shot, and re-bandaged her with sterile dressing. She was placed on a broad spectrum antibiotic and vicodin for pain. The vascular surgeon on call sympathetically informed us that the ear we'd brought with us on ice was no longer viable, and she was given an outpatient appointment with a plastic surgeon to discuss her options. Kelly was asked several times to fill out a police report, which she declined. We left the ER and walked over to Washington Square Park where I bought her an ice cream cone. We sat there like that, enjoying the end of summer.

I said, "So tell me what happened. How did Sergei get you?"

"Not much to tell. Yesterday afternoon, when I left you at the Starbucks, I was walking back to Pam's apartment. There was a Suburban parked on the curb. I didn't think much of it, but as soon as I walked by, the doors flung open and someone called my name. Before I could even react, two big guys grabbed me and put a bag over my head. Next thing I remember, I was lying in that closet with my hands tied and a terrible pain in the side of my head. No one spoke to me at all. He put me on the phone with you for three seconds, but that was it. Other than that, I had no idea what was going on. The only other time the door to the closet opened was when you came."

"I'm so sorry, Kel."

"Who helped you with the colonoscopy?"

"Vito."

"Vito?" she laughed. "Get out of town."

"Really. I set up the cart and had everything opened and prepared to go. He just handed me things that I pointed to. He was so scared. You should've seen him, quiet as a mouse the whole time."

"So, I see he isn't going back to Albany."

I shook my head. "It doesn't look like it."

"Isn't the FBI going to be pissed that he left witness protection?"

"I'm fairly certain that Vito doesn't care what anyone thinks."

"I called Pam this morning while you were sleeping."

"How are they, Pam and Gina?"

"Pam's doing better. They both slept most of the whole day yesterday and woke up with a new outlook. Gina's going to stay there tonight as well. They seem to be hitting it off and getting along well, and they both need company right now. They would love it if we could drop by later."

"And what would you like to do?"

"I would like to talk to you—seriously. No jokes, okay?"

"I'm all ears."

"I said no jokes." She chuckled and tried to punch me, but I grabbed her, giving her a big hug.

"Sorry. I couldn't help myself. Go ahead."

"Actually, that's what I want to talk to you about, John. Your not being able to help yourself. Now I'm going to say a few things and I want you to listen without interrupting, but first promise me that you won't get upset or run away."

I didn't like where this was going, but I nodded and she slipped her arm through mine, nuzzling closer.

"When I was having my coffee this morning, I overheard Vito talking on the phone to someone. He mentioned your name several times."

Uh oh.

"Really?"

"John, please stop pretending. It was pretty obvious from the tone of the conversation that you're working with Vito again, and to be honest, it even sounded a little like—he was working for you."

"Kel...I don't know what to say."

"Don't say anything. I'd rather you not lie to me."

I turned my head away in shame and felt the urge to run. She gripped my arm more tightly, as if reading my mind. "I want you to look at me." I turned back toward her and saw tears in her eyes.

"I love you, John, with all my heart and soul, but I can't live like this, never knowing when somebody from your past or present is going to show up and cut off some body part, or worse. Maybe I'm just not strong enough, I don't know. You promised me a long time ago that you had put that life behind you, but I realize now that you can't. It's always going to be there, whether you want it to or not. I'm just a simple girl from a small town in Ohio. I'm just not cut out for this." She paused and we sat there silently for a minute. I was afraid to speak.

She continued. "I need some time to myself to reflect on things—on us. I need to do some serious soul searching. I don't know when, or even if, I'll find the answers I'm looking for. I'm going back to the apartment tomorrow, but I'd like you to stay with Vito or wherever. I know this is hard for you to hear, but if you care about me, then please show me respect by letting me think things through on my own."

I nodded and whispered hoarsely, "I love you, Kelly." I was feeling very weak and was quite sure I couldn't stand on my own.

"I know you do, John. I've always known it."

"Can I call you?" I asked softly.

"I'd rather you didn't for a while. I'll let you know when I'm ready." She stood up. "I need to be alone right now, okay? Please don't say anything. This is hard enough for me." She was crying as she walked away.

R̶x 66

"**I'm** bloated all the time, Doctor. Even now. Look at me. I don't look like this normally. I feel like I'm pregnant." She leaned back and raised her garment up so I could see her exposed abdomen. It was almost five p.m. and I just couldn't take much more of this.

"You can put your blouse down, Mrs. Cardillo. I understand what you're saying, but since I've never met you before, I really don't have a reference point as to what you look like normally."

"Well, it's not like this. That's for sure."

"I understand." She was fifty years old and very distraught over the fact that she had been gradually gaining weight despite the fact that her diet hadn't changed. A twenty pound weight gain over the last year without newer, looser clothing had left her feeling uncomfortable. Like many people, she was unable to accept weight gain as a natural consequence of the aging process, slowing metabolism and decreased physical activity.

"You were referred for a colonoscopy. Is that correct?"

"Yes," she replied. "There has to be some reason for why I feel like this."

"Abdominal bloating is one of the most common complaints we hear, Mrs. Cardillo. Most of the time, there is no explanation. As you are fifty years old, a screening colonoscopy is definitely recommended, but I don't want to give you the impression that it will give you the answer to your problem. It might, but it's important that we both have realistic expectations for the outcome of your exam."

She didn't like that. "Well, we need to do something, so we might as well start there."

"All right then, why don't you follow me and I'll have my secretary, Marilyn, schedule your colonoscopy? If there are any dates that you prefer, please let us know, and we'll do our best to accommodate you."

"Thank you, Doctor. I'd like to get it over with as soon as possible. I just know something's wrong. Somebody at work said it could be cancer."

Reassuring her that it most likely was not cancer, we walked together to my secretary's desk to make her appointment. When the patient had left, Marilyn came looking for me to say goodnight. She found me in my office, finishing up paperwork.

I looked up at her from my desk, and she looked back at me sympathetically, shaking her head. "Sorry, boss, no calls from Kelly today."

I nodded, again disappointed, as I had been every day when she'd brought me the same news. It was Friday and had been almost a full three weeks since I'd last seen or heard from Kelly. She wouldn't return my calls or acknowledge the flowers or cards I sent. I was afraid to push any harder. She needed to make up her own mind, but I was losing hope. I was also losing my appetite and wasn't sleeping well because of it. I knew that I was rapidly becoming depressed.

My cell phone rang and I practically jumped out of my skin, but it wasn't her.

"Hello, Cheryl."

"Hi, Cesari. Got a minute?"

"Sure. What can I do for you?" I hadn't heard from her either in several weeks.

"Well, an interesting bit of information came across my desk today, and I thought I would share it with you. I don't know if you saw it on the news, but they found a John Doe in a dumpster up in the Bronx several weeks ago."

"I don't really watch the news too much these days. Too political."

"Well, it turns out that the John Doe's DNA and fingerprints match those we found all over your dead boss and his secretary."

"You don't say."

"I do say. They also found a knife on him that my forensics people are almost one hundred percent certain was the weapon used to kill Dr. Griffin. We still have no idea who the guy is, though, or why he might have killed your boss."

"Wow, that's pretty good detective work, Cheryl. My hat's off to you. I always knew that you'd go far."

"Hmm, yes. Unfortunately, the knife itself was wiped clean of fingerprints."

"Too bad, but what does this have to do with me?"

"Yeah, too bad, and I'm getting to that part. I was thinking through the case and something came to me about where the John Doe was found, something that rang a bell. It took a while, but eventually I remembered. He was found in a dumpster behind a restaurant on City Island called The Seashore. You know the place?"

"Yes, I think so. Why is that interesting?"

"I suddenly remembered that when you and I were dating, you were always trying to take me to one of your favorite restaurants in the Bronx. I used to laugh at you because we both lived in Manhattan and were surrounded by thousands of the best restaurants in the world. I mean, why would we go all the way up to Bronx for food, right? Do you remember those discussions?"

I didn't like where this was going. "Yeah, I remember."

"Do you remember the name of the restaurant you were always trying to take me to?"

"Not really," I lied.

"It was The Seashore. Remember? 'The best lobster ravioli in the city.' The same place we found the John Doe. Talk about coincidences. Isn't that amazing?"

"I guess I don't have as good a memory as you, Cheryl."

"Yeah, I bet. Anyway, that got me thinking. So I started to do some old fashioned sleuthing and found something else you might find interesting."

"And what would that be?"

"The John Doe was missing his right ear and guess what? Your boss, Dr. Griffin, was also missing his right ear."

"Yeah, you're right, that is interesting, but I still don't see what any of this has to do with me."

"I'm getting there. Be patient. Well, whoever cleaned the knife could have done a better job because traces of blood had seeped inside the spring mechanism. In fact, we found three different blood types there. One matched your boss, another matched the John Doe, himself, and the last was from an unknown source."

"Okay, I have to admit this is fascinating, but once again..."

"I'm almost there, Cesari. I'm almost there. Three weeks ago, the same day the John Doe was found, a nurse in the ER at Saint Matt's called in a report of a possible assault as she is required to do by law. A young black woman apparently lost her right ear traumatically and came to the ER for treatment. The alleged victim was described as being in her late twenties, accompanied by a white male. The woman declined to file a complaint, but the police opened a file on her anyway in case she changed her mind. A very astute officer at the precinct made the connection with the other cases and forwarded the information to my office. Are you still with me, Cesari?"

I groaned inwardly. "Yeah, I'm still here."

"Well, it took a while to put all the pieces of the puzzle together, but I eventually did. So, I called St. Matt's ER today and spoke with the nurse who treated the young lady. She vividly recollected that day and the people involved. Apparently, the victim was a friend of hers who worked as a nurse there and her male companion was a doctor who also worked at St. Matt's. Can you believe that?"

I sighed deeply as the noose tightened, but didn't say anything.

She continued. "Do I need to give Kelly a call and ask her to submit a blood sample?"

"Please don't do that, Cheryl. She's been through enough."

"Why don't we have dinner? Off the record, okay? I just want to know what's going on and I'm sure you're explanation will be very entertaining."

I resigned myself. "Sure, when?"

"You tell me. I don't want to interfere with any plans you might have with Kelly."

"That won't be a problem. Kelly and I are going through a transition period. We're sort of re-evaluating things, you know? Actually, I haven't heard from her in three weeks."

"I'm sorry to hear that," she said sympathetically. "You two looked so happy up in Vermont."

"Thanks, and I'm sorry to have to say it. So, tonight would be fine if you're free."

"Where?"

"How about Dempsey's on 2nd Avenue? It's a classic Irish Pub and I could use the atmosphere right now. Maybe we can get a chorus of "Oh Danny Boy" going."

"See you in an hour, John."

I finished work at six and took a cab over to Dempsey's. I was a little early, took a seat at the bar and ordered a shot of Jameson's. It was pretty crowded as happy hour was in full swing. I downed the shot for courage and thought through what I was going to say and how I was going to say it.

Cheryl walked in just as I was thinking of ordering another drink. She wore a blue, knee-length dress and black heels. I stood as she approached. "Hi, Cheryl."

"Hey, Cesari. Been here long?"

"Just a few minutes."

She glanced around. "Maybe we should grab a booth for privacy?"

I signaled the bartender that we were going to sit somewhere else and he nodded his approval. Cheryl and I ordered drinks and he promised to send them to the table. I sat across from her and a waitress handed us menus.

"You look great, Cheryl. I like the earrings."

"Thanks, and you look good, too." I wore a white dress shirt, blue tie and shoes. I had flung my jacket onto the bench seat next to me. We made small talk for a minute or two like that and thanked the waitress when our drinks arrived. We both ordered shepard's pie for dinner. She sipped her Glenlivet and looked at me hard, her blue eyes penetrating right into my soul. She'd make a great D.A. or Attorney General one day.

"Okay, Cesari. Let's get to it, if you don't mind? So, tell me what you can without incriminating yourself too much. Let's start with how's Kelly and why did someone feel the need to cut her ear off?"

I took a sip of whiskey and mulled over how best to tell the story. "Physically, she's fine, but emotionally, you can imagine how traumatic an experience like that might be." I paused as Cheryl nodded sympathetically. She had been in law enforcement a long time and had seen it all.

I continued. "Well, to make a long story short, Reg, Dr. Griffin, had a business relationship with the guy you found in that dumpster. The guy was a Russian national named Sergei and they had met while Reg was on vacation in Moscow. The guy felt strongly that Reg had double-crossed him, and so he acted impulsively and slit Reg's throat. He erroneously got the idea that somehow I could help him out with his business. I couldn't, but to encourage me to greater effort, he decided to kidnap Kelly and send me a piece of her as a warning that I might find the rest of her in pieces as well if I didn't do as I was told." I thought that sounded very plausible.

She nodded and took another sip of scotch. "What's the significance of the ears?"

The waitress served our meals and we started eating. The bar area overflowed with noisy customers and Irish music piped in from overhead speakers. Several people started doing a jig nearby.

"Our late Russian friend spent some time in a Siberian prison camp where some of the other prisoners apparently got hungry one night and tried unsuccessfully to eat him, starting with his ear. He liked to remind people of just how much he'd suffered."

She looked at me in disbelief. "You're kidding?"

I shook my head. "I wish I was. That was his calling card, I guess."

"And so you killed him because of what he did to Kelly?" It was more of a statement than a question.

"I have no idea what you're talking about," I said between mouthfuls of shepard's pie and whiskey.

"What was the nature of the business relationship between Dr. Griffin and Sergei?"

"I don't know."

"Yeah, right. Did this have anything to do with the Russian diamonds you were asking me about a couple of weeks ago?"

"I don't know what you're talking about."

"You're such a liar, Cesari, and don't insult my intelligence. I know you're in this up to your eyeballs."

I didn't say anything, choosing to sip my whiskey quietly instead.

She sighed in frustration, took a deep breath and let it out. "Sorry for prying, but what happened to you and Kelly? I mean on a personal level."

I looked down dejectedly. "She got tired of people trying to kill her because of me. I don't blame her. She said she wanted some space and time to think things over. That was three weeks ago, and I haven't heard from her since. She won't return my calls. I know she's alive because I've seen her in the ER where she works, but she runs away whenever she sees me coming."

Reaching across the table, she placed a hand on mine. "I'm sorry, John. Break-ups are never easy."

"Thank you, and considering the way I handled our break-up, I really appreciate your not gloating right now. You'd have every right to, and I wouldn't blame you one bit if you did."

She looked at me sympathetically. "I would never do that, John. When we were dating, I really cared about you very much and maybe I still do. You could have been a little more delicate with me than you were, but I don't want to see anything bad happen to you."

"Thanks."

"So, did this Russian guy have a last name?"

"Sergei is how he introduced himself. No last name."

"Were those his friends in the Crowne Plaza in Times Square? We found Russian passports in their room."

"Yes."

"Very messy, Cesari. Do you think you're in Iraq or something?"

"What can I say?"

She looked exasperated. "Do you really think you can just go around handing out justice to those you think are in need of it?"

"First of all, I want to go on record that I didn't admit to anything, but the short answer is yes. If they hadn't hurt Kelly, they would all still be breathing today. Guys who hurt women ought to be removed as quickly as possible from society before they infect the gene pool. The city ought to give me a medal."

She sat back in her chair, rolled her eyes in disbelief and downed the rest of her scotch in one gulp, at the same time signaling the waitress for another. "I should cuff you right now, Cesari, and remove *you* from the gene pool."

I chuckled. "You're a lawyer, not a cop, remember. The only handcuffs you own are lined with velvet and hidden in your bedroom." I smiled at her. "That's right. I don't forget things like that."

She sat back, giggling. "Then maybe we should go there where I could make a citizen's arrest, and interrogate you more thoroughly. I'd make you tell the truth." Her cheeks were a little flushed.

"I'm going to warn you right now, Ms. Assistant District Attorney, that I've been known to resist arrest, and I don't think you could handle me."

She laughed out loud this time. "Please, if I can't handle a pansy from the Bronx like you, I should just retire early and sell cosmetics for Mary Kay." She practically inhaled the second scotch.

There was an awkward silence as we stood on the precipice. She looked at me for a long time and I held my breath. After what seemed like forever, she surprised me by suddenly standing up and grabbing her purse.

"What are you doing?" I asked, a little bewildered by her sudden movement. We were doing so well there for a minute. This was just what the doctor ordered.

"Making the biggest mistake of my life, I'm sure. Why don't you get the bill while I go to the powder room and buy us a condom? Are you still in decent shape, Cesari?"

"Pretty good, why?"

"Then I'll get two condoms," she said, smiling and I started to tingle. I watched her butt as she walked away. Very nice indeed. She knew I was staring, too, and abruptly turned around, catching me in the act. Busted! I hated when they did that. She smiled triumphantly and turned back.

I looked at my watch. It was almost eight p.m. There was a guy named Nicolai waiting in the ER for his colonoscopy later tonight. He had about half a million dollars in diamonds in his colon. Uncle Boris had sent him. Uncle Boris and I had worked things out. I thought about Cheryl and the velvet handcuffs as I strummed the table and looked at my watch again. It was cutting it close, especially if Cheryl and I went into overtime, so I called the ER to let them know I might be late.

"Hello, this is Dr. Cesari. I'm going to be—tied up for a while. I'll call you when I'm free."

The End

1. DECEDENT'S LEGAL NAME (First, Middle, Last) **SERGEI**   2. **M**   3. SOCIAL SECURITY NUMBER

4a. AGE-Last Birthday (Years) | 4b. UNDER 1 YEAR (Months, Days) | 4c. UNDER 1 DAY (Hours, Minutes) | 5. DATE OF BIRTH (Mo/Day/Yr) | 6. BIRTHPLACE (City and State or Foreign Country) **MOSCOW**

7a. RESIDENCE-STATE | 7b. COUNTY | 7c. CITY OR TOWN

8. STREET AND NUMBER | 9a. APT. NO. | 9b. ZIP CODE

10. EVER IN ARMED FORCES? ☐ Yes ☐ No | 11. MARITAL STATUS AT TIME OF DEATH ☐ Married ☐ Married, but separated ☐ Widowed ☐ Divorced ☐ Never Married ☐ Unknown | 12. SURVIVING SPOUSE'S NAME (If wife, give name prior to first marriage)

13. FATHER'S NAME (First, Middle, Last) | | 14. MOTHER'S NAME PRIOR TO FIRST MARRIAGE (First, Middle, Last)

15a. INFORMANT'S NAME | 15b. RELATIONSHIP TO DECEDENT | 15c. MAILING ADDRESS (Street and Number, City, State, Zip Code)

16. PLACE OF DEATH (Check only one, see instructions)
IF DEATH OCCURRED IN A HOSPITAL: ☐ Inpatient ☐ Emergency Room/Outpatient ☐ Dead on Arrival
IF DEATH OCCURRED SOMEWHERE OTHER THAN A HOSPITAL: ☐ Hospice facility ☐ Nursing home/Long term care facility ☐ Decedent's home ☐ Other (Specify)
17. FACILITY NAME (If not institution, give street and number) | 18. CITY OR TOWN **BRONX** | 19. COUNTY OF DEATH

20. METHOD OF DISPOSITION ☐ Burial ☐ Cremation ☐ Donation ☐ Entombment ☐ Removal from State ☐ Other (Specify) | 21. PLACE OF DISPOSITION (Name of cemetery, crematory, other place)
22. LOCATION-CITY, TOWN, AND STATE | 23. NAME AND COMPLETE ADDRESS OF FUNERAL FACILITY

24. SIGNATURE OF FUNERAL SERVICE LICENSEE OR OTHER AGENT | 25. LICENSE NUMBER (Of Licensee)

ITEMS 24-28 MUST BE COMPLETED BY PERSON WHO PRONOUNCES OR CERTIFIES DEATH | 24. DATE PRONOUNCED DEAD (Mo/Day/Yr) | 25. TIME PRONOUNCED DEAD
26. SIGNATURE OF PERSON PRONOUNCING DEATH (Only when applicable) | 27. LICENSE NUMBER | 28. DATE SIGNED (Mo/Day/Yr)

29. ACTUAL OR PRESUMED DATE OF DEATH (Mo/Day/Yr) | 30. ACTUAL OR PRESUMED TIME OF DEATH | 31. WAS MEDICAL EXAMINER OR CORONER CONTACTED? ☐ Yes ☐ No

32. PART I. Enter the chain of events—diseases, injuries, or complications—that directly caused the death. DO NOT enter terminal events such as cardiac arrest, respiratory arrest, or ventricular fibrillation without showing the etiology. DO NOT ABBREVIATE. Enter only one cause on a line. Add additional lines if necessary.   Approximate interval: Onset to death

IMMEDIATE CAUSE (Final disease or condition resulting in death)   a. **Death by Cesari** Due to (or as a consequence of):

Sequentially list conditions, if any, leading to the cause listed on line a. Enter the UNDERLYING CAUSE (disease or injury that initiated the events resulting in death) LAST   b. Due to (or as a consequence of):   c. Due to (or as a consequence of):   d.

PART II. Enter other significant conditions contributing to death but not resulting in the underlying cause given in PART I. | 33. WAS AN AUTOPSY PERFORMED? ☐ Yes ☐ No
34. WERE AUTOPSY FINDINGS AVAILABLE TO COMPLETE THE CAUSE OF DEATH? ☐ Yes ☐ No

35. DID TOBACCO USE CONTRIBUTE TO DEATH? ☐ Yes ☐ Probably ☐ No ☐ Unknown | 36. IF FEMALE: ☐ Not pregnant within past year ☐ Pregnant at time of death ☐ Not pregnant, but pregnant within 42 days of death ☐ Not pregnant, but pregnant 43 days to 1 year before death ☐ Unknown if pregnant within the past year | 37. MANNER OF DEATH ☐ Natural ☐ Homicide ☐ Accident ☐ Pending investigation ☐ Suicide ☐ Could not be determined

38. DATE OF INJURY (Mo/Day/Yr) | 39. TIME OF INJURY | 40. PLACE OF INJURY (e.g., Decedent's home; construction site; restaurant; wooded area) | 41. INJURY AT WORK? ☐ Yes ☐ No
42. LOCATION OF INJURY State | City or Town
Street & Number | Apartment No. | Zip Code
43. DESCRIBE HOW INJURY OCCURRED | 44. IF TRANSPORTATION INJURY, SPECIFY: ☐ Driver/Operator ☐ Passenger ☐ Pedestrian ☐ Other (Specify)

45. CERTIFIER (Check only one)
☐ Certifying physician-To the best of my knowledge, death occurred due to the cause(s) and manner stated.
☐ Pronouncing & Certifying physician-To the best of my knowledge, death occurred at the time, date, and place, and due to the cause(s) and manner stated.
☐ Medical Examiner/Coroner-On the basis of examination, and/or investigation, in my opinion, death occurred at the time, date, and place, and due to the cause(s) and manner stated.
Signature of certifier **John Cesari MD**

46. NAME, ADDRESS, AND ZIP CODE OF PERSON COMPLETING CAUSE OF DEATH (Item 32)

47. TITLE OF CERTIFIER | 48. LICENSE NUMBER | 49. DATE CERTIFIED (Mo/Day/Yr) | 50. FOR REGISTRAR ONLY- DATE FILED (Mo/Day/Yr)

51. DECEDENT'S EDUCATION (Check the box that best describes the highest degree or level of school completed at the time of death)
☐ 8th grade or less
☐ 9th - 12th grade, no diploma
☐ High school graduate or GED completed
☐ Some college credit, but no degree
☐ Associate degree (e.g., AA, AS)
☐ Bachelor's degree (e.g., BA, AB, BS)
☐ Master's degree (e.g., MA, MS, MEng, MEd, MSW, MBA)
☐ Doctorate (e.g., PhD, EdD) or Professional degree (e.g., MD, DDS, DVM, LLB, JD)

52. DECEDENT OF HISPANIC ORIGIN? Check the box that best describes whether the decedent is Spanish/Hispanic/Latino. Check the "No" box if decedent is not Spanish/Hispanic/Latino.
☐ No, not Spanish/Hispanic/Latino
☐ Yes, Mexican, Mexican American, Chicano
☐ Yes, Puerto Rican
☐ Yes, Cuban
☐ Yes, other Spanish/Hispanic/Latino (Specify)

53. DECEDENT'S RACE (Check one or more races to indicate what the decedent considered himself or herself to be)
☐ White
☐ Black or African American
☐ American Indian or Alaska Native
☐ Asian Indian
☐ Chinese
☐ Filipino
☐ Japanese
☐ Korean
☐ Vietnamese
☐ Other Asian (Specify)
☐ Native Hawaiian
☐ Guamanian or Chamorro
☐ Samoan
☐ Other Pacific Islander (Specify)
☐ Other (Specify)

54. DECEDENT'S USUAL OCCUPATION (Indicate type of work done during most of working life. DO NOT USE RETIRED)
55. KIND OF BUSINESS/INDUSTRY

About the Author

JOHN Avanzato grew up in the Bronx. After receiving a bachelor's degree in biology from Fordham University, he went on to earn his medical degree at the State University of New York at Buffalo, School of Medicine. He is currently a board-certified gastroenterologist in Geneva, New York, where he lives with his wife of twenty-five years.

Inspired by authors like Tom Clancy, John Grisham, and Lee Child, John writes about strong but flawed heroes. He is currently working on his third novel in the Cesari series, *Temperature Rising*.

Made in the USA
Middletown, DE
22 September 2015